MAKE MY HEART RACE

GRACE MCGINTY

ALSO BY GRACE MCGINTY

Hell's Redemption Series: The Redeemable/The Unrepentant/The Fallen

Damnation MC Duet: Serendipity/Providence

The Azar Nazemi Trilogy : Smoke and Smolder/Burn and Blaze/Rage and Ruin

Dark River Days Series: Newly Undead In Dark River/Happily Undead In Dark River/Pleasantly Undead in Dark River/Seductively Undead in Dark River

Black Mountain Mates: Hunting Isla

Eden Academy Series: The Lost and the Hunted (Prequel)/Heart of the Hounded (Prequel)/ Rebels and Runaways (Book 1)/Sweethearts and Savages (Book 2)

Shadow Bred Series: Manix/Frenzy/Feral/Crave

Stand Alone Novels and Novellas: Bright Lights From A Hurricane/The Last Note/ Inside The Maelstrom Part 1 and 2/8 Seconds to Fly/Pay-Per-Heart/The Daymakers/ Make My Heart Race

Penalty Box Players: Sticks and Stone/Break My Bones

Omega Lottery: Tryst In The Dark

For the girlies out there hustling to achieve their dreams. I believe in you. You've got this, you sexy little badass!

Also for the ladies who like their men fast, but their cars faster. Vroom, vroom, bitches!

Lastly, for the ladies at the BBC: I dropped some Poet easter eggs just for you! Also for Kat, thank you for checking the vibes!

MAKE MY HEART RACE

PROLOGUE

TALLY

THERE WERE ONLY three things in life that gave me the same risk-to-reward thrill as motor racing.

Discounted end-of-day sushi.

Petting an orange cat.

Sleeping with another driver on the grid.

So far, only one of those things had blown up in my face, as evidenced by the sports commentators talking way too loudly outside my garage.

"After crashing out in last week's race, Ryclo Racing must be wondering if Tally Palmer's head is in the game at all. I'm not sure she has the stamina to make it out here, racing with the big boys. She's the third driver for the team, but I don't think her position over there is quite as solid as she'd like, and there's still some who say she stole the position from a more deserving driver."

The other commentator made a disgusted noise. "More like she stole the heart of the right man, wouldn't you say, Dan? The Romeo and Juliet of NASCAR—that's what they call Tally Palmer and Buck Willtot of Willtot Racing. Of course, Buck's father, Brick, is the owner of Willtot Racing, and it can't hurt having someone as powerful as Brick in your corner when you're trying to find a team, even if it is with your most fierce competitor."

I knew that voice. Rupert Ballantyne was commentating royalty, but he was also an epic dick weasel. Not just your average douchebag either; he believed he was God's gift to motor racing, even though he'd never been behind the wheel of any vehicle professionally.

I snorted as I secured myself into my suit. You'd think they'd have the decency to loudly question my talent and integrity somewhere other than in front of the very garage where I was getting ready to race.

Besides, they were so fucking wrong. Brick hadn't helped me get onto Ryclo at all, not even a little. In fact, he was one of the loudest naysayers about women in NASCAR.

No, my hard work had gotten me here, from racing three-quarter midget cars in the rain when I was six and could barely reach the gas pedal, to fighting my way onto podiums and proving my worth every weekend for as long as I could remember.

It had also been my dad's hard work, driving cabs on nights and weekends to pay for the thousand things that needed to be bought as I progressed through my career, while legacy kids like Buck Willtot got it all handed to them, as if it was their birthright.

Not that I begrudged Buck his place on the track. He was so talented—and fucking hot, I might add—that it was hard to begrudge him anything, including my body.

Rolling my shoulders back, I pushed down the swelling emotions in my chest. Thoughts of my father made my heart squeeze painfully. He was the reason I was here, driving in the Cup series for the first time, but he wasn't here. He would never see this moment. It had been five years since he died, and the best way I could make him proud was by going out there and driving like the skilled driver I knew I was.

I repeated the words my therapist had told me for years in my head. *My dreams are worthy. I'm making my family proud.*

"Tally, let's go!" one of the mechanics yelled.

I sucked in a deep breath, told myself I was a badass bitch once more, and walked through the garage. Some of the guys slapped me on the back, while Hayes handed me my helmet and the rest of the gear I'd need.

"You got this. Leave everything out on that track and prove to everyone you deserve to be here." Hayes wasn't chief mechanic, or anything like that. He was almost as far down the totem pole as I was, but he'd been one of the few who'd gotten friendly enough to give a shit if I won or lost.

I gave him a tight smile, pushing my sunglasses up the bridge of my nose. "Thanks, Hayes."

They'd already moved the car out onto the track, and I sucked in a deep, fortifying breath. This was it.

Either I won this one from the back of the field and got into the playoffs, or I went home.

I smiled and waved at the crowd, though it was more jeers than cheers. Ignoring the negativity, I thought about the fact that out there in that crowd was probably another little Tally Palmer who wanted to drive stock cars, or ride bikes or bulls, or fly fighter jets. I could be someone they looked up to, and I would race for them today.

The team went over all the last-minute details, but my head was already in the race. I was playing scenarios over and over in my mind, and even if they never happened, I had a backup for that backup. I was ready.

We stood for the anthem, and as I watched the fighter jets fly over, I tried to talk myself out of puking. I was shaking so hard that I'd curled my fingers up into my fists and held them tight to my thighs. I couldn't let anyone see I was rattled, because the other drivers on this track were like sharks; they'd smell my fear, the blood in the water, and it would be all over for me.

Pulling on the head sock that went under my helmet, I looked down the row of cars and drivers, searching for one pair of sparkling blue eyes.

Buck met my gaze and winked at me, and my heart fluttered in my chest. The press called us the Romeo and Juliet of NASCAR, but it wasn't that serious yet. Maybe one day it could be, though. Buck was every-thing an All-American NASCAR driver should be—handsome enough to tempt a nun, with that Southern, good ol' boy charm and a smile that could drop panties. And he fucked like he drove; like getting you to the line first was the only thing that mattered on God's green earth.

I blew him a kiss, even knowing the cameras would pick it up and probably play it on the late-night recaps of the race. He grabbed it, mimed slapping it onto his cheek, then shoved on his own helmet.

Chuckling softly, I got my head in the game. I could put kisses on those high cheekbones myself later. Dragging myself up and through the window of my car in a maneuver I'd done hundreds of times before, I put on my helmet. The team continued to give me instructions while strapping me in, and I just nodded along. I knew my job. I trusted that they knew theirs too.

"Drivers! Start. Your. Engines."

Giving my team one last smile, I pulled down the visor on my helmet and started the car. The feel of the engine vibrating below me mellowed out the nerves that were threatening to make me throw up what little food I'd had earlier.

I'd made it here. That was something my dad would have been proud of.

The fact that Rupert Ballantyne and Dan Baker thought I'd slept my way onto a team was beside the point. I hadn't. I'd done the time on the tracks. I'd clocked up more hours iRacing at home than was probably healthy. I'd sweated my way into this spot, and I was going to enjoy being here.

We rolled out onto the track, and all too soon, came the words over the radio. *"RACE. RACE. RACE."*

Time to go to work.

It was a fucking mess. A win here could send any of us into the playoffs,and we were all driving like we knew it. I'd barely missed a huge wipeout earlier, when #34 went into the wall and got himself all the way around. I was twelfth back in the pack, all but landlocked in place, but there were still ninety-six laps to go. Anyone could get it.

Both of my teammates were ahead of me, running fifth and sixth, according to the team radio. My job was to be the little yappy dog snapping at the heels of the people who wanted to take them out.

No one wanted me to win. I couldn't win, not really. But I'd be fucked if I wasn't going to try.

The thing I loved most about the sport was the unpredictability of it, and when another huge smash had smoke flying into my windshield, electricity raced through my veins. I dodged the cars ping-ponging around the track, just in time to see a car bounce off the outside wall, flipping end over end as it rolled into the infield. Just a flash of color, but it made my heart pound.

"Whose car was that?" I demanded over the radio.

"Just checking," came the voice of Tyler, a gruff older man in his fifties. "It was Willtot."

My heart thundered. It was bad. I knew it was bad.

We saw crashes every single fucking race, but some just made your blood freeze. "Is it rough?"

"Yellow flag, Tally. I'll let you know when I know."

As the cars slowed, I couldn't help but look over. The car was on fire, but that was okay. We wore fire suits for a reason. He could still be okay.

"Get out. Get out. Get out." I chanted the words under my breath as the safety cars raced in, fire extinguishers already out as they landed on their feet to extinguish the blaze.

"Red flag."

Almost out of muscle memory, I stopped my car, angling it infield. "Ty. Is he out?"

"Not yet." Something in Ty's voice had me on edge.

Why the fuck wasn't he out yet? "Come on, Buck. Come on."

I kept half an eye on the track, enough to see the paramedics fly to the infield. I could hear my blood whooshing in my ears.

No, no, no. "Ty, tell me what's going on!"

"They're choppering him out. It seems serious."

Fuck.

"Hold your position and then come in."

I watched helplessly as two medics loaded Buck onto a stretcher and tore out of the infield, even as the track maintenance team cleaned up the debris from the crash. The amount of cars remaining in the race had nearly halved, with eleven cars knocked out by that crash. I couldn't care less. Not when I knew deep down that something was really wrong with Buck.

"Yellow flag. Maintain position, Tally."

Distracted, I didn't even remember replying to Ty's directions. Instead, I lost myself in the pattern of the drive.

The second I climbed out of the car at the end of the race, I ripped my helmet off my head. "Is there any news?"

No one would meet my eyes. Every single person in the pit had something they needed to do right then, and dread washed over me.

"Someone fucking *tell* me!"

Hayes gave me a look filled with sympathy, and I was already shaking my head when Ty appeared beside me. "He didn't make it out of the infield, Tally. They worked on him all the way to the hospital, but he was pronounced dead on arrival."

I shook my head furiously. Ty was wrong. He was *wrong*. "No."

"I'm sorry, sweetheart. It was a freak accident. They think a piece of debris came through the window at a high enough speed and hit between his Hutchins and his helmet, getting the jugular. He lost a lot of blood before they could get the fire under control." He swallowed hard. "I'm so sorry."

My knees gave way, shock sending me to the ground. My head battled with my heart, like that traitorous bitch wanted to scream *I told you so* to the aggressively beating organ in my chest. This sport had fatalities. We knew every time we drove out onto the track that we might not come back.

I'd known that Buck was a driver—a wild and aggressive one at that—before I started dating him. I should have been at least a little bit prepared for this.

But my heart screamed and screamed at the loss of what could have been, even if I did just sob silently with my head hanging, defeated. Arms picked me up, shuffling me out of view of the crowd and the garage crew.

I looked up at Hayes, and something about the concern on his face made me pull myself together. I cloaked myself in numbness. Shook away the pain in my chest, and replaced it with a black abyss of nothingness.

Wiggling out of his arms, I stood on my feet. "I'm okay," I said weakly.

Hayes shook his head. "No, you're not."

I swallowed hard as the tears threatened to well in my eyes once more. He was right; I wasn't. "I'm okay enough to get out of here."

Sam Ryker appeared in the doorway of the garage we were standing in. His face was a mask of neutrality, though I could see regret in his eyes. "Tally, can we talk?"

I knew, deep down in my bones, I wasn't going to like what he had to say.

ONE

TALLY

I WAS BEGINNING to really relate to those old-style country and western singers who sang mournfully about how Lady Luck had abandoned them, then kicked them in the balls while stealing their dog.

Luck hadn't stolen my dog, but it had killed my boyfriend. Luck hadn't kicked me in the balls, but it had gotten me fired and black-listed from the profession I loved, all because some grieving father decided it was my fault his son crashed and veered into the path of flying debris.

Brick Willtot had sunk my career, because he was convinced that I was bad luck. That Buck had been thinking about me when he'd hit the wall that sent him careening into a bunch of other cars, before flipping end over end. That it was my fault his own mechanics hadn't secured down the piece of framing that pierced his jugular.

It was "just bad luck," as the commentators kept

saying over and over. A freak accident. A one-off in the history of the sport.

I'd made myself watch the accident over and over on Youtube. The sports broadcasters had stopped showing the footage out of respect for the family, but people on the internet had no respect. So I forced myself to sit there, rewatching the crash for hours to figure out who was really to blame. But no one had fucked up but Buck himself, and there was no one to blame but the sport of motor racing.

Slumping back against the sagging couch in my studio apartment, I closed my eyes against the memories of that moment. It had been six months ago, and as luck would have it, I now had bigger fucking problems.

Problem number one: I had no money whatsoever. Apparently, Brick Willtot had teabagged his giant fucking brass balls into the mouths of all the other teams, so no one would pick me up after Ryclo dropped me. Worse than that, I couldn't get a job *anywhere* in NASCAR.

Right now, I was waitressing at a diner down the street, but I wouldn't even be able to do that for much longer. I only had one real solution; it was dangerous as fuck, but the payoff would be worth it.

I flicked through my phone to find the number of Willy Love. His real name was William, but his parents had called him Willy, and it kind of stuck. Our parents had been best friends, so we'd grown up together, and while I pursued racing, he'd gone and gotten a great job

as an investment banker. Where was the thrill in investment banking?

Anyway, he was the closest thing I had to a family
now, though I hadn't spoken to him in six months, so I
wasn't exactly sure how this would go. As the phone
rang, I switched it to speakerphone, putting it carefully
down on the coffee table like it was an explosive device.

"Hello?"

"Willy? It's Tally."

"Tally? Jesus fucking *Christ*, it's good to hear from
you. I was worried. Colin! It's Tally."

While I'd been pursuing grease monkeys with dirty
fingernails and aw-shucks smiles, Willy had come out
as gay to his parents and presented Colin, a guy so
unproblematic and sweet, Willy's parents couldn't help
but accept him. I could hear Colin thanking cheese and
RuPaul in the background. He had his own deities.

"Where the hell have you *been*, Tally? We've been
worried sick. You just fell off the face of the earth."

I felt kind of bad, but I hadn't been in a fit state to
talk to anyone without screaming in rage, and I
wouldn't run the risk of ostracizing Willy and Colin.
They were the last two people on the earth who'd care if
I disappeared completely.

"I'm in San Francisco."

"Why the fuck would you be here and not tell us?"
Willy demanded, like San Fran had personally offended
him at some point. It was a damn good question. It was
the last place I had come to beg for a spot in a team
before running out of hope and money. There'd been

cheap studio apartments that I could afford, even if they were in a crummy area of town.

Plus, it had seemed as good a place as any to fade into obscurity, away from the memories of my family and the burning ashes of my career.

It was also close to the only people in my life who gave a shit, even if I hadn't wanted them to know I was here at that point. Willy and Colin were the closest thing I had to a home base, and as luck would have it, I'd need them more now than ever.

I didn't say all that to Willy, though. "Just where I landed. I would have come to see you eventually. I just needed a little time to sort everything out."

The silence down the end of the line was loaded, but Willy knew me. He knew not to push.

"Are you coming to visit?" Colin asked, filling the emptiness.

I winced, because my next request was going to be hard for them to fathom. It definitely would've been better if I'd asked in person, but I was a chickenshit. "Kinda. I was kind of hoping you'd come and meet me somewhere, and uh, bring the Porsche."

"Tally—"

"It's safe with me; you know that. I'm broke, Willy. One little race could set me up until I find something else to do with my life, other than waiting tables in a bad area of town." That might've been a small piece of emotional blackmail, but still, desperate times and all that.

Willy sighed heavily. "We could loan you money until you're back on your feet."

I was shaking my head, even though they couldn't see it. "I don't want your money, Willy. I can do this. I'd bring it back to you in one piece, I swear."

He made a growling noise in the back of his throat. "I don't give a shit about the Porsche, but if I'm comprehending the things you *aren't* saying, you want to use it for fucking street racing. *That* shit, I have a problem with."

"I'll wear a suit. And a helmet. Not that I'm going to crash your car." I let the words sit between us. "I need this. I…" I almost told him, but if I did, I knew he definitely wouldn't give me the car. "Please."

Willy sighed heavily. "Fine, Tally. But if there's the smallest hint that they're going to be cowboys, I want you to pull out. You hear me?"

"I swear." I wasn't worried. They'd be chasing my taillights before they knew it.

Another heavy sigh. "I'll pick you up. I'm not letting you go alone. Colin can stay here, in case he needs to bail us both out of jail."

The tension in my chest unfurled slightly. "Thank you, Willy."

We rolled up to San Gregorio State Beach just after one in the morning. The roads were pitch black, and the only sign that everyone wasn't tucked up in bed was the collective light of the group of cars and bikes parked off the Cabrillo highway. Music pounded and car engines revved, and I could see everyone and their girl-friend swigging from beer bottles.

"Feels like old times." Willy still seemed unimpressed to be here, but he was right. He'd been driving me to street races since before either of us had a license. We'd lived in a small town, where there hadn't been anything to do but race down darkened streets and get pregnant at fourteen.

Luckily, after a huge growth spurt in our freshman year, Willy had become the cool kid that no one fucked with. Also, well and truly in the closet. It meant no one came near me with a ten-foot pole to get in my pants, but Willy had no interest in me either.

I looked over at the one man who'd never let me down. "I love you, Willy Love." With a name like that, maybe his parents had created a self-fulfilling prophecy.

"I love you too, though you're giving me my first fucking gray hair, Tally. Luckily, Colin loves a silver fox. And call me Will. If you call me Willy out there, some-one's going to get the shit beaten out of them."

I laughed. He'd always been built like a linebacker, but he'd obviously been working out lately too. If it came to fists flying, my money was on him.

I climbed out of the car, and Willy uncurled himself from the driver's seat. A guy in tight black skinny jeans came over, his patchy goatee not doing his weak jaw any favors. "You here to drive, man?"

Willy shook his head, and I stepped forward. "I'm here to drive."

Goatee guy looked me up and down, and I knew what he saw—a small blonde with booty shorts and a holey, oversized Harley Davidson sweatshirt. I looked like someone's kid sister. "You even old enough to drive?"

"I'm twenty-two, asshole. I can drive just fine." My outfit choice was deliberate. I *wanted* the other drivers to underestimate me. Winning races started long before you got behind the wheel. But this guy wasn't a racer, and I didn't need to take his bullshit.

Goatee lifted a nonchalant shoulder. "It's a five-k buy-in. Winner takes all."

Raising my chin, I pulled an envelope full of hundreds from my back pocket. It was the last of my savings, so I *had* to win this race or I was fucked. I handed it to him, and he had the balls to raise an eyebrow at me.

"You sure? No one's gonna go easy on you."

I stepped around him. "I'm sure."

Goatee shrugged. "Whatever. It's your ass." His voice dropped into that skeevy note guys assumed was alluring, but really made most women's skin crawl. "And what a sweet ass it is."

Willy stilled, but I gripped his arm and dragged him along. Goatee was just the money guy; he wasn't the person we needed to see.

A girl in dirty, ripped jeans and a Halestorm t-shirt torn off at the waist was deep under the hood of a Supra. Finally, she stood. "No NOS?" she asked the guy in front of her. "If you use it during the race, you're disqualified. We want our races to be entertaining, not some kind of dick-measuring competition over who has the most mods."

"Cat…"

"Don't wanna hear it. If you can't win without it, go see Mankles now and get him to give you your money back. This shit is about *skill*." The guy huffed and sat back in his car, and the woman—Cat, I guess—turned toward me. "You racing?"

I nodded. "Yeah, the 911 GT over there."

"Any mods I need to know about?"

I looked over at Willy, but he shook his head. "She's stock."

Cat raised an eyebrow. "Care if I check?"

Willy shook his head again, leading her over to check out the engine, while I looked around at my competition. Other than the Supra, there was a Civic that looked like it was going to race, as well as a bright yellow Camaro and a sleek gunmetal Corvette. Most worrying was a Dodge Demon. Those fuckers were fast as hell, and if anyone was going to give me a run for my money with sheer horsepower, it was going to be that one. There were a bunch of other cars, the kind that you always saw at these kinds of gatherings, though I wasn't sure which ones would race.

Finally, Willy appeared beside me and I watched Cat walk over to the Demon. Yeah, I'd check that bastard out too, purely to drool.

I looked up at the frowning face of my oldest friend. "Did it go okay?"

Willy nodded, but the frown didn't leave his expression. "Are you sure about this?"

I nodded, not sure I could cough up the words. There was no other option but this. Leading him back to the car, I grabbed my gear. There was only twenty minutes until go time, and I needed to get my head in the race.

There was a hell of a lot more riding on this race than five grand.

TWO

TALLY

SUITED UP and sitting in Willy's 911, I breathed a sigh of happiness at being back behind the wheel of anything. I revved the engine, feeling my muscles immediately relax. Being without a car for six months had been like being without a limb, but I'd left my team-issued sponsor car behind when they revoked my contract. I couldn't justify buying another car with my savings, especially once I landed in San Francisco. There had been more important things to spend my money on than fast cars, especially since I needed a roof over my head.

We were lined up across the road after pulling names to determine our positions, and I breathed a sigh of relief to see the Demon wasn't in the line-up. I could take the rest of these easy enough.

I was surprised to see a bike beside me, though. Seemed dangerous to race two wheels against four; the guy must've had a death wish. I lifted my helmeted head at him, and he nodded back.

Along with the bike guy, there were six other cars in the grid, which was a lot for a street race, but meant that the pot would be forty grand.

The fire suit and helmet were getting me some strange looks, but that had been the provision from Willy. I had no doubt he'd take back the keys, get me back my five grand and take me home, if I didn't keep my word.

Goatee stood off to the side with a walkie-talkie to his ear, while a girl stood in front of us with a thong in her hand. It was lacy and pink, and I was fairly sure I'd get a UTI just thinking about wearing something like that. The taillights of the guy in front of me were beginning to burn my eyes, but I didn't care. I was focused on that fucking pink ass floss like it was the last vestige of my freedom.

Finally, she raised her panties high, gave the drivers an exaggerated wink, then dropped it. The car in front of me burst off the line. Adrenaline burned through my veins as the bike beside me jetted between the front two cars, narrowly missing G-string Girl.

Now I saw how a bike could compete.

Focusing on the race, I went through my strategies. We would speed down the mostly unlit seaside highway for twenty-five miles, which should take roughly twelve minutes, given the sharp corners and thin, two-lane road. I kept pace, but didn't try to make any serious moves yet. Let them jockey for position first; I'd just sit back and ride their slipstream. Happiness surged through my veins right on the tail of the adrenaline.

The darkness was all-encompassing, with only our headlights bouncing off the road reflectors, showing us the way. Another reason I didn't want to be up front just yet.

Two cars up front got a little too close, and both ran off the road into the dunes on the right. Lucky for them, because fifteen seconds later, they would have been off the side of a cliff.

We slowed to hit a sharp bend, but I'd spent all afternoon studying this road. I knew the lines I wanted to take; I knew every inch without ever having driven it. I went around the Supra, the Porsche revving hard as I cut in, forcing the Supra to brake on the turn.

Seven more minutes. I pushed the Porsche past one-twenty on the straight, and she purred her agreement. "Good girl," I muttered at the car, keeping my eyes trained ahead of me, my fingers loose, my breathing even. "We've got this."

A big stretch in front of us had me trying to push her harder, but I was blocked by a 350z that was riding tight to the Camaro. Fuckers needed to move, because it was almost time for me to school them.

As they continued to be a rolling roadblock, I knew I'd have to get creative. Soon, there'd be a turnout, and I could use it to go around them, but it was dangerous. At this speed, I could hit the gravel and go careening out of control. But if I stayed back here, I would be in trouble.

I was weighing up my options when the Camaro slowed around the corner, shifting to the high line. It was dangerous. Risky as fuck. But I pulled up onto the left and zipped tight on the inside, the Camaro barely missing the back of the Porsche by a fish's dick. I zoomed away before he could try and regain his position.

"Fuck *yeah!*" I screamed through the windshield.

Four cars down, three to go. I couldn't see the bike anywhere, so maybe he'd wiped out earlier. Even better. Only two to go.

Quickly flicking my eyes to the clock, I knew I only had three minutes to make this drive count. A lifetime in a race. They might still knock themselves out, but I knew exactly where I wanted to make my move. I'd wait a little longer.

I stared at the taillights of the Corvette and the 350z; they were fucking close. Whoever was behind the wheel of the Corvette could really drive, but that little 350z was handling like a fucking pro, and it was light as fuck.

Wouldn't matter. I was almost there.

The road squeezed into a tight two lanes, with barriers on both sides, which was my sign. It was almost time. "One mississippi, two mississippi... There it is." I breathed and focused. Watched the cars in front of me. "Let's do this, girl."

Gunning the accelerator, I swerved hard to the left

and hit the paved shoulder. The road spread out before a bridge, allowing three of us to sit side by side for a split second, before I pushed the Porsche to turn hard in front of the Corvette. I slipped in front of it before I hit the bridge, missing the guardrail by a margin that would give Willy a heart attack. As I opened the Porsche up, I could see the finish line just ahead.

I did it. I fucking did it.

I began to laugh. "Fuck YES!"

Then, out of nowhere, the bike pulled up beside me, and my mouth swung open as he got across the line barely a wheel in front of me.

My foot dropped from the accelerator, and I down-shifted almost by muscle memory. "No," I breathed as the bike slowed in front of me. "No, no, no, this can't happen. Fuck!" I slammed my hand on the steering wheel, shocked as hell. "*FUCK!*" I screamed.

Pulling into a lot where spectator cars were parked, I rested my head against the steering wheel and tried to calm my racing heart. It would be okay. I'd try again. There'd be something else.

I didn't have another buy-in, but I could save it. I'd be okay. I breathed heavily, trying to calm myself when I heard the crunch of gravel.

Willy pulled open the door, and I took off my helmet. "I lost." I didn't want to cry, so I blinked that shit back. I'd lost races before. You didn't fucking cry at the finish line, because no one would ever take you seriously again.

But Willy knew me. "You can try again." He didn't

say how, or when. It would be harder next time, because I'd lost my element of underestimation. I wouldn't be able to pull the same back-of-the-pack trick, because they'd be watching for me.

"I can try again."

The cars from the starting line started to trickle in, and with them, pumping music and shouts of disbelief. The bike pulled into the lot, and the rider hopped off. It was definitely a guy, because he was tall, easily over six-four. I climbed from the Porsche, and despite the disappointment flooding my veins, walked over to the winner. That was a lesson my dad had instilled in me—you were only as worthy as your sportsmanship, so no matter how angry you were at your loss, you shook hands out of respect. I didn't know if that really applied to street racing, but I wouldn't dishonor my father's memory by being a bitter hag.

The guy took his helmet off and accepted the crowd of people coming to gush over him and his win. *Dammit.* Not only was he a good racer, he was sexy as fuck. Wasn't that always the way? I could see the tattoos climbing the column of his neck beneath his collar. The guy was basically a cliché of a bad boy street racer.

It was a humid night, and I was sweating my ass off in my fire suit. Peeling it off my shoulders, I tied it around my waist as I waited for the crowd around the guy to dissipate a bit.

Finally, he looked up and met my eyes. He seemed surprised, but he quickly chased away the expression into one of grudging respect. Excusing himself from the hordes of guys wanting to stroke his bike—and the girls who clearly wanted to stroke something else—he made his way over to me.

"Good drive out there." His voice was deep and gravelly, and I heard Willy whistle softly. He was smoking. But I could maintain my professional demeanor.

"Thanks. You too, obviously. You must have been riding without your headlights?" When the guy nodded, I shook my head. "That's fucking crazy. Genius, but crazy. I didn't even see you until you were past me." And that fucking *burned*. He'd been like a ghost in the race.

"Sorry about that, but you know how it is." The guy put out a hand. "I'm Jesse."

"Tally."

His face folded into a frown. "Did you say Tally?"

I was almost used to this. If you were a NASCAR fan, you inevitably knew my name. Mostly because Buck's death, and the resulting blow-up, had been big news for a while. But I didn't offer him any more than that, because I just wanted to forget that period of my life, before the other shoe had dropped.

Fuck, it was basically raining shoes at this point.

Someone came running up, holding an envelope that was bulging with cash, tackling Jesse around the back and slapping the winnings into his chest, forcing Jesse to grab it. "That was fucking amazing! You smoked that Porsche right at the—" His head snapped up at my gasp, and I met the eyes of a guy I didn't think I'd ever see again. "*Tally?*"

"Hey, Hayes."

Shit. I didn't need this blast from the past right now.

His gaze ran over my body, snagging at my belly, and I mentally cursed. Was it too late to put my fire suit back on? His eyes went comically wide, and I could see the flash of headlights in their deep blue depths.

"You're *pregnant?*"

THREE

TALLY

EVERY SET of eyes in our small group fell to my waist. Willy stumbled back like I'd shot him, and Jesse seemed more perplexed than anything. I hadn't even thought anything of it. It wasn't like I was carrying a watermelon down there. I was barely showing at all, which is why I'd had no fucking idea until this week. Hell, I didn't know how Hayes could even tell. The doctors had called it a cryptic pregnancy. I called it a kick in the uterus—quite literally.

"Yep. I'd appreciate it if you kept that to yourself." I didn't know if he was still working for Ryclo, but mechanics gossiped nearly as much as a knitting circle.

I was worried if word got back to Brick Willtot that I was possibly knocked up with his grandchild, I was in for a world of trouble. Even the thought made my blood turn to ice. He was rich, powerful, and grief-stricken. I was a nobody, with a dangerous job and no support system. If he tried to take the baby in court, I'd stand no fucking chance.

So I was going to lie out my ass. "Five months along. I made some mistakes after… everything." I could have a baby a month early. It happened a lot. Let them think that my baby was from a seedy one-night stand.

I should have known Willy wouldn't drop it. "Who's the father?"

Lie, lie, lie. "Some loser I met in a bar while I was drowning my sorrows. Also, none of anyone's damn business. It's mine, and that's all that matters." Willy's eyes promised this wasn't over, but he dropped it.

But the question had drawn Hayes's focus to Willy. "Who are you?"

"Will Love. Tally's *friend*." He basically chewed on the word *friend*; that was how much emphasis he put on it. His tone suggested we were way more than friends, and that, ladies and gentleman, was the reason I'd never gotten any dates in high school.

They eyed each other up and down, like they were going to brawl. Finally, Hayes gave a sniff. "Can't be too good a friend if you couldn't tell she was pregnant. It's obvious as shit to anyone who's spent any time with her."

I sighed and rolled my eyes to the heavens. "Neither of you have ever seen me naked, so you can stop the damn posturing." Jesse laughed, and I was glad one of us was enjoying the moment. "What the hell are you doing here, Hayes?"

My old mechanic shrugged. "Same thing you're

probably doing here—answering the call-out in Palo Alto. I thought while I was in town, I'd catch up with Jesse. We're friends from way back."

I blinked dumbly at him. "Uh, I'm here because I need the prize money, so I don't have to raise my kid in a mold-infested roach hotel."

Jesse frowned at my words. "You really don't know? It's been the talk of the industry for the last couple of months."

I swallowed down the ache in my chest that came from knowing I'd lost my dreams. Someone had stolen them away, and there was absolutely nothing I could do about it. "If you haven't noticed, I'm not exactly on the Christmas card list anymore."

Rage flashed across Hayes's face. "I know. I left Ryclo soon after you. I couldn't give everything to a team who'd do that shit to one of its drivers. I told Ryker where he could shove it. I've drifted around for a couple of months, but when VANT Enterprises announced they wanted to get into racing—particularly open-wheel—well, I wanted in. They have the money and the drive to do big things."

His passion was a mirror of my own, or it had been, up until a few months ago. Now he was talking about a dream I no longer had a place in.

I pasted a smile on my face. "Sounds great. Indy-Car? Or Formula racing?" I'd never driven anything but stock cars at a competitive level, but if it went *vroom-vroom* around a track, I was here for it.

And just like that, we were back to being coworkers,

as Hayes told me all about VANT's supposed trajectory. IndyCar first, then maybe try and petition the FIA for a team status, perhaps buy out an existing team and rebrand it.

I ate up his words, even as my heart broke. Hayes had always been as passionate about motorsports as I'd been, and one of the few people on the team who used to sit and talk with me about it like we were buddies, not like they thought I was just a novelty to appease the fans.

The only other person who'd talked like that with me had been Buck. But Buck was dead.

A sleek red Ferrari pulled into the lot, and to say it turned heads would be an understatement. People stopped and watched as it purred past them. It was like a beautiful woman walking down a catwalk—you held your breath until they were gone from sight once more.

It pulled up beside the Dodge Demon, and an older man slid from the driver's seat. "Holy shit," Hayes whispered, but I was too busy staring at the woman who'd just climbed out of the passenger seat of the Demon. She must have been in her fifties, but man, if I could look half that good in my fifties, I'd sell my soul to the devil right then and there.

The guy, who must have been a similar age to the woman, leaned forward and kissed her softly. He was handsome, his Mediterranean features obvious, even in the darkness.

Another guy climbed out of the driver's seat of the Demon, coming over to stand beside them. To say they stuck out in this crowd would be a gross understatement. Apart from being at least thirty years older than most people here, they screamed money. Everything about them dripped with wealth and affluence.

Cat, the woman who'd checked out Willy's Porsche for enhancements, went over and spoke to them. She smiled brightly at them, before looking over in our direction. The entire group turned toward us, and I had the sudden urge to hide.

Jesse chuckled softly. "Like Candyman, you said their name too many times and they appeared, Hayes."

The guy from the Ferrari walked toward us, and I whipped my head toward Hayes and Jesse. "Who's that?"

But I was surprised when Willy answered. "Antony Barbieri. One of the best lawyers on the West Coast and co-founder of VANT Enterprises."

Now it was my turn to stare, wide-eyed. The man had that swagger of someone who knew their own power. The dude was a silver fox, that was for sure—if powerful older men were your thing. Unfortunately, it had never been my thing; I was always a sucker for the wild boys with little to no regard for their own physical wellbeing. I was doomed to this heartache. It had been all but written in the stars.

Antony Barbieri stopped in front of Hayes. "Mr. Davis, it is good to see you again so soon."

Hayes flushed, reaching out to shake hands. "Uh, absolutely, sir. But please, call me Hayes."

The silver fox grinned broadly. "Call me Antony, then. Do you make a habit of street racing?"

Whoops. Guess who got busted with their hands down their pants?

"Uh, no, sir—I mean, Antony. I was just here supporting my friend, Jesse." Hayes frantically indicated the tall biker. "Jesse, this is Antony Barbieri, who I interviewed with this week for the VANT Racing team." As Jesse and Antony shook hands, Hayes eyed me, something mischievous crossing his features. Before I knew it, he was tugging me forward. "Actually, I'm glad you're here. This is Tally Palmer. She's a former NASCAR racer. Youngest woman to ever race at Daytona. She's an amazing driver."

Antony eyed me, one eyebrow raised. "Nice to meet you, Miss Palmer." His eyes dipped to my stomach, which was still exposed.

Fucking hell.

Whatever, though. I didn't care what some random person thought.

"And you, sir. That's a really nice ride." I lifted my chin at his Ferrari. "I think I'm beginning to see who was behind VANT's desire to start a racing team."

Antony threw back his head and laughed. "What can I say? I'm an Italian at heart, and Ferrari and Formula One are basically coded into our DNA." He glanced between me and Hayes. "My wife, Vanessa, said you drove with quite a lot of expertise tonight, and I guess we know why now. But Hayes says you're a *former* NASCAR racer?"

My whole body tensed. "Yes. My team released me from my contract partway through the season." I hoped my frosty tone meant he wouldn't press.

To his credit, he didn't, but I felt his eyes appraising me. Man, no wonder he was a good lawyer. I felt weighed and measured. "I see. Well, Hayes, I'm glad we ran into you tonight—it'll save me a phone call. Welcome to the VANT Racing team."

Hayes let out a whoop and shook Antony's hand again. "Thank you so much, sir."

They sorted out a few details, then Antony left, promising to email Hayes all the paperwork. He walked back over to the little group that included who I assumed was his wife Vanessa, though maybe not, when she turned and kissed the other guy with her too. Whatever, rich people could do what they wanted; it was the boon of being rich.

Which I very much was not.

Exhaustion weighed down my bones, stress and sleep deprivation making me more tired than I'd ever been in my life. I turned to Willy. "We better go home before Colin calls the cops because he thinks we're dead." I smiled at Hayes, though I could feel it strain against my cheeks. "It was good to see you, Hayes," I told him softly. It really was. It was so fucking good to see him, but it was also a painful reminder of everything I'd lost.

Surprising the shit out of me, he stepped forward and hugged me. I tried to hold myself stiff, but I melted into his arms. Hayes had been there for me in my worst moment; it almost seemed poetic that he was here right now too.

"If you need anything, call me, Tally," he whispered against my hair.

I murmured something unintelligible against his chest. I wouldn't be doing that, but it was nice of him to offer.

He pulled back, his brows lowered in a serious expression. "I mean it. Call me anytime. You still have my number."

Sighing, I stepped out of the comfort of his arms. "Yeah, Hayes. I do."

Jesse was closer than he was before, and he gave me a crooked grin. "I hope I get to race you again soon."

I smirked back. "I won't let you past me so easily next time." I reached out and shook his hand, and the feeling of his long, strong fingers wrapping around mine made me a little breathless. The adrenaline was definitely catching up with me.

I climbed into the passenger seat of the Porsche, and Willy gave the guys a little nod as he slid behind the steering wheel. The tenseness of his jaw told me I was definitely going to get a lecture, but instead, he gave me the silent treatment all the way back to his side of town. He didn't take me back to my place, just pulled up in front of his townhouse, walked around and opened my door, waiting.

Sighing heavily, I climbed out. Honestly, I didn't really want to be alone tonight anyway. On the way past, I squeezed his arm. "I'm sorry I didn't tell you, Willy. I would have eventually."

He sucked a deep breath. "You're lucky I love you, Tally. Go inside before you freeze." The fire suit was actually toasty as hell, but I didn't tell him.

Despite the late hour, Colin opened the door. Willy ushered me in and kept walking toward the stairs that led to their bedroom. "Tally is pregnant. She drove a hundred and fifty miles per hour, in the pitch black, while pregnant. *You* deal with her," he said to his long-time lover, then stomped up the stairs like a drama queen.

Colin's mouth hung open as he looked between us. Well, between me and the disappearing shoulders of his partner. "Ah, sweet thing. You look tired. Come on, I'll grab you something to wear to bed, and we can talk about all this tomorrow."

Colin's softness was in direct contrast to Willy's anger, and it almost made me cry. I swallowed it down, following him to the downstairs guest room. He flitted around, showing me the ensuite and grabbing me some sweats and one of Willy's oversized tees from the laundry room.

Finally, he left, shutting the door, and I let the tension flow from my body, like purging poison from a snake bite. I'd survived the night; that's what mattered most. I tried not to think of the loss, or even worse, how it had felt to lean into Hayes. I peeled my fire suit off the rest of the way, letting it land with a muffled thump.

Looking down, I realized one of the sleeves was

sitting weird. Picking it up and shaking it out, I couldn't believe my eyes when a yellow envelope fell onto the bed. My head knew exactly what it was, but my heart couldn't believe it.

Flicking it open, I found eight rubber-band-wrapped stacks of hundreds. The buy-ins.

"How the fuck did this end up in my suit?"

Even as I asked those words out loud, I knew. Jesse had slipped it in there. The last time I'd seen the envelope, he'd been holding it.

But why would he give me forty thousand fucking dollars? And should I keep it?

FOUR

HAYES

I DROVE MY BABY—A.K.A. my lime-green 1963 Chevy Nova—behind Jesse all the way back to Avalon. I followed him into the garage, parking as far to the right as I could to accommodate his bike. He'd always preferred two wheels over four, and it was the one argument we couldn't resolve.

I followed him up the internal stairs to the main living room. He'd rehabbed this place from a falling-down foreclosure into something to be proud of, and it showed. Little pieces of Jesse's personality were littered through the place, like the hardwood floors, because he liked to work on bike engines while watching football, or The Bachelorette, depending on the season. The rustic kitchen cabinets were all handmade by him, and they gave the place this kind of homey feel that some modern homes lacked.

He could sell the place and double what he paid for it, but he wanted to stay here, despite it being miles too big for him and still in a kind of sketchy neighborhood. *"I'll know the right time to sell."* That was all he ever said when I brought it up, and I had to give it to him, the next suburb over was going through some kind of gentrification, so he might've been right.

Honestly, he really didn't need the money. His dad had worked for the Feds, and had a huge life insurance policy. When his dad had been killed back when we were fifteen, his uncle had made him invest the money. Some safe investments later, and Jesse had made so much money, he didn't have to work unless he wanted to. He flipped houses. He raced his stupidly fast bikes. He lived life on his own terms, and I could respect that. Not that I'd give up either of my parents for any amount of money, but still, it must be good to not have to work unless you wanted to.

"So, are we going to talk about the girl?" Jesse asked as he stripped out of his leathers, hanging them on a rack right by the door.

I slumped onto his couch. Tally Palmer. Fucking hell, fate couldn't have punched me in the dick harder than it did tonight.

When she'd first joined Ryclo, she was sweet but fiery. She didn't take any of the garage talk to heart, but she also didn't take any shit from the guys. She knew the sport, knew her way around the engine, but more than that, she knew how to drive. Tally Palmer had balls as big as an elephant, dipped in pure brass. Not going to lie, I'd fallen a little in love with her the first day I saw her.

However, before I knew it, Buck fucking Willtot had her in his sights, then his bed. I couldn't speak ill of the dead; Buck had been a good guy. A golden boy who the sun had shone on every day of his life, until it didn't anymore. Though, if you asked any driver, at least he went out leading the pack, doing the very thing he loved, and that was a good way to die.

Buck and Tally had been a good match. But Brick Willtot was a surly old fucker, and I hated him to the very marrow of my bones for what he'd done to Tally.

Jesse flopped onto the couch beside me, and I knew he wouldn't drop it. At least he'd brought me a beer to wash down my pathetic crush.

"She was the third driver for my team. She got a raw deal after another driver died and his daddy decided it was her fault."

"The Buck Willtot fatality?" I nodded; his death had been big news for weeks. "Did she nudge him into the wall?"

I shook my head. "Nope. She was way back in the pack. Nowhere near him or the accident."

Jesse screwed his nose up. "I'm struggling to connect how it was her fault?"

"They were fucking. Her and Buck were an item. The star-crossed lovers of NASCAR. Willtot Senior decided his son had been distracted by her boobs or something, and it made him crash. So Brick got her blacklisted from the sport."

"What a fucking cunt," Jesse snarled, and I couldn't agree more. "The woman can drive, though." He cleared his throat. "So, when did you realize you wanted to fuck her into a different universe?"

I gave a mirthless laugh. Clearly, I wasn't as subtle as I thought. I could only hope that Tally didn't pick up on it. "When she told McSweeny that not only could she beat him in any race, she could steal his wife and give Mrs. McSweeny the first real orgasm she'd had in forty years."

Jesse's jaw unhinged. Yeah, it was hard to imagine those words coming out of the mouth of such a sweet thing, but she'd proved then and there that she could take anything those old boys could dish out. Not only that, she'd serve it back to them so hot, it burned.

Leaning back, Jesse continued to chuckle softly. "She sure is pretty too." My eyes slid toward my best friend.

We'd met back in high school, when he'd transferred to Texas. His mom had ended up having a breakdown not long after his dad's death, so Jesse had been shipped down to an uncle. One weekend, he'd found me ass-up in a piece-of-crap old Mustang that was being held together by some cable ties, cloth tape and rust.

Jesse had been flailing. He'd needed an anchor, and I'd needed a purpose in a town so small, it was like looking down the barrel of death as soon as you were old enough to vote. We'd talked to each other in a language we both understood, despite his East Coast accent, and we were friends from that very moment on.

I'd introduced him to NASCAR. He'd done up an old Indian while I'd worked on my Mustang. He'd gone off to travel down the West Coast on his bike, while I'd apprenticed with a racing team, and the rest was history. It was pure luck we'd both ended up in San Fran.

It felt almost like fate that Tally had ended up here too. "Do you think the guy with her was actually her boyfriend?"

Jesse snorted. "Fuck no. Did you see his face when you dropped that she was pregnant? His shock was funny as fuck." He turned toward me, his eyes assessing. "Do you want something from her? Not to bust your bubble, but she's having a baby. Some other guy's baby. She's hot, but that's a lot of baggage to take on for a nice body and some common interests."

He didn't understand. He'd spent his life in the fast lane, jumping from one place to another, one bed to another. He didn't understand what it was like when you met someone your soul connected to. He probably also didn't know the heartache you felt when her soul connected to someone else's first, and you had to watch them from the sidelines like some weird-ass creeper.

I really hadn't thought I'd ever see her again. After telling Ryker to suck my dick when he told me he'd ditched her at Willtot's request, I'd kind of sequestered her to that part of my life. She was somewhere mourning a guy she loved, and I went and licked my wounds over a girl I'd never had.

Now I had a second chance. But she came with a baby. "I don't know, Jesse. I don't care if she has kids. I love kids." I was the oldest of eight. Like I said, there wasn't much going on in my hometown, except mining and making babies. "I don't want to compete with a ghost, though, you know?"

He nodded. "Yeah, man. I get it. On a different note, what the fuck were Vanessa Sumich and Antony Barbieri doing at an illegal street race?"

That was a really good fucking question. I doubted they'd been there to see me, and that Dodge Demon had definitely been watching the race. They'd been there for a reason—maybe to scope out drivers. I hoped so, because I knew the driver they needed, and she'd been right there in front of their faces.

"I don't know for sure, but man, that would have made front-page news if the cops had rolled up. Can you imagine some of the city's finest citizens out in the middle of the night with the rest of us hooligans?"

We drank and talked shit for a bit. I'd forgotten how nice it was just to be with Jesse. Being with him, just hanging, was like sleeping in my childhood bed—so comfortable, you wondered how you slept anywhere else.

Finally, I yawned and stretched. It was time to hit the sack, and I downed the rest of my beer. "What are you going to do with the forty thousand? Invest in another property to flip?"

Jesse stood and cracked his spine, leaning left and right. "Nothing. I gave it to the girl," he said, like it was nothing.

I blinked at him slowly. "You gave Tally forty thousand dollars?" *Holy shit*. That was a lot of money, and sure, Jesse didn't hurt for cash, but that was a chunk of change.

He just shrugged. "She needs it more than I do. Besides, she drove the best out there; I sneaked her from the back. It's only fair."

Sometimes, I thought I knew Jesse, but then he'd go and do shit like this. It made me realize there were so many layers to this man I'd thought of as a brother for most of my life. He had a heart as big as fucking Texas under that gruff, tattooed, bad boy exterior. He looked like the kind of guy mothers warned their daughters about, and god knows, many mamas back home certainly had. They didn't know him, though. He was aloof and quiet, but he'd give you his last dollar if you needed it.

I slapped him on the back. "That was a nice thing to do, Jesse. I know she'll appreciate the buffer."

Selfishly, it also meant I didn't have to find another way to see Tally, because if I knew her at all, she wouldn't accept forty thousand without a word. She was never one to take hand-outs; despite what the NASCAR pundits had said, she'd *earned* her place on the track at Daytona.

No, she wouldn't just accept that amount of money. She'd be back, and I already couldn't wait.

FIVE
TALLY

THE FOLLOWING DAY, I stared at all the money in that envelope on the nightstand, trying to work out what to do with it. It felt like charity, and that didn't sit well with me. I wasn't anyone's charity case—a fact I knew was going to cause problems once I finally dragged myself from bed and stood in front of Willy and Colin, while they asked all sorts of questions I had no answers to.

It was a point of pride for me. I'd worked hard for everything I had. In that envelope was a shitload of money that I hadn't earned. I'd lost. Jesse had won, fair and square.

But I was a single mother-to-be, and I wasn't sure I had room for pride anymore.

Sighing, I stood, Willy's shirt falling to my knees. I grabbed the envelope and stuffed it in my helmet. I'd figure it out later, once I was back at my apartment. Right now, it was time to face the outrage of my friends, now that they knew I'd been keeping secrets. More than one, but this one especially.

They didn't know I'd been booted from NASCAR. No one did. The story peddled by the team and the media was that I'd been suffering from PTSD after seeing my lover die on the track. It made me seem weak, but at the time, I'd been in too dark of a place to fight back. Well, that, and I'd had to sign an airtight NDA, which meant I couldn't run my mouth about why I was fired.

Fuckers. All of them.

The smell of food was making me hungry, which was a lot better than the urge to puke I'd had for a couple of months there. For a long time, I'd just thought I was stressed. I'd always been a little bit of an anxiety puker. When I was younger, before a really big race, I always used to lose my breakfast. It was like clockwork really. I'd thought I'd grown out of it, but once I started puking in the mornings a couple of months ago, I'd just assumed the stress was getting to me.

Boy, had I been wrong.

I stepped out into the kitchen, where Willy was sitting at the breakfast bar, reading on his tablet. His hair was messy, and he was boyishly handsome; Colin was a lucky dude. Actually, Colin was attractive too, if in a slightly softer way. Not physically softer—he had the lean body of a professional diver, and I doubted there was an ounce of fat on him. No, he was less emotionally shut down than Willy, who'd had to overcome expectations of who he *should* be, according to society, so he could be finally happy. And they were happy, stupidly so.

I needed a guy like either of them, a guy who'd love me the way they loved each other. That wasn't in the cards for me right now, but it was something to hope for, right? Even with Buck, I wasn't sure I could've had the kind of love these two did.

"You're awake!" Colin said happily, spotting me standing in the doorway. "Come in. I made you waffles with strawberries and chocolate sauce."

Tears welled at his thoughtfulness, but I swallowed down the emotion. "Thanks, Col." Walking over to the breakfast bar, I leaned my head on Willy's back. "Sorry I didn't tell you."

I felt the stiffness leave him, and he turned until he could loop an arm around my waist. He hugged me tightly, and it just felt nice. I'd been missing human contact for the last few months.

"It's okay. I know you would have, when you were ready. Not like you could have avoided me for the next eighteen years. I was only saying to Colin last week that I was giving you one more week, then I was going full PI and tracking your ass down." I felt him smile. "Besides, you'd never deprive me of being Lug Nut's favorite uncle."

Colin snorted. "You cannot call the baby Lug Nut, Will." He winked at me. "Plus, we all know I'll be the favorite." He came around the counter and hugged me too, until I was squished between them, safe and warm.

"We love you, Tally. And we'll love this baby too. We're your family, and you can lean on us."

Willy grunted. "What he said."

A few seconds later, Colin pulled away and put a plate of food in front of a stool. "Sit and eat and tell me everything we need to know. Appointments you need. Your due date. Who the daddy is, because I *know* you weren't out fucking random guys in bars, Tally."

Yeah, I knew that line might've worked on Hayes, but it definitely wasn't going to work on Willy. I guess it was time to come clean.

"After Buck's accident, I was pulled into the office trailer of Ryclo…"

They were silent as I told my whole tale of woe. Meeting Buck and falling in immediate lust. Honestly, that was probably the most relatable part of the story, because anyone who'd ever met Buck would fall in lust with him. He'd been so handsome and so fucking personable that he lit up any room he entered, and was the center of attention if he remained in it for more than five minutes. He'd swept me off my feet and into his bed before you could say, "Howdy, ma'am."

Colin waggled his eyebrows at that, because he got it. Willy was like a true brother figure. He didn't think anyone deserved me, and had chased off potential boyfriends for years. My dad said he'd always wondered if Willy was secretly in love with me, but Colin had dispersed that notion easily.

I knew it was just because he was protective; Willy might be gay, but he was also a guy. He once told me that he knew how guys thought, and quite frankly, none of them were worthy of my attention. It was sweet, in its own way.

I continued with the story, and when I got to the accident, my voice became monotone as I recounted the race, seeing the burning car in the infield, having to drive the remaining laps without knowing if Buck was alive or dead.

By the time I got to being let go by Ryclo for "underperformance"—but really, because Brick had thrown a tantrum—Willy was irate as hell. "We'll sue the *fuck* out of those assholes for wrongful dismissal. They broke the contract; there'll be rules against that."

I shrugged, like it didn't mean anything, like there wasn't a huge, empty abyss in my soul. "It was in my contract; they had every right." They'd had to pay out my contract, but still, a few thousand dollars was an insulting consolation prize to end my dreams. I shook my head, because I'd been over this a hundred times in my mind. I'd even taken my contract to a lawyer.

"Anyway, I didn't realize I was pregnant until a couple of weeks ago. I went to the doctor, where they did an ultrasound and told me I had a cryptic pregnancy. It's not as unusual as it sounds, apparently. I didn't purposefully keep it from you guys."

Willy frowned. "And the baby is Buck's?" I nodded. "So you're six months along?" One more nod, and he swiped a hand down his face. "Jesus Christ. So we have twelve weeks to get you completely ready for a baby? Colin, grab a notepad. We need to write a list."

Willy loved lists. I had to admit that while it felt good to share this burden with someone else, I was sad that it wasn't with Buck. Willy and Colin would help, of course, but they were funcles, not fathers. I was looking down the barrel at a future of raising this baby solo.

And that scared the shit out of me more than any race.

Breakfast turned into coffee on the back deck of their townhouse, though they would only give me hot chocolate now. I didn't tell them I'd been drinking double espressos just to stay on my feet before realizing I was pregnant.

Finally, the conversation turned to last night, and I knew my reprieve from lectures was over.

"You can't do that shit anymore, Tally. If you'd crashed, it wouldn't have just been you who died—you owe that little life inside you some consideration. Not only that, if you'd crashed and needed surgery, no one would've known you were fucking pregnant and told the doctors. You aren't an irresponsible teen who goes to street races to get their kicks. I know you didn't ask for this, but the truth is, it's your reality. If you don't want to be a mother, you could consider adoption—"

"No!" I wanted the baby. I did. I'd thought briefly about it, but I'd also thought about how disappointed my dad would be in me if I didn't at least try to make a life for me and the baby. I'd had such great parents. How would someone else raise him or her, and what if they were mistreated? No, I wanted to keep it. "I needed the money, though. Babies are expensive, and I don't have any skills, other than driving fast."

"What about Brick Willtot—" Colin started, and I shook my head.

"No. He can't know. He'd take it off me quicker than he could throw thousands of dollars at a lawyer and call me a destitute whore."

I didn't feel the least bit bad of depriving Brick of the last piece of his son left in the world. He'd crushed my entire future over an accident. He didn't care if I ended up in the gutter. It felt vengeful, but I didn't want to inflict someone who thought that was okay on my child. My baby would learn morals and ethics—the ones instilled in me by my parents, not the entitlement of the wealthy.

Still shaking my head, I shrugged. "Doesn't matter. I won't have to race again. The winner of last night's race stuffed the prize winnings in my fire suit, without me knowing."

Both Willy and Colin looked shocked. "Jesse gave you the forty grand? Why?"

"You can win forty thousand dollars street racing? Holy *shit!*"

I laughed softly at Colin's amazement. Yeah, it was a lot. But when the possibilities included death, jail, or getting your car impounded forever, the reward had to be worth the risk. "I don't know why he did it. The money was stuffed in the sleeve. Maybe he thinks I'm a charity case."

Willy narrowed his eyes at me. "Tally Palmer, you

keep that money. The guy stealthed you anyway; it was basically yours. Do not give it back. Think of it as a gift."

Yeah, Willy knew me too well. I was definitely giving the money back, and we both knew it. "Sure thing, William."

He sighed. "Come on. I'll drive you home."

SIX

TALLY

I SAT on the money for another two days, as I went back and forth on whether to keep it. I'd hidden it inside of my couch cushion, which wasn't exactly a revolutionary hiding place, and after forty-eight hours, I was convinced I was five minutes away from an aggravated burglary where it would all be stolen and I'd be fucked again. I was stressed the entire time I did my shifts at the diner. It was awful.

Finally, I caved and called Hayes. It rang a few times, making me start to think he wasn't going to answer. Maybe that was fate. Maybe that meant I should just—

"Hello?" His voice was always pleasing. I'd spent hours talking to him while we were out on the road, and the deep, rumbling tone of his voice had sometimes made me forget I was supposed to be digesting his words, not just imagining him talking dirty to me. Very awkward, especially when I'd had a... well, not a boyfriend. I guess we'd had a "situationship." Hell, Buck hadn't even wanted to make us public. It was just an unlucky snap posted to social media that had outed us. Either way, we hadn't been seeing other people, so I'd always felt a little guilty I found Hayes so attractive.

"Hayes? It's Tally."

A little puff of laughter echoed in my ear. "I wondered when you'd call. I was beginning to think you wouldn't."

I frowned. "You knew Jesse gave me the money?"

"Not until after we got back here."

I still didn't understand it. "Why?"

There was some rustling on the other end of the line. "I don't know, Tally. You'd have to ask him."

I made a little frustrated noise in my throat. "Well, do you want to give me his number?"

"I mean, I could, but I wouldn't want to breach his privacy like that. You'll have to come over and have dinner tonight."

"So he can give me forty thousand dollars, but not his number?" I asked incredulously, and Hayes just laughed in response. Damn, it was a nice laugh, though. "Fine, I'll come over for dinner. But I'm bringing that money back. I'm not a charity case."

The mirth still hadn't left his voice when he asked, "Do you want me to pick you up, or do you want to drop a fifty on getting an Uber here?"

Damn the bastard. But I wasn't going to give him the satisfaction. "I'll get a rideshare. What's the address?"

He rattled off an address down in South San Fran, and I promised to be there at seven, before hanging up. Looking at my watch, I decided to take a tiny nap. Growing a human was exhausting.

The incessant vibrating of my phone woke me. Rolling across the bed, I grabbed it. My home screen showed sixty-two missed calls. Fifty-three from Hayes, and nine from Willy.

Looking at the clock in the corner of the screen, I realized it was ten at night. *Ah, fuck.*

Turns out, it wasn't my phone that had woken me up, but the pounding thump of the front door. I pulled it open to find a pale-faced Hayes filling my doorway. Behind him was an equally frazzled-looking Jesse.

"Oh Jesus, thank fuck," Hayes muttered, his phone to his ear. "Will, she's here. She looks like she was just asleep. What? Yeah, I'll put her on."

Damn, two lectures in a week was going to be a new record for me. "'Lo?"

"Fuck me, Tally. Are you trying to age me two decades this year or what? Why weren't you answering your phone?"

I grimaced. "I had a nap. I must've overslept." *Okay, understatement.*

"Your friends went full detective, tracked me down on LinkedOut and called me. Said you were meant to meet them three hours ago, but never turned up. They thought you were dead." The subtext there may as well have been shouted. *He'd* thought I was dead. "They asked for your address, and they were closer, so I gave it to them. But Colin and I are on our way over."

"Willy, you really don't have to. I'm fine. Go take Colin out for ice cream or tacos or something. I didn't mean to ruin your night."

There was a long silence at the other end. "Are you sure?" It was Colin this time. "If you need us, Tally, you know we're here."

"No, I'm fine. I swear, guys. It was just a nap. Have some shrimp tacos for me, because I'm not supposed to eat seafood anymore. I'll call you tomorrow."

Another long silence. "First thing, Tally. If you don't call by nine a.m., I'm calling the cops to do a welfare check," Willy grumbled. I had a feeling that last line might've been for Hayes and Jesse.

"Before nine, I promise. Love you guys."

Hanging up Hayes's phone, I handed it back and looked at them kinda sheepishly. "Whoops?" I stepped back into my apartment. "I guess you guys better come in."

My mother would have said something about letting two men into my apartment after ten o'clock, but she'd been gone for a decade, so the little voice inside my head that was hers was disappearing. And god, that made me so freaking sad.

Before I could tear up at the thought that my baby wouldn't have grandparents, I searched my fridge. "Would you like something to drink? Uh, I have water or… milk?"

"I'm good," Jesse replied, the first words he'd said at all. He looked around the tiny studio apartment. The whole place was one room, essentially. It was well decorated, and the Murphy bed also became the couch when it was pushed up. I mean, it was a cheap hovel, but at one point or another, someone had clearly had big aspirations to make affordable housing actually nice. I'd done my best to make it my own, even when I didn't want to do anything but lie on the couch and stare at the ceiling.

I dragged my eyes from Jesse to Hayes. His blue eyes looked at me like he was trying to decide how to save me, and honestly, it felt like too much. I cleared my throat, and he dragged his eyes away. "Water is fine. Thanks, Tally."

I grabbed a glass from the cabinet and poured him some from the filtered jug in the fridge, taking a moment to cool my face. When I turned back around, I felt calmer. "I'm so sorry I missed dinner. Though, I guess now I don't have to worry about crossing town in a cab with forty grand."

Jesse's face was impassive. "Keep the money. I gave it to you for a reason."

Well, at least he didn't beat around the fucking bush. "And what reason is that?"

"Babies are expensive."

I went to the nightstand and pulled out the envelope. "Then donate it to a charity or a women's refuge or something. You won the money; it's yours. I don't need it." *Lie, lie, lie.*

Could eyes actually smolder? I felt like they were barely banked coals, and I was about to fall into the fire. "Yes, you do. You live in a room smaller than my living room. You have no baby stuff. No crib, no bassinet. No baby clothes or change mats or anything that would even *hint* that you're about to have a child. So either you don't have the money for it, or you don't plan on keeping it."

I couldn't help but snarl at his words. Who was he to judge me? I was keeping the baby, but he didn't have any right to an opinion either way. "That's none of your fucking business. *I'm* not your business, and this baby definitely isn't."

He shrugged. "Didn't say it was. But that money is my business, and I want you to have it. So stop being a stubborn asshole about it and get out of this fucking roach motel. Move somewhere safer for you and your baby."

"Jesse," Hayes growled in warning.

Huffing out a disgruntled noise, Jesse turned and looked out the window into the night. Well, into the brick wall of the building opposite me. I frowned at him until Hayes's fingers touched mine.

"Sorry, Tally. Jesse's missing the part of his personality where he actually *has* a personality. When they were handing them out, he was still in the brooding asshole line. He got that in abundance," he said more to his friend than to me.

I made a non-committal noise. He'd got that right.

Apparently, Jesse had also spent a little time in the hot line, because he did hot, brooding asshole far too well.

"We'll head out and leave you in peace. I just wanted to check you were okay," Hayes said softly, and I realized I didn't really want him to leave, though I'd never admit that.

I missed having him as a friendly face. I missed the way he made me feel when we talked about cars and life. I missed the chance I might've had with him, if I hadn't been so caught up in Buck and now the baby.

I pushed those feelings right down deep. There was no room to start a relationship in my life right now. None whatsoever. "I'm okay, Hayes. I've been doing just fine by myself for a long time. I haven't met a challenge I didn't approach head-on, and it'll be the same now."

Hayes opened and closed his mouth a few times, and I could see the conflict written all across his face as if it were scrawled in Sharpie. But ultimately, he gave a short nod.

Jesse turned, his face looking way more intense with the darkness behind him. "Do you want to go into business with me?"

The hell? This guy had lost his fucking mind.

SEVEN

JESSE

I'D LOST my fucking mind. Tally was gaping at me, and so was Hayes. Actually, Hayes was looking at me like I'd just lost my marbles, and he wouldn't be wrong. I wasn't even sure why I cared. I could take the money back and move on with my life. Hell, I could do what she suggested and donate it to an animal shelter, or a food bank or something.

I wasn't prone to lying to myself, though. It had less to do with feeling like I didn't deserve the prize money —I'd ridden a damn fine fucking race—and more to do with the fact that the girl in front of me, with big, wounded eyes and wild hair, captured something inside my chest. I wanted her to be okay.

Maybe her situation reminded me of my mom, the stress she'd felt having to raise me by herself after my dad died. The breakdown she'd had, which I'd always felt was a little my fault.

"There's a house beside mine that I was going to

buy, restore, then flip for a profit when the time's right. That's what I was going to do with the money." I kept my voice neutral, like I didn't care what she did. Which I didn't, not really. "You help me renovate it, and when we sell it, you keep half the profits. I figure that once the baby comes, you're going to struggle to work at the diner and care for a child, so this might be an option." I shrugged. "Whatever you want. You could even live in the place while we renovate."

She narrowed her eyes. "You want me to buy a house with you?"

Hayes scoffed, but she was making it sound weirder than it was. "I want you to work your ass off rebuilding a house that's basically dilapidated, as a business proposal, yes."

It wouldn't hurt that she'd be right next door. I knew Hayes would like that. You only had to look in his eyes to know he was smitten with this tiny little racer. I mean, she was basically his dream girl, so it made sense.

"Can I think about it? Because I don't know you."

Well, at least she had some common sense. "Sure. Come out tomorrow and look at the place before you make up your mind. Hayes is living with me next door, if that helps ease your mind or whatever."

I was already making a list of things I'd do before she moved in. The bathroom and kitchen were in good working order, but the master bedroom would need to be redone before it was habitable. I'd put in a good security system, because she'd still be there alone with a tiny baby, and us being next door wasn't really close enough.

She eyed me appraisingly once more, then nodded. Hayes let out a tiny, relieved breath that I wasn't not sure she heard. "I'll come around and pick you up at about ten? I start work on Friday, but I have tomorrow free."

It felt like time to go. I strode toward the door of this tiny little hovel and tried not to let it tug too strongly at my heartstrings. This was just the right thing to do. For Hayes. And it was what my dad would've done.

With that thought, I opened the front door and walked out into the hallway, waiting quietly as Hayes said something softly to her. Probably apologizing for me. He'd spent a lot of time apologizing for my surliness when we were teens. He stepped out, and the door shut behind him, but neither of us moved until we heard the deadbolt and chain slide into place.

My area was a little shady, but this one was worse.

Both Hayes and I were silent as we made our way back to the haphazardly parked car. When Tally hadn't turned up an hour after she said she would, Hayes had panicked. I had too, though I'd tried to keep it cool.

She was a pregnant woman, alone. What if she'd slipped in the shower? What if something had gone wrong with the baby? What if she'd passed out and hit her head on the kitchen counter? The possibilities were endless for anyone living alone, but a pregnant woman in her sixth month was just exponentially worse. So I hadn't told him to calm down, just went to work tracking her down like a fucking stalker.

Hayes slid into the driver's seat, and I climbed in beside him. He didn't speak until we pulled out onto the main arterial road back to my place.

He snuck a look in my direction. "That was unexpected."

I grunted noncommittally. "She keeps the money, turns it into some more, and I don't have to move next door so we don't get squatters. Works for me."

"So, it was purely a selfish offer?" he asked lightly, but I could hear the sarcasm in his tone. "Don't bullshit a bullshitter, Jesse. You like her."

I snapped my head around. "Nah, man, I'm not trying to move in on your lane. I can see your big heart eyes every time you look in her direction."

He kept his eyes on the road, so I had time to judge his profile. He didn't seem jealous or angry. Instead, he raised an eyebrow in my direction. "You don't know her well enough yet. We might be choosing lanes, but it's Tally's road, and she doesn't give a fuck what you think you want or deserve. I had my chance, and she chose someone else. I'd rather see her happy, and if that's with you, even better."

Jesus fucking Christ. "Man, I offered her a job, not my dick. You're getting ahead of yourself."

He hummed as he got off at our exit. "Hmm. We'll see."

I believed in the bro code. If he wanted her, I'd keep my hands to myself. I mean, she was beautiful, but he was my best friend, and I loved the shit out of him. I wouldn't ever jeopardize that.

I arranged with the realtor to meet us at eleven the next day, and it didn't hurt that I'd put feelers out already about the place next door. Where mine was a split-level, this one was a single-story bungalow, and while rundown, had some potential.

I would have bought it with or without the money I'd given Tally, but I let her think I needed her money to do it. I wasn't above stacking the odds in my favor. I might be making a mistake, because she was basically a stranger, but my dad had taught me how to read people early on. She had a wide, open face, and her every thought flashed across her features. She'd tried to give the money back, even though keeping it would have made her life insanely easier. Plus, Hayes liked her, which was worth a lot on its own.

No, I wasn't second-guessing my offer.

Hayes pulled up in his car, but I saw that it was Tally in the driver's seat. Hayes loved that car; it was his baby, and he wouldn't even let *me* drive it. So if I needed further proof of his smittenness, it was there, with Tally behind the steering wheel. She was grinning widely, talking animatedly as she gave the engine a little rev, making it purr.

Yeah, it was pure joy on her face, and his too. Definitely the right decision.

As she climbed out of the car, I raised a single brow

at a flushed Hayes. "Damn hooligans. There goes the neighborhood," I deadpanned, and Tally threw back her head and laughed.

"This baby drives like a dream! I want to marry this car."

"You'll have to wait until Hayes files for divorce, and I have it on good authority that he's still in love with the old bird." I waved them toward the door. "Come on over to my place while we wait for the realtor, and I'll show you my baby. Two wheels are far superior to four," I teased them both, laughing at the outrage on their faces.

"Never!"

"Fuck off."

I laughed harder, and it felt good. "You say that, but you haven't seen Jeanette." Leading them into the garage, I walked past my racing bike and toward my one true love—my 1988 Softail Springer Harley. Grabbing the keys from just inside the doors, I walked over and started her up, the sound as relaxing as a cat purring. "Climb on and tell me that isn't an exhilarating feeling."

She grinned at me and didn't even hesitate to throw her leg over the machine. Giving it a little throttle, she laughed. *Yeah, baby. Feel that horsepower rumbling between those sweet thighs.*

"She's nice, Jesse," she said huskily. "I can see why you love her so much." Her smirk had me mesmerized. "But I still prefer four wheels on the ground than two, you crazy person." She winked at me and slid from the bike, but I was too busy wondering what it would be like to fuck her over it.

I pushed that thought right out of my head. Hayes had seen her first. Worse than that, I was about to make her a business partner, even if it was in name only. You didn't fuck your business partners. If *that* wasn't enough, she was about to be someone's damn mother, and I wasn't daddy material.

Well, not that kind of daddy anyway.

"You have a sidecar? That's kind of funny," she said with a chuckle, and I did my best to look imperious.

"What, a twenty-something guy can't have a sidecar for his bike?" I didn't use the sidecar on the Harley, but it was good to have, especially when Norton rode along. "Where else would this guy go?"

I opened the door that led into the house. Norton ambled down the stairs from the living room, but he was a patient boy, waiting for my command to greet the newcomer in the room. A long-haired German Shepherd—well, mostly—he was smart. Though his tail wagged furiously, he eyed Tally suspiciously. I probably should've warned her, given I didn't know how she felt about dogs.

"He's gentle. He won't hurt you."

Norton took that as permission, as he stepped tentatively into the garage and toward Tally. Despite her surprise, she didn't look scared as she reached out, fingers curled into a soft fist, letting Norton sniff her fingers. When he licked them like she was made of cotton candy, she giggled.

"Oh my god, who is the handsomest boy? Aren't you just the sweetest, floofy boy!" With those words, Norton went full lovebug.

I'd picked him up on the side of the road as a puppy on my way down the West Coast, just past Tijuana. He'd been discarded with his siblings on the side of the road like trash. They'd been way too small and way too sick to ever survive out there by themselves, and I'd never hated humanity as much as I did the moment I found them.

I'd driven them to the closest vet, who'd checked them all over and declared his siblings were healthy enough, just infested with parasites. However, Norton had a significant heart murmur, and the vet had informed me it would be most humane to put him to sleep, since it was unlikely he'd ever be adopted with a possibly life-threatening defect.

That hadn't sat well with me, so I'd waved his siblings goodbye, but Norton became mine. He'd seen the best puppy cardiologists—which apparently was a thing—but thankfully, by the time he was a bounding six-month-old puppy, the murmur had almost gone. By the time he was a year old, you wouldn't have even known.

Now he was almost four, and aside from Hayes, was my best friend. He went to jump up on Tally's legs, and I whistled sharply. "Stop. Gentle, Norton." He sat back down on his haunches and nudged at her hands insistently for pats, which she gave him liberally.

"Your dog is as much of a manwhore as you are,"

Hayes whispered to me, and he wasn't wrong. Norton was a flirt, but he loved everyone: men, women, mailmen, other animals. Even the ducks at the park we went to. Occasionally, he was wary of people, and I always paid more attention to those people. And he was personally offended by one Boston Terrier we saw sometimes at the dog park. But otherwise, he was the best-natured dog anyone could ask for.

A car pulled into the driveway next door, and Norton curled around Tally's legs to stand in front of her, between the intruder and his new friend. Did I mention he was also protective? Not usually over a stranger this quickly, but always of me, and Hayes when he was here. I wondered if Norton could tell she was pregnant?

"Heel, Norton," I commanded, and he gave a pitiful whine, throwing a look up at Tally, but coming back to my side. "Stay."

Ushering Tally out, we met Chet in front of his car. "Mr. Banks, so glad to hear from you again." I bet he was. No one else was going to offload this place from him. "Let's do a last walkthrough, shall we?"

Optimistic of him. Still, I put my hand on the small of Tally's back and followed the realtor, Hayes close behind.

EIGHT

TALLY

IF I'D THOUGHT that Jesse was just giving me a freebie so I'd keep the money, one look at the house made me second-guess that. It looked like someone had pictured themselves as one of those social media renovators, because they'd done the kitchen, and it was *gorgeous*. Sage green walls with a butcher-block countertop? Beautiful. Gold fixtures and a matte black sink bigger than my fridge? Magazine-level perfect.

But the rest of the place didn't even have drywall. Obviously, someone had just decided to demolish everything all at once. Now, it was basically framing and studs with a roof. Even the master bedroom was just an empty shell, with an ensuite straight out of the seventies, which included mustard-colored tiles that had discolored to baby-poop brown.

It was way more than a slap of paint and some new carpet. According to Chet, the bank had foreclosed, and now it was on the market for basically nothing.

Sitting in Jesse's living room, which had been done immaculately right down to the crown moldings by his own rough—and honestly, sexy as fuck—hands, I wondered what I'd even bring to the table.

Norton snuffled at my lap, and I went back to stroking his head. I hadn't committed to anything yet, though Jesse had told the realtor to draw up the paperwork, so I assumed he was going to do it with or without me. And why wouldn't he? His commute to work was twenty-three steps outside his door. If I agreed, my commute would literally be just out my bedroom door.

The baby kicked me—not wind, like I'd convinced myself it was for ages—and I rubbed my stomach. Norton whined and nuzzled closer, as if he knew I was pregnant. "You're such a sweet boy, Norton."

A big empty ache churned inside me at the thought of a career other than the one that I'd dreamed about, but that was life, right? You just had to roll with it, and that's all there was to it.

"I'm in. You take the money back now."

Jesse poked his head out from the kitchen, where he was getting pizzas out of the oven. He might have a beautiful kitchen, but apparently, neither of them knew how to cook. "You're in?" I nodded, and a small smile curled his full lips. "Good."

He disappeared back into the kitchen, while Hayes laughed from the recliner across from me. "I for sure thought you'd look at the place and think *hell fucking no*. I know I did."

I shrugged. "I need to do something, especially once the baby comes, and this means I won't have to find childcare while I work. You'd vouch for him, right?"

Hayes looked at me intently. "I trust Jesse with my life." He leaned forward. "Once, when we were sixteen, my next-door neighbor fell and broke her hip. She was old as dirt, but she had twelve cats and refused to stay in the hospital if there was no one there to look after her pets. My parents promised to feed them, but Brenda said that wasn't enough. They needed love and affection, and that if there wasn't someone there, they'd pine and get sick. She loved those cats."

He dropped his voice further. "Anyway, Jesse heard my parents argue about it once, and volunteered. He moved in next door the whole eight weeks that Brenda was in hospital. The cats hated him at first, and one day, they just accepted him. I couldn't work it out, because those cats were skittish and only really liked Brenda. One day, I went over to peek through the window, and there was Jesse, dressed in Brenda's nightgown and robe, petting those cats like he was a crazy cat lady. The gown was floor-length and floral, and had lace right up to the neck. Funniest shit I've ever seen."

He laughed and sat back. "Brenda came home and lasted another year before she died. Jesse personally oversaw the rehoming of those cats. When I asked why he didn't keep one for himself, he said it was because he was allergic."

I leaned back on the couch, which Norton took as an invitation to climb all the way into my lap. Well, until

Jesse returned to the room. "Norton, down," he grumped, and the dog huffed a put-upon sigh and climbed down to lie at my feet instead.

I took in the huge, gruff guy, with the tattoos that spread down both arms, and even up his neck. He looked scary. He looked like a bad boy who meant nothing but heartache. But there was something about him, in the softness in his eyes, in his vibe, that just made me feel safe rather than fearful.

I was a strong believer in trusting my gut. It hadn't led me wrong yet.

Telling Willy that I'd gone into partnership and moved in next door to a man I didn't really know went down about as well as you'd imagine. He thought I was insane, but he didn't really argue against it like I thought he would. Apparently, the two of them had bonded over my "disappearance."

Besides, I'd laid it out to him and Colin in a very logical manner, as the business proposition it was. The amount the realtor believed we could get for a professionally finished home in the area, and what the projections were for the next few years. All very official.

I knew Willy was just happy to know that there'd be someone close by, that I was out of my one-room studio. He didn't say so, though, even as he and Colin helped me pack everything up into two tiny suitcases a couple of days later. But I'd known him long enough that he didn't even have to say a word. I could see it in the way his eyes skimmed the worn-down couch, the chipped countertops, the leaking tap in the bathroom. The fact there was no aircon.

I didn't have the heart to tell him the place I was moving to didn't even have walls, but at least I stood to make around eighty thousand after the new place sold.

If Willy was silent and brooding, Colin was the polar opposite, which was why they worked so well. Colin filled the empty air with conversation, talking about the baby and my appointments at the community health clinic, and gossiping about people who were on his diving team. The man loved gossip when he wasn't involved.

I knew he'd keep my shit locked down, but he was more than happy to tell me how Clarissa and Melanie were fighting over the same piece-of-shit swimmer who was legit fucking half of the training center. Or about the two office interns he'd caught fucking at Willy's work Christmas party. The man was an endless run of anecdotes. I loved it, and I loved him.

Finally, we loaded everything into Colin's SUV—because the Porsche wasn't made for moving anything but giant egos—and drove over to my new neighborhood. Jesse and I had worked out logistics and expectations yesterday, and I'd signed all the paperwork. Given that the place had been empty for so long, the city was happy to waive the normal cooling-off periods, so I could move in immediately. It worked out well, because my sublease had just come up again, and I could break it without penalty.

Lady Luck was handing me this olive branch, and I was going to take it with both hands.

"Are you sure you don't want to come and stay at my parents' place in Santa Barbara for the weekend? They'd love to have you," Colin offered again as we pulled up in front of Jesse's house.

I shook my head. "No, but thank you, though. Tell your parents I said hi, and your sisters." The guys were on their way down the coast, but had postponed to ensure I had someone to help me pack my meager possessions. I was also fairly sure Willy just wanted to ensure where I was staying was safe, the big mother hen.

Hayes stepped out from Jesse's house, coming over to shake the guys' hands. "This is Will's partner, Colin," I introduced, as Hayes and Willy hefted my bags and walked toward the new house.

"Nice to meet you, Colin. Jesse's just next door, making sure everything is set for you to move in. He had someone come in and put a security system in yesterday, so you'll be safe here. It's also got an alert button that'll call us, and then 911, in case you need it."

I rolled my eyes. "That's really not necessary, Hayes."

Willy grunted his disagreement, and I led them into the new house. Norton scrabbled on the floorboards as soon as he saw me, and I laughed as I bent down to get puppy kisses. It wasn't until half my face was damp that Norton noticed Willy and Colin behind me. He stiffened automatically, putting his body between me and them.

Luckily, Colin was a huge dog fan. He didn't meet his eye, just put out his hand to be scented, and Willy did the same. Finally assuring himself that the guys were okay, Norton went back to wagging his tail.

"Good security system, aren't you, boy?" Colin cooed, and Norton leaned in for a scratch before returning to my side. We followed Hayes further into the house to the master bedroom. It had an ensuite and a spacious walk-in wardrobe, which was pretty lux for this area. I wouldn't need it, but it would make a good nursery eventually.

As we stepped into the bedroom, we found Jesse putting last-minute touches on the room. Drywall had been put on and painted, and there was a bed in the middle of the floor. Although it was still just unfinished hardwood flooring, there were huge area rugs covering the floorboards.

Jesse was sitting on one in front of me, constructing a bassinet. It had mesh sides, with Scandinavian-style pale wooden legs. It took me a minute to notice the small set of drawers beside a change table as well, all of it matching. The whole place was light and beautiful, and made me want to cry.

Hayes came up behind me. "We wanted you to have somewhere comfortable for you and the baby that wasn't a construction zone. There's also a state-of-the-art Hepa air purifier over there, to make sure nothing hazardous to the baby drifts in."

Jesse had stopped what he was doing to watch my reaction, and my cheeks flushed as I swallowed hard. "You guys didn't have to do this," I told Hayes, who just shrugged.

"Consider it a baby shower gift. Plus, the work on the room had to be done anyway. We just sped it along a little."

"It's nothing. You were coming from a furnished apartment. We knew you wouldn't have much." Jesse stood and shook the bassinet to make sure it was sturdy. "Won't be needed for a while yet anyway, but it's good to have the basics. We'll leave you to get settled in." He squeezed my shoulder as he left, and the small amount of contact felt electrified.

Hayes flung an arm around my shoulder. "Let us know if you need anything. We're right next door." He left too, and I took in the room. It was beautiful. Simple but lovely.

"Well, if no one else is going to say it, then I will," Colin announced. "Holy hell, girl, they are *swoonworthy*." He dragged my suitcase into the walk-in. "You need to lock one of them down. Or both. We're progressive out here."

I shook my head and laughed, but I had a sneaking suspicion that no matter how much my head told me that was a terrible idea, my heart was getting a little caught up. It had a short memory for how messily heartache could kill you.

NINE

HAYES

THE FIRST DAY at any job was nerve-wracking. But the first day at a brand-new race team made me feel like I was about to jump out of my skin. Here, I had a chance to make something of myself. For my name to be written into history books, even if it was just as a lowly mechanic.

The compound where VANT Enterprises had set up VANT Racing was huge, more like a plane hangar than any workshop I'd ever been in. There was technology here that was revolutionary. I tried not to walk around like Charlie in some creepy old guy's chocolate factory, but it was hard not to gawk.

"We're just going through the motions of building the car at the moment, and while there are very few modifications we can make, there's always something, am I right?"

Antony was showing me around, and everything had that shiny newness about it. Even the other employees. Eventually, we'd be a team, where we could lean on each other and know that we had each other's backs, but that would take time.

I nodded, pointing out things I would change, things I was excited about, just generally fangirling about even being here, but trying to be cool. "How about drivers?"

"Rocco Passero has just lost his seat in F1, and we've managed to convince him to sign on for two years as our primary driver."

"Holy freaking *shit!*" I gasped, making heads turn.

Rocco Passero had been the wünderkind of F1, but suffered from a severe image problem. He partied way too hard. He also didn't play well with his teammates or the press or the team bosses, or just about anyone.

I cleared my throat. "Uh, well, that's a bold move."

Antony laughed. "Indeed. But we needed a bold driver to break into the game, and no one can drive like Rocco Passero."

That was true. "Just the one driver then?" I asked lightly.

My new boss raised an eyebrow at me. "I think we should start our working relationship with open and honest communication, don't you think? So how about you ask me what you want to ask me, hmm?"

I chuckled nervously. *Way to make a first impression, Hayes.* "I guess I didn't expect to see you out at that race the other day." I mean, we might be in a brand-new company, but you never knew who was a snitch. "Do you, uh, go to those kinds of events often?"

Antony snorted a laugh. "Not as much anymore, but it might surprise you that once upon a time, I attended those kinds of events regularly… from behind the wheel. But I'm a little too old for that now, and Vanessa would murder me if I died in a fiery car crash."

He continued around the factory. "No, we were doing exactly what you thought we were doing—scoping out racers. Mostly for sim driving and testing while we get the car race-ready, but maybe even for seats on the team. Rocco is excellent on road circuits, though he lacks some of the experience of street circuits and definitely on ovals. He was a little derisive of 'racing in a damn circle.'" Antony shook his head, like Rocco was just a wayward child and not a twenty-odd-year-old veteran of elite motorsports.

I nodded, and didn't hesitate when I said, "You should get Tally in. She can drive in circles, on the street, on a track, anywhere you need her to race. She's amazing behind the wheel of anything. She could make a shopping cart race downhill competitively."

Antony made a non-committal noise, but didn't outright say no. We continued the tour, before sitting down to talk logistics in a meeting with the rest of the team. I met the team manager—a legend of IndyCar, Ari Rome. I'd thought he'd retired, but apparently, enough money could pull anyone out of retirement.

When the day was done, I waved to Antony as he slid into that beautiful fucking Ferrari that made me want to weep. I knew the team wanted to get into Formula One eventually, but they were looking at probably six years or more before they could get FIA to even consider letting them in as a new team. They could buy out the interest in one of the existing teams, but Antony had big ideas of starting something great from the ground up. He was happy to pay his dues in IndyCar for now, but he'd be developing an engine in the background that could make us a contender.

Fishing my keys from my pocket, I jumped a little at the shouted, "Hayes!" As I turned, Antony pulled up beside me. "Tally… Why did she get booted from Ryclo? I know what the media said about it afterwards, but everyone is very tight-lipped about it."

Dammit. I could tell him the truth and break Tally's trust, but possibly get her a job back in her dream industry. Or I could be vague and hope he gave enough of a shit to look into it further. "I'm not sure I can say, but it didn't have anything to do with her driving ability. She was an amazing driver, and had one of the best rookie years in the last decade. If you're thinking of hiring her, you won't regret it."

Antony nodded slowly, staring through the windshield. "And she's pregnant?"

I bristled. "Yes, but I promise you that won't slow her down. I'll work with her to get childcare figured out, if you give her a chance."

He shook his head. "Calm down, kid. I'm just putting out feelers, not drawing up contracts." He gave me a lopsided grin. "You should know that while motorsports is my passion, Vanessa has one true goal in life: to put deserving women in male-dominated arenas and watch them fuck shit up. Miss Palmer being a woman won't count against her at all. See you tomorrow, Hayes."

"See you tomorrow."

Driving home, I decided not to tell Tally that Antony had been inquiring about her. If something came of it, then great. But if nothing came of it, I couldn't watch her heart break one more time.

Holding her in my arms that day, first when Buck died, and then when Ryker fired her, was the fucking worst thing I'd ever experienced. Not as bad as it was for Tally, of course, but watching someone's world shatter was so heart-wrenching, I wouldn't wish it on my worst enemy.

She'd changed that day. I'd watched it happen before my very eyes; she'd gone from a fresh-faced, happy-go-lucky driver living her dream, to a crushed bug beneath the heel of powerful men who gave more of a shit about their boys' club than anything else, including winning races.

Even now, it pissed me off. The only thing that chased away the anger was the fact I was going home to her.

I wanted to woo her without pressuring her, but I'd be damned if I knew how. I didn't want to push, and I could wait for her to come to me, if that's what she wanted. It was so freaking hard, though—every time I saw her with her head thrown back, laughing in that loud, honking laugh she had, I'd fall a little more in love with her.

Part of me didn't want her to work at VANT with me, because then we'd have to go back to being coworkers and teammates once more, and I wanted to be so much more than that. I hadn't believed in love at first sight until that first moment I saw Tally.

Letting out an aggravated huff at my pathetic self-ishness, I turned up the music and sang along to Tom Petty at the top of my lungs. By the time I pulled into Jesse's driveway, I was excited about seeing her. Did that make me whipped?

As I climbed from my car, I could hear Tally laughing, and Jesse's own deep-throated chuckle. Jealousy poured through me, but not at Jesse making her laugh. I mean, even the thought of Jesse flirting with her, or actually pursuing her, didn't make me jealous. No, if anything, I was just envious of the time he got to spend with her, making her happy. I wanted that.

Slowly, I warned myself again. She'd been through a lot, and the last thing she needed was me to barrel into her life with my heart bleeding in my hands.

Rolling up the sleeves of my button-down work shirt, I walked over to the new house. The sounds of some eighties rock band reverberated around the place, and Norton picked his head up from the floor where he was lying near the front door. I swear, he rolled his eyes, like he was saying, "They're nothing but pups, am I right?"

When I made it further into the place, I saw Jesse in a paint-splattered tee, beside what I could only assume was someone here to investigate a crime scene. Dressed head to toe in a white jumpsuit, Tally looked like she was turning off a nuclear reactor rather than undercoating a room.

"Rocking that body condom there, Tally," I teased to get their attention, and she whirled around. Her eyes lit up, making my heart thud in my chest. What I'd give to come home to that expression every day.

"Hayes! Jesse is convinced that if even a drop of paint gets on me, the baby will turn into an alien," she laughed, walking toward me and ripping the respirator mask from her face. She was grinning, her cheeks flushed pink.

"You'll be a great mother to little E.T.," I said solemnly, and she swung the respirator at me, gently whacking me in the gut.

Shaking her head, she looked between me and Jesse. "Honestly, you're as bad as one another." I looked over at my best friend, and I knew that expression. The wall around his heart was being kicked in, one laugh at a time, by the woman in front of me. "How was your first day?"

I led her out of the living room where they were painting and into the kitchen. The fumes couldn't be good for her, and I was glad Jesse was making her wear all the protective equipment.

She grabbed a beer from the fridge and handed it to me, and I smiled gratefully. "It was amazing. Tally, the tech they have in that place would blow your mind. The simulator itself is like Formula One grade. It's…" It was the stuff of motorhead wet dreams. "So fucking amazing. And you'll never guess who they're lining up as their primary driver?"

Her big eyes were so focused on me that it was a heady experience. Maybe that's what was so intoxicating about Tally; she made you seem like no one else in the world existed at that moment but you.

I drew out the silence for dramatic effect. "Rocco Passero."

"No fucking way!" she squealed, and I laughed.

"That's what I said! Apparently, he's lost his seat, and Antony Barbieri managed to woo him to IndyCar for a two-year contract. And guess who they got to be team principal? Ari Rome!"

Her eyes were so fucking wide, and I just wanted to pick her up and swing her around. I hated that she wasn't in this world anymore. I'd do everything I could to get her into VANT Racing too. I didn't give a shit if it was like, insider benefits, or whatever. She deserved everything the world could give her and more.

"Ari Rome! I thought he'd retired. Oh my god, what I'd give to work with Ari Rome. Did you know when he was a driver, he won the most back-to-back championships in history? He still holds the record…"

As she rattled off more racing facts, her face all lit up like there was a supernova burning inside her, a fragile thing in my chest awoke, and I knew I'd do whatever I could to make her happy forever.

TEN

TALLY

JESSE HAD FOUND several rotting floorboards in what was the laundry room, which meant that we had contractors coming in to fix the subfloor. Which worked out, because today, I needed to buy a car. At Jesse's insistence—and Hayes's too, if I was honest—I'd kept some of the race winnings to prepare for the baby. I wouldn't see any money from the sale of the house for at least six months, and babies were expensive. First thing I needed was a car, though, because getting to appointments on the bus was tedious as hell.

Hayes came with me, because who better to take to look at used cars than a NASCAR mechanic? I mean, I knew a bit; you couldn't drive cars professionally without knowing about them. I knew enough not to be ripped off by an unscrupulous salesman, anyway. But Hayes could pop the hood, eyeball the motor while it was running, and tell me exactly what was wrong or what was wearing down. You didn't turn down that kind of help.

We took Jesse's banged-up pick-up truck, because we needed to pick up several cans of paint and other stuff from the hardware store on the way back, and Hayes refused to even consider putting that in his baby.

"What about a minivan?" he asked me, and although his face was completely neutral, his eyes were laughing.

"How about you get a minivan, asshole," I grumbled back, and he burst out laughing. Man, such a good laugh. The kind that made you happy. "I want something a little cool. But also extremely safe." I had complete faith in my own driving skills, but I shared the road with a lot of other people, and some of them were idiots. The fact was, every person would likely make one stupid or reckless decision on the road at some point in their life, and I wanted to know that my baby would be safe.

Which also reminded me that I needed to talk to Willy and Colin about what would happen if anything happened to me during the birth. If I died, I'd want them to have the baby. But that was definitely something to have a conversation about first.

Man, being pregnant made you morbid and practical. Adulting sucked.

We climbed out of the car at the used car lot. "All right, Hayes. Your mission, should you choose to accept it, is to find the best car we can get under five grand. You in?"

He raised his eyebrows at me. "Let's do this shit."

An hour later, we hadn't found a car that suited me, and the salesman was loitering around like a vulture over a dying rabbit. Frustrated, I eyed an oversized SUV. It would be safe, and it was within budget, but it would be expensive to run. I was getting hungry and tired, which made me more than a little snappy as the salesman tried to tell me that it was the car chosen by most expectant mothers.

I wanted to punch him.

"You know what? We might come back later, I think," Hayes said as he checked out the engine. The salesman looked panicked, like his commission was leaving.

I pouted, then hated myself for pouting, and then I felt like crying, because this wasn't going right. *Definitely hangry.*

The salesman shook his head. "Pregnant wives, am I right? It takes their already naturally emotional selves to a whole new level of irrationality," he joked to Hayes.

I blinked at the guy. "*Excuse* me?" The guy suddenly realized he'd fucked up, when Hayes didn't laugh and agree like a good old boy.

Oh, man. I was about to show this asshole irrationality.

"Listen here, you little weasel. My ability to make a decision has *nothing* to do with my pregnancy and *everything* to do with this car lot's policy of shining up turds and trying to tell me that they're gold bars. You think I'm emotional now? You're about to see a whole new emotion, you stupid son of a bitch."

I stepped toward the guy, about to charge him and slap the crap out of his smug face, but Hayes grabbed me under my arms, carrying me away. I furiously flipped the salesman off with both hands.

"We won't be back, fuckface!" I yelled. Maybe that was a little over the top, but screw that guy.

Hayes put me on my feet and led me back to the truck. I was so enraged that I was huffing and puffing.

"How dare he? I was a world-class fucking race car driver, and he was calling me an overly emotional little woman. *Aw, gee shucks, what could she possibly know about cars?'"* I mocked in the salesman's smarmy voice, and Hayes swallowed down a snort as he let me rage. He opened the side door, so I could climb in. "I know more about cars now than that fucker has ever known in his entire damn life."

"I know, Tally," Hayes said soothingly, reaching over to help me with my seatbelt after I futilely jammed it into the wrong clip over and over.

"I was a fucking champion. I was *someone*, you know? My face was in magazines. Little girls asked me for my autograph. And now…" I hiccuped and realized I was crying, like the irrational little woman that guy had suggested I was. "And now I'm going to be a single mom, scraping by, and I'm already fucking it up. I resent the baby, do you know that? Last night, I thought about how I could be back on the circuit if it wasn't for it. That makes me the worst person in the world, because how could any mother think that about their child?"

Hayes unclipped me and pulled me back into his arms. He hugged me so tightly that it felt okay to break down. For the first time since realizing I was pregnant, I let myself feel all the things.

Fear. Worry. Joy. Regret. Wonder. They all spread through me one after another, like the shuffling of tarot cards. How could I do this, without giving everything up that I'd worked so hard for?

Hayes stroked my hair, whispering soothing sounds. "Hey, hey, it's going to be okay."

"I'm so damn scared, Hayes. I never thought I'd have to do this alone."

He stroked my back and squeezed me tighter. "You're not alone, Tally. You have Will and Colin, who love you so much that Will threatened to break both my hands—in kind of graphic ways for a pen pusher—if I ever thought of hurting you." He pulled back a little. "You have me and Jesse for as long as you want us, because we're one hundred percent Team Tally, you know? And we'll be Team Baby too."

"You can't say that. You barely know me. And Jesse has been my friend for all of a week."

"We were on the road together for months. I know enough about you to know that if you need me, I'll be there." He laughed. "As for Jesse, he sat on my toolbox the first time I met him and spoke to me for three hours. At the end of the day, he said, 'We're best friends now,' like that's all there was to it. When I tell you that Jesse doesn't need to know you for long to be a hundred percent behind you, I mean it. You're already up a week on me, so he's about ready to give you a kidney."

I smiled, letting my head rest back on his chest. He smelled good, like cologne and motor oil. He smelled like happiness. I wished I knew what they wanted from me, why they would bother taking all my shit on, but when I'd looked up into his face, his sparkling blue eyes shining down at me, part of me knew.

The part of me that recognized the look in his eyes was deep in my chest, and it thumped a little harder at the possibility that I was reading his expressions right. But I couldn't take the leap and be wrong. I couldn't ruin what we had by making it something it wasn't.

Rejection would break more than my heart. Besides, when I was with Jesse, a long, shutdown part of me woke up too, and I would never, ever come between their friendship.

No, the best thing to do was remain friends with them both. Treat them how I treated Willy and Colin.

"Want to go get some ice cream?" Hayes asked softly, and I nodded, not lifting my head.

Tomorrow, I'd treat them with the same affection as I treated Willy. Today, I'd take the comfort Hayes was so freely offering, and try not to catch feelings that I didn't deserve.

ELEVEN

JESSE

I WAS FUCKED. Head over heels, absolutely fucked. We'd been working on this place for a month now, and the more I worked with her, the more enamored I became with the woman next to me.

Tally held a piece of drywall in place as I screwed it. "What do you think about Benny, after Benny Parsons? It's unisex, so it could suit either gender."

I looked down at her and raised an eyebrow. "You wanna call your kid Benny? May as well call it Crystal Meth. Or better, you can call it Dale Earnhardt and be done with it."

She gave me the finger, but still held the sheet still. It really was good to have an extra set of hands, though I made sure she never lifted anything heavy or climbed any ladders. "Don't be mean. Both the baby's parents were NASCAR drivers when it was conceived, so I kind of want to give it a name that's a nod to my dreams."

She always sounded so sad when she talked about

her racing career, and I hated it. "What about Bobby? There are lots of great Bobbys in NASCAR history. Bobby Labonte. Bobby Allison. Ricky Bobby," I teased. "It's unisex too."

It helped that Hayes had always been a NASCAR fan. He'd been talking to me about iconic drivers for as long as we'd been friends. I'd been so surprised when he left Ryclo over the firing of a random driver, though now I'd met Tally, I could understand. The idea of anyone being cruel to her made me irrationally angry.

If I saw Brick Willtot anytime soon, I was going to punch that fucker in the face.

"Bobby... I like it," she said, grinning up at me like sunshine personified. And that was the reason I was fucked.

I liked her. The more time I spent around her, the more I *liked* her. Worst friend ever. Hayes had told me about her breakdown at the car lot, and it would make me the worst kind of asshole to catch feelings for this girl.

Let me list all the ways in which me thinking of Tally romantically was fucked up.

One: my best friend liked her. And I mean, seriously liked her. There was a bro code for this kind of situation, and if I made a move on Tally? Well, it was like breaking the code, then throwing the code into the ocean, where it'd be eaten by the Shark of Treachery and then shat out into tiny little flecks of asshat, which would then be consumed by the Whale of Betrayal.

Two: she was obviously in a vulnerable place. I

would be all kinds of scum if I tried to pursue something with her right now, while she was still figuring herself out.

Three: she was about to be someone's parent, which meant she came as a package deal. I had nothing against babies, but I honestly knew nothing about them. I wasn't parent material at all. My dad had been gone most of the time with work, and my mom had sent me as far away as possible after her mental breakdown. While logically, I understood that they'd both loved me, that shit left a guy with a little bit of trauma.

Repeating points one to three in my head, I climbed back down the ladder. She held it with one hand, like she could stop it toppling over with her featherlight weight. Once I was on the ground, she stood there, hands on her hips, looking up at the wall we'd just hung.

"It looks beautiful."

It was unpainted drywall. It was the furthest thing from beautiful in the world, but as I looked at it, it did seem just a little bit nicer somehow.

"You're beautiful." It just fell out of my mouth. I slammed my jaw shut so fast, I definitely chipped a tooth, but it was too late. *Fuck me.*

But she was beautiful. She looked like a Renaissance painting of some wild goddess, her hair poking out at odd angles, her stomach definitely popping now, and a satisfied smile on her face.

Well, she *had* been smiling. Now she was frowning in my direction.

So I did the manliest thing I could think of—I ran away while changing the subject. "So, I think we're definitely done for the day. I feel a bit like Thai food. Or tacos? What do you say to tacos?" I'd made it all the way into the kitchen by the taco speech, and I grabbed my water bottle and chugged the cold liquid, like it was going to cool the fire in my blood.

I'd need to be frozen for that to happen.

She sounded amused by the time she made it to the kitchen. "Sure, I could go for tacos. Let me grab my purse."

She moved toward the back of the house where her room was, and I gave myself another pep talk, which was mostly calling myself every derivative of asshole I could come up with. I was just going to ignore that I'd opened my big mouth. Maybe if I pretended that it was no big deal, Tally would forget about it.

Solid move.

I grabbed my wallet and keys, stuffing them in the pockets of my jeans. When Tally emerged, she'd changed into leggings with a cropped t-shirt. The leggings accentuated the bump of her stomach, and when she bent down to slip on her Chuck Taylors, I noticed they also accentuated the curves of her delicious ass.

We climbed into my old truck, and I listened intently as Tally chatted about all sorts of things. Appointments Will was taking her to, stats for Rocco Passero that she'd Googled, what the plumber had said about underfloor heating, and the fact that she was negotiating with a lady on social media for a crib.

"Take one of us with you if you go to look at it. I've seen that episode of *Law and Order*."

She raised an eyebrow at me, but agreed easily. The whole thing was so fucking domestic, that if I didn't know our circumstances, I'd think *we* were a couple expecting our first child, living the American dream.

What was even more surprising was that the idea didn't make me want to run for the hills. So we'd come full circle; I was so fucked.

Clearing my throat as we pulled into the parking lot hosting the taco truck, I interrupted her recount of the differences between IndyCar and Formula One. "You should message Hayes and see if he wants any tacos."

She blinked those big eyes up at me. "Shit, of course. I'll call him." Pulling out her phone, she dialed his number. "Hello?" She paused, frowning in concentration. "We're getting tacos. The one down by the park. Yeah. Okay, we'll wait for you... What is it? Hayes, I hate surprises." She huffed, and it was cute as fuck. "We'll see you soon."

I raised an eyebrow as I parked, coming around to open her door. I held out a hand, and she took it easily. The way her small fingers curled in mine made my heart thump in my chest, and I felt like such a sap in that moment.

She grinned up at me. "Thanks, Jesse. Hayes says he's got news, but wouldn't tell me what it is. You think VANT got one of the Ferrari guys to defect to IndyCar?"

she teased, and I couldn't help but laugh too. Her face lit up. "Holy shit, feel this."

I realized she was still holding my hand as she tugged it toward her stomach, and suddenly, I was cupping the small mound of her belly in my palm. I felt the flutter of something beneath her skin. A kick. Or a headbutt. It was hard to know.

Her eyes were shining, the flash of the taco truck lights making them sparkle with happiness. "Guess I can't call it a cryptic pregnancy anymore. Lug Nut is making himself known. Or herself."

I stared down at her stomach, nothing in my brain but white noise. We stood there, in this silent bubble moment, the setting sun making her skin a soft pink and so damn kissable.

Our eyes caught, and I could see it then—the attraction she felt for me too. My eyes dropped to her lips as they parted, her tongue darting out to wet her puffy lower lip. I wanted to kiss her more than anything. My eyes darted back to hers, all the impossibilities suspended in the silent moment stretching between us.

I leaned closer, infinitesimally, hoping she'd see the invitation and want to kiss me enough that she'd close that distance between our lips. That she felt this thing between us as much as I did.

A car door slammed, jolting us from the moment, and then Hayes was there, grinning wildly as he picked Tally up and spun her around.

She laughed, her eyes flicking briefly to mine, before she focused on my best friend. "Oof, Hayes. Put me down." He settled her back to her feet, and she looked at him like he'd gone nuts. "What are you so happy about? Did you win the lottery? Did someone give you a Hellcat for free?"

"Better!" He was all but bouncing from foot to foot. "I got you a job. Well, another job." He flicked his eyes to me briefly. "Well, basically a glorified interview. They want you to do some testing on the cars."

Emotions crossed her face like camera flashes. Elation. Fear. Happiness. Worry. Doubt.

"They know she's pregnant?" I couldn't help but ask.

Tally rolled her eyes. "The whole underground racing circuit in this city knows I'm pregnant now, thanks to this guy." She lifted her chin at Hayes, who was giving me the stink eye, like I was shitting all over his grand reveal. I felt like crap as some of the excitement left her face. "He makes a good point, though. I can't test drive pregnant. Also, I'm about twenty pounds heavier than I should be."

"And still thirty pounds lighter than most male racers. Plus, it's all sim driving for a while anyway. You can do this, Tally. It's not the same as before, but you can dip your toes back in, and who's to say that it won't lead to something more? Something different, but just as good. Not your exact dream, but dream-adjacent." He lowered his voice. "Maybe even better than NASCAR," he whispered, like Richard Petty might appear from behind the food truck and declare him a traitor to the sport. "But first, they've invited us to a team cookout, and I guess they'll give you an informal interview. Antony said you should come too, Jesse."

I raised an eyebrow at him. Why would I be invited, unless they thought Hayes and I were... a thing? Whatever, I'd take the opportunity to suss out the VANT group and their intentions, and make sure they weren't going to take advantage of Tally.

Happiness had made her whole face light up, and I vowed that one day, she'd look at me like that too. I'd just have to work harder for the privilege.

TWELVE

TALLY

"TALLY! WE HAVE TO GO!" Hayes yelled from the doorway to the house. I'd only just washed the paint from my hair and my hands, but at least the primer coat of the plasterboard was done. I was enjoying renovating the house; there was something satisfying about it. It also gave me something to focus on in the long, lonely evenings, like Googling how to use a nail gun without piercing vital body parts, or studying how to recess lights. Between that and reading about all the shit I was probably going to fuck up once the baby was born, I was distracted from the past that haunted me.

Right now, though, I was trying on ten different dresses to decide which one made me look less pregnant. If everything went right, I could converge my old life with my new one, and create something better for me and the baby.

Huffing a frustrated sigh, I threw on a floral dress and pinned my hair up. Realistically, they'd either want me for my driving skills, or not at all. Slipping my feet into sandals, I grabbed a denim jacket and rushed out of the house.

Locking up, I met Hayes on the front porch. He was grinning, as if he hadn't just hollered at me like a fisherman's wife. "You look beautiful," he said, his eyes sliding over me quickly before meeting mine again. "Are you ready? Because if you aren't, I'm stuffing you into the car anyway. We're running behind schedule."

Pit crew mechanics, man. They were all about being on time. I held up my hands. "No need for stuffing anyone anywhere. I'm ready. Lead the way."

Hayes turned, and I took a moment to really take him in. He was so fucking handsome and kept himself in great shape. His ass was the kind you wanted to sink your nails into, while you held on for dear life as he dicked you right into the mattress. He was wearing classic blue jeans that looked well loved but still neat, and a button-down shirt with the sleeves rolled up as a concession to the summer heat. He looked like the kind of boy you took home to your mama, and she'd tell you what a sweet man he was.

And after you finished your Georgia peach pie, he'd take you home and eat your pie.

Something low in my body clenched, and I groaned. He looked over his shoulder, but I quickly schooled my features. I had to get my head in the game, right now, or I was going to fuck up this chance.

As if to bamboozle my libido in a tandem attack, Jesse appeared. He was dressed in all black. Black t-shirt. Black jeans. Black boots. The only colorful things about him were the tattoos running across his exposed skin. He was holding a bottle of wine, and Norton was looking at him pitifully from the front window.

While Hayes's eyes had taken me in quickly, Jesse's gaze was like a caress as it slid down my body, taking in my curves, the spot where my hem brushed the middle of my thighs, even my feet, before traveling back to my face. "You look nice."

I snorted at the faint praise. "Thanks, Jesse. You both look good too. Now let's go, so I don't make a terrible first impression."

"Your first impression was at an illegal street race. I'm not sure you can change that now," Hayes teased. "But we can get you there for a good second impression."

We slid into his car, though I had to insist I sat in the back seat. I couldn't even imagine Jesse trying to fold his legs into the space in the back. These muscle cars weren't really made to be people movers.

Antony Barbieri and his family lived in an area that was so rich, we went through two security checks, got ticked off a list, and had to hand over our ID before we were let in. It would probably have been easier to get into Fort Knox.

The houses were few and far between, all surrounded by high fences and sprawling lawns. Honestly, there was rich, and there was whatever the hell the VANT owners were. Obscenely wealthy. I assumed that was why Antony Barbieri could just wake up one morning and decide he wanted to start a very costly racing team from scratch.

We pulled up to a small camera, which I think scanned Hayes's face, before letting us in. "Welcome, Hayes Davis," it said in a robotic voice, and I gaped as Hayes rolled down the driveway.

"Sometimes, I forget they made their money in tech," Jesse grumbled. "That's some science-fiction bull-shit." I couldn't agree more.

As we pulled up to a spot, a valet came over and collected the keys from Hayes, who eyed him warily. The guest parking was a mish-mash between pick-ups and SUVs, though there was one shiny red Ferrari parked amongst them, like a diamond in a pig pen.

We walked up the beautiful steps to a house that was far more earthy than I'd expected, especially compared to the other houses in the area. Wood, glass and concrete sat together in architectural chaos, but somehow managed to work.

Vanessa Sumich, Antony's partner, answered the door barefoot, in a beautiful dress that flowed behind her. Her hair was beginning to gray, and somehow, it only added to her beauty. She was gorgeous.

"Hayes! It's good to see you again." She leaned forward and kissed his cheek, like they were old friends and not employer-employee. Then she stepped back, reaching out a hand toward me. "And you must be Tally. I've heard a lot about you over the past few weeks, and I saw you race. Very impressive."

I wasn't sure if she meant she'd seen race footage of

me, or she was referring to the recent, slightly illegal street racing, but I didn't press. "Lovely to meet you, Ms. Sumich."

Waving a hand, she turned to Jesse last. "Mr. Banks, thank you for coming also."

Jesse raised an eyebrow. "Thank you for inviting me, Ms. Sumich, though I'm not sure why you did. Hayes and I aren't a couple."

I looked over at Jesse like he'd lost his goddamn mind, and Hayes's eyes were almost as wide as his mouth.

The elegant woman in front of us threw back her head and snort-laughed. "Oh my goodness. Well, you know what they say—never say never." She gave us an outrageous wink. "You're still very welcome. Please, come in, all of you." She was still chuckling, and I gave Jesse a *what the fuck* look.

He shrugged unapologetically, and Hayes elbowed him in the ribs, but we pulled it together as we were led through the house.

And holy shit, what a house. It had vaulted ceilings and huge windows, with so much light, it was like being bathed in sunshine. There was gentle art on the walls, in a color palette that was earthy and neutral. The place was like a warm hug; you could do cartwheels across the kitchen floor, but also snuggle down in front of the fireplace—which was kind of unnecessary in California, aside for aesthetics.

Finally, we stepped through the open back doors, onto a deck that was humming with people. Vanessa disappeared to get us some drinks, and we made our way further into the crowd. Some faces I recognized from my time in the sport, like Ari Rome, who was surrounded by people like he was holding court. A few other faces I recognized from my time coming up in NASCAR, but honestly, the progression of both sports was vastly different.

One face I hadn't expected to see was that of the bassist from my favorite masked rock band. I nudged Hayes. "Holy shit, it's Poet, from The Daymakers." It wasn't like he was wearing the mask right now, but they'd recently revealed their identities, because of doxxing or some shit. This was why the world couldn't have nice things.

It was also how I knew that Poet was Moss Aguilar, son of one of the biggest names in Formula One driving history. He was making conversation with someone I couldn't see, his arm around a girl I knew was his partner, Charlotte. If their interviews were true, she was the girlfriend of the entire band. *Lucky bitch.*

Actually, I'd recently discovered that the VANT owners were also known polyamorists. Maybe that was why Vanessa had assumed that me, Hayes and Jesse were all one big love triangle. Boy, they couldn't be more wrong, but I let myself imagine for a moment, a world where I could have them both without ruining our burgeoning friendship.

Then I snorted. I couldn't maintain a relationship with one man, let alone two.

"Want to go introduce yourself?" Hayes murmured to me.

Fuck no. But Hayes was already dragging me along, stepping to the outside of their little group. I cast a panicked look over at Jesse, who was leaning back against the railing, looking amused.

"...it would mean a lot to the foundation if you could just come to one session. No pressure, though," Moss Aguilar was saying to someone in the group.

When I saw who they were talking to, my feet stopped dead, like I was knee-deep in quicksand. They were talking to freaking Rocco Passero. *The* Rocco Passero was right here, right in front of me, next to one of my favorite music artists of all time.

"Breathe," a soft voice said to me, and I looked up into the beautiful face of Charlotte. Or Dreamer, as the fans knew her. "If you pass out at their feet, you'll give them even bigger egos than they already have."

Sucking in a deep breath, I looked everywhere but at the two men in front of me. The ground needed to open up and drop me into the abysmal pits of mortification forever. I continued to stare at Charlotte. "Do you think I can blame it on the pregnancy brain?"

She laughed, giving me a conspiratorial nod. "I think so, yes." Her eyes dropped briefly to my stomach, then back up again.

A hand appeared in my peripheral vision. "Hi, I'm Moss. It's nice to meet you...?"

Sucking in another deep breath, I shook his hand

and forced a smile that I hoped wasn't as awkward as it felt. "Tally Palmer."

Hayes stuck out his hand too. "Hayes Davis. A mechanical engineer over at VANT Racing. Nice to meet you. And you too, Mr. Passero."

"I bet it is," Rocco Passero crooned, like he was talking to a child.

Hmm. I frowned, doing my best dumb blonde look. "Rocco Passero. Your name sounds familiar. Are you in the music industry too?" I fluttered my lashes in slow swoops. "What's your band's name?"

Hayes was looking at me like I'd lost my mind now, but I didn't like the snarky way Rocco had replied to him. My Hayes, who was kindness personified. *Nuh-uh.*

Charlotte made a noise, but when I looked over at her, she was keeping it together. However, her eyes were sparkling, like she was about to explode with laughter.

Rocco frowned. "I'm not in a band."

I raised my eyebrows at him. "Well, keep at it. You never know when you'll make it."

That was too much for Charlotte, who choked out a laugh halfway through sipping her champagne, and spat it back into her glass like a small fountain.

Moss looked amused. "Rocco here is in Formula One. Well, formerly in Formula One. I don't believe he has any musical talent whatsoever."

"Oh, wow. I used to race karts when I was a kid. My dad was a NASCAR fan," I said to Moss, and he must have caught on to Charlotte's amusement, because he decided to play along.

"Really? I run a foundation that gives kids in low socioeconomic areas the opportunity to learn racing skills and achieve sponsorships."

This time, I didn't have to feign my interest. "Your father was a racer, right?" I could feel Rocco's eyes on the side of my face. *Oops, might have just given away my hand, but whatever.*

Moss nodded, smiling sadly. I felt like a dick, but it was a pain I could relate to. The pain didn't go away just because you didn't say their name.

Hayes gave him a sympathetic look. "Arguably one of the best of all time." He flicked his eyes quickly at Rocco, who definitely fit into that category but didn't need any further inflating of his ego.

"You run your foundation here in California?" I asked, but Moss shook his head again.

"No, over on the East Coast, but I'm working with VANT to set up a satellite foundation on this side. I was just asking this guy if he wanted to get on board, help out a little."

What I would've given to have had a foundation like Moss's when I was a kid, rather than my father working himself into an early grave to pay for all the things I needed. "Let me know if you need any help. I'm happy to get out there with the kids and give them pointers."

Rocco raised a perfect, dark eyebrow. Goddamn, he

was handsome. "And why would he want the girlfriend of a mechanic to help teach children to kart?"

What a pompous ass. I gave him a tight smile. "Sorry, maybe I didn't introduce myself properly. Tally Palmer, NASCAR driver." I leaned forward. "That's the one where you actually have to be a better driver than the person next to you, not just have the best car."

The corners of his lips quirked. He reached out and gripped my hand, lifting it to his lips. "I didn't introduce myself properly either. Rocco Passero, the best Formula One driver in history." He brushed barely a whisper of a kiss across my knuckles. "But I assume you knew that already."

I shrugged. "You know what they say about assuming."

Charlotte was belly-laughing now, looking up at Moss. "Poet, can we keep her?" She hooked an arm in mine. "Come on, let's leave the testosterone behind and go get some of those fancy little pastry puff things."

THIRTEEN

TALLY

I'D PROBABLY FUCKED up my chances at interviewing for VANT Racing already, by opening my big mouth on their star driver, but I wasn't ever going to be the person who let someone with a huge ego talk down to my friends.

As much as I wanted to work for VANT, I was also happy flipping houses with Jesse right now. I told myself that over and over as I ate some kind of mini hamburger with Charlotte, who grilled me for information like she was in the CIA, while telling me very few details about The Daymakers or their lives. Honestly, it was a masterclass in being good at PR.

Antony walked over, and I stiffened. Charlotte leaned closer to me, dropping her voice low. "I love my guys, but holy hell, what a hottie."

She was right, of course. Antony Barbieri was universally sexy. Perfectly straight men would look at him and question themselves. His hair was a dark gunmetal silver, his skin a warm gold that seemed to defy age. He was clean-shaven, and his jaw had clearly maintained its sharpness. I wondered if that was due to cosmetic surgery or just good genes. His eyes had crow's feet, the only hint that he was older than you might think.

But the most attractive thing about him was the way he looked at Vanessa. His face softened as he gazed at her, like the sun rose just for her. It was sweet, and it made my heart clench in my chest. One day, someone would love me like that. I wouldn't accept anything less.

He held out a glass of wine to Charlotte, and another to me. "Sparkling apple juice," he murmured. I smiled gratefully at him, more touched by the small gesture than I normally would be, because... hormones.

Charlotte coughed. "Mine definitely isn't apple juice." She sipped again. "Delicious, though." She smacked her lips, and Antony laughed.

"Thank you. We have a vineyard just north of here, and we like to pretend to be vintners."

Charlotte tipped her glass to him. "I'm no expert, but it tastes better than the stuff you can get at Costco." She smirked, then looked over her shoulder. "I think Poet wants to leave. Thank you for inviting us, Mr. Barbieri. We'll be in touch?"

He nodded. "Absolutely. We look forward to working with you."

Charlotte hugged me. "Stay in touch. I like you!" Then she bounced away. I watched her go, Moss following her with his eyes, as if he wanted to devour her right here on the lawn.

Antony shook his head, amused. "I remember being that young. Everything burns red hot all the time." He turned back toward me. "I assume Hayes has informed you that we're looking for test drivers over at VANT?"

I swallowed hard. "He has. Mr. Barbieri—"

"Please, call me Antony."

"Antony, I promise you, I can get the most out of any car you put me in, either on the track or in sims. However, I have to tell you that I kind of come with an extra for a little while." I made a vague motion toward my stomach. "And it doesn't really sit right with me to leave the baby at daycare from the day it's born. So I wouldn't be much good to you for a while. To be fair to the team, maybe you should find someone else. Someone who can make VANT Racing their number one focus."

Antony made a noise of disagreement. "Just bring the baby with you. I remember the newborn stage— they sleep and eat a lot, and you'd have one hundred percent permission to do what you need to keep the baby happy. Hayes will also be there. In fact, as we get a little further into establishment, I might look at putting in a creche. The days of families being able to live on single incomes are long gone. To be honest, it's getting difficult for families to even be able to live on dual incomes.

"We want to get the best people, and to get the best people, you have to pave roads to help them succeed.

Best to start as we intend to go on, hmm?" I could see him considering the idea as I just gaped at him. "Something for the board later. If you wish to test drive for us, the opportunity is yours. We'll figure out the rest when it becomes an issue."

I was nodding slowly, as I tried to form words. "Yes. One hundred percent yes. I... You won't regret it, Antony. I promise."

He gave me a broad smile, and in that moment, I could see the young man Vanessa must have fallen in love with. "I know I won't. You have a hunger I recognize. I saw it in a young woman breaking into an industry that had no space for her thirty years ago." I had a feeling he was talking about Vanessa, and when he looked over at her in the crowd, I knew I was right. "As a testament to that young woman who wouldn't give up, we try to provide opportunities to other women in male-dominated industries."

It might not sit quite right that I was getting this position because I was a woman, but I didn't care. I'd come up against so many drivers who had their seats because of who their daddy was, or their mentor, or simply because they were rich enough to pay for their seat. It wasn't an industry that gave opportunities for fairness, so I'd take whatever hand-ups I could get.

My eyes snagged on Rocco Passero. "Uh, in the interest of starting off with honest communication, Antony, I might've already offended your star driver by pretending not to recognize him. And perhaps telling him that if he tried hard, he could also be a rockstar like

Moss Aguilar one day." I winced at my own words, but I was determined to start on a clean slate.

Antony threw back his head and laughed. "I am fairly sure Rocco's ego can take it, Tally. Actually, I'm fairly sure his ego could take being run over by a monster truck several hundred times with no ill effects." He shook his head, still chuckling. "That being said, we'll soon be a team, so please, do not antagonize him on purpose."

I nodded noncommittally, because as I found Rocco in the crowd, I found his gaze burning back at me. I wasn't sure I could completely keep that promise. Something about his arrogance got a rise out of me.

However, this was my second chance, and I wasn't about to fuck it up over a guy.

Again.

As the night wore on, I drifted back to Jesse. He was still holding up the railing on the deck, but had been talking to different people during the night, beer in hand. Every time someone came up to us, though, he introduced me first.

However, how he introduced me varied. Sometimes it was, "This is Tally; she's my business partner." But other times, it was, "This is Tally; she was the youngest rookie to ever drive in Daytona." Either way, I flushed every time.

There was something about Jesse that drew people in. It was the casual way he held himself, like he didn't care that he was in a mansion, surrounded by people who had nothing to do with him. He belonged wherever he said he belonged.

I shivered lightly as the sun set, taking the last vestiges of warmth with it. Jesse wrapped an arm around my shoulders, pulling me closer without even skipping a beat in the conversation he was having with one of the VANT marketing guys. They were discussing wine from southwest California, of all things, but Jesse somehow kept up with the conversation, even though I'd never seen him put a wine glass to his lips in the time I'd known him.

I rested my head against his chest, soaking in his warmth. He smelled so damn good, it should be against the law. Some kind of woodsy scent that one hundred percent came out of a bottle, but still made me want to lick him from head to toe.

Wait. No. Bad, Tally. Bad.

Warning signs were flashing in my brain, but my touch-starved soul hit the override button. Just for a moment, I could appreciate the warmth of holding another human being.

Where's the harm?

It wasn't like I was going to strip down on the back patio of my future employer's house and ask him to take me. This was just a harmless hug between friends. That was it. If I couldn't help but curl my fingers into the strong muscles of his back, that was on me, not Jesse.

His arm tightened around me a little more, his hand

coming down to rub the top of my arm vigorously to warm it, as the topic moved on to burgeoning suburbs for real estate in San Francisco.

I breathed out deeply, feeling the steady thump of his heart against my cheek. This was getting a little desperate, but I'd take it. I closed my eyes for a moment. Man, this pregnancy thing was making me tired all the time. I really needed a cheeseburger and a nap.

Lips touched the top of my head. "You okay there, Tally? Want to head out?"

Sighing, I straightened. "Yes, please."

His fingers trailed down my arm one last time. "Let's go find Hayes."

It didn't take long to find Hayes, who was talking to what looked like a group of cowboys, judging by the hats and boots, as well as one of Vanessa's other partners, Nathan. They were all laughing, and I felt almost bad dragging Hayes away.

Then the baby kicked me right in the bladder, and I wondered if there was a countdown of how many times it could do that before I peed myself.

Hayes reached out and grabbed my hand, dragging me close. "Tally, this is Tessa May. She was the first woman in professional bull riding. You might know her as T.M. Moore? She's sponsored by VANT. And these are her partners, Branch and Frankie." I looked at the two guys, who looked like they'd climbed straight out of *Yellowstone* and straight into any hot-blooded woman's spank bank.

I blinked a little as shit suddenly came back to me. "Holy shit. T.M. Moore! I watched you ride in your debut season. You were *amazing.* You signed a rider number for my dad once in Texas. I still have it framed somewhere. Wow." I shook her hand hard. She had to be in her early thirties now, not that you'd know it. I remembered watching her on the television, thinking if she could make it in bull riding, then I could definitely be a race car driver. "I got into NASCAR because I was inspired by you."

Tessa May frowned. "Your dad was a cab driver?"

I nodded furiously. "Yes!"

She smiled widely. "I remember him. He said you wanted to be a driver. I'm so glad you got there! He really made an impression on me on that day. I was worried I was going to fuck everything up, and your dad was there, telling me about you, and how you looked up to me, and it made everything clear again. I owed him a lot more than an autograph. What a small world." She shook her head like it was unbelievable, which it definitely was. "How is he?"

I swallowed hard, fighting to keep my smile on my face. "He died a couple of years ago."

She gave me a look filled with empathy. "I'm sorry for your loss. I'm sure he'd be proud of you, though. He definitely was back then."

I nodded, not trusting my voice. Jesse stepped closer, touching my back with gentle reassurance. "We should get Tally home," he said softly to Hayes, who looked at me, his face softening with sympathy.

"Yeah, of course." He stuck out his hand and said his farewells, and I did too.

Jesse's hand remained on the small of my back as we navigated our way out of the still-thick crowd. It had been a hell of a night, but I was looking forward to being back in our little bubble. I hadn't realized how secure I'd become in the routine that Hayes, Jesse and I now had.

The valet brought Hayes's car, and we climbed in. I let my head flop back onto the head rest. "Is it just me, or was there a disproportionate amount of group relationships at that party?" Jesse asked, and I snorted a laugh. I'd noticed the same thing.

Hayes tapped the steering wheel as he waited for the gate to open. "Not just you. Maybe they have, like, a group-relationship social club or something? But they all seemed happy, right? I don't know, man. It would be hard not to be a jealous asshole in that situation."

I was keeping my mouth shut, because I'd struggled holding down a relationship with one guy, let alone five, like Charlotte and The Daymakers. But I mean… I could dream of a perfect world. A world where I could be loved by more than one partner. I could rely on them. I would never be alone again.

And the sex. Man… imagine the sex.

I swallowed the moan in my throat, letting out a choked sound. Hayes looked at me in the rearview mirror, and I worked to keep my face impassive. Oblivious to my inner thoughts, he continued. "I mean, it obviously works some of the time, because Vanessa and her little polycule have been together, what? Thirty years? I think, with the right person, I'd be open to it too."

Jesse's face whipped toward Hayes. "Seriously?"

Hayes's eyes met mine, then darted away. "Sure. I mean, I don't want to fuck another guy, but I wouldn't mind sharing a woman. Especially if it was with the right person. Or people, I guess."

Jesse looked out the windshield. "Yeah. Me either, for the right girl." He pointed to a fast food place. "Let's go through the drive-thru. Tally's hungry."

Holy shit. I couldn't believe what I was hearing. I kept reminding myself that they weren't talking about me in particular. They hadn't been anything but friendly, really. But there'd been that moment with Jesse the other day at the taco truck. And there were a lot of those moments with Hayes.

Had we just soft launched the idea of a three-way relationship?

"Can I take your order?"

I'll have a threesome with two handsome guys, who already take care of me better than any of my exes ever have. And a side of fries. Thank you.

FOURTEEN

HAYES

TALLY HAD BEEN quiet for the rest of the ride home last night, but she hadn't seemed uncomfortable. More like she was deep in thought, either about the topic of conversation, or the double beef burger that she'd ordered.

I hadn't imagined the tension between us as we walked Tally to her door, but we'd said a friendly good-night and walked next door. However, as soon as we made it through the front door, I'd turned to Jesse.

"You're interested in Tally." It was a statement, not a question. I wasn't oblivious; I could see how much he liked her, just from the way he watched her. Jesse and I had a long friendship, and some things you just *knew*. For instance, I knew he wanted her. I also knew that he loved me and wouldn't make a move on her, because he believed in the friendship code, despite the fact I had no claim whatsoever on Tally. She was her own free woman, and if she chose Jesse, I'd be happy for them.

But he'd never pursue her, knowing that I already had feelings for her.

So I hadn't been surprised by his hesitant, "Yes."

Last night had been eye-opening in more ways than one. I hadn't known that group relationships like that were even an option. I'd spent so many years thinking that relationships could only look the way my parents' did. My mom and dad had met at work when they were in their twenties, fallen in love, gotten married. They'd bought a house, and my older sister was born the same year.

They were the perfect representation of a nuclear marriage, and even to this day, they loved the hell out of each other. They'd been the ideal I'd looked up to as I grew up. Their love was one I aspired to for myself. But they'd been firmly working class, which meant life hadn't always been easy, even though I hadn't realized that fact until I was older.

When my youngest sister had gotten sick when I was eight, my mom had moved to the city with her to get medical care, leaving my dad to take care of me and my older sisters. However, he'd had to work a full-time job to pay for the medical expenses. Those years had been tough—not just for him, but for my mom in the city with my sister and zero emotional support. No one to lean on. No one to give her a break. That year had aged them both.

What would it have been like for them to have had a third adult in the family? Someone to help my dad out so he didn't have to do it all, or someone to swap out with Mom so she could have a break.

Hell, not just in times of crisis. If there'd been two incomes in the house, my dad wouldn't have had to work overtime to make ends meet. Would we have been closer if I'd been able to see him more often? If he'd had time to interact with us and not be bone-tired?

All those questions had been running around in my head as I said, "She's having a baby. She's a package deal."

Jesse had just shrugged. "I know, man. She's been talking baby names with me. She's letting me feel it kick. I can't explain it, but there's just this *excitement* in my chest. Like, this anticipation that's buzzing around my body to meet this little human we talk about daily. But on top of that, there's this fear. That something will happen to Tally, or to the baby. I'm so twisted up, but something I know for sure is that there's no other girl quite like her, and if I didn't take my chance because I was scared, I'd regret it."

He was so fucking right. She was a once-in-a-life-time kind of girl. Brave and sweet, and so fucking talented, it was awe-inspiring to watch.

"I'd like to pursue something with her too. And if you meant what you said in the car, I don't see why we can't both pursue her. Together."

We had come to some kind of gentlemen's agreement, and now it was all I could think about as I went through schematics for the car at work today.

The difference between a Formula One car and an

IndyCar was the fact that the car was standardized between teams. In IndyCar, you could only use approved bodies, engines, and parts on most things, but that didn't mean we didn't have room to wiggle.

VANT Racing had been set up with bigger things in mind, namely Formula Racing. So we could machine our own dampers and bearings on premises. There was no end to the small tweaks we could make to ensure these cars had the best build money and technology could buy. I didn't have three mechanical engineering degrees, but what I did have was a lot of hands-on experience building machines.

No matter how exciting this was, I couldn't stop thinking about Tally and Jesse. Would he bring it up to her while they were working today? Would she say yes? Was I imagining her interest?

I managed to make it through the rest of the day without losing my mind, though at the end of the day, I caved and texted Jesse.

H: *We should talk to her tonight.*

J: *You have absolutely no chill, man.*

H: *I've been waiting for this moment for nearly a year. I've been patient.*

J: *All right. She said she's been craving zucchini noodles, so I'll find a place and order in. Bring your A-game.*

. . .

Decision made, I decided to pull into a strip mall on the way home. It had a florist, and flowers could only make things better, right?

The mall was bustling at four in the afternoon, and I noticed a baby store halfway up the collection of store-fronts. Before I knew it, I was stepping into the giant building. It was a kaleidoscope of pastels, and there was so much stuff. Surely babies didn't need all these things.

I drifted toward the toys, and there were aisles and aisles of things. My eye snagged on a little red knitted race car in a bin filled with bunnies and bears. As I picked it up, it rattled softly, and I smiled. Could I be someone's dad?

Immediately, I knew the answer was yes. My dad mightn't have been around a lot when I was growing up, but he'd been a wonderful role model. He was always tired, but there was never any doubt in my mind that he loved me and my sisters with everything in him.

I wanted that. Tucking the toy under my arm, I took it as a sign that I was doing the right thing. After paying for it—and avoiding the gently interested questions of the girl at the register—I went and picked out a bunch of flowers from the florist as well.

Driving home, my palms started to sweat. I was nervous. Maybe more nervous than I'd ever been. I was out of my element, and it was equal parts exciting and terrifying. I didn't have any doubts about Jesse, though. I'd meant what I said to Tally the other day; I trusted no one more than I trusted Jesse. He was the best man I knew.

His truck was in the driveway next door, but the place appeared to be locked up tight. You only got your lumber stolen once before you learned to keep that shit stored away.

I climbed from the car, grabbing the flowers and the toy. *Fuck.* Was this weird? Maybe flowers were weird. I mean, as far as she knew, we were just friends right now. I dropped the flowers on the porch swing. Maybe I could come back out for them if the conversation went well.

Pushing open the door, I yelled, "Honey, I'm home!" Then cringed. Man, how I'd ever gotten laid in my entire fucking life was a miracle.

Jesse poked his head around the wall separating the kitchen from the living room. He raised an eyebrow in an expression that clearly said *what the actual fuck?*

Tally laughed, and I shifted my focus to her. The golden-brown of her hair poked out in fizzy little curls from the bun on top of her head. She had a dirt smudge on her cheek, and she looked tired. But that soft little smile hit me right in the chest.

I held out the toy to her. She reached out to take it, her tongue dipping out to wet her lips. "For the baby," I said. *Obviously.* I could hear Jesse snort a laugh in the kitchen, and I glared over my shoulder in his direction.

Tally shook the soft toy with a smile. "Thank you. It's perfect."

Jesse appeared in the doorway. "Dinner's warming in the oven. Creamy lemon-zucchini noodle bake."

Her face lit up. "I've been craving that all day."

I looked at Jesse, and he gave a barely perceptible nod. Sitting at the coffee table across from her, I physically held myself back from reaching out to grip her hands. I didn't want her to feel pressured in any way. "Tally, Jesse and I were wondering... uh, do you remember what we were talking about yesterday?"

"Shifting aerodynamics in NASCAR?"

"No, after that."

"Whether a snake that had just eaten a golden poison frog before it bit you was venomous or poisonous?"

"Uh, no."

"When we were talking about the idea of polyamorist relationships," Jesse interjected, looking between us like we were insane. Hey, we'd burned through a bunch of topics. "What Hayes is trying to say —without much success—is that we think you're fucking amazing. Beautiful, funny, tough." He squatted down so they were eye level. "In the last month, I haven't been able to stop thinking about you. I want to take you out, make you smile."

She was blinking wildly, and I leaned closer. "I've been completely smitten by you since you won your first race. You climbed from the car and did this little happy dance, and I thought I'd never seen anyone more beautiful in my entire life. I still haven't."

"And Hayes is my best friend. I knew he was totally

whipped by you, and I love him more than any other person on the planet. I wanted him to be happy. Which meant you had to stay firmly in the friendzone. Until last night."

She swallowed hard. "Last night?"

"If you're open to the idea, both Jesse and I would like to take you out on a date," I said, and there it was. All out there.

Jesse was nodding. "And if you aren't interested, we can just forget this conversation ever happened. We'll go back to flipping the house and supporting you as friends. Because we are adults, in control of our own emotions. No one will get all bent out of shape."

I let out a long exhale. "Absolutely. Your happiness is what means the most."

Tally's eyes were so wide, I wondered if they'd fall out of her head. "Just so we're all on the same page, you want to both be in a relationship with me? As in, joint boyfriends? Would we... uh... would we, um, go to bed together?"

I imagined Tally stretched between me and Jesse. I mean, we'd been friends for a long time. We'd fucked girls together. We worked well. But if it was Tally, sucking my dick while she rode Jesse?

I swallowed down the groan, working hard to keep my thoughts from my face. "If that's something you'd like. We've shared women before; it's definitely something we're open to. But I'd be just as happy to have you all to myself."

Jesse nodded. "You're in the driver's seat here, Tal.

We can experiment with whatever you want, or keep it solo. Whatever makes you happy. But there's absolutely no rush to decide on any of that. We can go slow."

She was silent, her eyes flicking between the two of us. I began to sweat more, a rivulet sliding down my spine. Her face was so expressive, but I didn't let myself hope. Not yet.

She let out a shuddering breath. "And if I want to go fast?"

Relief washed over me, but hot on its heels was desire. I leaned forward, capturing her mouth. She kissed me back, and it was electrifying. Better than I could have ever imagined, as I swallowed her little squeak of surprise, and then her moan as my tongue tangled with hers.

When I finally needed to breathe, I wrenched my lips away. "Yes?" I asked hopefully.

She looked at Jesse, who was now kneeling at her side. "Yes," she breathed.

Thank fuck.

"I forgot you only knew one speed," I teased, then leaned in to kiss her again.

FIFTEEN

TALLY

AT SOME POINT, my life had taken another sharp left turn. Lady Luck had lost control, but I was going to ride this wacky train all the way to the final destination.

Jesse plucked me from Hayes's arms like I weighed nothing, wrapping my legs around his waist. His lips captured mine, and I was suddenly pressed between two bodies. While Jesse's lips dominated mine, Hayes pressed soft kisses down my nape.

Holy hell.

Jesse pulled away. "More?"

I nodded furiously. *More. So much more.* I was going to experience the full effect of this moment before they changed their minds and realized I came with way too much baggage.

Hayes nipped the skin of my shoulder. "Words, baby. We want to hear you tell us what you want. If this is enough and you need to take a breath, we can go back and eat dinner. This isn't a one-time offer."

I reached back and gripped Hayes's hair, gently pulling him closer until I could find his mouth. I could feel Jesse's eyes on my face as I made out with his best friend. I felt sexy and powerful, these two men looking at me like that, their pupils blown out with desire, and their chests heaving against mine.

"Take me to bed, please," I murmured against his lips, and Jesse laughed.

"Because you asked so damn nicely." He spun and carried me up the stairs easily. "Norton, stay," he commanded, and the dog pouted as he wandered back to his bed.

Hayes ducked around us, opening the door and stepping into the room first, already peeling off his shirt. Holy hell, he was beautiful. Broad shoulders and chest, with a light brush of hair across his pecs, he was a solid mountain of a man. I wanted to taste every inch of exposed skin.

Jesse laid me down on the bed, stepping back to peel his own clothes off, but Hayes was there to take his place almost immediately. "I've dreamed of you like this," he murmured huskily. I doubted when he was having dirty dreams about me, I was seven months pregnant. But I still didn't have a huge stomach—more like I was just bloated after eating too much queso and chips.

He knelt between my thighs, stretching up to kiss me again, like he couldn't get enough. We kissed and kissed until his lips traveled down to my jaw, along my throat. He ran his hands under my shirt, dragging it up until my shitty t-shirt bra was exposed. I mean, I wasn't exactly dressed for seduction, but the way Hayes's eyes lit up told me it didn't matter even a little. He all but swan-dived between my breasts.

Jesse chuckled, that deep, rich sound that always thrummed right between my thighs. "Thank fuck I'm here. This jackass knows sweet fuck all about seduction, apparently."

I wasn't so sure about that. Hayes had managed to liberate one of my nipples from my bra, and was doing this thing with his tongue that was making me see stars.

I gripped his hair, holding him to my chest in case he even thought about stopping. "Holy shit. He makes up for it with enthusiasm," I moaned.

Jesse gripped my leggings, wiggling them down my thighs until my legs were bare, then he shoved Hayes over to one side of me. "No pressure on the belly, bro. But don't worry, I've got plenty of ideas for positions," he purred, and I shivered with pleasure. "Are there any other limits we should know about?"

At this point, I couldn't even think with Hayes's lips around my nipple, let alone think of things I *didn't* want. I shook my head. "No."

Jesse looked up at me from where he'd positioned himself between my thighs. "We'll work on that later. We'll keep it all about you tonight. You tell us if there is something you love, or something you want to stop. Just say the words, Tal, and we'll make it happen."

Then he tongued my clit over my freaking underwear, and I died. Or maybe I was brought back to life, because my body jerked like I was being electrocuted. *Oh my god.* This was something else.

Hayes came back up to kiss my lips, swallowing my moans, which elicited his own. Jesse was dragging down my underwear, and I kicked it off eagerly as he traced his lips back up the inside of my thighs. Hovering over my damp core, he took his time flicking his tongue over my clit, testing me, tasting me. Teasing me.

I tried to press my thighs around his head, but he gripped them in his large hands. "Hold her open for me, Hayes. I want to see every inch of what I'm about to eat."

And he did. He ate, like my screams of pleasure were the only sounds he ever wanted to hear again. His fingers came up to slide in and out of me as he sucked my clit, and I was done for.

"Jesse, *please.*" I didn't know what I was begging for, because my orgasm was already pulsing through my body, setting me on fire.

Hayes seemed to know, though. "Don't worry, baby. We aren't done yet." He rolled onto his back beside me, and Jesse stood up, shifting me onto Hayes's waist. I gripped his cock, notching it with my entrance as Hayes thrust upward. He filled me in one swift movement, and choked on a gasp. He curled up, leaning on his elbows, so I could lean down and kiss him. My hands on either side of his head, I rolled my hips, dragging him slowly along all the pleasurable places inside me.

A hand gripped my chin, and Jesse turned my face

toward him, kissing me as Hayes's hands fell to my hips, helping me move, finding that rhythm that made me gasp for breath. I wanted us all to come, wanted us to cement this moment together.

Grabbing Jesse's cock, I twisted toward him where he knelt on the bed, gloriously naked. Fuck, he was beautiful. His tattoos ran up his thighs, some even wrapping around his hip, and I wanted to catalog the details of every single one. But first, I wanted to taste the giant cock that was straining toward me.

"Holy hell," I moaned. Every part of that guy was huge. Tugging him closer by his dick, I leaned forward the best I could and sucked the tip, working my hand up and down, riding the rhythm of Hayes as he thrust up into me. "More," I groaned at Hayes. "Faster… I'm so damn close."

My beautiful Hayes delivered, fucking me faster and faster until I was sloppily sucking the head of Jesse's cock, and my hands had lost all rhythm.

"Hayes! I'm going to—" I broke off into a moan, as I sucked Jesse's cock down as far as it would go, making him curse.

"Fuck!" he shouted, holding my head tightly, fucking my face. "Baby, I'm coming." Pulling out of my mouth, he exploded all over my chest. Hayes's face was slack-jawed with his own release, hot spurts of his cum unloading inside me.

We definitely should have talked about contraception, but at least I couldn't get pregnant, right?

Leaning down to kiss me once more, Jesse moved

away from the bed. "Don't move. I'll grab a towel." He disappeared into the ensuite, while I leaned down to kiss Hayes.

"I hope I lived up to your imagination."

The gentle kiss he gave me said far more than words ever could. "You're everything I could've ever dreamed of, Tally Palmer." He gave me a crooked smile. "I didn't expect to have my best friend's cum on me at the time, though. That's a curveball."

Whoops.

Jesse had thrown on a pair of sweats by the time he walked back into the room. Shifting me off of Hayes, he laid the towel down beside his best friend and helped me shift my stretched and strained body over, then cleaned me up with a warm washcloth while I flushed bright red. He'd literally just had his mouth where the cloth was, but this seemed more intimate somehow.

"You better help me up so I can pee." When I came back out of the bathroom, I nearly ran into Jesse, who was balancing three bowls of zucchini noodles and an entire foil-wrapped garlic bread in his arms. "You're going to spoil me, I can tell."

Kissing my temple, he herded me back toward the bed. I pulled on one of their discarded shirts and climbed into the bed beside Hayes, who'd dragged his boxers back on. He pulled me close to kiss me again. "I'm never going to get enough of the taste of you," he growled, and something warm in my chest glowed a little bit brighter.

Jesse placed the bowls on the nightstand and sat

beside us, leaning back against the headboard and pulling me between his thighs, so I was pillowed by his chest. Hayes stuffed pillows behind Jesse's back, then his own, before grabbing the TV remote and putting on a documentary about marmosets. We snuggled in to relax and eat, and honestly? I could get used to this.

When Jesse kissed the top of my head, and Hayes hooked my leg over his, I let myself hope that this could be something good for once.

SIXTEEN

JESSE

WE FELL INTO THE RELATIONSHIP, like it was always meant to be this way. It helped that Tally soon started working at VANT Racing a couple of days a week, helping fine-tune the simulator. Apparently, the whole simulator setup was hush-hush, but she always came home with banked excitement. On those days, Hayes let us have time together, and I spent that time worshiping her in whatever way she'd let me. Usually between her thighs.

Alternately, on days when Tally worked with me, when Hayes got home, I'd go work on my bike, or take Norton to the dog park, or something that'd give them one-on-one time. The whole arrangement worked surprisingly well, and some of my favorite moments—with the exception of any time I was naked with Tally—were the ones where we all sat around on the couch, watching a race or a new TV show.

It was domestic in a way I'd never thought I'd enjoy

until now. Slowly, our lives were intertwining, and it gave me a settled feeling in my chest that I hadn't experienced in years.

Right now, Tally's head was in my lap, and I stroked my fingers through her soft hair. I was only half-watching the show about a British soccer team. Instead, my gaze kept drifting to the soft slope of her nose. The thick brush of her eyelashes. The freckles that kissed across her cheeks.

Her gaze flicked up to mine. "Stop staring, you big creeper," she teased, her eyes dancing with laughter. Hayes chuckled, squeezing her thighs where they sat across his lap. She looked at him, then back at me. "I was thinking… I have my ultrasound tomorrow, if one of you wants to come?"

My heart did this weird little flip-flop thing in my chest, and I was nodding before I'd fully processed what she was saying.

Hayes had a better grasp on language, because he was leaning forward and kissing any piece of exposed skin he could reach. "Pretty sure I speak for both of us when I say we'd love to. Maybe we'll take it in turns, so we don't freak out the ultrasound tech?" he asked softly. I could only imagine how that conversation would go, but I had a feeling that ultrasound techs saw a *lot* of shit; maybe they wouldn't even be fazed. "I have a meeting tomorrow with one of the engine manufacturers, so Jesse, you might be up first?"

He looked like it almost pained him to say it, and I understood. I'd want to experience this first, serious milestone with her too. But I appreciated him handing me the opportunity. That was the joy of our unorthodox relationship, right? That one of us was always here to meet her needs?

I lifted her hand and kissed her fingers. "I'd love to. You can go to the next one, man. I hear there's a bunch of scans as you get closer to your due date."

Tally raised an eyebrow. "Been doing a little research, Jesse?"

I shrugged, trying not to flush. Hell, I'd been doing research before we were a thing. I'd wanted to know how best to support her, and whether or not she might have the baby while hanging drywall, like this was some kind of eighteenth-century labor nightmare. After that, I'd researched the later stages of pregnancy, and the first few weeks postpartum, and then a few days ago, I'd moved on to milestones of the first few months.

Babies were hard work. They needed a lot of things. They were so damn fragile and delicate, and they couldn't tell you if anything was wrong. I wanted to stay ahead of any problems, and maybe make Tally's life a little easier. Sometimes, learning together was better than doing it all alone.

And it wasn't just the baby. The first few months for Tally would be wild too: crazy hormones, lack of sleep, the fact that a woman's body had to recover from hauling around a whole watermelon-sized human, then pushing it out of her vagina. And that was if she didn't have to have a C-section, or any of the other hundred possibilities that could happen during birth.

The whole thing gave me cold sweats.

"Just wanted to make sure I wasn't completely oblivious."

Hayes reached between the couch cushions and came up with a battered copy of *What To Expect When You're Expecting*. "Same."

Tally laughed, but it was a soft, gentle sound, her eyes glassy with tears that I prayed didn't fall. I wasn't sure I was prepared for Tally tears. She pushed up on her elbows and kissed me, just a gentle brush of her lips on mine, then pulled Hayes up closer so she could kiss him too. "You two really are something else—you know that, right? Thank you."

Hayes nipped her bottom lip. "It's nothing. The literal bare minimum." He gave an exaggerated sigh. "But if you really want to show your gratitude, you can scream my name so loud that the neighbors hear you while I eat this delightful little pussy."

She paid him back all right, twofold.

"Okay, Miss Palmer. Let's see how the little one is doing, shall we?" The tech pulled out a magic wand covered in what I assumed was lube, then squirted a heap on her stomach. "Your notes say this was a cryptic pregnancy? Bit of a surprise, I bet. To you too, I'm sure, Dad."

It took me a really long moment to realize she was talking to me. "Oh. Uh, yeah. A real surprise," I muttered, and Tally snorted a laugh.

Honestly, if I didn't know she was pregnant, I'd just think she was an average, midsize woman who'd binge-eaten a bunch of carbs. I hadn't known her when she was a tiny NASCAR driver, the way Hayes did. I loved her curves. I intended to memorize every single one of them.

The ultrasound machine picked up the subtle whoosh of a heartbeat, and there was no denying that the woman in front of me was pregnant. Heavily pregnant. You didn't need to be an expert to see the face of a baby hiding inside the woman I'd had my dick in literally twelve hours ago.

I turned a little green. I tried to recite what I'd read on the internet.

Having sex during pregnancy is healthy.

The baby is safely tucked away and cannot see my dick.

I'm not going to hurt it if we take precautions regarding positions.

I repeated it again as the tech measured the baby, pointing out its tiny hands and feet. Tally's eyes were transfixed by the screen. "Do you want to know the gender?" the tech asked, and Tally nodded vigorously.

I held my breath as the lady moved the wand around. "These things are never one hundred percent certain until they're born. Plus, he's a little shy. But in my professional opinion…" She paused, looking over at us. "Congrats, guys. You're having a boy."

She printed out pictures while I stared at the screen. A boy. Tally was having a son, and I guess, by extension, so were Hayes and I.

Oh, shit.

What if I fucked it up, and somehow traumatized the kid for life? Panic crawled up my throat, but I swallowed it down. It would be okay.

Tally reached out and gripped my hand, threading her fingers through mine. "You look like you're about to pass out. Are you okay?"

Taking a deep breath, I nodded. "Just seems a lot more real now." I looked at her, so she knew I wasn't about to run out of there. "What if I fuck him up somehow? What if I say something one day at the breakfast table that he has to talk to a therapist about in fifteen years' time?"

The ultrasound tech held in a laugh and excused herself, so Tally could get cleaned up. "Jesse, I worry about those same exact things every single night before I go to sleep. The only difference is that I know it won't be because I don't love him. It'll be because I have no fucking *clue* what I'm doing, but we can learn, and Google is free. We've got this... if you still want this. I know it's a lot." She chewed her lower lip, and I couldn't help but lean in to kiss her.

"We've got this. Let's go. I need a beer and an ice cream, but not necessarily in that order."

SEVENTEEN

TALLY

ROCCO PASSERO WAS AN ARROGANT DOUCHEBAG. Whoever his PR people were, they deserved a raise, because he one hundred percent believed his own press. He was gruff, recalcitrant and didn't want anything to do with the promotional side of the job. He just wanted to be behind the steering wheel of the car, and that was it.

Normally, that was something I could understand—even relate to, on a fundamental level. I'd also hated the dog-and-pony show that came with sponsorships and building a team brand when I was in NASCAR. But Rocco Passero was the face of VANT Racing, and we still didn't have a second driver to pick up the personality slack.

The team was having a press conference today, and I was hiding at the back, listening to the familiar shuffle of journalists talking to each other in hushed tones, the snap of camera shutters. Rocco had rolled in late, hungover as shit. There was still smudged lipstick on his neck. He looked like he'd just rolled out of the clubs and into this press conference.

Hayes was beside me. In fact, the whole team was standing at the back of the room, dressed in our team uniforms—black with the deep purple *VANT Racing* across the front.

"He smells like a distillery," one of the mechanics muttered, shaking his head as Rocco stumbled up onto the stage. His smile was lazy and cocksure, and Ari Rome gave him a look that probably would've made me wither into nothing more than a husk. But Rocco just smirked. I had to give Ari kudos for not punching him in his smug face.

Antony strolled in, barely casting a look at Rocco or Ari as he sat in the middle of the long table at the front of the room. "Thank you for waiting, ladies and gentleman. I'm very excited to be sitting in front of you today, launching a new name in IndyCar." Antony launched into a spiel about IndyCar, VANT Racing, the research and technology we were putting into the cars, and the goal of being the premier force in IndyCar within three years.

Ari Rome spoke next, giving a brief overview of his goals as team principal, changing from his former team to one being built from the ground up. Basically, all the boring, predictable questions.

The PR person, Luella, stepped forward. "We'll take questions now."

Almost all the hands in front of us rose. There were

journalists that I knew from my time on the NASCAR circuit, and I pulled my VANT cap lower over my face.

"Paul Camwood, MotorDrive. I have a question for Mr. Barbieri. You've been seen around the Formula One circuit for many years now. Is IndyCar a stepping stone for VANT Racing to reach the bigger leagues of Formula racing?"

Antony gave a lopsided grin. "I don't think anyone would be surprised to hear that I am a lover of Formula One. I think we can all agree that if you love one side of this sport, you likely love them all, from NASCAR to Formula One. That being said, I wouldn't consider our place here to be a midway point to anywhere. You'll see VANT Racing in the Indianapolis 500 for decades to come. Will we perhaps branch out further into different international Formula competitions? Perhaps, like many other teams, we will make that leap. But for now, we are focused on our current plan of dominating the IndyCar competition."

More hands went up, and Antony pointed to a guy in the front. "Oscar Ruiz, Drive Away Magazine. My question is for Rocco. Does your move from Formula One have anything to do with Lucia Christian, and the rumors that you and she had an affair right under the nose of your teammate, Mattias Christian?"

Anger flashed across Rocco's face, but he quickly shut it down. He leaned forward lazily in his chair, eyeballing Oscar Ruiz like he was trying to melt him to his chair. "No." He leaned back, his arms crossed over his chest.

Oscar waited for more, but there was just silence. "Do you have anything else to add in response to those rumors?"

Rocco leaned forward once more. "Not really, no."

Luella looked like she was about to have a heart attack, and she quickly picked someone else for the next question. The questions mostly flicked back and forth between Ari and Antony, but whenever someone would try and draw Rocco into the conversation, he'd give them nothing. He was a nightmare for the publicists.

I missed the name of the journalist in the back, but he stood up tall, notepad in hand. "So far, you've only named Rocco Passero as your driver. Have you approached any other drivers, and did you have reservations about hiring a driver with such a checkered personal history? I mean, from crashing cars to trashing bars, Rocco has been front-page news for the length of his career."

Rocco leaned forward, clearly angry again, but Antony placed a hand on his chest. "While Rocco might be... boisterous"—the crowd laughed—"he is also the youngest five-time world champion in Formula One history. He's won more races than many of the greats put together. His record speaks for itself, and VANT Racing is honored that he has come on board for something a little new and exciting. We have no regrets or worries about his performance on the track, which is where it counts."

Antony's expression brooked no further questions on Rocco's suitability to the team. "As for our second and possibly third team drivers, we have a few feelers out, not just from IndyCar drivers, but from other motorsports too. For instance, we have the very talented Tally Palmer, who has come over from NASCAR to help us run sims."

He pointed to the back of the room, and almost as one, the journalists turned. I almost hid behind Hayes, whose shoulders had gone stiff, but I didn't. I lifted my chin and eyeballed every single one of those fuckers who'd written about me like I was some grease-covered jezebel after Buck's death.

Oscar Ruiz laughed. "You have certainly gathered a team that's no stranger to being in the tabloids, Mr. Barbieri. The Lothario of Europe, and who some refer to as the Delilah of Willtot Racing."

Hayes was all but vibrating now, and I grabbed the back of his belt before he did something stupid, like punch a journalist at the team's first press conference. Rocco met my eyes, and his gaze assessed me in a new light. Obviously, he was the last person to pay attention to tabloid bullshit.

Antony gave Oscar Ruiz what could only be described as the stink eye. "I guess that is why I am the billionaire, and you are the reporter, Mr. Ruiz. I see their performance on the track and the benefits of their experience for the team, not the sensationalized fabrications made up to sell cheap magazines." He cleared his throat. "Now, does anyone have questions that people actually interested in motorsports might like answers to, or are we devolving into some kind of soap opera?"

The questions continued from the more professional pundits, but I could still feel the eyes of some
journalists on me. I looked over their heads at the front
of the room, trying not to tug at the bottom of my shirt
so that my stomach bulge was covered properly. I told
myself that it was okay. No one would know. And
even if they did, they'd never guess it was Buck's
baby. I wouldn't be front-page news again. It would be
fine.

I kept repeating that to myself as they wrapped up
the conference and the journalists filed out. This time, I
purposefully hid behind Hayes, though I pretended it
was because I was talking to Stephie, a software engineer who was working on the simulator with me.

The girl was insanely clever, just a little socially
awkward. Her hair was a fuzzy red, her skin was so
pale she basically glowed, and every time she spoke to
anyone, she flushed bright red. But Antony had
poached her from VANT Enterprises over to the racing
team, and I could understand why. She was a prodigy,
that was for sure.

She fanned her face. "Why was that so stressful? No
one gives a damn about me, but when they all turned
around to stare at you, I thought I was going to wet
myself," she squeaked out. "I'm definitely not doing
this again."

Hell, if I could get out of it, I'd also avoid more of
these conferences. "Me too. I was thinking, the percus-
sion of lap sixty at Iowa Speedway is off. By that stage,
there'd be a fair amount of marbling on the road, and

you want to factor that into your handling through that on both hard and—"

"Tally Palmer. I thought you'd slunk away into obscurity."

My spine snapped straight, and I tried not to externally freak out. I looked over my shoulder at Rupert Ballantyne, one of Brick Willtot's cronies and one of the premier race pundits for NASCAR.

Pasting a tight smile on my face, I turned. "Rupert. What are you doing covering IndyCar? Get demoted? Did they find out you were taking bets on races?" I teased, though it might have been a little too sharp to ever be considered good-natured. "Did they find you jerking off to pictures of Brick Willtot in the garages again?"

Stephie let out a high-pitched gasp. *Okay, that might have been too far.*

I had no good feelings when it came to this old fuck. Brick might have blacklisted me with the teams, but it had been Rupert who'd ensured that my reputation went into the trash right along with it. He was the one who'd painted me as the distraction to the NASCAR viewers, and he was the reason I was painted as—how had Oscar Ruiz put it?—the Delilah to Buck Willtot's Sampson. Like fucking me was akin to cutting his hair and losing his ability to drive around the track without crashing.

It had been Rupert who'd insinuated I was the cause of Buck's death in the media. I fucking hated him.

Rupert gave me an equally sharp-toothed smile. "A

new team is big news in motorsport. The magazine wanted to run a story on it." It didn't help that Rupert was one of the key writers for the biggest motorsports magazine in the world. "Though, given the professional quality of the drivers, it might be a footnote in the archives rather quickly."

Hayes snorted. "I've always wondered how your career was so long. You never did know jack shit about racing."

Rupert slid his crocodile eyes to Hayes. "You're one of the former mechanics for Ryclo, right?" He lowered his voice. "That tracks for the Jezebel of NASCAR, doesn't it? Were you fucking this one too?" He sneered at me, before flicking his gaze back to Hayes. "At least *you* only threw away your career, and not your life."

I felt like I was being stabbed in the heart, but I wouldn't give this old bastard the satisfaction of knowing that. "How about you go fuck yourself, Rupert?"

"Listen here, you little—"

"Palmer. It's time to get back to work." My gaze whipped to Rocco Passero, who was standing behind Rupert Ballantyne, looking annoyed.

Rupert pasted one of those smarmy expressions on his face. "Rocco, welcome to IndyCar. I'm sure it was quite a coup for VANT to get you. How much are they paying you?"

Rocco gave Rupert an expression that I wanted to take a mental snapshot of, so I could recall it every day just to make myself happy. A little serotonin boost. He stared at Rupert, as if he was somewhere between stinky dog shit and an annoying little fly. He eyed him up and down slowly, then dismissed him as inconsequential as he met my eyes again. "Let's go."

Swallowing hard, I gave a tight nod. "Sure."

Rupert, the snake that he was, couldn't let it go without one more barb. "Watch yourself, Passero. This one is a black widow." He curled his upper lip. "I'll let Brick know I saw you."

The threat was there. If Brick knew I was working again, he'd fuck my career just as some weird, fucked-up form of vengeance.

I gave him the sweetest smile I could muster. "Sure, tell him I said to go fuck himself too. I mean, if he takes his cock from your mouth long enough for you to get a whole sentence out."

With that, I spun on my heel and left the room before I did something completely uncool, like burst into tears.

EIGHTEEN

ROCCO

MY HEAD WAS POUNDING, like a bull was stomping on it, and there were two bikini model influencers asleep back in my hotel room. Well, maybe not asleep now, but waiting for me. Yet, instead of being balls-deep in some golden Californian girl, I was under this glaring fluorescent lighting that was making my head hurt even more.

I entertained some of the bullshit questions from the reporters, but when that fucker brought up Lucia, I wanted to jump the table and beat the shit out of him. I wouldn't forget the face of Oscar Ruiz anytime soon.

I'd been so relieved that the stupid press conference was over that I almost sprinted from the room. I was already at the door, listening to some fucker praise me as if I was going to become his best friend just because he could repeat my stats, when I spotted the girl in the back.

Something about her body language made me stop.

She was smiling, but it was more of a grimace. Her hands were at her sides, but her fingers were curled into fists. She was talking to one of the older journalists, who I didn't recognize and who hadn't asked a question.

A little more curious than my hangover warranted, I walked toward the group. I turned up just in time to hear him besmirch the quality of the team drivers, which I couldn't have given a shit about, as I was used to it. Besides, my skills spoke for themselves.

But whatever barb he threw at the girl next had her rearing back, pain flashing through her expression like he'd slapped her. I didn't know her, except for the shit she'd given me at the team get-together the other week, but she was still part of my team.

That was enough for me to interrupt. Besides, the mechanic behind her, Hayes, looked like he was ready to throw it all away and punch this old bastard in the face. I knew for a fact that punching reporters was bad for your career.

"Palmer. It's time to get back to work." I'd get her to run me through the sims or some shit, so she didn't think I was coming over here to save her.

The journalist turned around and started waffling about some bullshit that I couldn't be bothered wasting brain cells on digesting. I dismissed him as a waste of my time and the oxygen surrounding us.

"Watch yourself, Passero. This one is a black widow. I'll let Brick know I saw you."

Again, she pulled back like she'd been struck. I

didn't know who the hell this Brick guy was, but the little driver clearly had some secrets. She grew a pair of balls, drawing herself up to her full height. "Sure, tell him I said to go fuck himself too. I mean, if he takes his cock out of your mouth long enough for you to get a whole sentence out." I laughed as the man turned bright red, watching her stomp away.

Hayes leaned into his space. "Stay the fuck away from her, Ballantyne, or I'll visit you somewhere a little more private and we can talk about this like men." He marched after Palmer, and I was left standing there with the shit stain.

The guy looked at me, shaking his head. "This is why women shouldn't be in motorsports." He said it like it was an obvious conclusion.

I looked down at him, screwing up my nose. "Don't talk to me."

Moving through the other team members, I headed out the back exit of the conference room. I didn't really need to go to the sims, but it wouldn't hurt to get to know the car already. I knew the computer guys had been tinkering with it so I could get used to the difference between a Formula One car and an IndyCar, without booking in track time. Track time was expensive, and honestly, not that helpful at this stage.

That was the excuse I gave myself for heading to the sim room, and while I did, I Googled the name of the sweet little driver with the smart mouth. There were at least five techs in the sim room, but not Tally, so I headed to an empty office and sat down in the office chair as I binged the history of Tally Palmer.

There was a surprisingly large amount of information about her online; I could track her stats right back to when she was a kid. She was good, and if she'd been a boy, she might have been scouted by some of the Formula academy teams, rather than being left to progress to NASCAR.

Not that she hadn't done well in NASCAR. There were pictures of her at sixteen, holding a trophy for one of the lower level championships, and it seemed she'd lazed around in there for a few years before being picked up by Ryclo Racing. I sifted through her stats, and although I'd never personally driven in NASCAR, I was impressed by the short videos of her skills. It was wildly different to open-wheel driving, way more Wild West Wreck'em derby than a sport for gentlemen. Or gentlewomen.

There was an article about the death of her father in a carjacking, and right beneath it was a huge article on the death of a driver named Buck Willtot. I read through it, frowning at the amount of times her name came up, considering she'd apparently been nowhere near the crash. When the article mentioned that her and Buck were dating at the time, lightbulbs in my brain flashed on.

Like the old superstition of women on ships, some believed that women had no place in motorsports. It was a sport for men, like pressing some pedals and moving a wheel was somehow too complex for womenfolk.

I couldn't be too superior about it, because Formula One was also pretty bad, especially in Europe. I'd never believed women couldn't race. If they trained for it, there was no reason they couldn't drive. At this point, I'd appreciate the challenge from whatever gender wanted to come for my crown.

Finally, there were the opinion pieces about why she was dropped from her NASCAR team, and even more articles calling her the downfall of the Willtot racing dynasty. I looked at the dates on the articles.

Less than a year ago.

"You know you don't actually need me to do sim runs."

I didn't even look guilty as I glanced up beside me, at the woman I was reading about. She would've had to be a hell of a lot closer to read the words on my screen, and I would've smelled her sweet, summery scent well before then.

I shrugged. "You've raced the tracks. I would like to discuss lines with you before I climb into the machine."

Tally narrowed her eyes. "Really..." She seemed suspicious, which was probably fair, considering what I would *actually* like to have been doing were the two blondes in my bed, about ten miles in the other direction. Inhaling deeply she wrinkled her nose. "How about you come and see me when your blood-alcohol level isn't enough to kill a horse?" Her voice was stern, but her lips twitched.

I raised both my eyebrows. "I am sober as a judge." She snorted, and I grinned. "Okay, well, a little less than a judge. But I could still outrace you and anyone else in this building."

"You think?"

I nodded solemnly. I wasn't being boastful. I definitely could. "Even in that rally car driving you Americans are so fond of. NASCAR," I snorted.

"Wanna put your money where your mouth is?" She was shorter than me, a little thing, maybe just over five-four, but she was fiery.

"I don't want your money," I said in that pompous voice that sometimes passed my lips, picked up from spending too much time with rich fuckers.

She rolled her eyes. "It's just a saying. Not all of us are multimillionaires, Passero. If I win, you have to do at least three workshops for Moss Aguilar's Karting Academy. If you win... well, name your price."

What did I want from this girl? "If I win... Hmm, I don't know. You take me to a NASCAR race and change my mind."

Something dark flashed across her face, but it was gone as quickly as it came. "Deal." She grabbed my arm. "Let's go, Pretty Boy. You're about to get your ass handed to you."

She pulled me into a room next to the sim room, and inside were two computer set-ups with huge screens and the kind of booths you'd see in arcade driving games. With a grin, she stuck her head back out the door toward the main area of the garage.

"I'm about to kick the great Rocco Passero's ass in iRacing!" Several heads looked up, and she all but danced back into the room. "Same car. Same specs. May the best racer win?"

She stuck out a hand, and I shook it. Her skin was soft and warm, and maybe I held it just a little longer than necessary. She blinked those big green eyes up at me, and they were alight with happiness. It was a thrill I knew all too well—the chance to show everyone what you were made of.

The mechanic who'd looked like he was going to thump that journalist appeared, along with at least a half a dozen other VANT Racing employees. He walked over and ran a hand down her spine. It was a familiar gesture, one that claimed her subtly, both to me and every other person in the room. Were they dating?

"Are you sharking the Italian, Tally?" he murmured softly, and she looked up at him with big doe eyes. Yeah, they were definitely having sex. I didn't examine the disappointment in my chest. Was it his baby she was carrying? The journalist had implied some kind of relationship between them.

She shook her head, but she was grinning. "Nope. He made a big claim, and now he has to back it up. Come on, Passero. Let's do this."

Shaking my head, I climbed into one of the little pods. I'd been familiarizing myself with the steering wheels for the IndyCars, but this one was different again. More like one you'd find in an average car.

Tally quickly cued up the race, and I did a little practice lap. Once I had a feel for the controls, I was ready. I turned to her, a smirk on my face. "May the best racer win."

NINETEEN

HAYES

TALLY RACING REALLY WAS a thing of beauty, even if it was just on the digital big screen. She was racing Passero, and the guy was a prodigy behind the wheel. When she'd announced she was racing Rocco Passero on a NASCAR sim, I'd immediately come to watch, of course. As they got further and further into the race, more people appeared.

Passero was great, but my girl? She was just as good. She was ruthless, and you could tell that Rocco wasn't used to the more tactile racing of NASCAR. He swore in Italian when she bumped him, but managed to pull it off the wall. Tally was hyper-focused, and I could see her slipping back into the groove. It was like she was back there, on the track, jostling for position.

Twenty-five laps later, Rocco had gotten the idea, riding the railing around the outside to cut in front of her and take her right at the finish line. There was a smattering of applause around the room, and Tally threw back her head with a laugh. "Good race. Maybe you are worth the hype."

Passero looked at her with an expression I knew all too well: desire. I wanted to punch him, but managed to restrain my more caveman tendencies. She looked happy, and I wasn't going to march in there like a jealous boyfriend.

He raised his chin at her. "Double or nothing, but this time, we race IndyCars."

She smirked. "You're on."

They slipped into a different cockpit position and loaded up the Indy tracks and cars. Once they were ready to race, they both looked serious. This time, there was a lot less jovial smack talk.

She held her own, though; running sims had definitely helped her adjust to the style of car and racing. But soon enough, Rocco pulled just a little ahead. Not as much as you'd think, with Tally right there at the back of him, only a fraction of a second behind. They both chose good lines, and it was a close-run race.

By the time the twenty-five laps were up, Tally was sweating lightly, coming in mere seconds behind one of the best drivers in the world. There was applause, and I noticed Antony beside me, an impressed expression on his face. How long had he been watching? He winked in my direction and disappeared from the room.

Tally unbuckled herself and climbed out of the cockpit, taking Rocco's hand to steady herself. "Looks like you owe me two races now, Palmer."

She rolled her eyes at him, but she was smiling

widely. Man, to see that look on her face again was a gift in itself. I hated that I wasn't the one to put it there.

"A deal is a deal."

He nodded. "In good faith, I'll call Moss today and arrange a couple of mentoring sessions or something." He grumbled it, like it was the worst thing in the world, but Moss had told me the other day at the party he'd already agreed to at least two weeks of guest mentoring.

What an ass.

Tally spun toward me, grinning. "Did you see me almost kick his ass?" she teased, and I wandered over to her.

I kissed her temple, breathing in the scent of her hair. "I did. You're still damn good, Tally Palmer."

Ryclo didn't know what it had lost. Even just thinking about that fucking team made my blood boil, and I still itched to punch Rupert Ballantyne in the dick. That old fucker needed to retire, and I was happy to force the issue with a broken jaw.

I met Rocco's eyes, and we had one of those weird, macho silent conversations.

She's mine.

He inclined his head. *Message received.* But I didn't like the shit-eating grin on his face that said, *For now.*

I wrapped an arm around Tally's shoulder. "Come on, Speed Racer. You put our driver through his paces right up until home time."

She looked at her watch and gasped. "Oh, shit. The bosses are going to think I'm a lazy ass. Where's

Stephie? I hope she wasn't waiting on me to do those calibrations."

I led her from the room and back toward the lockers where we kept all our stuff. "Stephie was in there, taking bets on who would win. I had twenty bucks on you," I told her, and she thumped me in the chest.

"You should have saved your money. He's the best driver in the world. I didn't stand a chance."

I pulled her into my arms, pressing her against the lockers. Leaning forward, I brushed my lips across hers. "I have nothing but faith in your abilities, Tally Palmer. You could drive us into Hell, and I'd still believe in you."

She stroked my face, the soft curves of her features making my heart beat faster. Someone wolf-whistled from the garage, and I moved away. Man, I wanted to take her home and lay her on any flat surface available so I could make her scream my name.

Unfortunately, we had to collect Jesse, then head over to Will and Colin's house for dinner. Tally had talked to us about her backup plans when it came to the baby and birth, and she was going to ask them to be guardians. We were also going to tell them about us.

I grabbed the shirt I'd hung in my locker and headed into the men's bathrooms. "I'll be back in a minute." Tally nodded, grabbing her dress and disappearing into the women's.

It was kind of nerve-wracking. William Love was not a small man, that was for sure. And he was super protective of Tally, though by all accounts, she hadn't made that easy. But without a doubt, he adored her. There was very little he wouldn't do for her, and I wanted to suss him out more. Was he in love with her, despite the obvious love he had for his boyfriend? If anyone knew that love was a complex emotion, it was me.

Tally was quiet on the way back to the house, and I knew it probably had something to do with running into Rupert Ballantyne. His words had been honed to hurt her, though what he got out of inflicting that kind of pain on Tally was beyond me. As far as I was aware, they'd never had a relationship outside of the professional one that all drivers had with the media. However, you only needed to look at the venom in Rupert's expression to know that he hated her, or maybe what she represented.

I made a note to talk to Antony about it, because I didn't want Brick Willtot or Rupert ruining this opportunity for Tally. I reached across the center console to grip her fingers. "Do you want to talk about it?"

She shook her head, but directly contradicted herself when she asked, "Do you think he could tell I was pregnant?"

I shrugged, because to me, it was blatantly obvious and always had been. But that was because I'd always been professionally aware of her build. I'd had to create the cockpit for her cars in the team; I'd had all her measurements. I knew how much she weighed, how tall she was, what she looked like after six beers and two tequila shots. We'd been professional colleagues, and it had been part of my job. But more than that, we'd been friends.

Rupert had never been anyone's friend. If he'd been able to tell she was pregnant, I'd be surprised. She had popped a little more lately, but not enough that you'd think she was nearly seven and a half months pregnant. I couldn't rule it out, though.

"If he did, he wouldn't think it was Buck's. You look three months along, at the most. He'd probably think it was mine." I lifted her fingers to my lips.

"You'd be okay with that? God knows what the rumor mill will say back at Ryclo, if it gets out."

"One hundred percent okay with me." I smiled at her. "I don't know if I've said this, but I'm in this for the long haul, Tally. Me, you, Jesse and the baby are going to be a family. So if he thinks the baby's mine, then he's right. It's ours. I'll love and take care of him, because he's a little piece of you."

She let out a shuddering sigh. "You make it very hard not to weep like a baby, Hayes Davis. I don't know what I did to deserve your… care, but I promise, I'll take care of you right back."

We fell back into a comfortable silence, each deep in our own thoughts. I meant every single word I'd just said, although I was just skimming the surface of my feelings for Tally. She wasn't ready for the big words yet, but I could wait.

Jesse and Norton were standing on the front porch when I pulled up, and my best friend had put on his finest button-up. With his hair combed back, he looked like he'd stepped out of a sixties issue of GQ. He was a handsome fucker, and he knew it. Even Norton was brushed within an inch of his life, wearing the jaunty little bowtie that Tally had bought for him off the internet.

They both loped down the porch stairs, and Jesse put a blanket down over my upholstery in the back so Norton didn't scratch up the leather. We really needed that family car already.

Norton was a good dog, though, and he knew to sit in the footwell behind the passenger seat. Jesse closed him in, leaning through Tally's open window to kiss her soundly. "Hey, baby." He jogged around to the other side, climbing in the back seat.

"What, I don't get a kiss?" I joked, as I reversed the car out of the driveway.

Jesse snorted. "Nah man, you aren't my type."

"Too handsome?" I teased back.

"Too hairy. I've seen your ass; you're one stray spark away from a forest fire back there."

I gasped, my eyes flicking to Tally. "That's a lie! My ass isn't hairy at all!"

Tally laughed, giving me a mock sympathetic look. "Of course not…"

"Assholes," I grumbled, but I was smiling. This right here was perfect.

TWENTY

TALLY

WILLY WAS GIVING the guys the stink eye, and it was kind of hilarious. Both Jesse and Hayes had been nervous, and I got it. Willy was the closest thing I had to family, and his approval meant a lot to me. Colin was happy as long as I was happy, but Willy had taken on that protector role early in our lives, and if it hadn't been for him, I would have crumpled after my dad's death.

I owed a lot to Willy, and to Colin. But their opinion about this arrangement wouldn't change my mind. I'd hate it, but I wouldn't leave either of the guys just because of Willy.

"I want to know if I've got this correct. You're all together. The three of you. Is that plausible in the long run? Maintaining a relationship with one person is hard. Adding another person is… insanity. What if you fall out of love with one of them?" he asked me, and I mean, it was a question I'd asked myself many times.

I shrugged. "I didn't say it was going to be easy. But we're going to work hard at it, because it feels right, Willy. So far, there haven't been any issues, and we're committed to open communication."

Willy went to argue again, because that was his default, but Colin slapped his forearm. "Leave it, Will. Can't you see she's happy? You can worry like an old woman about the what-ifs later."

Jesse leaned forward, his forearms bulging against the table top. "I swear on my life, I will make sure she stays that way. Both Hayes and I only want what's best for her, and the baby. They won't lack love and support. Every day, they'll know they have someone to lean on." Hayes nodded his agreement.

Willy looked between us all, letting out a sigh. "You're all grown, consenting adults who know that I will literally throw your dismembered bodies into the ocean as shark food, if you even consider hurting her."

I looked at Colin and rolled my eyes, but Hayes was very solemn as he said, "I'll help you throw me off the Golden Gate if I hurt either of them."

Ugh. Definitely giving him a blowjob after this.

Colin clapped his hands together. "Well, now that's decided, I made crème brûlée for dessert." Behind Willy's back, he gave me two big thumbs up, mouthing, *You go, girl!*

Willy topped up the guys' wine and got me another soda, while Colin made his grand re-entrance, holding a platter of desserts. As he placed one in front of every-one, I took the opportunity to squeeze his arm.

It had always been me and Willy against the world, but when Colin had appeared, he'd fit in seamlessly. He'd never tried to freeze me out, never tried to insist that Willy drop me. He'd just opened his arms, accepted me with all my issues, and saw me as a peer, not someone who needed protection. I wasn't so sure that I would've been as open-minded if I was in his position. Colin had merely insisted I was his sister-in-law, and basically incorporated both Willy and I into his big, happy family.

Which was why I felt completely at ease with this next part. When he finally sat back down, I swallowed one last mouthful of soda and began. "All that being said, our relationship is new. It wouldn't be fair on the guys to expect them to take on the commitment of a child, if anything happens to me, considering we haven't been dating long." I cleared the lump in my throat. "We all know that childbirth is kinda risky, so I wanted to ask, if anything happens to me, would you guys be the legal guardians of the baby?"

The silence in the room was almost a physical caress. Colin and Willy looked at each other, then back at me, then at each other once more.

I started to panic a little, but I wouldn't push this issue. I could figure something else out. "There's absolutely no pressure. A child is a big deal and would completely change your lifestyle."

"And we'll absolutely love and care for the baby ourselves, if it comes down to that. The child wouldn't end up in foster care, or up for adoption, or anything like that," Jesse added.

I nodded, feeling overwhelming appreciation for Jesse and Hayes in that moment. "But there's no one on this planet that I trust as much as you guys to care for my child. In a year, or two, or five, if the guys and I are ready to reach a different level of commitment"—I tried not to choke on the C-word—"then we can reassess, you know?"

Will and Colin were still having one of their silent conversations, the kind that only ever occurred once you'd been with someone for a long time. Colin frowned, Willy raised an eyebrow, Colin rolled his eyes. Then they turned back toward me in synchronization. Honestly, it was almost creepy how in sync they were.

"Of *course* we'll be guardians to your baby, Tally. As if you even have to ask," Colin said sternly, shaking his head at me, like I was just asking dumb questions and not foisting a baby on him. "As if Will would let it be any other way."

The man in question lifted his chin in agreement. "He's right. No offense, but you hardly know these guys, and there's no way I'd let them raise the last piece of you."

I grinned, because I'd known them both well enough to know that this was a forgone answer. "Okay, that's the last heavy topic of the night, I promise. Did I tell you I almost beat Rocco Passero at iRacing?"

. . .

Waking up sandwiched between two hot men was possibly my very favorite way to wake up. Lips traced over my shoulder blade, making me hum happily in my sleep. I pressed back against the very large erection resting on my ass cheeks and wiggled softly.

"I have to go to work," Hayes grumbled, even though he ground himself against me a little more. "We have a nine a.m. meeting, and I can't be late." His lips and hands roamed over my body in direct contrast to his words.

"We could be quick? Or multitask and do it in the shower?"

He rolled away, and suddenly, strong hands were around my feet, dragging me to the end of the bed. He hauled me into his arms and was kissing me even as I squealed.

"God, I love that you're a problem solver," he murmured, as he carried me toward Jesse's ensuite bathroom. I looked over his shoulder at a now-awake Jesse, a contented smirk on his face as he watched Hayes haul me around like a sack of potatoes.

As he set me on the bathroom vanity, the cold marble chilled my ass cheeks, making me yelp. Hayes set about getting the water to the perfect temperature.

"I've been thinking about making love to you in the shower for a week." He helped me peel off Jesse's shirt, which I'd already stolen as a night shirt. Slotting between my thighs, his dick still hampered by his boxers pressing against my core, he kissed me softly.

"Dreamed about how I'd get you nice and wet and slippery, then press you against the tiles and slide in."

I tugged at his boxers. "I'm not sure I understand. I think I'm going to need a hands-on demonstration."

I squealed again as he picked me up and walked me into the shower stall, not dropping me back to my feet even as we stood under the showerhead. My belly got in the way a little, but I hardly noticed it when he leaned forward and sucked on my tits. He might have had a tiny obsession with my breasts.

I threaded my fingers through his hair, gripping it tightly. "You want me to slide into that wet pussy, baby? Fuck you against these tiles?" he purred. "The way it grips me so fucking tight." He groaned, his hands on my ass digging in a little firmer.

"Please, Hayes. Fuck me, hard and fast."

"Yes, baby."

He lined himself up, and with one hard thrust, buried himself all the way inside me. My head thumped back against the tiles as his dick stretched me. I held on for dear life as he began to move.

"Like warm silk. So soft. I could live inside you, if you'd let me," he growled. "I'm not sure if I'm allowed to say this, but the belly really does something for me. I just want to fuck you over and over and over again, so you stay big and round with child."

I laughed softly. "That's some primal bullshit right there, Hayes Davis."

He chuckled into my throat, as he bit the column of my neck. "You make me lose my fucking mind." The hot water flowed down our skin, making us damp and slippery as he fucked me like he wanted to own me forever. "You're mine, Tally. I've waited so fucking long for you, and I'm going to make your life so good, please you so good, that you'll never want to leave."

I wasn't going anywhere; I'd never felt so happy in my life. "Then you better fuck me like you love me," I purred, and his groan had him shifting the angle of his hips and fucking me harder. *Holy shit.* "Oh god…"

"No god here, baby. Just you and me."

I held on tight as pleasure crashed through my body over and over, my hand sliding down to rub my clit to just prolong my pleasure a minute more, chasing that feeling for just a little longer. Finally, with a groan that echoed around the bathroom, Hayes came inside me.

My knees felt like jello when he lowered me to the ground. "I think we're going to be late for that meeting, baby girl."

Licking the water droplet that hung right there on his nipple, I laughed when he moaned. "I think you might be right."

TWENTY-ONE

JESSE

PANTING, I rolled onto my back beside Tally on the floor. Sweat made her skin glow, and I wanted to lick the salt from her skin. I didn't know what it was about her, but I couldn't get enough. I was *obsessed*.

"You know, we don't have to christen every single room," she told me, breathing equally as heavily.

I rolled to my side so I could take in her post-sex expression. That soft flush of pink might be my favorite color. "Are you complaining? Because it didn't sound like it, when you were like 'oh my god, Jesse, right there, *right there!*'" I teased in a fake falsetto.

She whacked my chest, but her palm quickly came back down and stroked over the abused skin. I almost purred. "I do not sound like that." Her indignation was cute as fuck.

Oh, she sounded way better than that, but I just kissed her instead of arguing. She kissed me back, yawning and stretching a little. Her stomach was a little round ball between us, and she looked like a fertility goddess.

Honestly, it was too easy to imagine her round with my baby, and that should have shocked the shit out of me. Three months ago, I might have been horrified by the very thought. But now? A primal part of me really enjoyed unloading inside her tight little cunt. We'd quickly produced medicals so we could abandon condoms, at least for this last part of her pregnancy. She had dreams that didn't involve being barefoot and pregnant forever, so once the baby was born, we'd reconsider contraception.

"Do you really not want to fuck in every room?" I asked her lightly. She was horny as hell, and the internet said it was because her hormones were wild. I had zero problems with that. I was here to satisfy every desire she had.

She flopped back. "We both know I do. You take your shirt off, then the sweat drips down your back muscles, and I'm helpless to resist. I'm like a savage."

I leaned over her. "My savage."

Weeks were slipping away so fast, it was hard to imagine she was getting close to her due date. I'd worked hard at getting this place finished, because I wanted her to be able to relax after giving birth. I'd set up the spare room in my house for her too, though she hadn't moved into it. Apparently, we could renovate a house together, but it was a little soon to move in together.

But she'd agreed that after the birth, she'd move in

with us at least temporarily, so she would have help during the night. Will had put his foot down about that, and I was kinda glad it had been him and not me, even though we were in complete agreement. He'd told her that for the first month, she either moved in with us, or with him and Colin.

My phone buzzed somewhere across the room, which I knew was my signal. My job today had been to keep Tally distracted until Hayes messaged me. Turns out, the VANT Racing team had fallen in love with Tally as easily as I had, and wanted to hold her a surprise baby shower.

I mean, not that I loved her. Well, not yet. But I was definitely going that way. I mean, I really cared about her. The thought of anything happening to her produced a panic in my chest that felt like a heart attack. Her laugh was the best thing about my day.

Yeah, that's not love at all.

Dragging myself from the spiral where I'd admit things to myself that I wasn't ready to even say out loud, I grabbed my phone. "Stay there, baby. I'll grab a towel."

I climbed to my feet and ducked into the bathroom. Looking at my phone, I saw the message I'd been waiting for.

H: *We are good to go.*

. . .

Pulling on my jeans, I walked back into the sitting room. We'd been christening another finished room. At least we'd laid down a drop cloth.

"Hayes messaged. His car won't start, and he wants a ride home." I'd told him that was a stupid excuse, considering he literally worked at a glorified mechanic's workshop, but he'd insisted it was fine.

I knelt between her thighs, stroking the wet washcloth over her core, making her moan softly. This little part of the ritual of fucking satisfied something deep inside my chest. The urge to care for her needs.

I moved away before she could tempt me back between her thighs. Pushing to my feet, I reached down and hauled her to hers. She rubbed her stomach and sighed heavily. She was frowning, which wasn't the face I wanted on the woman I'd just made come. Twice.

"All good?"

She nodded. "No one tells you that hefting around another human being in your body is exhausting. And painful."

I was pretty sure everyone told you that, but I wisely kept my opinion to myself. We were mere weeks away from the birth, and she was uncomfortable in a way I couldn't help with now. I hated that. "Come on, we'll go get your boy toy, then I'll give you one of those calf massages you like when we get home."

This time, she sighed happily. I watched her walk through to her bedroom, then went to the kitchen to find my shirt. I'd taken it off earlier, partly because I wanted to keep it clean, and partly because I liked the way she watched me with hungry eyes when I worked shirtless.

She emerged from the bedroom in a soft dress, and I internally fist-pumped. She looked like a goddess, and I knew that she would've murdered me if she'd shown up to a party dressed in her old painting clothes.

After locking Norton in the backyard, I ushered her to the truck. I gave her a little boost as she climbed into the passenger seat, and kissed her shoulder, just because I could.

She gave me that crooked smile that had me in a chokehold. "You look like a bad boy, but you're really just a marshmallow, aren't you, Jesse Banks?"

I gave her my best panty-dropping smirk. The one that had gotten me out of bad grades and speeding fines, but had also gotten me into almost every bed I'd wanted, and more than a few fist fights. My mother had told me it was dangerous, and she hadn't been wrong.

"Don't tell anyone. I've got a reputation to maintain." I shut the door and walked around to the driver's seat. She chatted happily as we drove across town to the VANT warehouse, and she only really expected a few responses from me here and there. She seemed so damn content, and that felt like my greatest accomplishment in life right now.

Pulling into the guest spot in the complex's parking lot, I feigned looking around for Hayes. "He must still be inside."

She frowned, but leaned back in the seat. "He

might've gotten caught up talking with one of the guys. We can wait."

"Or you could take me in and show me around? I've never been here before. It would be nice to see where my partners work."

Tally raised an eyebrow at me. "Partners?"

I shrugged. "I mean, I've seen his hairy asshole way more than polite society would consider necessary, so I'm pretty sure that makes us closer than friends now. I still don't want to fuck him, though," I joked, and she rolled her eyes. "We are all partners in this relationship. You're my girlfriend, and he's my Brofriend."

She let out that honking laugh that I loved so much, gripping the bottom of her stomach. "Stop, I don't have the bladder control I once had," she hissed out between laughing breaths. "Brofriends. That's perfect."

I moved around the hood of the car and opened her door for her. She put her hands on my shoulders, allowing me to lift her down. I didn't let her go, as I looked down into her sparkling sea-green eyes.

"You're perfect." I leaned down and kissed her, my lips telling her things my voice couldn't just yet. Finally, I pulled back, my dick getting uncomfortably hard behind my jean zipper. "Come on, before we make an unintentional sex tape on your bosses' security cameras."

She flushed that pink again, but she threaded her fingers through mine and led me inside. There was a girl behind the reception desk, and her excited face would have given it away, if Tally even remotely suspected what was about to happen.

"Tally!" she said, all but bouncing in her chair. If she'd been a dog, her tail would have been wagging faster than the speed of light. "I think Hayes is back in the engineering offices."

"Thanks, Valeria," Tally replied, seeming unfazed by the girl's excitement. Maybe she was like that all the time. Tally led me through the office doors. "This is where everyone works, except Antony. His offices are off the garage." She went toward a set of swinging double doors. "The workshop is just through—"

"SURPRISE!"

Tally jumped a foot in the air, and I put my hands on her hips to hold her steady. The workshop was filled with blue balloons in all different shades, with a big *Congratulations* sign in an arch. It looked like everyone was here, including the higher-ups in VANT Enterprises and all the mechanics. There must have been thirty people in that room.

"Oh. My. God," Tally squeaked out as Hayes bounded over, lifting her into the air and spinning her around.

"Are you surprised?" he asked, giddy.

She looked around at the trestle table of food and the giant cake shaped like a baby bottle. "When... How?" She shook her head. "You guys did this for me?" she asked, her voice unsteady.

Valeria from the front desk skipped in. "We did! We've been planning it for weeks." She grabbed Tally's hand and dragged her further into the room, where everyone crowded around and congratulated her. Hayes and I stood back, watching her fight back tears as she hugged all the gruff mechanics, the slightly awkward Stephie, the PR girls, and Antony.

"She looks happy, right?" Hayes murmured. Honestly, she looked overwhelmed and like she was about to burst into tears, but the grin on her face made my chest feel all warm.

I slapped him on the back. "Yeah, I think she's happy." With this. With us. We were doing the right thing.

TWENTY-TWO

TALLY

SOMEONE PULLED up a chair and sat me in it. Valeria was handing out cake, and she seemed so excited about the party, I wondered if she'd missed her calling. Hayes was chatting to one of the engineers, while Jesse was talking to Trent, who was yet another one of Vanessa Sumich's partners.

How they'd managed to remain together all this time was impressive, but when I saw Antony run a hand over Trent's back in a way that could only be a caress, it made a little more sense.

Sometimes, I felt like the sun in our little solar system relationship, with Hayes and Jesse rotating around me, and I adored that. But it appeared with the VANT owners, they were all stars, each burning brightly together to make one beautiful galaxy.

Alphonso, one of the engineers, appeared in front of me, and in his hand was a wrapped package. Alphonso was easily in his sixties, and there was no one on the team who knew more about how to put cars together than him. Even Hayes looked up to him.

"For you," he said, grinning broadly. "My wife wishes you the best with your baby, and said that while it seems like a lot, he will lose booties at an alarming rate."

Inside the present was a little ribbon-wrapped package of hand-knitted baby booties. There was also a small knitted cardigan in a sage green, in the softest wool I'd ever felt. Beneath all that, was a sage and white baby blanket.

I swallowed down the emotions that had just swelled up in my throat. "Alphonso... this must have taken hours. Please thank your wife for me. This is so *beautiful*."

Alphonso smiled toothily. "Ah, she loves to knit and crochet, and we were never blessed with children of our own. She enjoyed making them."

I stood up and hugged the short man, and he patted my back awkwardly. *Gah.* I couldn't cry. If I started, I wouldn't stop. Clearing my throat, I stepped back. "Thank you."

The older man flushed, and someone cleared their throat. "Stop. If you cry, the old man will cry too." Behind Alphonso stood Rocco Passero, and he was throwing a teasing grin in Alphonso's direction.

"Not too old to kick your ass, kid."

Rocco threw back his head and laughed heartily. "I believe it, Fonzo. Now, out of the way. There's a pretty girl, and I have a large package."

Alphonso looked over his shoulder at me and lifted his eyes skyward. I smiled at his retreating form before switching back to Rocco. Damn, he was handsome. He was the kind of man that made your blood run a little hotter. Which made me feel guilty. But I was a woman with eyes; I could appreciate he was attractive without pursuing anything.

Beside him was indeed a large present, wrapped in racing car paper, which was kind of cute. "Thank you, Rocco. You didn't need to get me anything."

Honestly, I was wildly surprised he was even here. I mean, he barely came to press conferences and training days. A baby shower would've been the last place I'd expect to see him.

He shrugged. "This is a party. It is expected to give the mother a gift for the baby." He pushed the box forward, and I took it hesitantly. It was half my size.

I opened it up, and inside was a car seat and stroller system. I'd eyed this one while researching, so I knew how much it cost, and there were four digits in its price tag. "Rocco... I can't accept this."

"Do you have one already?"

I shook my head. "Well, no. I haven't gotten to that just yet." I'd been buying things second-hand and online, but car seats were one of those things you needed to buy new, and I was still looking.

Rocco tilted his head. "Then what is the problem? Don't you like it?"

I gaped up at him. "No, I love it. But it's too expensive as a gift."

He snorted, waving a hand. "I looked; it has the best safety ratings of any car seat on the market. I have more money than I can spend in a lifetime. Take the gift, *Stellina*."

I chewed my lip. "Thank you, Rocco." I stood, and he kissed both my cheeks. "I appreciate your thoughtfulness." My brain couldn't compute the idea of Rocco Passero Googling car seats himself.

He stepped back and winked. "You're welcome." Then he just turned and walked away.

Holy crap.

Valeria appeared with a plate, some blue-tinted cake resting in the center, and handed it to me. Beside her was Stephie, and we all watched Rocco walk past Antony, saying something softly in his ear, then head out the door.

"I know we aren't meant to say this about our coworkers, but that man went straight into my spank bank the moment I saw him," Stephie said softly. Valeria made a hum of agreement.

If I was honest, I'd had more than one dirty dream about Rocco Passero, long before I met the man. He'd been in my fantasy arsenal when he first came onto the racing scene, back when I was sixteen.

I made a non-commital noise, which shook them from their drooling trance, and they both handed me small packages. "Our turn!" Valeria had bought me a onesie with a teddy bear on the front, as well as a giraffe teething ring. Stephie had bought a board book about Amelia Earhart and a nasal aspirator.

I thanked them both, and they sat around as more people came up to give me gifts. I was overwhelmed by the generosity of these people I had known just a few months. The gifts ranged from pacifiers to sleep sacks and everything in between. By the end, I'd had three slices of cake and was as close to being overwhelmed with emotion as I'd ever been.

Lastly, Vanessa and her partners appeared in front of me. I stood, shaking my head. "Thank you all so much. I can't believe this." I felt like I was living in a dream. I hadn't had a party since... I couldn't even remember when. Before my mother died, that was for sure.

Antony rested a hand on his shoulder. "You deserve it. You're a valued member of this team." He cleared his throat. "And on that note, follow us." He led me through the crowd, out into the parking lot.

Sitting in front of us was a large Lexus SUV, and I looked over at them. "Mr. Barbieri..." I started, but he waved a hand.

"Don't panic, Tally. This is a company car, on lease to you for a duration. At the end, we'll trade it in. It's a tax write-off, at best." He said it all airily, but the lopsided smirk on his face told me that it might be a company car, but they'd bought it *for* me. "You need a way to get to and from work, and if two of my employees are using it for transportation, all the better."

Hayes stood on one side of me, Jesse on the other. The shock on their faces told me that they hadn't known this was going to happen either.

"It's got one of the best safety ratings of the year," Hayes murmured softly.

I'd had company cars before, especially back when I'd been driving professionally. The difference was that this felt like I didn't really deserve it.

I looked between Vanessa and Antony. I felt like I should turn it down. "Are you sure?"

Vanessa nodded. "Absolutely. Look, we have company cars. We'll write it into your contract, if that makes you feel better."

The tears that I'd been holding back were now sliding down my cheeks. Antony pulled out the keys from his pocket and held them out to me. I hesitantly took them, while everyone clapped and cheered, like I'd just come in P1.

I hugged Antony, even though it was probably inappropriate, then I turned to his wife. Vanessa reached down and hugged me close. "You're going to be a wonderful mother, Tally."

The tears flooded up and poured down my cheeks as she held me. I'd needed to hear that, even though it probably wouldn't be true. I'd be a fuckup, but it wouldn't be because I didn't love the hell out of this baby.

She continued to hug me like she knew how much I needed it, stroking my back in circles, until I finally pulled my shit together and stepped back. I gave a damp kiss to her other husbands, Trent and Nathan, and walked toward the car. It looked brand new, and smelled like they'd rolled it off the factory floor today.

I needed to find the words to say thank you to these people, who'd made me feel like I was part of a team once more. Several people were now chanting, "Speech, speech, speech!"

"Uh, first of all, thank you! Thank you to every single one of you for taking time out of your lives to attend this surprise for me. Thank you to everyone who organized this baby shower, to VANT Racing for letting me be part of the team." I scrubbed the tears from my cheeks with the back of my arm. "Sorry, everything makes me cry right now."

A little ripple of laughter moved through the crowd.

"Antony, Vanessa, Trent, and Nathan—thank you for seeing enough in me to take a chance, and for all your kindness since." I looked at Hayes and Jesse, who were still standing over by the bosses. "A very special thank you to Hayes and Jesse, for everything."

God, at that moment, I wanted to say the words. I wanted to tell them that I loved them, but it was too soon, not the right time.

I cleared the lump from my throat. "I appreciate you all, and I can't wait to be back with the team, along with this bonus employee." I rubbed my stomach. There was a smattering of applause, and we all headed back inside.

Lady Luck was on my side now, and happiness was within my grasp.

TWENTY-THREE

TALLY WAS TOSSING and turning in bed, like she couldn't get comfortable. She'd popped a lot last week, and the last ultrasound showed that the baby was starting to turn, so the uncomfortableness was only going to increase. Right now, she basically had a basketball strapped to her front, and that was never going to be the easiest way to sleep.

I nuzzled her cheek. "Baby, are you okay?" Sleep was sitting there at the edge of the darkness, because when Tally couldn't sleep, none of us could. Jesse and I had been switching out every night, just so one of us was in the land of the living each day.

She sighed. "No. I think I'm having contractions."

Any drowsiness fled, like she'd just shot adrenaline right into my veins. "You *think* you're having contractions?"

Another heavy sigh. "No, I know I'm having contractions. For a couple of hours now."

I shot out of bed, staring down at her calm face. I was panicking. I'd told myself I wouldn't panic when this moment came, but fuck that. "We should head to the hospital," I said softly, when really, I wanted to say *why the hell didn't you tell me earlier?!*

She nodded, pulling herself into an upright position. I grabbed my phone and called Jesse, who answered on the third ring. "It's go time. Call Will and Colin."

I hung up and started gathering all the things she'd need. *Does she need her body pillow? What about that inflatable ball thing?*

"The bag is in the corner, Hayes."

I was supposed to be the calm one. She was the one about to push out a human.

Grabbing the bag she indicated, I picked it up and resisted the urge to pick her up too and sprint to the car. I walked around her in circles as she pulled on her sleep shorts and a hooded sweatshirt.

I looked for her keys, but couldn't find them. *Where would she put the keys?* I checked the kitchen bench, the coffee table, and the fridge.

"They're on the hook by the door," she said softly. Sure enough, there they were, hanging by the door.

Jesse appeared, and I'd never been so relieved to see anyone in my whole life. "Thank fuck you're here."

He gave me a wide-eyed look, then moved toward Tally. "Ready to have a baby?"

She winced, holding her stomach. "No. Can we skip this part?"

Wrapping an arm around her shoulder, he looked over at me. "Go put the bag in the car and take several deep breaths, man. You look like you're about to pass out."

I escaped out of there so fast, you could probably smell burning rubber. Well, you could've, if I'd been wearing shoes. *Fuck.*

I loaded her suitcase into the car, then raced back to the front door, pulling on my sneakers without any socks. Jesse led Tally out of the house and over to the car, talking to her quietly about how far apart her contractions were, and all these other things that I *knew* were important but had escaped my brain.

Jesse held out his hand for the keys, and I gave them over quickly. I didn't trust myself to push a shopping cart right now, let alone drive Tally to the hospital. I climbed into the back seat with her, holding her close. She had three more contractions on the fifteen-minute drive to the hospital, and every single time, I held my breath through the entire thing.

She was squeezing my fingers so tightly that I was worried they might break, but I'd let her pulverize my entire body if it helped.

She panted as the latest contraction eased. "I'm scared, Hayes. What if I can't do it?"

I held her tightly to me. "You can do this, sweetheart. You're Tally fucking Palmer. You've conquered every hurdle the world has put in your way. In a few short hours, you'll have our baby in your arms, and you'll be the most beautiful mother on the planet." I lifted her fingers to my lips. "I'm scared too. Petrified. But I know deep down in my gut, you have this."

We pulled into the emergency department, and I gently helped her out of the car. Jesse kissed her deeply, then rested his forehead against hers. "I'll park the car and call Will and Colin. I'll be back soon."

She nodded and waddled into the reception area, where they sent her straight up to the maternity ward, after getting her a wheelchair. As soon as we stepped from the elevator, it was a flurry of activity. Nurses bustled around, getting her a bed, strapping her to monitors and doing visual checks.

When Jesse appeared with Will and Colin, I could have cried with relief. The nurse raised her eyebrows at so many men in one room.

Will marched over to the bed and kissed Tally's forehead, speaking to her in low tones. She burst into tears, and Colin looked like he was moments away from following suit. She clutched at her oldest friend's shirt as he held her close. Their bond was something Jesse and I could only work toward. There was unconditional love there that was beautiful.

It was why I hadn't protested when Tally had said she wanted Will to be the only one in the delivery room with her. I think Jesse had been a little disappointed, but he'd held it together. We respected her wishes, of course. She joked that it was because we'd only just gotten acquainted with her vagina; she didn't want us to see a flashback of it stretched around a watermelon every time we went downstairs.

Apparently, it didn't matter if Will did, since he already thought vaginas were gross.

She wanted us here in the hospital, though. She wanted us beside her as she labored, and that meant something. There would be plenty of time to see her give birth, because I was in it for the long haul. In two, five, ten years, when she was ready to have another baby, I would be there, holding her hand and telling her she was glorious.

When Will straightened, there were tears in his eyes, and that was all that was needed to push Colin over the edge. He burst into tears, and Tally laughed, waving him over so she could hug him too. They were family, those three, and soon, it would double in size. Because they'd be my family too. And given the look of peace on Jesse's face, they'd be his too.

Will left them cuddling, and I wasn't sure what Colin was saying to Tally, but it made her gasp and laugh through the next contraction.

Coming to stand beside us, Will dragged in a deep breath. "I'm fucking terrified."

Jesse slapped him gently on the back. "We all are."

His eyes flicked between us. "I'm glad she has you two. You're good for her. I haven't seen her this happy in so long, and you two play a big part in that." He let out a shuddering breath. "Thank you for letting me be here too. I know you guys have all gotten closer, but I'm not sure I could have let you do this alone. If she needed me, and I wasn't here…"

I squeezed his shoulder. "She wanted you, and we

understand. The next one is all mine, though, got it?" I teased.

He gave me a tight smile and nodded. "You got it."

Six hours later, Tally gave birth not to a little boy as expected, but a little girl. The ultrasound tech had said it was a guess, and apparently, she'd guessed wrong. When Will had walked into the waiting room to tell us, his face flushed and coated in tears, I'd been gobsmacked. Colin had cried harder, hugging Will tightly. I'd hugged Jesse, then Will too.

"Everything went perfectly. She's just delivering the placenta, and they kicked me out for that. Apparently, there are some things I did not need to see. They're just cleaning her up, then you guys can go and see her."

What felt like a heartbeat later, we were staring down at the most beautiful baby I'd ever seen. Tally was in an exhausted slumber on the bed, and if I couldn't see the monitors, I'd have been freaking out.

The baby was squishy and wrinkly, an odd shade between purple and pink, but she was gorgeous. I snapped a photo, then messaged my parents to let them know.

H: *Surprise. It's a girl. And she's the most beautiful little girl in the whole world. Everything is perfect. Tally is doing well, textbook birth.*

• • •

My parents were still in Texas, and we hadn't really told them about the whole polyamory thing. But they knew Tally was my girlfriend, that she was pregnant, and while the baby wasn't mine biologically, I wanted them to know that I was going to consider myself the baby's parent in every way that mattered.

I hadn't doubted that they would accept it easily. They'd talked to Tally on the phone a couple of times, and my mom had answered a bunch of her questions about babies and what to expect. She'd been great. They'd sent care packages, and talked about their grandbaby.

Mom: *She absolutely is the most beautiful baby ever. Give Tally all our love and tell her we are so proud of her. Can't wait to hold my brand-new granddaughter.*

Now I was going to cry. Jesse wrapped an arm around my shoulder. "I might be biased, but she's way cuter than any baby I've ever seen," he whispered.

A nurse appeared and pointed down at her. "Would you like to hold her?" I nodded vigorously. "You're Dad?"

Jesse couldn't take his eyes off the baby. "We both are."

The nurse didn't even blink. "Well, congrats to the both of you. Come sit over here. Okay, now hold your arms like this." She angled my arms, then slid the baby into them. She was so light, so tiny.

"Hello, beautiful girl," I whispered. "I'm going to protect you and give you the world."

Jesse's fingers looked huge against her cheeks. "Me too."

The nurse just grinned. "I have to wake your mama up to make sure she's okay, pretty girl." She gently shook Tally from her sleep, checking her temperature and asking about her pain and the stitches.

Stitches? Where would she have stitches?

Tally groggily answered all the nurse's questions, and once the lady had closed the door, I rose to my feet. Jesse hovered, ready to catch the baby if I so much as looked like I'd drop her. I slowly made my way over and kissed Tally's forehead and the exhausted lines around her eyes.

"God, you're amazing. Do you know that?" Leaning forward, I carefully placed the baby into her arms. "Look what you made, sweetheart. She's perfect."

She sucked in a deep breath. "Hello, beautiful girl. Hello, Bobbi-June."

The baby opened her tiny eyes and blinked up at her mama. Everything inside of me shifted and rearranged. Every priority I'd ever had, every dream I'd ever imagined, reformed itself around these two.

Jesse smiled widely. "Perfect. Bobbi-June Palmer. Welcome to the world, angel."

We sat in silence, just staring at the baby, for an indeterminate amount of time. It could have been minutes or hours.

Colin and Will arrived in the room later, with the biggest bunch of flowers I'd ever seen, and Colin cried some more as he cooed over Tally and the baby.

At that moment, I didn't think I could ever love two people as much as I loved the woman on that bed, and the tiny baby in her arms.

TWENTY-FOUR

TALLY

I STAYED in the hospital for two days, and tried not to think about the medical bills. My vagina felt like it was on fire, and my milk had come in like a tsunami, so my boobs also felt like they were on fire. I couldn't sleep.

And none of that mattered, because Bobbi-June was the most perfect baby that I could ever ask for. I wished Buck could have seen her. He would have adored her; I knew it. He probably would have preferred her to be a boy, but he still would've loved a little girl.

I'd received a huge balloon bouquet from everyone at VANT Racing, and another one from Vanessa Sumich herself. A gift basket from Hayes's parents also arrived, which had made me cry again. I would be glad when my hormones were my own again.

There had been someone here almost the entire time I was awake, but right now, everyone had gone home. Jesse and Hayes needed to shower and feed Norton, and Will had to work, as did Colin. I smiled as I thought about them cooing over the baby. Bobbi-June was going to be the most loved child on the planet.

There was a knock at the door to my room, and I looked over quickly to make sure the sound didn't wake Bobbi-June. "Come in." The door swung open, and my heart stopped.

In the doorway was Brick Willtot.

Fuck. Fuck.

I reached out and grabbed the buzzer in one hand, the crib in the other. Not that I thought Brick Willtot could just walk out with my baby, but I wasn't being rational.

"Tally." His tone was cool and calm, but I knew this man. The cooler he appeared, the more rage-filled he was.

"Brick. How'd you get in?"

He looked over at Bobbi-June, but didn't get any closer than a few feet away. "I told them I was here to see my grandchild, and money makes the world go round. My sources said you were having a boy."

I tried not to think about who would have been feeding Brick information. "What are you doing here, Brick?"

He sneered in my direction. "Don't be ridiculous, Tally. We both know why I'm here. I can do simple math. This baby is Buck's. The last piece of my son that you stole."

"NASCAR stole your son. I had nothing to do with

it," I argued, though I knew it was pointless. "You aren't welcome here," I added for good measure.

He tilted his head at me. "You'd keep my grandchild from me?"

Fuck yeah, I would. "This isn't your grandchild," I lied.

"Don't insult my intelligence. That doesn't look like a premature baby, and I can count backwards by nine."

"I don't give a shit what you think."

He stepped toward me, his cheeks beginning to flush. I pressed the buzzer in my hand. "You're nothing but a whore, Tally Palmer. I know that baby is my grandchild." He leaned closer. "When I'm done, you'll never see her again. I'll have my lawyers paint you out to be the fickle slut that you are, and I will seem like a benevolent saint in comparison. Someone who can provide that child with all the love, care and opportunity a destitute single mother can't. The best education. The best opportunities.

"You're a mother who already tried to keep that baby away from its biological family. You'll have no job, no prospects, no money. When I'm done with you, you won't have a box to live in. I'm going to ruin you, and people will let me, because I'm rich and important, and you are noth—"

"Are you okay, Tally?"

I looked past Brick at Rocco. I'd never been so relieved to see anyone in my life. "Brick was just leaving."

"Like fuck I am," the man in question growled,

lurching toward me. Rocco was immediately there, stepping between Bobbi-June, me and Brick.

I couldn't see Rocco's face, but every muscle in his back was tense and ready. "I suggest you leave before I get security to do it for you. And then the police."

Brick took a step back, but the expression didn't leave his face. "You'll be hearing from my lawyers, Tally. I'll get a DNA test ordered, then that baby is coming home with me."

He spun and left as the nurses arrived, barging them out of the way. "Excuse me!" the nurse snapped, then she looked over at me. "Is everything all right?"

"I want that man banned from this room," I told her. "I... I don't want to see him ever."

The nurse frowned, but determination firmed her jaw. "I'll tell Security. He won't get past our desk again. Is there someone you want me to call?"

I shook my head. I'd message Hayes and Jesse myself in a moment. The nurse left, and I let out the breath that had been burning in my lungs. I wanted to collapse into a ball beneath the blankets, but I was far too aware that Rocco was still here in the room with me.

"Deep breaths, *Stellina.*"

I covered my eyes, pressing the heels of my hands into their sockets until I saw stars, and sucked in oxygen. Bobbi-June was still oblivious to the tension in the room, and for that, I was thankful.

"You're okay." His voice washed over me, that absolute confidence that it was fine, and I let myself delusionally believe him for a moment. I looked up at him, and he was staring down at the baby. *"Bambolina.* You got your mama's beauty, didn't you?" he said softly. He looked back up at me. "You're glowing, Tally."

I gave a slightly hysterical laugh. "Liar. But I appreciate it."

He presented me with a huge bunch of pink and purple hydrangeas. "Congratulations."

I grabbed the giant bunch of flowers and laid them across my lap. "Thank you, Rocco. For these, and for before."

He waved a hand, like it meant nothing. Maybe to him, it was nothing. But it meant something to me. He sat down in the chair. "They tell me at work that everything went well." I nodded again, because this was a little awkward. "Bobbi-*Giugno.*" He pronounced it almost like Juno, and I laughed.

"Bobbi-June. Like the name, not the month."

He grinned. "Beautiful name." He looked back at the door. "And the man? He was the father?"

I tried not to dry-retch at the thought of fucking Brick Willtot. *Ew.* I mean, he might have been handsome if he wasn't so ugly on the inside, didn't have a beer belly, and wasn't as mean as a rattlesnake.

"God no." I hesitated, but I guess the secret was out. If Brick managed to get a DNA test, he was going to find out the truth. "His son was Bobbi-June's father. He died on the race track."

Rocco nodded sadly. "I'm sorry for your loss."

I blinked at him. He was the first person to give me their condolences, except maybe Hayes and Ty back at

Daytona, when I first came off the track. No one else had ever acknowledged that I'd lost anyone at all, even though Buck and I had been seeing each other for six months.

It had gotten lost in the rest of the bullshit.

"Thank you. I feel sad that she'll never get to know him."

Rocco reached into the crib but paused. "May I?" I nodded, and he stroked a steady finger across her cheek. "So small. Her nose is the size of my fingernail," he said softly. "That is sad, but she will have you to look up to. As well as your lovers."

Squinting in his direction, I tried to work out if that was a jab at my lifestyle or not. It didn't appear to be, though. "They're more than lovers. They're partners."

"They are very lucky to call this *bambolina* theirs. And you." He gave me a crooked grin, and his dimples did something to me. Honestly, this was the most I'd ever heard him say, and this soft version of Rocco Passero seemed totally at odds with the man who was featured on the covers of magazines. He stood, giving me one last smile. "I look forward to seeing you when you return to work." With that, he left.

I was still sitting there, kinda stunned and confused about the last thirty minutes when the nurse reappeared. She gave me a soft smile and took the flowers from my lap. "I'll put these in water, shall I?"

She disappeared back out of the room, and I reached into the crib and gently picked up Bobbi-June. Bringing her to my chest, I nursed her. As I looked down into her tiny face, with her weirdly shaped head, I knew deep in my soul that I would stand in front of a bullet for her over and over again.

I would definitely protect her from Brick Willtot and his lawyers.

TWENTY-FIVE

JESSE

"OKAY, hear me out, kid. We are gonna get you wrapped, snacked and back down to nap before your mama wakes up." I looked up at Hayes. "You ready?"

He nodded, baby powder in one hand and a diaper in the other. "We got this. Smooth pit stop. We've been practicing."

"The bottle's in the warmer?"

"Yep."

Hayes and I had taken over the night-time feedings to let Tally sleep. It had taken a couple of weeks, but we had it down to a fine art now.

"All right. Let's do this. Box box!"

I made funny faces as I unsnapped Bobbi-June's sleep suit. I gurgled and blew raspberries, doing anything I could to keep her distracted as Hayes wiped, swiped and floofed baby powder. I lifted her legs up, snapped the new diaper into place and slipped her back into her onesie, then back in the sleep sack.

I lifted my hands in the air. "Clear!"

"Clear!"

I gave her a tiny high five. "Great work, team."

Picking her up gently, I laid her in the crook of my arm. It had taken at least two weeks before I could be convinced that she wouldn't break like glass if I held her. I sat down in the rocker that Will and Colin had gifted Tally, and rocked the baby gently. She yawned and let out a kitten noise of protest.

She was a great baby, who barely ever cried, and was so alert and precious. Possibly the smartest baby on the planet, already trying to hold her head up and look around. But she was grumpy if she wasn't fed, especially if she'd given you enough warning already.

I rocked her gently. "Don't worry, baby girl. Hay-Hay has already gone to get your bottle. He won't be long."

As if her little noises had summoned him from the kitchen, he appeared, a sleepy Norton in tow. My big dog wasn't mine any more. He was firmly one hundred percent Bobbi-June's dog now. He'd sit there and look at her in the bassinet for hours on end. When she had tummy time, he'd lay beside her and stare at her lovingly. When Tally nursed her, he'd sit there with his big head on Tally's lap, like a living nursing pillow. When she cried, he was the first in the room.

Hayes handed me the bottle, a yawn stretching his face.

"Go back to sleep, man. I've got this. I'll put her down."

It was a testament to how tired he was that he just nodded, leaning down and kissing her cheek. He patted the top of Norton's head, then headed back down the darkened hallway.

I gave Bobbi-June the bottle, and she latched on beautifully. *What did I say? So smart.*

"Your mama has a big day tomorrow. And you do too. It's your first day of work. I gotta say, twenty-three days old and already having to go in for the daily grind seems kinda rough. This current economic climate, am I right? Craziness." I murmured soothing nonsense to her as I rocked. "Honestly, I can't believe your mama is even thinking about heading back already. She just pushed a baby out of her body—I think she deserves a few more weeks of rest and relaxation, right?"

The baby blinked slowly up at me.

"Yeah, I knew you'd agree. But your mama's a warrior; she won't let anything keep her down. I hope you get that trait from her. I hope you're a tiny little mini-mama, because I can't think of anyone more perfect in the world. Except you, of course."

I rocked and hummed the words to "Everyone Wants To Rule The World" while she finished her bottle, then placed her over my shoulder—the spit cloth already there, because you only needed to be puked on once before you learned. I'd Googled the best way to burp a baby, because I still wasn't convinced my giant hand wouldn't hurt her if I patted her back too hard.

As she burped on cue, I laid her back against my chest and rocked her until she fell asleep again. I was ready for her to sleep through the night, but on the other hand, I liked these quiet moments. I felt like her real father in moments like this. Like I was doing something right. Maybe I was meant to be a stay-at-home dad.

I laughed at the idea. My father would have had a coronary at the very thought—hell, maybe my mom would too. They'd had pretty strict ideas about what roles a man and woman should have in a family. But that had meant that when my dad died, my mother had crumbled to pieces. She'd been so busy being Mrs. Banks, she didn't know what to do when there wasn't a Mr. Banks to give her purpose and personality.

I'd never have that problem with Tally. She was so gloriously her.

"Ugh, I'm feeling all sappy, baby girl. Let's put you down before I wake you up again," I whispered, though she was sound asleep. Gently moving toward the bedroom, I laid her down in the bassinet in the corner of the room. The nursery and all her stuff was in my living room for now, but she still slept in the spare room with Tally.

I held my breath, but she stayed asleep. I wasn't sure if it was meant to feel like disarming a bomb every time I put her down, but it did.

I climbed in beside Tally as carefully as I could, but I should have known she wouldn't stay asleep. "Okay?" she asked sleepily, and I kissed her arm.

"Everything's perfect. Go back to sleep."

She snuggled back down into the pillows, her

breaths already returning to their soft rhythm. "Okay. Love you," she mumbled, and my whole body froze. But she was already humming soft, sleepy breaths.

I resisted the urge to drag her into my arms and kiss her. "Love you too," I whispered back, knowing she wouldn't hear.

I did, though. So fucking much.

The morning came and went so fast, and then I was alone. Just me and Norton, and I wasn't sure which one of us stared more pathetically at the door, waiting for them to come home.

The house was almost finished now, and I had mixed feelings about it, really. I was excited to have this project that Tally and I had worked on finally completed, but the future after that was so up in the air. Would she take the money and get a place of her own, somewhere further away? Would she move in here, if I asked?

Everything was happening so fast. I felt like we'd skipped so many different steps, but I couldn't find it in me to regret it. Especially not after last night.

My phone rang in my pocket, and I fished it out. I groaned out loud, scaring Norton, when my mom's name flashed across the screen. We didn't talk much; she had her life and I had mine, and we didn't need to cross over that often. She was on the other side of the country, so that was always a decent excuse. I felt like we had started being strangers the day she'd shipped me off to Texas while I was grieving.

My uncle had become my support; he'd been Dad's older brother and had only died about two years ago. I usually spent my holidays with Hayes's family. My mom was a non-event in my life. Still, I answered when she called.

"Hi, Mom."

"Jesse. I thought you might call your mother, but after a couple of months, I figured if I wanted to speak to my only child, I better do it myself."

I cleared my throat. After I was sent to Texas, she hadn't spoken to me for six whole months. Talking to me was too painful, she'd said. She didn't get to be on her high horse now, but I let it go.

"Sorry, I've been really busy."

She snorted. "Riding your motorbike and having no responsibilities?"

I looked skyward, hoping I could make it through this conversation without saying something I'd regret. "No, I bought the house next to mine, and I've been doing renovations on it. I'm almost done, actually." I paused. "And I got a girlfriend, so I haven't been traveling as much."

The silence at the other end of the line was long. "Oh? What's her name, this new girlfriend? Anyone I'd know?"

I didn't know how my mom would possibly know her, unless she was in her fundraising circle or the lead actress on her daytime soap opera, but I still answered. "Unlikely. Her name is Tally. She's a friend of Hayes."

"Oh," she sniffed. "I see." Yeah, my mom wasn't a huge fan of Hayes. She thought he was a bad influence —like he was the reason I was a loner who didn't want to move back to DC. Hayes told me I had mommy issues. He was probably right.

You know what? In for a penny, in for a pound. "Actually, both Hayes and I are seeing her. We're in a polyamorous relationship, and she just had a baby, which I'm beginning to love like my own."

Mom snorted. "Very funny, Jesse. I don't know why every time I call, you have to be so flippant. I wanted to invite you home for Christmas, but I think I might just go with the girls to Cabo."

I would bet my entire fortune that had been her intention the entire time and she was just guilt-tripping me. "I couldn't have made it out there anyway. Enjoy Cabo, Mom."

I expected her to hang up, but she paused a little, then asked, "Are you really dating the same girl as your friend?"

Well, shit. I'd been kind of hoping she'd just continue to believe I was kidding and let it go. Might as well rip off the bandaid. "Yes."

"And she has a baby?"

"Three weeks old, yesterday."

There was a long silence. "Is the baby yours?"

"Not legally. Or biologically." But that baby had

already become the center of all our worlds, and hopefully one day, that wouldn't matter at all.

She let out a long breath. "Thank goodness for that. I thought some girl was baby-trapping you," she snapped. "I think I might need to come out there and ensure that you aren't blinded by a pair of perky breasts and your best friend. You're financially well-off, Jesse. You need to be careful of people's intentions."

Anger washed over me. This woman, who hadn't even seen me in five years, had the nerve to lecture me about people's intentions? Plus, I was hardly generationally wealthy. I had a couple of houses and enough money in the bank that if my place fell down around my ears, I could rebuild it without stress. I wasn't on the *Forbes* rich list, for fuck's sake.

"Don't bother, Mom. Have a great time in Mexico." Then I hung up, hissing out a breath through my teeth. "Come on, Norton. Let's go get a pup cup and go to the hardware store." The dog stared up at me, his head cocked. "What? Coffee and power tools are cheaper than the therapy I so desperately need after that conversation." He still stared. "Fine, we'll get fries on the way home."

Norton barked and sat near his leash. I'd been hustled.

TWENTY-SIX
TALLY

BOBBI-JUNE WAS A HUGE TIME WASTER. Not just for me, either. Everyone at VANT Racing had stopped to coo over her in her tiny little knit cap and booties. Alphonso had looked all sparkly-eyed when he saw her wrapped in the baby blanket and booties he'd gifted me, and had taken a photo for his wife. He told me that the baby was going to have so many knitted blankets soon, I wouldn't know what to do with them.

Even Antony had held her, making baby talk, asking if she would come and race for them in sixteen years' time, which made me laugh. I loved racing, but the idea of my baby flinging herself around a race track at over two hundred miles per hour filled me with terror. I had no idea how my dad had ever let me race.

True to Antony's word, VANT had set aside a little room off the office with a recliner that I could use for nursing, as well as a baby monitor and bassinet if I needed it. Their thoughtfulness made my chest feel full.

But the baby mostly just stayed in her stroller, sleeping or playing with the mobile that hung across the top.

I was halfway through the day when I finally made it to the simulations room. I brought Bobbi-June in with me, and she was thankfully sound asleep.

Stephie looked panicked when I parked the stroller beside her desk. "What do I do if she wakes up?"

I shrugged. "Just rock her with your foot. She's just been fed, so she should sleep for a little while. Unless you don't think you can do math and jiggle your extremities at the same time?"

Stephie huffed. "I could drink tequila shots and juggle, and still do the math needed for this." She might be timid, but no one second-guessed her mathematical talent.

Luckily, the room was pretty dark and silent. We'd had to adjust for the fact I was smaller than the last time we'd run the simulation, and I knew I'd have to get back into shape sooner rather than later. My brain was always kind of on the baby, but eventually, I was deep into the drive.

There were differences between open-wheel and stock car racing, obviously. They were a world apart physically, but driving was driving. The fundamentals were the same, but your skills had to be tweaked between the two.

I'd shout stuff at Stephie, and she'd adjust on the fly, which was a testament to her skills more than anything else. Especially since she'd admitted that before starting at VANT Racing, she'd never seen a race car in her life. She didn't even own a normal car. She rode the bus to work, and didn't ever want to drive. Said she'd seen the statistics. You were less likely to die on public transport than in a personal vehicle.

The project that Stephie and I were working on would create the standard settings for the vehicles, and then they'd be tweaked to the drivers and engineers. Honestly, it was such an awesome experience, it felt like I was playing instead of working.

As we stopped the simulation, I glanced down at my watch. The room was still silent, even though Bobbi-June was normally awake by now. Panicking slightly, I climbed from the simulator and stopped when I saw Rocco holding her, swaying from side to side, baby-talking to her in Italian.

"My ovaries," Stephie gasped when she noticed him in the room too.

I frowned at her and stepped toward the large man holding my tiny, cooing baby. He looked up at me with a soft smile. "She was fussing. I think she wanted to get out and see the world," he said placatingly. "You seemed to be in the zone, and she didn't seem unhappy with my presence. I should have asked for permission."

I mean, yeah probably. I was probably a shitty parent for not noticing her fussing. Maybe I shouldn't be bringing her to work, if I was doing both of my jobs badly.

However, the baby was flailing her tiny arms in Rocco's direction and seemed perfectly content in the arms of a stranger. "It's fine. Thank you for holding her."

He tucked Bobbi-June back to his chest, and Stephie sighed. Yeah, I got it. The normally gruff driver was smiling down at the baby, and if I hadn't just given birth, I might have become spontaneously pregnant again.

"It's nothing. She is a good *bambolina*." He handed her over to me and turned to Stephie. "I believe we have a meeting?"

Stephie cleared her throat, and I could see the flush of her cheeks even in the almost darkness. "Uh, yeah, we do. Just need to get your measurements for the simulator."

I clutched Bobbi-June to my chest, where she began to nuzzle hungrily. "I'll leave you to it." I placed her back in her stroller, and she started protesting, her tiny wails sounding like a kitten crying more than the cater-wauling you'd think of. She really was the best baby.

Rocco looked over at us. "Just feed her here, *Stellina*. I won't look." He lifted his chin at the chair over in the darkened corner, then climbed into the cockpit of the simulator without sparing me another glance.

I looked over at Stephie. She shrugged, as if to say *go for it*. So I did. I also wanted to watch Rocco in the simu-lator, if I was honest.

I slipped my arm out of the oversized work shirt that I was wearing. I had a maternity tank on, but I still looked around to make sure everyone was distracted before I pulled out a boob. Bobbi-June latched quickly, and I held her close to my body. Rocco was still figuring out the simulator, pointing out the differences between it and the one he used to use for the Formula One team he drove for.

Stephie was one hundred percent focused as she made calculations to account for his slightly increased body weight, height, and the track he was testing. I knew there were about fifteen other people who worked on the software for this thing, but they lived at the VANT Enterprises offices most of the time.

Finally, Rocco began racing, and it was a thing of beauty. He drove with so much ease, despite the fact that Stephie had set the simulator to provide haptics. It had taken me a while to get used to them today, as we'd kept them to a minimum when I'd been pregnant. If I crashed into the wall, it provided enough physical feed-back that your wrists would hurt, as it would if you crashed into a real wall. It was a great motivator to take it seriously. Not that Rocco would know anything about that, because he maneuvered the imaginary vehicle around the track easily.

Bobbi-June finally finished, and I popped her over my shoulder to burp her as I stood, walking over to Stephie. "This part here, the track was made for stock cars. It's going to drag for IndyCars, so you want to make sure it's reflected in the sim."

Stephie made notes as I watched Rocco continue to drive. I couldn't wait to see him out on an actual track in the prototype car.

I snuck out as quietly as I could, going to find

Hayes. As predicted, he was in the garage, tinkering with the nose cone of the car. Seeing us, he laid down his tools and grinned. "My favorite girls." He dropped a kiss on Bobbi-June's head and then one on my lips. "Want to have lunch?"

I tucked Bobbi-June back into her stroller. "Well, she just ate, but I'd love to."

He shouted to Alphonso that he was going to lunch, then threw an arm around my shoulder as we walked toward the big double doors. "How's the first day back going?"

I shrugged. "Everyone's been really good about Bobbi-June, but I'm sure eventually the novelty of having a baby in a workplace will wear off."

"We'll deal with it when it comes to it. Pretty sure Jesse's dying to be a stay-at-home dad," he said with a chuckle.

It was hard to imagine Jesse—tall, tattooed, gruff-looking Jesse—as someone who changed diapers and gave baby bottles, but I'd seen it with my own two eyes. Both he and Hayes had stepped up for me when they didn't have to, and I could admit to myself that I loved them. It was hard not to when they celebrated every time Bobbi-June burped, like the house was a frat party and she'd won a belching competition. They tried to see who could make her smile first, even though I was ninety percent sure it was a gassy face.

"Hayes?"

"Hmm?" he asked, making faces at the baby as he pushed the stroller.

I pulled him to a stop. "I love you?"

He blinked in my direction. "Was that a question?" he teased.

Flushing pink, I slapped him gently in the stomach with the back of my hand. "No, I mean, I love you."

Grabbing me around the waist with the hand not holding the stroller, he pulled me close. "I love you too, Tally Palmer. So fucking much."

I kissed him until my knees felt like jello and I was breathless. "That's a relief, otherwise this unrequited pining thing might have gotten real old, real fast."

He laughed and kissed my temple, then walked me to our new favorite deli around the corner. It was one of those places that only served the workers in the surrounding industrial zone, and the decor was as varied and rough as the clientele, normally a weird mish-mash of office workers in matching suits and guys in high-vis vests with hard hats under their arms. But the place did a mean sandwich, and I was excited about eating my body weight in processed deli meats, now that I was no longer pregnant.

After ordering, we grabbed one of the open tables. There weren't separate tables; most people were happy to sit at the huge counter that wrapped around the grill and chat with the cooks or each other.

I parked Bobbi-June beside us, and a guy could have come in here shirtless, covered from head to toe in grease, and it would look less conspicuous than a baby. We got some weird side-eyes, but mostly, people ignored us. *Maybe I should buy her a bright yellow vest so she fits in.*

The short-order cook dropped off our food, made a funny, happy face at Bobbi-June which was made slightly more comical by his complete lack of teeth, then went back to the kitchen without saying a single word to us.

I'd just had my first bite when another guy walked up to stand beside our table. He looked almost as out of place as the baby, with his beige chinos and fleece sweater-vest. "Excuse me?"

"Yeah?" Hayes asked, his eyes flicking between me and the guy, like I should know who the hell he was.

"Are you Tally Palmer?" he asked, and I smiled. Maybe he was a NASCAR fan. It didn't happen often— out of sight, out of mind and all that—but occasionally, I was recognized.

Nodding, I put my hand out for him to shake. "Yeah, I am."

Instead of placing his palm in mine, the guy slipped an envelope between my fingers. I didn't even know where he'd pulled it from. He didn't even look at me as he said, "You've been served," in a bored tone. Then he turned and walked out while I stared, my brain struggling to catch up with what had just happened.

I dropped the envelope. It felt like a rattlesnake, curled in a ball, waiting for me to move so it could strike. I knew exactly what was going to be inside that envelope, and I wanted to set it on fire.

"Tally?" Hayes said hesitantly, as I peeled open the

sealed envelope and looked inside. Brick Willtot's name jumped out at me, like the boogeyman of my nightmares.

"Buck's family is suing me for custody of Bobbi-June."

TWENTY-SEVEN

TALLY

THE NEXT WEEK WAS HELL. Brick might have all the money, but I would bankrupt myself fighting him in court, if I had to. There were no depths I wouldn't sink to when it came to keeping my baby.

The guys had been great, but they didn't know what to do either, not really. They'd offered me up their savings, and Jesse had called a lawyer he knew for recommendations. They'd talked me down off the ledge several times, and had spent all night holding me while I cried.

Willy and Colin had been excellent too, and Willy came with me when I went to see the lawyer. While she'd been outraged on my behalf, she hadn't been as confident that the whole thing would be thrown out as I'd hoped.

"Look, you're a single mother with a dangerous job. You don't own any assets, have minimal support, and you're coming up against one of the richest families in the country, who are extremely well connected. You're going to have your work cut out for you." Will protested, but I just sat there in stunned shock. "Look, it isn't hopeless. The baby is well cared for and obviously well loved."

"What if I married her? Would that help her case? I'm not exactly in the poorhouse," Will asked, and I turned to stare at him.

Had he just offered to marry me? That was fucking weird.

The lawyer, Serena, raised an eyebrow. "You are comfortably well-off, Mr. Love, but you aren't Willtot rich. You're worlds apart. He's in the top hundred richest men in the country."

It had been so fucking awful, but I didn't care. I was going to beat this, and if I had my way, Brick Willtot wouldn't see a hair on Bobbi-June's head ever again.

Unfortunately, despite my current turmoil, life still went on. It meant that I still had to work; in fact, it was more important than ever. Antony had given me a week off after I'd mentioned I was having some family issues, but I couldn't remain on leave forever. It was hard when all I wanted to do was load her onto a plane and run away.

Because when it came down to it, no matter how much I loved the guys, I would choose my baby over them. I knew in my heart they'd understand too.

But we weren't there yet.

Hayes helped me unstrap her carrier from the car when we parked in our designated spot, and I felt like my whole body was made of lead. I was exhausted from sleepless nights and the stress, and a bad feeling in my gut.

My first sign that something was off at work too was Valeria looking at me with wide eyes and a frown.

The second sign was the yelling coming from Antony's office.

"What's wrong?" Hayes asked Valeria, handing me the baby.

"Brick Willtot arrived with his lawyers. He owns—"

"Willtot Racing, I know," he replied, his eyes darting to me.

Dread made ice spill through my veins. I hadn't told anyone at work who Bobbi-June's dad was, just that he was not in the picture. I was pretty sure most people assumed she was Hayes's baby.

I stepped toward the door, handing Bobbi-June back to Hayes. "You shouldn't go in there. Mr. Barbieri isn't seeing—" I ignored Valeria's warning. I knew I was the topic of discussion anyway, so I was fairly sure that Antony wouldn't care if I joined their conference.

It didn't sound like it was going well, though. "Listen here, Barbieri. I get that you want to join the racing world because you're bored, but there are *rules* here. A hierarchy across American motorsport. You're at the fucking bottom of it right now, no matter how much money you want to throw at this degenerate team you've gathered. Rejects and has-beens from across the world, from what I can see. But me, I'm sitting right at the top of the damn heap. I can make your entrance to this sport smooth like butter"—Brick leaned forward— "or so fucking hard, you'll have wasted *millions* of dollars on a team that will never see a race start."

He was clearly trying to intimidate Antony Barbieri, which would've been kind of hilarious in any other situation. He looked like he was attempting to loom threateningly, but Antony had a couple of inches of height on him.

"Let me see if I can tell you this in a language you'll understand, Mr. Willtot. I don't *care* what you want. I don't care how big of a fish you think you are in NASCAR—your reach isn't quite as long as mine." Antony leaned closer. "I don't care how deep you think your pockets are or how big of a deal you think you might be. My pockets are deeper, and my influence is broader. So for the last time, I am not firing any of my employees on your say-so." He stepped away, heading back behind his desk. "You can leave now, or I can get the police to remove you."

With a glare on his face, Willtot turned. I was too damn slow to hide before he saw me. The sneer on his face would have terrified me once upon a time. Now, it just filled me with a rage so deep, I wanted to claw his flesh from his face.

"I'm coming for you, bitch." He barged past me, his lawyer-slash-lackey right on his heels. I watched him until he was out the front door, everyone in the office also watching him go. Then I stepped into Antony's office and closed the door softly.

He looked at me and pointed to the couch. "I think

it's time we had a talk about why you quit NASCAR, don't you think?"

Slumping down into the overstuffed chesterfield, I dragged a hand down my face. "Bobbi-June's father was Buck Willtot, Brick's only son. When Buck died, Brick lost it. The accident wasn't anyone's fault; Buck just misjudged the distance to the wall, spun off and died in a truly freakish set of circumstances." I let out a shuddering breath as my shoulders curled in. "But Brick got it into his head that Buck's mind wasn't in the race because it was on me. That his son's death was my fault.

"And he was right about one thing—his reach in the motorsports world is broad. I was blacklisted before the day was even done." I let out a mirthless laugh. "It wasn't hard; most teams don't believe motorsports is for women anyway. They'd just kept me as a token female for the views. Before I knew it, I couldn't get a job anywhere."

Antony looked at the door, like he was wondering if he could go pluck Brick back from the parking lot and berate him some more. "I know the type."

I chewed my lip. "I never wanted to bring this to your door, sir."

Antony Barbieri actually grinned. A wide, dimpled smile. "I'm not sure you know this about me, Tally, but motorsports is only my *third* greatest love. First is my family, of course." Something sharkish appeared in his eyes. "Second is putting bigoted old men in their place. So don't worry about me or this team. If I have my way,

Brick Willtot won't be at the top of his so-called 'hierarchy' for long." The smile slipped from his face. "I have a feeling that if this is indeed about you, he isn't just coming for your job."

I shook my head, trying not to cry. "No. He wants custody of Bobbi-June."

Antony's lips twisted. "I see. I assume you've been to see a lawyer?"

I nodded. "Yeah. She said that he has a good chance. I'm a single woman with no prospects, basically. He's rich as hell, and my only real skill is to drive fast vehicles around a track all day."

He stroked his chin, deep in thought. "I'll give you the number for our law firm. They're on retainer, so please, use them as you feel necessary." He handed me a card from his desk drawer. "But I think I might have a solution for a couple of issues. I'll have to talk to a few people, but I don't want you to stress about this, Tally. I, and therefore all of VANT, have your back. Let's have another meeting this afternoon, say about two, and we'll go from there?"

I nodded and walked out into the reception area, my head feeling fuzzy. Hayes had the baby in his arms and a frown on his face. He was rocking Bobbi-June from side to side, and I stepped toward him, hugging her between us.

"Christ, Tally. Don't do that. You barged in there and left me holding the baby, and that guy looked like he wanted to strangle you with his bare hands! I was this close to handing the baby off to Valeria and going to knock his smug fucking head off."

I grimaced up at him, although I was trying to smile. "I can take care of myself. She can't. I wouldn't put it past him to try and snatch her."

Hayes shuddered, kissing my head and both cheeks. Then he kissed Bobbi-June's head too. The baby gurgled, lifting her head off his chest. God, I loved her so much. This was a nightmare.

"We should get to work before Antony decides we're too much drama," I whispered, taking Bobbi-June back from him. He kissed me once more and headed into the garage. I took some calming breaths and smiled down at my little girl. "Let's go race around a track and work out some of our frustration, hey?"

She gurgled again, and I walked into the simulation room. Stephie appeared in front of me immediately. "Are you okay?"

I nodded, swallowing hard. "I'm fine."

"I can hack Brick Willtot's emails and send fake dick pics to all the people in his address book, if you want?"

I tilted my head at her. "And why would I want that?" Stephie was scary smart.

She folded her arms over her chest. "Do you think I'm an idiot?" she asked, in direct contrast to my thoughts. "I Googled you, back when you first started working with me. A little math and maybe a few guesses, I know Bobbi-June is Buck Willtot's. I also know the Willtots had you fired from your old job." She shrugged. "I know lots of things."

I shook my head at Stephie, with her big glasses and her wild hair. "You're kinda scary, you know?"

She grinned. "I know. But the offer stands. I hate men like him. STEM is filled with the same kind of god complexes. We gotta stick together." She waved a hand. "Also, I made Bobbi-June a play corner, so she isn't stuck in the stroller so often. Valeria helped pick things, and Antony paid."

In the corner was indeed a little play area with a play gym over the top, a small bouncer that rocked from side to side with a mobile, and a white noise machine. I gave her a crooked smile. "Thanks, Stephie."

She flushed pink. "It's nothing. If she's going to spend so much time here, she's gotta be comfortable, right?"

I nodded, placing Bobbi-June down on the mat. She was such an inquisitive, independent baby. I'd gotten so lucky. She kicked her legs and waved her arms at the zoo animals hanging from the play gym.

"I don't deserve this team," I said to Stephie softly. She wrapped her arms around me and hugged me quickly. She wasn't normally a hugger, so I guess my face must've still looked like I'd seen a ghost.

"You deserve so much more." She stepped back. "Now, let's get to work."

TWENTY-EIGHT

ROCCO

MY MANAGER WAS RIDING my ass. I hadn't done the promotional shoots I was supposed to be doing. I had blown off my interview with GQ. I hadn't returned my father's calls, which meant he then called my manager and blasted him. The lawyers were all trying to get documentation from me, and I was tired of it.

I just wanted to *drive*. Not even partying was giving me a buzz at the moment. Everything just felt so fucking meaningless. I was on my couch, scrolling the the Gram, avoiding the pictures of Lucia and Mattias Fucking Christian that seemed to bombard me. I'd unfollowed their accounts, but they were deep in the world of Formula One, which meant that they were everywhere.

Throwing my phone across the couch cushions, I growled when it started ringing almost immediately. I contemplated ignoring it, but I hauled myself up and grabbed it. VANT's number flashed across the screen. They'd called me four times already this morning, all of which I'd ignored. However, Antony Barbieri didn't strike me as a patient man.

Of all the teams I've driven for, I liked these guys the best. Probably because they didn't expect as much from me. I wasn't a prize bull for them to lead around by the nose—not yet, at least.

Pressing answer, I switched the call to speaker. "Yeah?"

"Uh, Mr. Passero? It's Valeria from VANT Racing," the receptionist said hesitantly.

"I know." I was being a dick, but what else was new?

"Right." She let out a small, awkward laugh. "Mr. Barbieri is requesting your presence for a meeting this afternoon at two. He wanted me to emphasize the importance and non-optionability of it."

She sounded nervous, and I wasn't sure that was the effect I wanted to have on women. Other drivers, sure, but not on shaky receptionists. I felt a bit like an asshole. My mother would have my head if she knew that I was making women nervous.

I blew out a breath. "I'll be there." I looked at my watch. I had an hour to get across town. Whatever, I still had time to pick what to wear.

An hour and ten minutes later, I strolled into the reception area of VANT Racing. The receptionist still gave me that wide-eyed, star-struck look, and I smiled at her in greeting as I walked past. The door to Antony's office was closed, but the waiting area wasn't empty. Tally was there, her baby in her arms.

I came from a big family, and because I was the youngest son in a wicked web of thirteen children, some of my siblings, and half-siblings, were already having children during my teen years. Babies, I understood. They wanted nothing from me but to hold them, maybe make some weird faces or rock them to sleep. No, babies were easy. Adults were more complex, which was why I had twelve siblings, not all of them full-blooded.

Tally looked up at me and smiled. "Hello, Rocco."

She was beautiful, in an American way. She was small, with a roundish face and bright eyes. There was hunger in those green depths. A hunger that spoke to my very own competitive spirit. However, today, the skin below her eyes almost looked bruised from lack of sleep, and there was a deep furrow between her brows.

I frowned at her.

She raised an eyebrow. "The correct response is 'Hello, Tally.' Or has the alien that possesses your body gone over its word quota for the day? If that's the case, you could always just give a little wave. A nod of acknowledgement. Any of those work for you?"

"You look tired," I said instead, and she rolled her eyes.

"There's no hope for you. You're incapable of being

domesticated." She looked down at the baby, who was awake. "Some fish you just have to throw back for being too spiky, baby girl."

Bobbi-June gurgled, and I was mush at their feet. She was a cute baby, and the woman in front of me holding the baby made odd feelings churn in my chest. Maybe it was part of my ennui. Maybe meaningless sex was catching up with me, like my sisters had all said it would.

I snorted at the thought.

The door opened, and Antony was there, with the VANT legal counsel. I'd met with him a couple of times lately; I had a feeling he found me irritating.

"Great, you're both here. Come in."

Tally looked between me, Antony and the lawyer. "Uh, should I drop the baby off to Hayes?"

Antony waved a hand. "No, it's fine. She can sit in on the meeting. I'd like her opinion," he teased, cooing at the baby. Even stone-cold Antony Barbieri made cutesy noises in her presence.

Tally nodded, shifting the baby in her arms. I held out my hands. "Want me to carry her?"

Her gaze flicked over me. "If you could, just for a minute. My arms have gone numb." She handed me the baby, and I smiled down at her pretty blue eyes.

"*Bambolina*," I greeted Bobbi-June, shifting her into the crook of my arm easily. She weighed nothing to me. I gestured for Tally to walk in, and clocked Antony and the lawyer exchanging looks.

Rocking Bobbi-June softly, I sat carefully down on one of the soft couches in Antony's office. Laying her across my lap, I put a hand on her belly as I gently bounced her up and down. "Does anyone want to tell me what this is about?" I asked lightly, looking over at Tally, who just shrugged from where she sat opposite Antony's desk.

Our boss came around and leaned his ass against the desk. "I believe that you can perhaps help each other." He looked at Tally first. "Rocco here is struggling to get a green card because of some kind of 'moral turpitude' clause."

I clenched my jaw, but remained silent as her eyes ran over me before dropping to the baby, like I'd gone from someone safe to a possible threat to her child. "Moral turpitude?"

I huffed. "I beat the shit out of another driver after a race in Saudi Arabia, and people blew it out of proportion. *He* blew it out of proportion. Trust me when I say he deserved it."

She stared at me for another long heartbeat, then finally turned back to Antony. It felt like an acceptance that I wasn't a danger to her baby, or maybe that was wishful thinking.

"Okay? What does that have to do... Oh." Her head snapped back toward me, but I was still confused as fuck.

"Don't you hate it when people talk around you like you're a fuc—ducking simpleton?" I asked the baby, who gurgled her agreement.

"Tally here needs a husband with a lot of money and some sway in the racing industry. Her ex-father-in-law is trying to gain custody of Bobbi-June by using her lack of both financial security and the social frameworks needed to create a beneficial and secure environment for the child."

I frowned as it dawned on me too. I looked at Tally. "The asshole from the hospital?" She nodded, her lip wobbling. *Fuck.* I hoped she didn't cry. I wasn't sure I could deal with her tears. "I see."

She was already shaking her head. "Impossible. I couldn't do that to Hayes and Jesse. There has to be a different way that *doesn't* involve me marrying a man who doesn't even want to be married."

I was trying not to be offended by her quick refusal. "Who says I don't want to be married?"

She tilted her head at me. "The two women who got photographed blowing you in the back room of a club, like, three weeks ago?"

That had actually been well over two months ago, but it had been floating around in the tabloids for a couple of weeks now.

I shrugged. "That just means I like blow jobs."

She narrowed her eyes. "That didn't help your case like you think it did."

"I'll have you know, I'd love to be married." *Okay, not really true.* "And I'm totally open to this idea."

The baby on my lap was now starting to fall asleep. It was weird to have an entire conversation about an arranged marriage while rocking a baby on my knees, but somehow, that fit this moment.

Tally gaped at me. "You can't seriously be on board with this?"

I shrugged. "Why not? It's not forever, I'm sure. It'll get Immigration off my back, if I have both a sponsor and a wife. You'll get a husband who's wildly richer than that old fuck. And I know you aren't after my money, just my influence. Everyone's hearts will be safe and secure. Sounds like a neat solution to me."

Shaking her head, she looked between us all, like we were suggesting she hijack a plane. "And Jesse and Hayes?"

She has a point there. "See them on the side for a couple of years?"

"No."

"Fine, move them in too. Polyamory seems to be the flavor of the month in this country," I teased Antony. "It's not like we're marrying because of a grand love affair. You can all move into my place, and you can bang them on the downlow. You'll be my wife, but that doesn't stop you from being their girlfriend."

Standing, she started to pace around. "This can't be legal?" She looked at the lawyer. "It's insane, right?"

The lawyer cleared his throat. "Strictly, legally speaking, it would be a neat solution to both your problems. Not the only solution, but the most concise and possibly pain-free option. We might have to pay off a few bureaucrats to tick some extraneous boxes, but you wouldn't be the first sportsperson to secure their green card in this manner."

She shot a look at Antony, and he held out his hands in front of him, like a magician showing everyone there were no tricks up his sleeve. "It's your choice, Tally. I am just presenting you with a possible fix that is mutually beneficial. If you choose to go a different route, we'll support you in that as well."

Tally stared down at the sleeping baby, with her little rosebud lips parted. "I'll talk to the guys and let you know." She walked over to me. "There'd have to be rules," she said softly.

"Of course, *Stellina.*"

She lifted Bobbi-June from my lap, walking over to put her into the carrier. We all watched in silence as she strapped the baby in and lifted it over her arm.

I didn't think she would go for the offer; she seemed like the strong, independent type who hated relying on anyone else for anything. I found that so fucking attractive, which was an actual pain in the ass.

She turned at the door. "No matter the outcome, thank you for trying to find a fix for me. I appreciate it." Then she turned, shutting the door softly.

The room was silent for what felt like a long time. Antony walked to the other side of his desk and sat down with a huff. "It goes without saying that if you do anything to hurt Tally or that baby, I will ruin you. I don't care how rich you are."

Well, he could try, but he'd be unsuccessful. However, on this, I agreed. "I would expect nothing less." I looked at the lawyer. "Do you do prenuptial contracts? Because mark my words, I'm getting married."

Antony shook his head. "You're a cocky asshole, Passero, but you're an honorable man. If I thought otherwise, I never would have suggested it."

Honorable I might be, but my future wife was enough to tempt a saint.

TWENTY-NINE
HAYES

"ABSOLUTELY NO FUCKING WAY."

On this, Jesse and I one hundred percent agreed. "Seconded," I added. When Tally had sat us down and told us Antony's idea, the visceral need to shout, "*No!*" was only tempered by the sleeping baby in the bassinet, being watched over by Norton.

Tally had her arms crossed over her chest, and honestly, she didn't seem thrilled with the idea either. I kind of felt like an ass, because that made me happy.

"It would be just in name only. It would make my legal issues completely cut and dry. No one could possibly argue that Brick could give her a better life when Rocco's net worth is nine digits and climbing."

I snorted. "If you think Rocco wants a wife in name only, you've never seen the way he looks at you."

She rolled her eyes. "I love you two. I told them that I couldn't even consider it, if it meant breaking up with you guys. Rocco was totally okay with us having a relationship. Does that sound like a guy who only wants to marry me to get in my pants?" She snorted, as if it was craziness. "The guy was literally photographed with his tongue down the throat of a Victoria's Secret model four months ago. His last girlfriend was an actress known for her great ass—acting ability," she corrected. "I still haven't gotten my pre-baby body back, and everything is wrinkly. My boobs leak. I'm permanently tired, and have bags under my eyes so big, Delta would make me check them at the gate."

Jesse froze his pacing, walking over to her to kneel beside the couch. "You're the most beautiful fucking woman on the planet, Tally Palmer. I don't want to hear you talk about yourself like you're anything other than gorgeous."

Leaning forward, she put her hands on his shoulders and kissed him sweetly. Jealousy swept through me, though only because I wanted a kiss too, not because I hated the thought of her kissing Jesse.

That being said, Jesse was a whole different ball game to Rocco Passero, the fuckboy of Europe.

"I'm not ashamed of my body. I'm just saying, I'm not getting Rack Of The Year in *Playboy*. Honestly, if he wanted to, like, see other women too, I wouldn't even care." Her words said one thing, but her frown said something entirely different. "There's no waiting period in California for a marriage license. We could go down to the courthouse, get someone to officiate it, and be done in twenty minutes."

I shook my head. "It's not a twenty-minute thing,

though, Tally. You'll be husband and wife, and to convince the courts of that, you'll have to move into his house—"

"Mansion," Jesse corrected unhelpfully, and I glared at him.

"Right. And not just until the end of the court case. But for at least… I don't know how many years you have to be married to keep your green card. That's a long-term commitment, not just from you, but from all of us. We're a team."

She inhaled a shaky breath, and I knew then and there, that I'd have to adapt or I'd lose her. Her next words confirmed it.

"I love you guys, but if I have to choose between a surefire way of keeping my baby and you both, I'm choosing her. Always her." She leaned toward me, grabbing my hands. "I understand it's a lot to ask in a relationship that's so new. I wouldn't blame you at all if this was one thing too many." Her voice cracked, but she kept her jaw firm.

Jesse looked back and forth between us. "I told you, I'm all in with you and Short Stack. And I would never make you choose. This is just… a lot, like you said."

It was *beyond* a lot. I could see everything we'd been working toward slipping away from me.

Letting my head fall back on the couch, I tried to do the coping technique my dad had taught me for whenever I couldn't make a decision. I imagined the best-case scenario. That was us moving in with Rocco, and he turned out to be a eunuch with no interest in my girl, and we lived in a blissful kind of solidarity.

Then I imagined the worst-case scenario, though there were several that got progressively worse. She left us, and I'd fucked my chance at happiness. Worse again, she stayed and lost custody of Bobbi-June.

Then I imagined the likely outcome if Rocco and Tally got married. We all moved into his mega-mansion and lived in cordial harmony. Eventually, Rocco made a move on my girl, and she fell into bed with him. I mean, they'd be married, and I was secure enough to admit that Rocco Passero was a devilishly handsome guy. We added him to the relationship we had here for a few years, and either he stayed or we parted ways at the end.

Which outcome is worse—the likely outcome or the worst-case scenario? Because it will always end up in the worst-case scenario, if you dither too long. He who hesitates is lost.

I blew out a breath. "I'm with you, whatever you decide. We'll work through this, just like everything else," I told her, and the relief on her face made me feel like shit. I cuddled closer to her, wrapping her sweet body in my arms. "You're mine, Tally. And if I have to share you, it doesn't make you any less mine." I kissed her softly, letting her melt against me with a soft sigh.

Jesse sat on her other side, his gaze meeting mine over her head. *Ours,* his eyes said.

I nodded. *Let's show her that.*

THIRTY

TALLY

WE SAT at a diner in Avalon, waiting for Rocco to arrive. I'd decided that it was probably best if we all talked, without our boss or his lawyers being present. There were wrinkles that needed to be ironed out, ground rules that needed to be laid down to keep everyone comfortable.

I rubbed my temples. Jesus Christ, if you'd told me eight months ago that I'd be negotiating a marriage contract with Rocco Passero, along with my two other boyfriends, I would have laughed in your face.

Jesse held Bobbi-June in the crook of his arm, and it was insane to see how much she'd grown already. Every morning, I woke up and looked at her, thinking she'd gotten somehow bigger while I was sleeping. However, she still fit perfectly in his long arms, head pillowed against his bicep.

"I'm going to stress-eat my weight in pancakes," I grumbled at the guys.

The bell over the door jingled, and I looked up to see an incognito Rocco appear. Honestly, he probably didn't need to worry too much. He was a huge name in Europe, but most people here didn't follow Formula One. Or if they did, they weren't expecting to see one of the best drivers of the twenty-first century here in some dingy little diner. But the Clark Kent effect definitely worked, because no one even raised an eyebrow.

Okay, that was a lie. One grandma definitely checked out his ass.

He shook hands with Hayes and Jesse in that manly way guys do, like it was some kind of display of strength. However, I was surprised when he leaned in and kissed both of my cheeks. I flushed, hoping the guys would just write it off as embarrassment.

"It is good to see you," he said to none of us in particular. "Best thing about being out this season is the food. Is it too early for a burger and fries?"

The guys just continued to glare, so I shook my head. "It's never too early for a burger. Thanks for coming, by the way."

He shrugged. "Well, theoretically, you might be my wife soon. It's probably best that we get started on the one big happy family thing, right?"

Jesse shook his head. "Why would you even *agree* to this? There must be a hundred women who'd happily marry you. And that's just in a five-mile radius of this diner. What do you actually get out of this arrangement?"

Rocco was prevented from answering by the waitress. She was in her fifties and looked done with her shift already. "Ready to order?"

I nodded. "I'll have the egg white omelet and a Diet Sprite."

Hayes looked at me. "What happened to the pancakes?"

I poked my stomach, which still hadn't snapped back, though it wasn't as bad as I'd imagined it would be. "I have to get back to race weight."

He frowned, but nodded. Being a driver was a subtle balance between being strong enough to withstand the tough racing conditions, and being light enough that your added weight didn't slow down the car. It wasn't such a big problem in stock car racing, but in open-wheel racing, where everything was measured down to the gram? A stack of pancakes could be the difference between winning or losing.

Sure, I wasn't racing anytime soon, but I wanted to get the best out of the car, so they knew what it was truly capable of.

Hayes ordered a trucker's breakfast, and Jesse ordered the pancakes. "We can share," he said, winking at me. I mean, I wasn't going to turn down pancakes, and if I didn't order them myself, they were basically calorie free. Those were the rules.

Rocco looked up with a smile that seemed to stun the waitress, her eyes widening and her jaw going a little slack. "I will have the burger, rare please, with extra home fries."

The waitress—Patty, according to her name badge—

blinked several times and mumbled about it coming right up before scurrying away.

This was such a bad idea. The guy was a hopeless flirt. I was going to be a laughingstock. But at least I'd be a giant joke who still had custody of her own child.

Rocco turned back toward Jesse. "To answer your question, you are correct. I could propose to almost any woman, and if my reputation didn't sway them, my bank balance would. Which is precisely why I think marrying Tally would be for the best. We are using each other, and there's a nobility in that. Besides, I know she isn't in it for my money. She's made it very clear she doesn't care about my reputation." He raised a brow at me, though it wasn't strictly true. I'd fangirled just as much as anyone else when I'd first learned Rocco Passero was coming to drive for the team.

"Plus, we have a lot in common. So if I have to tie myself to someone for three years, it is probably best that we have shared interests, otherwise it would make for some terrible dinner conversation." He laughed at his own joke, before turning serious again. "And a little bit of it is old-fashioned chivalry. Tally is in a situation that I could make go away, and it makes me feel good to do it."

Hayes stared at him. "They're the only reasons? Shared interests, convenience and chivalry? It's not because you feel any desire toward Tally?" He dropped his voice. "Tally won't be coerced into something to show gratitude. I think you both should agree to keeping the relationship platonic."

I raised my eyebrows. That was some serious audacity. Part of me understood that he wanted some reassurance that I wasn't about to turf him out for a hot rich guy. However, the feminist part of me wanted to dickpunch him for believing he could just make sweeping statements like that.

Rocco chuckled. "I promise not to make any moves on your girl, unless she expressly, vigorously asks me for it."

They were all looking at me now, and I could feel the pink heat on my cheeks, so I was probably as red as a beet. *Well, this is awkward.*

I cleared my throat. "I, uh, I'm happy for you to see other people to meet your needs on the side, if you have to. Just keep it discreet, I guess?"

He gave me a long stare. "I was raised Roman Catholic. The sanctity of marriage and all that. Well, up until we get a divorce. I just won't tell my family about that one."

I gave him the side-eye. "So what, you're going to be a monk for three years?"

He screwed up his nose. "No. I'll possibly get escorts. Prostitutes don't count—at least, not in my family."

Ugh. I hated the thought. Although, considering I was going to be fucking two other guys right there under his roof, I didn't really have a high horse to climb on. Instead, I nodded, like I didn't give a crap. "Okay. Sounds good."

Just then, the waitress returned with our food. She

eyeballed Jesse with the baby against his chest, and the way Hayes had his arm over my shoulders. It was clear she couldn't quite figure it out, but it was none of her business.

"So, what next?" I asked the table, but no one really answered. Clearly, we were all just winging this and hoping for the best.

Although I'd been exaggerating when I told the guys that it would take twenty minutes to get married, it turned out I wasn't far off. The day after the diner, I signed a bunch of paperwork from Rocco's lawyers in a small conference room at the courthouse. Luckily, Antony had sent VANT's lawyers to ensure I wasn't about to sign over a vital organ or my first-born.

It was basically what you'd expect from a prenuptial agreement, except there was a clause that gave me a ten-million-dollar settlement, should we divorce, as well as another five million in a trust for Bobbi-June, which would go into effect as soon as we married.

I stared at the clause, then over at the enigmatic driver, who seemed to be lost in his own thoughts on the other side of the table. "Rocco?" I murmured quietly, and his dark eyes snapped to mine.

"Yes, *Stellina?*"

"That's a lot of money."

He rolled his eyes. "Merely a token, should we go our separate ways. It would look bad if I left you with nothing."

That seemed like a rather drastic guilt gift. I looked at my borrowed lawyer, who was giving me the professional version of the *are you stupid, take the money* look. "It's a generous offer, Miss Palmer."

So I grabbed the pen Rocco's lawyer held out, and signed on the dotted line. Then the lawyer handed me a marriage license, and I filled out the relevant parts.

Everything that was written about Rocco on that form was published on the internet, from his middle name to his birthday. Hell, I'd even seen pictures of his parents in the tabloids, as well as his brothers, who were also in the Formula One world, though not as drivers. They were good looking too, but he was definitely the most handsome of the four.

Rocco quickly signed his sections and handed them over to my lawyer. One of his lawyers lodged the application online, and then we were basically married, except for the officiant ceremony. I looked at my watch. Our appointment to stand before a judge was in ten minutes, and that would be it. I would be Tally Palmer-Passero.

The guys were waiting on hard plastic chairs outside the room, with Bobbi-June asleep in her carrier. They looked solemn, like I was walking to my execution, not to get married.

I gave them what I hoped was a reassuring smile. "Relax, guys."

Jesse gave me a sympathetic expression, while Hayes lifted his chin toward the other side of the corridor, where Willy and Colin stood.

Whoops.

I'd known they were going to be pissed. I'd intended to tell them, really. I hadn't been keeping it a secret on purpose; it was just everything had been moving so fast.

"Well, this isn't what it looks like," I said lightly, but it didn't make anyone laugh. *Eesh, big trouble.*

Rocco cleared his throat, and I hurried to fill the silence. "Rocco, this is my best friend Will, and his partner Colin. Uh, guys, this is my fiancé—and I guess in like, eight minutes, my husband—Rocco Passero."

Willy just raised a single eyebrow, like he always did when he thought I was doing something stupid, but not dangerous. Like, when I was twelve, holding a kitten I'd bought for ten bucks from Johnny Lipitski, and trying to get him to help me convince my parents I'd found it on the side of the road. He'd known it was a dumb idea that'd end in heartache when my parents made me get rid of it, but he'd backed me up anyway, even if he thought I was being an idiot.

Colin, bless him, stepped forward and shook Rocco's hand. "Nice to meet you, Rocco." His eyes bounced between the handsome Italian and the guys still sitting across from us, unanswered questions filling the hall.

"Palmer-Passero?" someone called from the end of the corridor, and I swallowed down the lump of trepidation that was threatening to choke me. This was the right decision. It was the best way to ensure I could keep my baby, and give her safety and security for a long time.

So I gave Willy one last imploring look and turned toward the attendant who was calling our party. We all walked single file into a small room with folding chairs and a judge in a black robe.

Willy grabbed my hand, turning me softly. "You're sure?" I nodded quietly. Letting out a heavy sigh, he kissed my forehead. "You look beautiful."

I'd found a white dress in a boutique on the way there, a simple sheath with white lace sleeves. Jesse and Hayes had helped me pick it out, a small contribution to a big decision. Jesse had paid for it, merely kissing me softly and telling me that if I was going to be a bride, I was going to do it properly.

"Thanks, Willy." He kissed the top of my head and went to sit beside Colin, who had somehow taken possession of Bobbi-June and was blowing raspberries on her cheeks and whispering to her. The lawyers also sat down in the room, and I gave a tremulous smile to my guys.

"Hello, folks. My name is Judge Jovianni. Let's get you two hitched, shall we?"

Forty-seven minutes after entering the courthouse, I emerged onto the steps as Mrs. Rocco Passero.

Sixteen-year-old me would have been losing her shit right about now.

THIRTY-ONE

JESSE

IT FELT like I was living in a telenovela. Or one of those holiday romances where the scrappy single mom married the billionaire. Except I wasn't sure where that left me.

Tally and Rocco hard launched their relationship with a courthouse steps photo shoot, complete with a ring that included a diamond almost the size of Bobbi-June's fist. They'd sat on the steps, and someone from Rocco's PR team had taken photos as he held her close and kissed her cheek.

It was… not awful. It was disconcerting, though. I wanted to marry her, and I guess Hayes might have wanted that too. I'd experienced my first true wave of jealousy when she stood up there opposite a man I hardly knew and said, "I do."

Now I was packing up my house and moving into a mansion across town. They'd rushed into this, and all I could see were problems and pitfalls. What if someone saw us kissing Tally? What if someone realized we lived with them too? What if the media got hold of the real story and made it somehow worse?

No, we just had to make it through the custody case, and then it didn't matter what happened at the end of the day.

Someone knocked on my door, and I instinctively knew who it was. It was like my body was as tuned to her as a flower to the sun. "Come in."

Tally moved into the room hesitantly. "I came to see if you needed any help packing?"

I was just taking essentials. I'd lock this place up tight, but I'd keep it, in case we ever needed a little escape. The house next door was already on the market. We'd done that the day after Tally had been served with legal papers.

I shook my head. "I have it all sorted, but I wouldn't say no to cuddling my girlfriend while *pretending* to pack." I gave her a lopsided smile, and she launched herself across the room and into my arms.

I fell back onto the bed with an *oof*, wrapping my arms around her back. She nuzzled her face into my neck, and I rolled us both onto our sides, so I could tangle our legs together.

"Are you doing okay, sweetheart?"

"I should be asking you that," she muttered against my chest. "I think Hayes is angry at me."

I kissed the top of her head. "No, he's not. We're all just figuring this shit out. Besides, we both know he'll take one look at the cars in Rocco's garage and be too aroused to be mad."

She laughed softly and squeezed me tighter. I wanted to hold her like this forever.

"I feel like a fool, though," I murmured into her hair.

She pulled back a little to see my face. "Why?"

"I should have offered to marry you first. You could have been my wife."

Her eyes softened. "I wouldn't have said yes. We were too new. Too involved. It couldn't have been just a business arrangement between us." She kissed my shoulder. "When I say 'I do' to you, I want it to be forever."

God, I didn't know you could love like this. I held her for a little longer, soaking in the warmth of her soft body. I wanted to freeze this moment, live in it forever. "I love you so much, Tal."

She raised her face, and I took a minute to soak in her features: those green eyes that ensnared me like a trap, the little upturn of her nose, the light freckles across her cheeks. She was so fucking beautiful that she stole my breath every damn day.

I kissed her softly, but she deepened it. "Maybe a little break would help rejuvenate your packing ability?" she murmured, her hands starting to wander down under my t-shirt to the waistband of my jeans.

Unfortunately, at that moment, the baby let out a cry, which made the dog bark as he scrambled around the house, searching for someone to help his tiny charge. I groaned, but kissed her lips softly once more, then pulled away.

"Norton really is the best dog," Tally laughed as she uncurled from my body. "Who needs a baby monitor?" She stood, looking down at me. "I love you too, you know that right? This"—she gestured at her obnoxiously large ring—"doesn't mean I love you any less."

I rolled myself into a sitting position, so I could pull her between my thighs and hug her close. "I know, sweetheart." I slapped that delicious ass. "Now, we better get moving. Hayes wants us there by dinner time, in case the media get hold of the story."

Why they'd even care was beyond me, but apparently, Rocco was a big enough deal in Europe that him being off the marriage market made headline news.

I'd thought Hayes was being paranoid, but when we rolled through the brand-new gated community that I'd only ever read about, I was surprised to see a photographer standing by his car, snapping pictures of people going past. A security guy was yelling at him, but the photographer seemed unperturbed by his aggression.

"Is he some kind of European prince, and we don't know it?" I asked Hayes, who was sitting in the driver's seat. Tally and the baby were in the back of the SUV, and I gave the photographer the stink eye on the way past.

Another security guard stopped our car. "Name?"

"Hayes Davis, Jesse Banks and Tally Pal—Passero,"

Hayes answered, and the guy looked down at his tablet and nodded.

"New residents. Welcome to the neighborhood." He waved us in, and Hayes pulled past the gates. There were only two streets in this community, bracketed by the ocean on one side and a large fence on the other. Less "exclusive" than the other gated communities in the city—which were reserved for politicians and generational wealth—this area still reeked of money and privilege.

Rocco's mansion was spread across sprawling grounds, and it was hard to believe this was so close to the city. The whole community had once been the grounds of an eighteen-hole golf course, but clearly, there was more money in real estate than golf.

The manicured yards and tall fences between properties definitely said the area was coveted more for the gated aspect than the community side of things. I could understand that; when your life was on display, privacy was paramount.

Rocco had given Tally a key fob, and the gate automatically opened as we rolled up. "Fancy," Hayes breathed.

Norton whined from the back seat, totally fed up with being jammed tight with the bags. "It's all good, buddy. We're almost there. Look at all this lawn you can shit on."

Tally laughed. "Basically doggy heaven."

It was human heaven too. There was no way Tally

would ever want to go back to my crappy split-level after this.

We pulled up at the front steps, Hayes parking the car. The door immediately swung open, and Rocco was there, a small smile on his face. He moved down the stairs, his eyes tracking us as we unloaded ourselves from the car

Reaching out, he shook my hand. "Welcome home." I couldn't get a read on this guy. Still, when Hayes let Norton out of the back seat, I caught a smile on his face. "Who's this?"

It was Tally that answered. "This is Norton. He's Jesse's dog, but I think he might have changed allegiance to Bobbi-June." She gave an awkward chuckle, the kind you give when you're the first person at a party, or you're meeting strangers you've never met.

Norton wandered over to Rocco cautiously, sussing out if he was a safe human for his people. Rocco sat down on the steps, placing a hand out, which Norton sniffed tentatively. Happy that Rocco didn't smell like the human equivalent of a rabid hound, he gave it a quick lick and bounded away to sniff out the perimeter.

"It's okay he's here, right?" There was a challenge in Hayes's voice, despite the pep talk I'd given him earlier about not fucking this up.

Rocco shrugged. "I like dogs better than humans. Plus, the estate is fenced. He can run where he likes." He stepped toward Tally, kissing both of her cheeks. "Welcome, *Stellina*."

I'd Googled what *Stellina* meant, and it meant little

star. I wasn't quite sure how I felt about him calling her that before they were even... whatever the hell they were now.

He grabbed one of the suitcases from Hayes, while I grabbed another two from the car. There was a removalist coming to the house tomorrow to collect the rest of the stuff we'd need to make this place our home —for a few years, at least.

The foyer had polished concrete floors, with staircases going up either side. Parking the suitcases at the base of the stairs, Rocco tipped his chin for us to follow him. "I'll give you the tour." He walked straight through, under the balcony landing and down into an open-plan kitchen and living room that was as big as my whole house.

"This is the main living area. The kitchen has the basics, but the main kitchen is in the butler's pantry over here." He opened what I'd thought was a cabinet door, but was really a hidden path to a second, full-sized kitchen. Hell, it might actually be industrial-sized. "Everything you could need is in here. Help yourself to anything. I get food sent in, but if you like to cook, don't be shy to use any of the appliances you find. Don't ask me how they work, though, because I have no idea about most of them."

He led us back out, then through giant glass doors that led onto a patio. A step below that was an infinity pool that looked out over the wide expanse of lawn. It had clear glass fencing, which would be good once Junie started walking. I was beginning to call her Junie because Bobbi-June was a mouthful, and her mama hadn't protested it yet.

We were silent, because what did you say to butler's pantries and infinity pools?

"There are six bedrooms upstairs; use whichever you like." He cleared his throat. "I had a room redecorated as a nursery for the *bambina,* but if you want to change rooms, or decorate differently, feel free."

"Six rooms? Why the hell did you buy a house with so many rooms?" Tally asked, as she climbed the stairs. I grabbed Bobbi-June's baby carrier and held it securely. With stairs this steep, we'd need baby gates too.

He shrugged. "I just rented it for the length of my contract. I liked the privacy. If you hate it, we can move somewhere else. Buy somewhere more permanent, if that would look better for your court case."

This place was worth at least fourteen million, and he'd casually mentioned going somewhere else, like it was nothing. I suddenly understood why this situation suited him. With this kind of money, would you ever be sure someone wanted you for *you*?

At least with Tally, he knew what he was getting into, and what she needed from him. Sure, it might be the same things that everyone wanted—a fat bank balance and some serious influence—but she was honest about it, not playing games with his head. I also knew for a fact that outside of keeping Bobbi-June, Tally didn't care if she lived in a mansion or a studio. Material things meant nothing to her. It's part of why I loved her so much.

Opening a door halfway down the hallway, Rocco pushed it wide and stepped aside. The nursery was a soft, buttery yellow, so different to the almost severe interior design of the rest of the house. There was a mural of cartoon ducks driving race cars around the walls, and a full-size crib on one side of the room. A pillowy patterned rug covered most of the white carpet. There was also a change table, closet and a wide, comfortable-looking chair in the corner.

Rocco looked almost nervous. As I walked further inside, I slapped a hand on his back. "Thanks, man. This is awesome."

The relief on his face made me feel like a dick for thinking terrible things about him when Tally first pitched the idea of marriage. He wasn't the asshole I normally saw on the television right now. There was no posturing about who had the bigger dick, or who was going to be the top dog in the house.

Maybe we really could help each other. Maybe he really didn't care that we were here too.

THIRTY-TWO

ROCCO

I HADN'T LIVED in a house this noisy since I was twelve. The removalists were carrying in boxes, dragging them upstairs to the rooms everyone had chosen. Tally was directing them around like a general, and the guys were unpacking as they went, to ease the stress on Tally.

Bobbi-June, Norton the dog and I had been banished to the lower floors.

I took the baby outside to the patio and sat in the shade, holding her against my chest as the dog sniffed around. He never strayed far from the baby for long, constantly coming back to make sure she was still here, still happy. *Man, what a good dog.*

The baby was as happy and content as anyone could ask for in a newborn. She was busy looking around at the bright colors and sounds of the backyard. "What do you think, *Bambolina?* Do you think you'll enjoy living here?"

The dog took off across the lawn to defend the baby from a squirrel. As I watched him, my phone vibrated in my pocket. Pulling it out with a sigh, I leaned back so the baby was resting safely on my chest, then answered the call. Rafa's face appeared on the screen. He only believed in video calls, because he was a distrusting asshole.

"Do you have your dick away?" he demanded before he'd even said hello.

You answer the phone during sex one time, and some people never let it go. "Yes, Rafa." I flipped the phone around, and Bobbi-June was lifting her head, looking at the camera. I snapped a quick screenshot of Rafa's face, because it was truly hilarious the way he was gaping like a fish.

"Rocco, whose baby is that?"

It was impossible not to fuck with him a little. "My baby. This is Bobbi-June. Say hello to your Zio Rafa, *Bambolina.*"

"Rocco…"

Once upon a time, that warning in my older brother's voice had meant he was going to punch the shit out of me when he got hold of me, usually because I was being a little asshole. Homesickness swamped me once again, the same feeling that had plagued me since I'd packed my bags and joined a racing academy at fourteen.

"Is that why socials are saying you had a quick courthouse wedding? Because you got some girl *pregnant?* Mamma is going to beat you if she finds out you had a baby out of wedlock. She's already praying for your soul." He muttered something not very complimentary under his breath.

He wasn't wrong. Mamma would come after me with a wooden spoon, if she thought I was impregnating girls and not marrying them. Though it wasn't like I could marry more than one. And if Papa had taught me anything, it was that you could be a happily married man and still impregnate women without marrying them.

That was how I'd ended up with at least seven half-siblings.

I shrugged. "Yes." Technically not lying. The baby was at least fifty percent of the reason why we had to get married. "And for a green card. Someone was holding up residency, and if I'm going to give this IndyCar thing a chance, I need to be able to work without being tied to VANT permanently." At least, that's what my lawyers had argued when we were writing up contracts. VANT had lured me here, but the nature of the racing industry was that drivers moved around. I needed to be able to legally work in the US for that. Not that I was going to leave VANT anytime soon, that was for sure.

Rafa pinched the bridge of his nose. "You knocked up a girl for a green card?"

The baby gurgled at the idea, and it sounded so much like a chuckle that it made me laugh. "Relax, Rafa. Bobbi-June isn't biologically mine. Though, legally, I am her step-father, so I guess that makes you her uncle, if you want."

I heard Rafa's wife, Theresa, ask something, and Rafa covered the phone to reply. I could imagine what she was saying, though. It was either, "Who's the woman in the photographs?" or "Did that manwhore really get married?"

Rafa made a little spinny motion, and I knew he wanted me to flip the phone camera so it was on the baby again. Heaving a heavy sigh, I turned the phone's camera back around, to show Bobbi-June asleep on my chest. She looked like the little doll I called her.

Thank goodness Rafa had the mic covered, otherwise Theresa's, *"Che cazzo é questo?!"* would have woken the baby right back up again. At least she'd said, "The fuck is this?" in Italian, so the baby's first word wasn't going to be a curse.

I snapped another screenshot. Man, I was going to put these as my wallpaper. However, I wouldn't get to surprise anyone else, because I had no doubt that by the end of this call, Theresa would have texted everyone in the family. And probably the extended family. Possibly even the neighbors.

I grinned, and Rafa rolled his eyes. "I think you better start from the beginning."

I weighed how much to tell them. I hated lying to Rafa, but he told Theresa everything, and in turn, Theresa told everyone else everything. I didn't want it to get out that this thing was anything but a love match.

At least, not until after Tally had the custody locked down.

"I met Tally at work. She's a former NASCAR driver. VANT Racing hired her to train the simulator. She's hot. I found myself thinking about her every day, seeking her out. When Antony told me I was struggling to get my green card, I propositioned her."

Rafa frowned. "What is she getting out of it?"

I gave him a cocky smirk. "What do you think, brother?"

Let him think what he would about that statement. "Rocco, tell me you—"

"I got a prenup, Rafa. I'm not an idiot." I didn't tell him I was giving her fifteen million dollars, regardless of how this went down. I didn't want her to struggle if things went sideways.

Rafa shook his head repeatedly. "Three months in that country, and you've already got a wife and a baby."

I didn't tell him about my wife's two boyfriends. That might get him on a flight over here to check me into the crazy house. I also didn't tell him of the contentment I felt with them here; like I'd been starving and alone for so long, and now here they were, a feast for my senses. Alive and full of comfort, when I'd been living with my loneliness until it was a familiar ache in my soul. Not that I'd tell Rafa any of that, because he'd be racked with older sibling guilt.

"Anyway, tell me about VANT. There's talk about them petitioning to be included in Formula E within five years."

We moved onto more comfortable topics, and it was like no time at all had passed since I saw him last. The whole time, the baby slept on my chest, and the dog eventually came to curl in a ball beside the lounger.

Inside my chest, the wall I built to keep myself safe from people who just wanted to use me, crumbled to dust.

The rumble of the removal truck leaving told me that the three other members of my newfound family would probably seek me out soon. "I should go, Rafa. Give my love to my nieces. Tell Mamma I love her when you inevitably call her straight after this."

Rafa shook his head. "I'm flying out at the beginning of the IndyCar race season to see your debut. I expect to meet your new wife then."

I winced; my brother was intense at the best of times. I gave him a small salute. "Okay. Bring the kids. I'll pay." I did it to needle him, because we both knew he wouldn't take my money, and he always acted so insulted when I suggested it.

He raised an eyebrow. "Perhaps you should bring your bride to visit the family instead."

I imagined showing Tally my country. Imagined her in the warm Italian sun, a smile on her face and her hair glowing like a halo of gold. "Maybe I will."

The snort at the other end of the line was definitely skeptical. "I'm sure. Love you, brother."

"Love you too, Rafa."

Hanging up the phone, I stroked my hand over the

baby's downy head. "Hope you stay an only child, *Bambolina*. No one drives you crazy like family."

Holding her close, I slowly—so fucking slowly—climbed to my feet. Walking on soft feet, I carried her through the house and up the stairs. I could hear laughter coming from one of the bedrooms, and a pang of longing hit me square in the gut. They were so happy.

When was the last time I was that happy?

It wasn't when I was balls-deep in some influencer from the Gram. It wasn't when I won my last race, though that had felt satisfying. But it didn't make me happy.

Laying the baby down in the bassinet beside Tally's bed, I picked up the baby monitor and tucked it in my pocket. Then I walked away from the sounds of that happiness, before I was tempted to stand outside the door and feed on it, like the emotional black hole I was.

THIRTY-THREE

TALLY

ROCCO'S HOME contained none of his personality, except for maybe the garage. All the guys were down there at the moment, drooling over Rocco's Ferraris the way some men would drool over porn.

I might have misinterpreted the look, but I think Rocco was almost as excited to show off his car collection as the guys were to see it. And why wouldn't he be? It was impressive as hell. If Rocco and I could talk about racing to make the next few years at least bearable, then he and the guys could talk about cars and bikes. I'd learned that Rocco really enjoyed superbikes as much as he enjoyed motor racing, so that definitely got him points in Jesse's book.

Slumping back on the couch, I watched Bobbi-June as she had tummy time. This whole thing had gone almost too easily. It was like having a really cool housemate in a really big-ass house, with nearly none of the weirdness I'd been worried about.

Flicking on the television, I watched the news. Doom and gloom, like most days, until it got to the celebrity gossip portion of the show.

"And European heartthrob Rocco Passero has surprised the sports world by getting married in a shotgun wedding this week. The woman who has stolen his heart? None other than former NASCAR driver, Tally Palmer. A source close to the couple said that they were very much in love, after meeting at recently founded VANT Racing. Many will remember Rocco Passero from the altercation he had with teammate Mattias Christian in Bahrain during last season's Formula One opener."

I blinked as the screen dissolved into two men in fire suits throwing punches in the pitlane garage of Rocco's former team. You couldn't hear much of what they were saying, except for Mattias Christian yelling, "She's my fucking *wife!*" from the ground as Rocco threw punches over and over at his face and his team tried to drag him off.

It cut back to the television presenter, who had her eyebrows raised. *"We wish the new Mrs. Passero the best of luck."*

They switched to a story about an NHL player who'd recently blown out his knee and been dropped from his team, and I blinked at the screen. I'd known Rocco was being blocked from his green card because of a fight, but I hadn't realized it was with his own teammate. Opening up ClockTok, I searched their names together. News articles would be filtered through the team's PR people, and then again through the media. But social media had no filter.

The first video that popped up was a photo montage to the tune of "Jessie's Girl" by Rick Springfield, and I turned the volume right down. It showed a woman with both Rocco and Mattias Christian. A photo of Mattias and the girl kissing. A photo of her talking to Rocco at an event, leaning in too close. Mattias and the girl walking the paddock, hand in hand. Another photo taken from far away, partly obscured by a wall, the girl's hand on Rocco's chest as she looked up into his eyes. The girl with a puffy, tear-stained face.

I ran to the comments.

Rocco the homewrecker.

I don't care how hot he is, you don't screw your team-mates' wives.

I heard that Mattias beats Lucia.

There were lots of comments under that last one, with some saying that Rocco fans were rabid and would make any excuse for his manwhore ways, others saying that Mattias's temper was an open secret in Formula One.

I flicked to the next video, which was an uncut version of the clip just shown on the news. Rocco and Mattias were talking with banked aggression in the garage, until Rocco pulled back a fist and punched Mattias fair in the face. You could hear him shout that Mattias was a piece of shit, with Mattias yelling back about her being his wife, all the while exchanging blows.

The comments under that video were full of speculation about what the fight was about, with theories ranging from Rocco losing his first seat to Mattias, to Mattias losing his wife to Rocco.

"It's not true, you know."

I threw my phone across the room in surprise, giving a yelp. Guilt flashed through me, making my cheeks heat. Rocco stood behind me, and I knew he would have been able to see exactly what I'd been looking at. Flushing, I looked at his chest.

"I'm sorry. It was on the news, and I didn't... I thought I..." *Ugh.* I wasn't making myself sound less guilty.

He shrugged. "It's fine. I'd assumed you'd seen it already. Most people have."

I shook my head. "I had my own issues this year, and I avoided news and celebrity gossip for my mental health." I waved a hand in Bobbi-June's direction, and he let out a little huff of laughter.

"I guess you did." He pointed to the seat beside me. "May I?" I scooched further over so he'd have space, and he sat beside me. "He was beating her. Not her face, but she'd have these huge bruises across her torso. I saw it once at a banquet we were forced to attend, just the flash of a bruise beneath her Versace. I asked her about it, and she was immediately defensive and told me to mind my business. But once she knew I knew, she kept seeking me out, like a refuge.

"Eventually, I got the whole truth out of her. But the tabloids saw something else, of course. My reputation didn't help me there." He let out a heavy sigh. "She wouldn't leave him. Then the footage of her in my arms got back to Mattias. I told him I knew he was violent, he told me she was his to do with as he liked, so I punched him. I lost my seat. My sponsorships. I begged her to leave the scene with me, but she chose to stay. The glamor and the fame were too much of a draw." He gave me a bitter smile. "Threw away my career for nothing."

I shook my head. Grabbing my phone, I showed him the comments about people speculating that Mattias beat Lucia. "Not for nothing. People will be watching now. That's one thing about social media—there's no hiding your secrets for long."

He nodded, and we sat in silence for a while. Bobbi-June eventually started to protest being on the ground, so Rocco leaned down to scoop her up into his arms.

"You're good with babies."

He shrugged. "Big family. Lots of little kids around all the time." He held her in front of him like a football. "They start making you look after the smaller children early, though normally it's just the girls that get stuck with the duty."

"You have many siblings?"

"Three older brothers and two younger sisters, and a lot of half-siblings. Plus, both my mother and father were one of ten children. Family gatherings were *big*. How about you?"

Holy shit, there was definitely a story there with the half-sibling thing. Maybe I'd extract one skeleton from his closet at a time, though. "I can't imagine having that much family." I shook my head. "Nope, no siblings. My mother died when I was young. My father died a couple of years ago. A carjacking gone wrong."

I said it so easily, but I'd locked that down in my brain so tightly, I was never dredging it back up again. It had been the worst time in my life, hands down. I took the emotion that tried to bubble to the surface, stuffed it in a box, and then threw that box into the ocean of my mind.

"Willy and Colin, who you met at the courthouse, are probably the closest thing to siblings I have. I love them like they're my family, and they love me the same way."

He huffed a laugh. "Indeed. Will, the big one? Threatened to castrate me in my sleep if I so much as thought about taking advantage of you." He lifted Bobbi-June to his shoulder, and I leaned forward to kiss her chubby little cheeks.

"I just bet. Did I mention he's protective?" I was still laughing as I looked up, suddenly realizing how close our bodies had become on the couch. He looked down with those dark, molten-amber eyes, his full lips only inches away. I could feel the soft gusts of his breaths on my cheeks.

Nope. No. Not happening.

I pulled away on a shaky breath. "I'm sure you're completely safe."

He gave a curt nod, a tight smile on his face as he handed a wiggling Bobbi-June over to me. "I'm not so sure I am," he said lightly, then stood. "The caterer should be here soon with food for the week. I had her cater for the whole household until you four get settled in and decide how you want mealtimes to work."

"Thanks, Rocco."

He gave me another tight smile and left. I settled back on the couch, propping one of the decorative pillows on my lap so I could nurse Bobbi-June.

Rocco and I had more in common than I'd thought; we'd both thrown our careers away on a pretty face, though in different ways. I thought about Lucia Christian, and her choice to stay. I couldn't judge another person, or their reasons for doing what they did, but what I'd seen in that video—the cold, almost evil look in Mattias's eye as he'd whispered something to Rocco?

No amount of money and glamor would make me stay.

THIRTY-FOUR

HAYES

GOING BACK to work had been interesting. The side-eyes. The way people watched us, like Rocco and I were about to start a brawl. The silence that descended on a room when Tally walked through. The only people who didn't seem fazed by Tally's new relationship status were Antony, because he knew the truth, and Stephie, who just figured we were all banging the whole time, so it was all good.

Stephie had been with VANT Enterprises for a long time before she came over to the racing side of the business. Apparently, the idea of her new co-worker having multiple partners was old news.

The hardest thing was watching the casual affection between Rocco and Tally at work, that we had all decided was necessary in public. Someone in the team had clearly gone running to Brick Willtot; otherwise, he never would have known Tally was pregnant, let alone shown up at the hospital after she'd given birth. It wasn't like we were posting about it in the newspaper.

So to maintain the ruse, Rocco would sometimes wrap an arm around her waist, or kiss her head as he walked past. Small things that weren't really that personal, but painted a certain picture among the team.

Luckily, we'd also decided that I didn't have to hide my affection. That would have been hell. Again, given the owners of VANT, no one's jaw dropped when Tally would kiss me, or when we'd go out to lunch.

Eventually, it stopped being quite so weird, but the tension was still there for the next few weeks. Simulations were almost done, and the car was almost constructed. We were getting ready to do physical testing on the cars, which meant soon Tally and Rocco would be driving it around the test track. It also meant that talks for a second driver were well under way, and I had a feeling we were going to get an announcement any day now.

Rumors were abound about who could drive with Rocco as a second seat, and while Tally's name had been thrown about, I didn't think she'd get the chance quite just yet. She definitely needed more experience driving in an open-wheeled car before they could send her out into professional racing. It had been a long time since karting, and there was a world of difference between a stock car and an IndyCar.

Still, the closer we got to testing day, the more excited Tally became. She was itching to be back behind the wheel of a race car, and I couldn't blame her. She was born to drive.

She was sitting in the cockpit of one of the cars now, as I gave her the grand tour. The sims had much of the same controls by design, but it was different somehow, sitting in the actual car that would race around St. Petersburg in a few months.

"The brake bias is shifted over a little, but otherwise it's pretty standard. Formula is where we get the chance to really experiment."

She sighed, resting her head back in the cockpit. Holding the steering wheel, she made vrooming noises and pretended to drive a track. I had no doubt that it was an actual track in her mind, and not just random movements, which somehow made it more adorable.

"Fuck, you're cute," I whispered, kissing the top of her head.

The baby had stayed home with Jesse today, who was working on selling the house that he and Tally had renovated. Today was our first full workday without her, and I could sense how anxious Tally was.

My phone buzzed, and I pulled it out of my pocket. Jesse had sent a photo of Bobbi-June reading the real estate pages of the newspaper, a slight frown making her look like she was concentrating.

J: *Junie looking for our next restoration project.*

· · ·

I showed Tally, and she laughed, her face soft as she stared at the baby. It was one of five photos Jesse had sent us today in the group chat, and I was fairly certain he was doing it as proof of life, to ease Tally's fears.

"Do you think they're doing okay?"

I smiled. "I'm pretty sure that Jesse has found his calling as a stay-at-home dad. He seems pretty content."

Jesse had been listless for as long as I had known him, but right now, despite the upheaval of the last week, he seemed pretty damn happy. This morning, we'd left him giving a bottle to Bobbi-June, and later, he had plans to finish the bike he'd started working on last year in the very impressive garage at Rocco's mansion.

Tally chewed her lip, but nodded. "I don't want him to think I'm taking advantage of him for free childcare."

Gah, this woman. Pulling her from the cockpit of the car, I dragged her into my arms, kissing her softly. "I promise you, if he had any issues, he'd let you know. But in case you miss the gooey way he looks at that baby, she's got him wrapped around her tiny finger, and she can't even burp on her own yet."

"Are you making out with my wife, Davis?" A teasing voice came from the doorway, and I rolled my eyes. Rocco calling her his wife was… difficult.

"Our wife, Passero," I taunted back, ignoring the stares of the other mechanics.

Tally blushed bright red as Rocco came over, twirling her softly and kissing her cheek, just beside her lips. "Our wife. Slip of the tongue." He winked, using that husky tone he only seemed to use with her.

Everyone else got either monosyllabic Rocco, or grumpy Rocco, but the more I got to know him, the more I wondered if his gruff, give-no-shits facade was just that—a mask to hide behind.

"Are you here for more sim testing?" I asked him.

Rocco shook his head. "No, Antony has an announcement."

Tally gasped. "He picked a new driver?" Rocco nodded. "Do you know who it is?" Another nod, then he mimed zipping his lips.

She huffed. "Am I going to be mad about who it is?"

He looked between us pensively, then shook his head. "He's young, but has a lot of potential. Antony wanted him in before track testing got fully underway, so he could ride the sims while you and I test the cars."

Valeria appeared in the garage. "Come on. Mr. Barbieri is announcing a new driver in the conference room."

Rocco waggled his eyebrows and followed along behind us. We ran into Stephie in the hall, who quickly wrapped an arm through Tally's. "Who do you think it is? Do you think he managed to woo another Formula One driver over? Poach someone from another team?" She looked over at Rocco. "Does one of your boy toys know?"

I huffed a laugh at being considered the boy toy for a woman at least two years younger than me. Rocco just shrugged.

Stephie screwed up her nose in disgruntlement as we piled into the conference room, staff already lining the walls. At the front of the room was Antony, Ari Rome, and a kid I couldn't name but recognized from somewhere. He was young, maybe eighteen or nineteen. He had floppy, curly hair and a big smile on his face.

"Holy shit, it's Mickey Macguire," Stephie breathed.

I leaned over to Rocco. "He looks like he's ten."

Rocco chuckled beneath his breath. "You aren't far off, my friend."

Stephie looked over her shoulder. "He's nineteen. He was the shining star of the iCar Development Program." I raised an eyebrow at her, and she flushed pink. "What? I do my research."

Ari Rome whistled to get the room's attention. "As I'm sure you've all guessed, we've secured the second seat for VANT Racing, and I am absolutely elated to welcome Mickey Macguire to the team. I'm sure you'll all give him a warm reception."

We all hollered and clapped, and Mickey went pink. So young. What would it have been like to achieve everything I wanted by that age? I was like, three years older, and it felt like an entire generation.

Antony waved a hand to calm everyone down. "To celebrate filling out the team, we'll be having after-work drinks. Well, except Mickey, who is still a bit too young." The team laughed, and Mickey flushed even more pink.

"But not too young to drive a car at 240 miles per hour around a race track," Rocco muttered to me out the side of his mouth. I mean, he made a good point.

That was a pretty insane double standard. Though I was fairly sure Rocco had been drinking red wine with his Wheaties as a kid.

Antony was still speaking. "We'll begin testing the cars after the Christmas break, and I'm sure you're all as excited as I am to see these machines we've worked so hard on come to life."

Ari and the team talked more about what would happen in the lead-up to the season, what the execs were doing, what the principals were doing—all crap that had little to nothing to do with the rest of us.

Finally, Antony ended the meeting. "All right, get back to work." He spotted our group in the crowd. "Tally, can I see you in my office?"

She looked over at me and Rocco, her eyes wide with dread. What the hell could that be about?

THIRTY-FIVE

TALLY

MY WALK to Antony's office was kind of terrifying. What if he was going to tell me he was letting me go? What if Brick had finally gotten to him, and he was going to fire me just because that old fucker hated me? What if my marriage to Rocco was causing too much negative publicity and he needed me gone?

I knocked on the door, and his muffled, "Come in," had me sucking in a deep breath. It didn't matter. I could find another job, or go back to waitressing or something. Everything was going to be fine.

Stepping into the room, I tried to be confident. "You asked to see me?"

Antony looked up from his computer. "Yes. Come in and grab a seat." He waved to the couch. "Stop looking so terrified. It's not bad, I promise."

All the tension whooshed out of me. I hadn't realized how much I'd catastrophized in the last five minutes. "Holy crap, you nearly gave me a coronary."

He laughed and came around to sit on the opposite side of the desk. I found he did that a lot, like he couldn't stand to be confined between the huge piece of antique furniture and the wall. "Sorry. Now that you've said it, I guess it would have seemed a little daunting. I just wanted to check in, discuss a few things. Coffee?" He pointed at an ultra-fancy Keurig machine, but I shook my head.

"I'm okay. Thank you, though."

"I need one. It's been a long day already." He turned his back to me, popping a pod into the machine. "It was hard to lure Mickey to VANT. He'd been promised to a bunch of different teams, and it took some heavy nego-tiating with his management to get him here. But I think he's the right choice."

I didn't know why he was telling me this, but his pause told me he wanted my opinion. "Stephie said he has the fastest lap times of anyone who's graduated out of the foundation program in the last decade. He's a solid second seat to Rocco. Plus, he's an all-American boy. He'll give the younger fans someone to cheer for."

Antony spun, an espresso cup looking teeny-tiny in his hands. "That's what the board thinks too. Some think he is a risk, though; that he's *too* good and will be poached by Europe to drive in F3 or perhaps even F2."

I shrugged. "It's better to have him make a good starting impression for the team before he leaves, then to not have him at all. He's going to be able to showcase the car and its speed, before he leaves. *If* he leaves." The high-pressure stakes of Formula racing wasn't for everyone, especially not when you could stay close to home and still have a really great career.

Antony smiled at me. "That's what I said. But that leaves us in a reasonably precarious position. We have two drivers who are just one lucrative contract away from abandoning IndyCar to move to the European circuits and paydays. We've decided we need a third driver, someone who can step in if that happens."

I frowned at him. "Are you looking for names?"

He grinned, and it lit up his normally serious face. "No, Tally. We are looking for *you*."

I blinked. And blinked again. He couldn't be suggesting what I thought he was suggesting, right?

"What do you mean exactly?" I couldn't let hope bloom in my chest just yet, so I held it tight, like a balloon that was just waiting for me to drop the string.

He came to sit on the coffee table across from me. "What I'm saying, exactly, is that the board and I would like you, Tally Palmer, to be our reserve driver."

I still couldn't believe what he was saying. "I've never even raced in an IndyCar."

"Hence the reserve part of your title. Don't worry, you'll get plenty of practice in the upcoming pre-season. What do you say?"

A million things filtered through my brain, like the shuffling of cards. My daughter, the court case, the feeling of being fired from my last job, Rocco, the guys —it all flashed through in brief glimpses before I opened my mouth and said, "I would be absolutely honored."

Antony clapped his hands together once. "Wonderful. I'll get the lawyers to draw up the contracts." His smile dimmed into a more serious expression. "I want you to know that you deserve this. You've worked hard for this team, logged more simulation hours than one person should ever have to, all during emotionally trying circumstances. You work hard, and that's all we can ask for here at VANT."

We went over some final points, including negotiation for pay—though honestly, I probably would've driven for free. Well, maybe not. I had a child to provide for now. Antony wasn't going to fuck me over, though; the number he'd suggested was more than reasonable for an inexperienced reserve driver.

Finally, I was released from the office to find a worried-looking Hayes standing there. Beside him was Rocco, chatting to Valeria at the front desk, making the girl look a little stunned.

I walked straight into Hayes's arms. "Is everything okay?" he murmured. "Did…" He trailed off, like the possibility of me being fired was too much to put into words.

"He offered me a contract as a reserve driver," I sobbed into his chest. I needed to pull myself together. But joy was coursing through my veins, and it was making me want to cry and laugh and run through the halls screaming.

Hayes pushed me away from him. "What?" he breathed.

"They want me as a reserve driver. I could *race*, Hayes."

He whooped, gathering me up in his arms and spinning me around. "Yes! I knew you could do this, Tally. I *knew* you could get back to where you needed to be. You were born to race, baby." He kissed me hard.

Someone cleared their throat, and I pulled back to see a grinning Valeria, and Rocco with a lopsided smirk. He didn't seem shocked at all. "You knew?"

I strode over to him, and he grabbed me up in his arms too, squeezing me tightly. "They told me this morning while I met Mickey that they were going to offer it to you. I didn't know if you'd take it. Didn't want to, er, jinx it?" He kissed my head, still holding me tightly. "You accepted? You're happy?"

I squeezed him in return. I wanted to ask if he'd pulled strings for me, but it didn't sound like it. That might be naive of me, but fuck it. Blissful ignorance was sometimes the best way to go.

Tally Palmer was *back*, baby. And I wasn't going to take even a moment for granted.

Jesse had been equally as excited for me, though his celebration had ended with me on my back on his bed, my thighs wrapped around his ears. But when we came downstairs again, it was to find a huge spread of Italian food and the guys chatting and drinking beers. Hayes had Bobbi-June in his arms, and Rocco was sneaking Norton fancy cheese. It looked almost… domestic.

"He's growing on us, I think," Jesse murmured in my ear. "You assume he's going to be the arrogant fuckhead that you always see on TV, but then he's stocking the garage with shit you need to restore the vintage Indian you've had your eye on for six months, even though you just mentioned it in passing." He huffed a laugh. "Hayes definitely wanted to stay pissed at him, but Rocco told him he could drive his Ferrari SF90 Stradale. I'm fairly sure Hayes would have sucked his dick if he'd asked for it in exchange."

Laughter burst from my lips, making the guys turn toward us. Gripping Jesse's hand, I moved in their direction like a moth to a flame. "It smells like an Italian restaurant down here. Where did this all come from?"

Rocco shrugged. "I know the owner of a little trattoria downtown, and he was happy enough to send us dinner for a healthy tip. It's as close to the food from home as I can get. To celebrate your promotion."

I leaned into Hayes, kissing his lips and Bobbi-June's chubby little cheek, then turned back to the man that was my husband. That shit still did my head in.

"Thank you, Rocco. I appreciate your thoughtfulness," I said softly. I appreciated so much more than that, but I didn't know how to express it.

Hayes passed me the baby, and I snuggled her close. She really was getting so big. "Were you a good girl today, sweet cheeks? Were you good for your dad—" I snapped my lips closed. *Oops.* We probably should've talked about that.

Jesse just raised an eyebrow, leaning in to kiss me,

amusement making his eyes crinkle at the corners. He tasted like me still, and that was a heady experience. "She was good for her daddy. We cleaned a carbie. We talked to Chet at the real estate agency. We napped in the middle of the day. It was quite eventful—wasn't it, sweet girl?"

I chewed my lip as I looked at the baby gurgle and wave her arms at Jesse, as if she were answering him. "That's good," I choked out past the emotion bubbling up in my chest. "Let me feed this little one, and then I think wine is in order."

I looked at Rocco, who was staring at us with such longing, it made my chest hurt. Yeah, I was definitely going to need wine.

THIRTY-SIX

JESSE

I STRAPPED Bobbi-June into her car seat as we headed out of the house. We needed to pick up Christmas presents, a new carburetor synchronization tool, and to pick up the mail from the old house.

We'd left Norton behind, and he'd looked thoroughly pitiful as we walked out the door. However, I was fairly sure the housekeeper who came every day, Elva, was sneaking him dog treats. She was wonderful, but I swear to god, she'd just appeared one day and we'd scared the shit out of each other. She was sixty, at least, and she fussed over Bobbi-June like she was the most beautiful baby in the world. Which she was, but I was a tad biased.

"Mail first, sweetheart, and then we'll hit up Target—what do you think?"

Junie gurgled in the back seat, and I knew by the time we left the gated community, she would be asleep. I tried to imagine what my dad would've said about me being a glorified househusband, but I couldn't imagine it would've been particularly positive. He and my mom had been very big into traditional relationship roles. My mom had given up her career as soon as she married, to become a housewife and care for me. It was why she'd been so lost after his death.

I didn't care, though. I might not say it to the rest of them, but I was loving this life.

Turning on the stereo, I played Bobbi-June The Beatles, specifically *Sgt. Pepper's Lonely Hearts Club Band*, because you were never too young to start your musical education. Hayes only liked dubstep, and I thought she might be a little young for Tally's favorite band, The Daymakers, just yet.

I was singing about a yellow submarine as we pulled up in front of my house across town. The baby was sound asleep in her car seat, as predicted, which was fine. She'd get her nap done early today.

Everything looked fine, and there was a *For Sale* sign in front of the house next door. We'd paid a company to stage the whole house to add to its appeal, and the agent felt positive that we'd get a little more than our asking price.

A car was parked across the road, a black sedan, and I wondered if the Hendersons had gotten a new car. "Come on, sweets. We'll check the mail slot and make sure the place is okay." It was getting cold, and you never knew when a pipe might burst.

As I walked, I felt eyes on me, and turned. There

was someone sitting in the dark sedan, and I was fairly sure I saw light glinting off a camera lens. *Paparazzi?*

Torn about what to do, I huffed out a frustrated breath. I hated the idea of being watched, but with Bobbi-June right there, I couldn't go and confront the guy. If he did something insane like pulled a gun or whatever, she'd be left unprotected. This helpless feeling was a new one.

I stepped into the house, scooping the mail off the floor and tossing it on the hall table. Placing the car seat in the living room, I peeked out the window. The sedan was still there. Pulling my phone from my pocket, I called Hayes.

"Hey, what's up?"

The guy was still snapping pictures. "There's a guy sitting in front of my house, and I want to go see what he wants. I've got Bobbi-June, and I'll lock her in the house, but wanted someone to know she was here, just in case. I'll call you right back."

"It's probably just the media. Leave it, man," Hayes said, but it sat wrong with me. Why would they be here and not at Rocco's mansion?

"If I don't call back in a few minutes, call the cops." I hung up, checked Junie one more time, and turned the deadbolt on the door. "Don't open this for anyone, okay?" I sing-songed at her, then locked it behind me.

Striding across the road, I rapped my knuckles on the car window. The guy inside only rolled it down a couple of inches. "Yeah?" He was probably in his late thirties. A nondescript-looking guy with pasty skin and dirty brown hair.

"What the hell are you doing outside my house, taking photos of me and my baby?"

The guy gave me a blank look. "I was taking photos of the houses. I like mid-century modern architecture."

"Bullshit," I spat. "Get the fuck out of here, before I call the cops."

The guy scowled at me. "This is a public street. I'm nowhere near your property line."

I narrowed my eyes. "Sure, fine. I'll tell the Hendersons—whose house you're parked outside right now—that you're a predator, trying to take photos of Lila through the windows, then? Lila Henderson is known to swing her Louisville first and ask questions later. I'll definitely support her statement that I saw you looking through her windows. Maybe she'll call the cops or maybe she'll call Hank, her husband, who once beat a guy until his jaw was in pieces for groping his wife."

Technically, that was completely untrue. Hank was a giant, but he was soft and sweet. I wasn't kidding about Lila, though. She was fiery as fuck.

My phone started to vibrate in my pocket, and I knew that if this fucker didn't move on soon, Hayes was probably going to call the cops himself.

The guy sighed. "Whatever, asshole." He wound up the window and started the car, peeling off down the street. I snapped a picture of his plates, then redialed Hayes.

"Thank fuck. I was about to call the cops." His

relieved voice poured down the line. "Was it a tabloid photog?"

I made a noncommittal noise. "I don't know. I don't think so, though. His camera was kinda crappy, and he had an attitude." I raced back up the stairs and unlocked the door. Junie was still safely asleep.

We were both silent for a moment as we chewed over who the guy could be. Finally, Hayes sighed. "Just head home. Keep an eye out, in case he's some psycho stalker. Maybe he's a Rocco fanboy?"

I didn't think so. Still, I grabbed Bobbi-June up and carried her out, locking the house back up tightly. "Maybe. I'll see you back at home."

Hanging up, I looked up and down the road for that black sedan or the guy inside it. It seemed all clear, but I was spooked. As I climbed into the car and started it, I checked in the rearview mirror. "How do you feel about online shopping, Junie?"

I hated the idea that some guy was going to chase us home, so I drove around for a while, going through the Starbucks drive-thru, down the highway along the coast, back around through the city. If I was being followed, they must've been pretty freaking impressive.

We ended up at a strip mall, and I was hungry enough to eat, despite the turmoil of the morning. Finding a little cafe, I grabbed the bottle from the warmer in the diaper bag and began to feed Bobbi-June. She'd definitely need changing after this.

"Jesse?"

Looking up, I saw Cat, who hosted the street races

in the area. Smiling at her, I waved her over. "Hey, Cat. How's it going?"

Cat looked down at the baby, then back at me. "I guess this explains why you haven't been to the last couple of races, huh?"

She reached me, and I stood up, hugging her close. We'd been friends for a long time; she'd been there when Hayes was still on the NASCAR circuit. We hadn't been close, but if I crashed out on a race, I was fairly sure she would have called an ambulance for me.

I'd been a regular on the street-racing scene for a while there, chasing something that was missing from my life, momentarily forgetting my loneliness by replacing it with the adrenaline of being reckless. I didn't need it anymore; I had Tally, and I had a purpose.

I shrugged. "I guess so."

Cat pulled a pretty, brown-haired girl with almond-shaped eyes closer. "This is Talia, my girlfriend."

I lifted the baby a little in my arms. "This is Bobbi-June."

"She's yours?"

This time, I didn't even hesitate. Her mama was mine. Which meant as far as I was concerned, this little piece of her was mine to love also. "Yep. Isn't she the cutest?"

Talia began babbling baby talk at Bobbi-June, and Cat rolled her eyes. "You're going to give her baby fever, and then who'll provide an outlet for the reckless adrenaline junkies of the city, hmm?"

I laughed. "I'm sure they'd be fine." I looked past

Cat, but froze as I saw what looked like the same guy from the front of my house.

How the fuck did he find us here?

Anger bubbled up in my chest, and I passed the baby to Cat. I trusted Cat more than I trusted most people. "Watch her for a minute."

"Jesse, what the—"

I missed the rest of her protest as I sprinted from the cafe, and the dude spotted me. He turned, running back to the parking lot, but I wasn't above chasing him down. "Stop!" I shouted, but the guy obviously didn't stop. If anything, he ran faster. But I'd run track back in high school, plus I had about ten years and half a foot of height on the guy.

I caught him easily by the cart return. Grabbing him, I thrust him against the bar. I spotted the gun at his waist and pulled it out, throwing it under a car. "Who the *fuck* are you, and why are you following me?"

The guy raised both hands. "Easy, man. Easy. I'm just doing my job."

"You're following me and my daughter while carrying a gun. I don't give a shit what your job is," I growled. "I don't give a shit how big of a story you think this is—if I catch you again, I'm going to kick your ass."

The guy frowned at me. "I think you've got the wrong idea. I'm a private investigator. I've been hired to get DNA from the baby. Apparently, the mother hasn't been responding to requests for DNA testing."

My blood froze. "Willtot hired you?" Rage washed

over me, and I shook him a little harder. "How exactly were you going to get her DNA, huh? You fucking weasel."

"Stop, man. I was just going to lift a bottle or something from the diaper bag if you walked away. I wouldn't hurt the kid."

I pushed the guy away from me. "If I ever see you again, it's your DNA that's going to be all over the sidewalk, do you hear me?"

I strode away, back to the cafe. Talia was holding a gently crying Bobbi-June, rocking her softly. I muttered an apology, gently taking the baby back and bouncing her in my arms the way she liked until she finally calmed. "Sorry about that. I have to go."

Cat looked at me, frowning. "Everything okay?"

I nodded, even if it was a lie. "Yeah, my girlfriend has a stalker." Small fib, but it went to show Brick Willtot would stoop to the lowest levels. "We'll catch up soon, Cat. It was nice to meet you, Talia."

I hightailed it out of the mall, and back home.

THIRTY-SEVEN

TALLY

JESSE WOULDN'T SAY IT, but he'd been shaken up by the whole private investigator thing, and he barely left the house with Bobbi-June for the next week. Hell, I was shaken up by it too. I shouldn't have been surprised that Brick would be underhanded and sneaky, instead of following the proper protocol and getting a court order. The guy wasn't used to hearing the word no.

I was ready for this to be over. So I got one of those at-home DNA kits, put a piece of her hair in it, and sent it off to a lab. Once it was back, I'd show it to fucking Brick. It wasn't like I was trying to sue him for Buck's inheritance. In fact, if he forgot all about us, I'd be happy.

I emailed my lawyer, who emailed me back promptly, telling me she had petitioned to expedite the trial due to harassment, and the date should be just after Christmas. The idea made anxiety eat at my chest, but we needed this to be done. I needed Brick to know that I would never, *ever* let him get custody of Bobbi-June, and if I had my way, he wouldn't be able to visit her either.

"Are you okay, *Stellina*?"

Rocco stood in the doorway of the study we all shared. He was in dress pants and an undershirt, like he'd half finished getting dressed when he'd stumbled across me.

I gave him a tremulous smile. "Yeah, just lawyer stuff." I let my head thump back against the office chair. "There's so many ways for this to go wrong, you know?"

He stepped closer, reaching out to stroke my arm in what I assumed was supposed to be a soothing gesture, but just made my skin tingle with awareness. Another thing to be guilty about—my growing attraction to Rocco. It was like my brain couldn't find the line between reality and make-believe. I was about to ruin the beautiful thing between Hayes, Jesse and me, just because my greedy vagina couldn't be satisfied with the two men she already had.

"It will be all okay, Tally. I'll make sure of it. Hayes has put the baby down, so we're just waiting for you to come down to eat."

Heaving myself from the office chair, I sighed. "Okay, okay. I'm coming."

He leaned in and brushed his lips over my cheek as I

walked past. "Enjoy the night. No need to borrow tomorrow's trouble today."

I held my breath as I nodded, brushing past him. There was absolutely zero body fat on that man, and he smelled so damn good. Like something spicy and woodsy that I just wanted to bathe in.

When Rocco had mentioned over dinner the other night that one of his family traditions was a large meal and gifts on Christmas Eve, none of us had hesitated to make it a thing. I'd done my research on *La Vigilia,* and I knew that it was done the night before Christmas. There was no meat, but it went heavy on the seafood. I could get behind that.

I'd also found out that Rocco was quite a cook. I never would have guessed that, considering how often we ordered in, and the fact he said he'd never used any of the appliances. But recently, he'd gotten up early and made pasta. By *hand.* I didn't know watching a man use a pasta machine could be a sexual experience, but watching him turn that little wheel had been a revelation.

Grabbing Rocco's hand, I led him out of the office and back downstairs. Jesse had lit the fire—though there wasn't a huge need for it, because the weather had been mild so far this December—and Hayes had bought enough booze to stock a ship. I'd gotten the food for tomorrow, which was Bobbi-June's first Christmas, and Jesse had taken her to pick out a tree earlier in the week, one of the few trips he'd undertaken. It was sitting in the corner of the living room, glowing brightly with lights.

Tomorrow, Willy and Colin would come on their way to see Colin's parents, and we'd have a huge lunch. But tonight, it was just us. This felt... right. Even Rocco being here felt good and not awkward, like he was meant to be with us all along.

The formal dining table was set, complete with intricate place settings and glowing candles. Swallowing hard, I walked over to it.

Hayes appeared with a cocktail. "Bobbi-June's midnight snack and breakfast are chilling in the fridge, so you can have this delicious cocktail and many more without worrying," he said, kissing my temple and handing me the glass.

Rocco started appearing with dishes, big bowls of pasta and risotto, a whole baked fish, and bread hot from the oven. He piled it onto the table, where the scent of cream and garlic and butter perfumed the air, creating a feeling of warmth and family that I hadn't had since... well, as long as I could remember.

"Rocco, this is... Wow," I breathed. Music came over the sound system, with Bing Crosby crooning "White Christmas." Jesse appeared with a grin, and Hayes handed both him and Rocco a cocktail.

Rocco made a sitting gesture, and we all did as we were told. He raised his glass. "To our first Christmas as a family." I swallowed down the lump in my throat as I raised my own. Rocco grinned. "Now eat. I didn't harass my nonna in the middle of the night for family recipes for you to let it go cold."

We ate and chatted, about the team and the upcoming race season, about Jesse's search for bike parts, about the house sale, about the baby. But we didn't mention the court case. The tabloids. Nothing even a little negative was brought up, and by the time we made it to dessert—this time in the form of a panettone and homemade tiramisu—I was so stuffed, I couldn't breathe. I was feeling pleasantly buzzed, my stomach was a little bloated, and I wanted to nap off my meal.

Stretching, I helped the guys move the leftover food to the fridge and stack the dishwasher. Hayes grabbed me in the kitchen, dancing with me slowly to the sound of the Rat Pack. Random selector had taken the wheel on the music streaming service, so we had everyone from Frank Sinatra to My Chemical Romance.

Hayes rocked me from side to side. "God, you're so fucking beautiful tonight," he breathed, also a little bit buzzed from the food and the wine and the good vibes. "I want to spend every Christmas Eve, New Years, and National Spaghetti Day with you."

I laughed, kissing him softly. "You say the most romantic things, Hayes Davis."

I was twirled away by Jesse, who also danced with me, his taller height meaning he had to stoop down even further to kiss me. "Merry Christmas Eve, sweetheart." I wrapped my arms around his neck and let him sway me from side to side for several songs.

A hand touched my elbow. "May I cut in?" Rocco asked quietly, but it felt like he was asking much more. Jesse gave me a small smile, his eyes telling me it was my choice. I looked at Hayes, who gave his own curt nod.

It was just a dance. Just a dance—they weren't agreeing to anything else.

"Of course," I murmured in Rocco's direction, holding out my hand. He wrapped his fingers around mine and drew me close. Not so close that it could be construed as anything but polite, but his thumb stroked the curve of my hip.

Tucking our clasped hands between our chests, he swayed me to the music, one song turning into another as we danced silently. "Thank you for celebrating *La Vigilia* with me. It has been a long time since I've had enough family around to warrant the effort."

"Thank you. It's been really special." It was an understatement, but I couldn't put into words how much it had also meant to me.

"I think she should kiss him for his hard work," Jesse said, and I whipped my head to the side and looked at him and Hayes, leaning against the kitchen counter, beers in hand like they were participants in our dance too.

Hayes shocked the shit out of me by nodding. "I think so too, and it might reduce the sexual tension in this house to something slightly more bearable," he teased, but there was something smoldering in his eyes.

I looked back up at Rocco, who was frowning at the

guys. Hell, even I was frowning at the guys. My heart was racing now. Could they really mean it?

Rocco looked back down at me. "She is not a gift you can just give away," he said softly.

Hayes didn't look at him, his eyes fixed on me. "No, you're right. She's a miracle that I'm thankful for every day. She's a ray of sunshine, and I'm not going to hoard her away if she wants to spread some of that light onto you too. She has enough warmth for all of us." He reached out and cupped my cheek. "If that's what she wants."

Jesse snorted. "The way she eye-fucks you whenever you walk into the room suggests she *does* indeed want that." He leaned forward to kiss me. "Take what you want, sweetheart. As long as I can watch," he purred, then bit my bottom lip softly. He stepped back, and it was just me and Rocco, standing chest to chest, the intense look in his eyes making my cheeks and my whole body heat.

"I…" I ran out of words. "It would mean something. To me. I want to, but it wouldn't be meaningless." *Way to say the same thing twice, Tally.* "Just so you know."

His hand came up to grip my chin. "It would mean something to me too." He leaned in and kissed me with so much fervor, it made me breathless. His lips pressed and conquered, like he was trying to steal the oxygen from my lungs. I threaded my fingers through his hair, like it was the only thing anchoring me to the earth.

Finally, he pulled back, heaving in oxygen. "Let's take this to the living room?" He looked between me and the guys. "And maybe some audience participation?" he teased, his lips brushing over mine again. "Would you like that, *Stellina?* My shining star. Would you like to be the center of our universe for the night?"

"Yes!" I shouted it, making Hayes laugh.

Fuck me. Christmas miracles really did exist.

THIRTY-EIGHT

ROCCO

I COULDN'T BELIEVE this was happening. I'd hoped, of course, but had meant what I said all the way back in the diner—unless she explicitly asked me for more, I was happy keeping it platonic.

Well, happy mightn't be the right word. Resigned. Suffering from a wild case of blue balls. But content to be part of this thing we had, even if it wasn't everything I desired.

But this moment right here? This was beyond my wildest dreams.

Moving her to the couch, I didn't let my lips leave hers. I devoured her until she curled into me, chasing the taste of my tongue, and I fed it to her. I couldn't get enough of our combined taste. I pulled her down until she was straddling my lap, and I finally got my hands on that sexy-as-sin, heart-shaped ass.

Flexing my fingers, I pulled her tighter to my body, wanting to feel every inch of her hot skin against mine.

I could feel the eyes of the guys on me, watching her move over me like this was live-action porn and the only thing missing was the pizza man.

I let my hands run up and down her curves, memorizing them. I slid my hands under her shirt, finding the soft skin of her hips. She was so beautiful, but I'd been with many "beautiful" women. There was something so magnetic about her that she had me obsessed, transfixed on doing nothing but pleasing her.

"Look at you, *Stellina*. You have us all transfixed. Just wanting to please you." I traced my lips down her throat, kissing the little hollow at the base before moving across her collarbone. "Wanting to hear your sweet sounds, make you come."

She was giving me those sweet noises now. Jesse stepped forward, hooking his fingers under the hem of her shirt. He hesitated a moment in case she wanted to stop, but she just put her hands in the air so he could tug it off easily. I grinned, moving my lips to the engorged swell of her breasts.

Was it weird that I kind of wanted to taste her breast milk? Maybe another time—I didn't want to freak her out right now and run the chance of shutting this all down. I leaned her further back so the other two men in the room had a good view as I kissed between her breasts.

"Do you want to taste?" I asked them, and Hayes dived for her, taking her lips with his. He had a painful looking hard-on, and I kind of felt bad for him. Kind of.

Deciding I was too hampered with her on my lap,

especially when I wanted to explore, I laid her on the couch, sucking and licking my way further down her body. I felt her suck in her stomach, and I frowned up at her, but didn't say anything. Was I in a position to tell her that she didn't need to do that shit around me?

Instead, I sucked the skin over her hip bone, leaving a hickey, marking her as mine. I gripped the waistband of her soft knitted pants, dragging them down those gorgeous thighs. She lifted her ass up to make it easier, and I appreciated the effort, because soon enough, I could settle myself exactly where I wanted to be.

Sliding her thighs over my shoulders, I looked up at her. She was stroking Hayes's cock through his pants while Jesse kissed her, but when I stilled, she pulled her eyes to me. "Fuck, you look like the sacrifice in some kind of pagan ritual," I breathed.

Hayes laughed, then groaned as she squeezed him through his chinos. "That's a bit sacrilegious on Jesus's birthday, but thank you."

Jesse rolled his eyes. "How does this work?" he asked, and I shrugged, dipping my mouth to her lace-covered core.

"However she wants it to work. But first I'm going to eat this pussy, because I've been *dreaming* of the taste."

Hayes unbuckled his pants, wrapping her hand around his cock and then covering it with his own. "Mmm, how could this work?" he said, stroking himself. "Maybe, while Rocco is eating you out like a feast, you could show Jesse how much you like his cock. You want to swallow Jesse's dick, baby?"

She nodded, reaching for the man in question. I watched it all, flicking my gaze between licking and sucking her clit, and waiting for things happening up there to unfold. I knew I'd found what she liked, because she folded in half like a sofabed and her grip on my hair was pleasure with a painful little bite.

"*Rocco!*"

Grinning smugly to myself, I continued working her over, getting her to where she needed to be. "Put her on her hands and knees, Rocco. Let's make her work for those orgasms," Hayes ordered, and I raised an eyebrow. I mean, I'd invited him to bed with me, but had never expected him to be quite so talkative. Honestly, though, I kind of liked it.

Doing what he suggested, I slipped her legs from my shoulders, and she protested wildly at the loss of my tongue pressing into her tight little pussy. Rolling her over onto her stomach, I dragged her up to her knees, then pushed her panties down her thighs, baring her to me completely.

Oh, yes. This was a great idea.

My dick jumped like he wanted in on the action, but I wasn't done yet. I dove back toward the apex of her thighs and ate her from the back, my fingers coming up to play with her clit as I plunged my tongue inside her. She ground back on my face, making me moan right into her pretty cunt. I pulled her ass cheeks apart and dived in there to tongue-fuck her like my life depended on it.

"Holy fuck," Jesse gasped, but I didn't look up to see what was happening up there. I had one job: to get my wife to come on my face.

Muffled moans told me she liked what I was doing, so I didn't slow down, not letting up until her pussy fluttered around my tongue. I needed to be inside her, right now. Climbing to my feet, I stripped out of my pants so fast, it was probably a world record.

Hayes raised a hand. "You clean, man?"

I nodded furiously. "I got tested for my physical, and I haven't been, you know, intimate with anyone unprotected."

He gave me an appraising look, like he was trying to work out if I was full of shit. I was more than prepared to run to my phone, find the email, toss it at him, and then bury myself inside my girl. But he nodded, and I appreciated the trust he had in my word. Hell, the trust that they all had in me. It was a humbling experience.

I pulled Tally off Jesse's cock, just for a moment. But I wanted to hear the words, the ones I'd been dreaming about for weeks. "You want this, Tally?"

"Fuck me, husband," she breathed, and I almost embarrassed myself by coming right then and there. Instead, I plunged my cock inside her, stretching her a little, listening to her scream my name like it was a banshee's call.

I plunged inside her, over and over again, and without my face buried between her thighs, I could see where we'd all ended up. Jesse's face was red as he fucked her mouth, and he looked like he was about to blow or pass out. I thrust hard into her, and she used the momentum to take him down further.

"Oh shit, Tally. *Fuck.*" His words were a garbled mess, and the feeling that I was fucking them both was surprisingly erotic. He grabbed her cheeks and then his hips were stuttering as he came down her throat, my sexy wife swallowing every drop.

Fuck me.

I wasn't going to last long at this rate, the tight grip of her around me like a drug haze I was lost in. Seeing my desperation, Hayes did me a favor, reaching beneath my girl to play with her clit and whisper filthy things in her ear.

"You take his cock like such a good girl." His words made her pussy clench, and I groaned as I held onto my control by a tenuous thread. "He's stretching you so wide, but I think that one day, you'll be able to take us both. What do you think of that, baby? You want us both sliding in that tight little pussy?"

She screamed something unintelligible as she came, and I was helpless but to fall along with her, my body unloading so much inside her that it leaked out around my cock. I pulled out, feeling light-headed, and stumbled to my ass, but not before I gathered her up, holding her back tight to my chest.

"*Stellina,*" I gasped. I actually had no words. I ran my hand up and down over her stomach, hips, breasts, trying to remember the very feel of this moment.

Hayes came and knelt on the couch. "She's not done yet, are you, baby? You can still take me?"

He leaned forward, seemingly completely unfazed that she was spread over my body like a feast. "Look at you, leaking cum all over his body. Maybe I'll have to fuck it all right back up inside you. Wouldn't want to waste it, right?"

Holy. Shit.

She made a begging noise, and Hayes quickly had her legs wrapped around his hips as he began literally fucking her into my body. My spent dick started to wake up at the sound of her sweet moans, the squelching sound of Hayes doing just what he said. I returned the favor from earlier, playing softly with her overstimulated clit, just gentle taps in time with his thrusts until she was coming all over again, the force of her orgasm making cum slide right out of her and all over my abdomen. It was chased by more of Hayes's seed as he shuddered through his own release.

Why the fuck was that so hot?

Hot liquid dripped down my ribs. Holy hell, had Jesse jerked off on me? But as I ran my hands up Tally's body, I realized her breasts were leaking milk. We all folded up into a sitting position, and I was probably going to have to get this couch dry-cleaned.

"Holy shit, my boobs leaked everywhere?" she gasped, her cheeks not flushed with orgasms, but embarrassment. Jesse knelt between her thighs and licked the milk from her skin, while I looked over his head at Hayes.

"Did we call for cleanup in the dairy aisle?"

Tally looked up at me, horrified, before her lips began to curl, first into a smirk, then into a full-blown grin, complete with dimples. "Watch it with the cow jokes, Passero." She slumped back against my chest. "Best. Christmas. Present. Ever."

I couldn't disagree.

THIRTY-NINE

TALLY

THE WIND HAD PICKED UP, but it didn't dampen my excitement even a little. Or maybe it was because Mickey Macguire was bouncing around like an over-enthusiastic puppy, which was kind of infectious.

It was track testing day, which meant I'd finally get to drive around a track for the first time in way too long. We were all in race suits, though they were just practice ones, and it felt so damn right on my body again.

My knee bounced where I sat beside Rocco, and he laughed. "If you two don't stop, you're going to need a nap before lunch time."

Mickey looked at Rocco like his every word was a biblical revelation. Man, had I ever been that awestruck by another driver?

Uh, yeah.

"Don't you still feel the excitement, Rocco? Or is it

just because it's an IndyCar and not a Formula One car?" Mickey asked.

Rocco shook his head. "I'm excited on the inside, kid. You'll learn how to be excited or nervous or scared without giving it away to other drivers, or the media who'll have their cameras in your face." Rocco pulled me closer, his hand wrapping around my thigh to stop the bounce. "Every good racer knows that the race begins as soon as you arrive at the track. Nothing but confidence. You're going to win every single time. And if you don't win that time, you think about what you can change so you'll win *next* time. It's about the mind as much as about your skills behind the wheel."

His hand slid further up my thigh, but Mickey didn't notice, so focused on the words coming from Rocco's mouth. I grinned, knowing he wasn't just talking about driving. I grabbed his hand before it could get too not-safe-for-work, though I was saved from permanently scarring the young driver when Ari Rome shouted, "Mickey!"

I reached out and bumped the kid's knuckles. "Be confident and all that shit, but remember to have fun too."

He grinned, such a wide, innocent expression. "Will do, Tally."

He jogged back into the garage, and I shook my head. He was nineteen, but I swear he'd lived and breathed racing for so long, he'd forgotten to have any social experience. The kid was about as socially inept as it gets, but he was sweet. It made me feel kind of maternal, which was insane considering I was only a couple of years older than him. Maybe it was motherhood.

With Mickey gone, Rocco pulled me closer and nuzzled my neck. "Are you excited, *Stellina*? Ready to be doing what you were born to do once more?"

I sighed happily. The only thing that could make today better was if I was starting, but I knew my limitations. I didn't even have close to enough experience behind the wheel of a live IndyCar, so I wasn't ready. But one day I would be, and then the world would know my name.

"Rocco!" someone called, and he kissed me softly and walked into the garage. "You too, Tally."

I skipped into the garage and saw Hayes standing beside one of the backup machines. It wasn't as fine-tuned as the starting cars, but it was still competitive. I stroked my hand up the side lovingly.

"Climb in, Tally. Let me know how it feels."

My heart pounded in my chest as I climbed in, slipping into the cockpit like it was a glove. So different from a stock car. What if I fucked this up?

Hayes squatted down beside me, holding out a helmet. "This is just like old times, baby. You're taking her out on a test lap, just to get a feel for it. We aren't competing for pole or points."

I nodded. We went over the rest of the checks and attached the steering wheel, then I was being pushed out onto the test track. I was glad they couldn't see my face from my helmet, because I was grinning so wide that my face threatened to break.

I'm back, baby.

I sat and watched Mickey go around the track first, his twenty laps getting progressively faster and faster until he was flying past at unbelievable speeds. It was amazing to watch.

But when Rocco rolled out, it only took him two laps to get the feel of the car before he showed us all why he was getting paid the big dollars.

Why commentators had been calling him a once-in-a-generation driver for so long.

Why I'd had posters of him on my wall, though I'd never wanted to drive anything but NASCAR.

The guy was poetry behind the wheel. He made it look so smooth, so easy, like he was out for a Sunday drive rather than edging close to two hundred miles per hour. In practice. He was definitely getting laid tonight.

Forty laps later, he rolled back into the garages, and it was my turn. Ari Rome's voice came over the radio. "Get your bearings, Tally, then put her through her paces."

The car was started, and once everyone was clear, I pulled out onto the track. I rolled it around the course once.

"Everything feel okay?" Ari asked through my earbuds.

I fiddled a little with the tension in the back anti-roll bar, and it was fine. "Feels good."

"Then green, green, green, make her go!"

I accelerated, my focus going to the track in front of me as I navigated the best lines. I'd studied this. I knew this track. Picking my lines into the corners, I got more and more confident as my speed increased and the scenery whipped by.

I was flying. This was magic.

Newton was a bit of an asshole when he said what goes up must come down. Sure, that was great for gravity, but it sucked when it came to emotions. After the pure elation of the test drive, getting a missed call from my family lawyer was like a lead weight there to drag me back down to Earth.

I waited until I got home to return her call, but I knew what it would be about. She'd given a copy of Bobbi-June's DNA test to the Willtots' lawyer, which meant everything could progress.

"Hello, Tally. How are things?" my lawyer, Serena, asked.

I slumped back against the office chair. "Fine, thanks."

"That's good. We have a court date for three weeks here in San Francisco, because it's the baby's home state. We've been assigned a judge, and honestly, he's got a pretty good record for finding in favor of the mother. I shouldn't have to say this, but I don't think he's easily bought either."

I let out a mirthless laugh. Not easily bought definitely doesn't mean he *couldn't* be bought, but I'd take it. "Thanks, Serena."

"No problem. Anything else I need to know?"

I chewed my lip. "Other than Brick having his private investigator following Jesse and the baby around town a couple of weeks ago, it's all been pretty normal. Jesse might have threatened him a little, though, just in case they bring that up." I'd told Serena almost immediately about Jesse and Hayes's place in mine and the baby's life. She had prepared against the idea that perhaps Brick's lawyers would use it as some kind of indication of my morals. It helped that we all lived together, were in a committed relationship, and all wanted what was best for Bobbi-June. We just had to hope that the judge was open to some new-age ideas, otherwise it might go badly.

We talked over some other things for a little while, including the fact that Bobbi-June may technically be the beneficiary of Buck's fortune, and his trust fund. I didn't want his money, and if they thought they could buy my baby, they were insane.

I finished up my call with Serena and headed downstairs. By the sound of it, Bobbi-June was awake. When I made it to the ground floor, Hayes was holding her out. "Look at that head control, Mama. Tell me you're the child of race car drivers without telling me. She'll be able to drive in Formula One before you know it. Isn't that right, Short Stack? You're going to take the racing world by storm in seventeen years, aren't you?" he cooed, and I shook my head.

"Maybe she'll hate cars. Maybe she'll want to be a librarian," I teased.

Hayes sniffed. "Then she'll be able to carry twelve books on her head, with this kind of neck control."

Jesse laughed from the couch. "That's not how librarians work. They have carts, and you know, hands?"

They bantered as I reached out to take Bobbi-June from his arms. One thing Brick would never be able to argue was that she wasn't loved completely and unconditionally. The guys had stepped up more than I could've ever imagined, and for that, I was so damn thankful.

I kissed her fuzzy head. "In three weeks, no one will ever be able to take you, not even for a moment. You might not have a lot of blood relatives, but you won't know anything but an absolute waterfall of love," I murmured to her, and she grinned, flailing her hands around.

Jesse stood and kissed me. "How was the test drive?"

I grinned, rocking the baby a little in my arms. "It was… amazing." I dropped my voice conspiratorially. "It might even be better than NASCAR."

Hayes let out a fake gasp, clutching his imaginary pearls. "Better than NASCAR?" He smiled. "Nah, baby, you looked amazing out there. Plus, you were only marginally behind the lap times of Mickey. I swear, soon you won't be a reserve driver; you'll be third seat. Antony was eyeing your lap times, like he was wondering if he could have three horses in this race."

Giddy at even the thought, I waved away the idea. "I'm not ready yet. But soon."

I was a fighter, and I wasn't giving up my dreams for anyone now. I could have my perfect life, and I would take down anyone who thought they could fuck with me.

FORTY

HAYES

THE DAY of the hearing was overcast. Tally had Bobbi-June strapped to her chest as she walked up the stairs. Serena had said the hearing shouldn't go for any more than an hour, and then it would be over.

Jesse and I walked a little behind Rocco and Tally. They were married, and it was important that they provided a united front. They were walking so close that their shoulders brushed, and Rocco had her hand tightly clasped in his. I hated that I wasn't enough for this moment, but even I could admit that it had all worked out for the best. If it had been me married to Tally, or even Jesse, the outcome of today would be a lot more ambiguous. Money could buy a lot of things in this country, and unfortunately, babies and judges were among that list.

The huge bank balance Rocco brought to this fight meant that if Brick Willtot wanted to steal our baby from us, he'd have to have some damn good evidence that Tally was anything but a devoted mother. No such evidence existed.

But it didn't mean I wasn't nervous as hell. That nervousness only doubled when we saw Brick and his wife Laverne in the hall of the courtroom. I watched Tally's feet stumble on the linoleum, and Rocco put an arm tight around her waist. He wouldn't let her fall. None of us would.

I hadn't seen Laverne Willtot since Buck's funeral— a funeral that Tally hadn't been allowed to attend—and she looked like she'd aged fifty years in the intervening months. A quiet and reserved woman, she'd always been overshadowed by her husband and sons.

The two older Willtot sons were also here, so apparently, it was a family affair. Bruce, the eldest, was the spitting image of his dad, and also an asshole. He helped manage Willtot Racing, and a couple of the other sub-branches of their business that made them so much damn money.

Buster Willtot had never been worth anything in his father's eyes, and that was a badly kept secret in the industry. Much more like his mother than his father, he'd become a kindergarten teacher, which was probably worse than useless in his father's eyes.

I had no doubt in my mind that Brick cursed God every day that it had been Buck who died, and not Buster.

The group spotted us, and the glares from Brick and Bruce were enough to peel paint. Laverne's eyes fell to the baby carrier strapped to Tally's front, and I watched the woman's face crumple. She stepped toward us, and I tensed.

"Laverne," Brick barked, and I saw her flinch, but she kept walking. "Laverne, come back here *now*."

Laverne looked over her shoulder, and I saw her spine stiffen as she ignored her husband and walked toward us quickly. Brick moved to go after her, but Buster got in his way. I couldn't hear what they were saying, but you didn't have to be a master in reading body language to know it was something angry.

As she came to a stop in front of Tally, the woman's big blue eyes looked watery. They were Bobbi-June's eyes, inherited from Buck. Tally took a deep breath. "Hello, Mrs. Willtot."

"Tally. You look well." Her voice was shaky and small. "I just wanted to say I'm sorry for this. Brick hasn't been the same after Buck's death and…" Another stuttering breath. "I fear he's ruined everything by bull-dozing his way through life once again."

Tally said nothing, her face a blank mask, but I could see tears shine in her eyes.

Nodding to herself, Laverne continued. "I wouldn't blame you if you cut all contact with us after this, so I was hoping, just in case, that I could see Buck's daughter, just once?" A tear slipped down the older woman's cheek.

Tally stared at the woman who seemed so small, like she was curling in on herself, preparing to shrivel away from the light. It was a pitiful scene, and it would affect even the hardest, most vengeful person. Tally was neither of those things.

Pulling the baby wrap to the side, she showed Bobbi-June's angelic sleeping face to her paternal grandmother. Laverne sucked in a deep, pained breath as she lifted a hand and traced the curve of her face. "So beautiful. Just like my boy. You named her Bobbi-June? You stuck with the B theme?"

I doubted it was intentional, but Tally wasn't going to contradict this woman who seemed like she was barely clinging to her sanity. "It's a good name."

Laverne nodded again, taking a step back. "You'll be a good mother. I know it. Buck really liked you. His eyes always lit up when he spoke of you, which is probably why Brick hated you." She touched Tally's shoulder. "I know it wasn't your fault. It was that silly sport that he loved so much."

This woman was breaking my heart. Jesse handed Tally a tissue that he'd pulled from god knows where, and that was when I realized they were both crying. For a boy who never got much of an opportunity to be a man. For Bobbi-June, who wouldn't get to know her grandmother or uncle, just because her grandfather was a narcissist. For Tally, who never got to say goodbye to her first love.

Serena, the lawyer, stepped up. "Mrs. Willtot, the proceedings are about to start. You better go back to your party." Her voice was gentle, like she too knew that this woman in front of us was one harsh word away from crumbling to dust.

Buster appeared behind his mother. He nodded at us, and I nodded back. "Look after her," he said to Tally.

My beautiful girlfriend lifted her chin at Laverne. "You too."

Buster's jaw tensed, but he gave her a curt nod as he led his mother into the courtroom. I watched them disappear completely before I came closer, pressing my hand to Tally's spine.

"You okay, sweetheart?" She shook her head, and I wrapped my arms around her shoulders. "It will work itself out, I promise. I know it feels like a lot now, but we can figure out the rest later."

I kissed her temple and stepped away, even though it pained me to do so. Rocco reached for her hand again, so she was never without the support of one of us. We were here for her. We all were. Now we just had to wait for this shit to be done.

We filed in, sitting on the left side of the courtroom. Tally unhooked Bobbi-June and handed her to Rocco, who placed the sleeping baby on his shoulder, rocking her so she didn't wake.

The judge grabbed the file in front of him, scanning through it quickly. "Mr. Willtot, Mrs. Palmer-Passero, I see we are here to decide who gets custody of Bobbi-June Palmer." The lawyers agreed, and the judge nodded. "Okay, proceed."

Twenty minutes later, I was tempted to leap across the courtroom and punch Brick Willtot in the mouth. His lawyer was trying his best to make Tally sound like a flake—an unstable adrenaline junkie, who'd probably die in a fiery car crash before she turned twenty-five. He'd also suggested that Rocco was a fake husband for the sake of this court case, who just wanted citizenship. That might have been true at one point, but good luck proving that now.

When he'd suggested that, the judge had raised an eyebrow at Rocco. "Is that true, Mr. Passero?"

I'd watched as Rocco had leaned forward, his eyes alight with passion. "Absolutely not. I love Tally, and Bobbi-June. I've set up a trust for Bobbi-June's future. I want to adopt her, so she can be a Passero like her mama. I want to watch her grow into a fierce and loving woman like my wife." He let out a sigh. "Did we expedite the natural progression of our relationship because of Mr. Willtot's aggressive tactics? Yes. However, it was inevitable. I have been smitten with Tally since the moment I laid eyes on her, the first time she put me in my place."

He gave a crooked grin, then it faded again, merely a flash before the sunset. "But I promise you that I meant what I said when I stood up in front of that judge. I intend to love her in sickness and health, in the good times and the bad. I will be there for both of them forever."

Man, I wasn't even married to the guy—or interested in dick—and I could swoon. The judge just nodded, making notes.

Willtot's lawyer scoffed. "How can he say that when we have proof that she is sleeping with two other men?

Does that sound like a committed, healthy relationship to you, Your Honor?" He passed a stack of photos to the judge, and it didn't take a rocket scientist to guess what they showed.

Serena took the stack that the opposing counsel handed her. She wasn't shocked. We'd prepared for this.

The judge raised his eyebrows at us. "I see. Mrs. Palmer-Passero? What do you say to this?"

Serena stepped forward. "Your Honor—"

"Counsel, I was talking to your client."

Tally stood. "Sir, I know it is unorthodox. Relationships have been between a man and a woman in the eyes of the law for a long time. However, I ask that you look at my relationship not through a patriarchal, traditionalist view, but an open mindset that reflects modern times. I love all three of these men, Your Honor. We love each other. We provide support, emotional and physical stability, for each other and Bobbi-June.

"At no point in the day is Bobbi-June without someone who would lay down their life for her. Instead of having one father to step into the shoes of the one she lost, she has three men who love and protect her. Who will love and protect me. Only one is my significant other in the eyes of the law, but in my heart, they are all my husbands."

Bruce Willtot muttered, "*Whore*," in a cough, and the judge raised a stern eyebrow at him.

"I understand it's unorthodox, but not unheard of in

this day and age, especially not here in California," Tally implored.

"Indeed. Okay, continue," the judge said, waving a hand at the lawyers.

It continued, but it was more of a joint character assassination than anything else, and Serena fired back as she mentioned Brick's underhanded tactics in getting Tally fired, and his aggressive stand-over tactics at the hospital after she'd given birth.

In the end, it went for nearly five hours before the judge was ready to give a decision. "It is in the best interests of the infant not to drag this out any further. Her wellbeing, both physically and emotionally, is the only thing that this court is concerned with. It is clear that in front of me is a happy, loved and well-provided-for child."

Brick Willtot growled low, a feral sound.

"This court grants sole custody of Bobbi-June Palmer to her mother, Tally Palmer-Passero. This court also denies the request for grandparent visitation rights." He looked at Brick. "You need therapy to help you deal with the tragic death of your son, Mr. Willtot. This child is not a replacement for the son you lost. She has no relationship with you, and will not unduly suffer from not knowing you, as is the mother's right. However, I fear that she might suffer under your influence."

The judge looked at Tally, whose whole body had sagged into the chair with relief. "Unorthodox as it may be, I believe that you provide a loving and stable home for your daughter. In the future, it might be beneficial for the child to know her grandparents, but that is entirely at your discretion." He looked down at the court stenographer. "Court dismissed."

I kissed the top of Bobbi-June's head, who'd been such a good baby during the trial, not even a little disgruntled about being passed between the three of us constantly. "Hear that, baby girl? You're ours for good now. Let's go hug your mama."

Rocco already had Tally in his arms, and she was quickly squished between his chest and Jesse's. We were a family, for real now.

FORTY-ONE

TALLY

THE FIRST RACE of the season was early this year, but we were ready. The Florida government had managed to woo both IndyCar and Formula One to happen within a week of each other, and it was causing a buzz across the racing world.

I wondered if it was because Rocco had defected, and they were trying to lure some of the die-hard Formula One fans to Indy. Already, Rocco had been bombarded with requests from the media for interviews, which his management had accepted. It was good for Rocco, it was good for VANT, and it was good for launching our relationship.

It also probably meant that we would have to walk the paddock at the Miami Formula One race, which terrified me. It was like a fashion show, and I was *not* a Brazilian lingerie model. I was just a girl with a fast car and a baby.

That was next week's problem. This week was the

launch of the race season, and I'd be watching Rocco and Mickey race for the first time. There was a buzz around the garages, as people stopped to snap photos, and Antony gave interviews, as did the rest of the VANT crew. The whole place was electric with energy, and I was part of it all.

Rocco had flown us all over on a private plane, which seemed a little excessive, but he'd argued that Bobbi-June was still too young to fly commercial. It was hard to believe she was almost twelve weeks old already.

Jesse had her strapped to his chest, and honestly, it was doing something crazy to my ovaries. Like I wanted to have my recently inserted IUD removed and let him impregnate me already.

I mean, I obviously wouldn't. I was nowhere near mentally ready for another baby, but I wouldn't mind practicing on any free surface.

"Babe, you gotta stop looking at me like that. I can't watch this race with a hard-on," he said softly. "We'll be up in the grandstands, cheering for our team, and then we can all celebrate properly tonight."

We'd created a monster when we'd decided to have group sex on Christmas Eve, but it was a hot monster, like Beast from *Beauty and The Beast*, or like, a dragon. Everyone wanted to fuck a dragon, right?

Kissing me on the cheek, he pushed me gently into the garage. Luckily, being a reserve driver meant I got none of the media attention, which was amazing, and I could hide with the mechanics and engineers out the back. Most of these guys were hardcore sports reporters and didn't give a fuck about Rocco getting married, especially now it was old news.

If they snapped a picture of me, it would be just a throwaway line at the bottom of their article on why Rocco Passero—a prodigious, somewhat contentious Formula One driver—had switched teams to come to IndyCar. The fight between him and his former team-mate was still far bigger news than him marrying a barely newsworthy former NASCAR driver.

We'd been here since Thursday, and both Rocco and Mickey had qualified well. Rocco was third, with Mickey a little further back, but both were in good spots for the team's maiden race. The whole of VANT Racing had been flown out for today to witness our hard work finally come to fruition.

Alphonso patted my back. "Exciting, right?" he whispered, and I sucked in a deep, shaky breath. I wasn't even racing, and I had nerves.

"I think I'm going to throw up. I'm so hyped."

Alphonso chuckled. "Trash can is over there, kid. Don't puke on the cars." I shook my head with a laugh.

Rocco finished his interview and moved back into the garage. Spotting me, he walked over, that little smirk on his face. God, he was beautiful in the black and purple VANT gear. It made him look like a villain, and it was sexy as hell.

"Are you eye-fucking me, my star?" He leaned closer. "*Baciami.* Kiss me, *Stellina.*"

Gah. When he whispered to me in that sexy Italian-

English mix, I was helpless to resist. I leaned forward, kissing him softly, as I chased the taste of him with my lips. He kissed with an expertise that made me weak in the knees. He should be locked away as a hazard to free-thinking women everywhere, because when his lips touched mine, my brain turned to mush.

"Wish me luck, beautiful."

I shook my head. "You don't need luck, Rocco Passero. Show these people why they call you *Il Diavolo* in Europe." It was because even if you got in front of him, the devil was always nipping at your heels.

"Because I tempted too many virgins into sinning?" he asked lightly, and I slapped his chest.

"I think it's poor form to talk about all the naive women you deflowered to your wife."

He kissed me hard. "You're the only woman who matters now," he whispered against my lips.

"Passero, let's go!"

He pulled back and winked at me, and I had to acknowledge the truth I'd avoided for a couple of weeks now. I'd caught feelings for my fake husband.

St. Pete in Florida was a hundred-lap race, and at some point, it became less about driving and more about fuel preservation. That didn't mean it wasn't tense as hell. As soon as the strategy engineer breathed, "Green, green, green," down the line, we were out there to win.

I sat in the garage, watching the race on the screens as Rocco maneuvered his way from third up to second almost immediately. I had the headphones on so I could hear the team radio, and it was absolutely electrifying. The high-pitched whine of the cars roaring past made my heart palpitate in my chest. It was *amazing*.

Hayes was part of the pit crew, and the mechanics rushed around, getting orders from the performance engineers up in the timing stand on the pit wall. A few wheel touches, a little bump and grind in the first chicane as they all jostled for a good position, but soon, it relaxed out into a proper race. Mickey had lost it a little, falling to eighth after someone nudged him, but he pulled it back and honestly, that was a testament to his skill.

They were going so fast, so few inches from the ground and so close to the driver next to them, it took some serious balls of steel. If I had my way, soon balls wouldn't be needed at all.

I watched it all with bated breath—every pass, every takedown, every decision I heard over the radio. They pitted Rocco, but they took way too long. Ten-point-six seconds, nearly four seconds more than acceptable. Rocco fell back to seventh, and after they pitted Mickey, at a minorly better seven-point-eight seconds, the team came back looking dejected.

Hayes was on the airjack, and it wasn't his fault, but I could still see the annoyance in his eyes. You wouldn't know it, though, by the way he slapped shoulders and told his team they would be better next pit. He boosted them all up, and as Rocco climbed back up to sixth, then fifth, then fourth, I could see the determination to be better settle on their faces.

Another forty laps, and they pitted again a little early, getting Rocco out in seven-point-one seconds, which was pretty fucking good.

Fist pumping in the air, I hollered for Rocco to go. He slipped back out well, getting into a good position to hopefully eat the distance between himself and the race leader as they all pitted for the second time.

Mickey got shoved into the wall, spinning him out and putting the track on a yellow. "Dammit," I breathed, but it happened. It had happened to at least three other drivers already today. A bunch of cars pitted under the yellow flag, and that would filter Rocco back up the front. Then he'd just have to keep the spot, for himself and for VANT.

Finally, we were down to the last five laps of the race, and Rocco was in an epic battle for one of the top three places. He was in a dogfight for first, but Powski was riding his ass like Mary on the way to Bethlehem.

Second. Third. Second again. First for a moment, before it was taken back on the second turn. I held my breath as they came up to the finish line, their speed on the straight hitting well over the two-twenties, and I couldn't believe it.

"And Rocco Passero and VANT get a podium in their debut race! P2 for Passero and for VANT Racing." The announcer's voice boomed around the paddock, and I jumped to my feet.

"Yes! YES!" I bounced over to the closest stunned

mechanic, wrapping my arms around him and jumping up and down. Hayes was down on the pit wall with the other mechanics, so this dude would have to do. "We did it! We podiumed on our first run!"

I spotted Mickey looking dejected in the corner, but that wasn't allowed.

"Get over here, Mickey Macguire! You're part of a podium team and you have to celebrate." Pulling him up, I wrapped my arms around his waist and hugged him tightly. "You should be so damn proud of yourself. You've achieved something today."

"Choking out and crashing in the final moments of the race?" he asked sullenly.

Teenagers, man. "We both know Millward touched your rear tire, Mickey. It wasn't your fault. It's just racing—you know this in that big head of yours. Celebrate with your team, and then next race, we're going to kick fucking ass! We'll be one-two on that damn podium, you mark my words."

That goofy grin I'd come to associate with Mickey finally lit up his face. "Yeah, okay."

I grabbed his hand. "Let's go and congratulate the team down in Victory Lane, you included. You did good, kid!"

We raced down to Victory Lane, where Rocco was in the second-place spot. I hopped the wall, stopping to congratulate Antony and Ari as they gave interviews to the press around them. Rocco was out of his car, talking to the trackside interviewer. I waited off at the side as he answered questions about the first disastrous pit, about climbing back up, about how it felt in comparison to Formula One.

As soon as he spotted me, though, he curled his finger at me, so I ran over and jumped into his arms. He kissed me hard on the lips, and I pulled back grinning. "P2, baby!"

He laughed, joy emanating from every inch of his face.

"I can't see Powski and Millward of Team Beerberg kissing in celebration, ladies and gentlemen. Tally Palmer, reserve driver for VANT Racing," the interviewer said, laughing.

I raised my hand in greeting at the cameraman, flushing a little, and moved back so they could finish the interview. Spotting Hayes, I went over and hugged him too. "You guys totally nailed that last pit stop," I yelled over the sound of the crowd, kissing him as he spun me around.

A throat cleared behind me. "Excuse me. You must be the new Mrs. Passero." I turned and met the disapproving features of an Italian guy in his late twenties, or maybe early thirties.

"Uh, Tally Palmer-Passero. It's nice to meet you." I put out my hand to shake, mostly out of instinct.

The guy raised a single eyebrow. "Rafa Passero. Your brother-in-law."

A brother-in-law who'd just seen me kissing a man who wasn't his brother. *Fuck.*

FORTY-TWO
ROCCO

TALLY WAS GIVING me the silent treatment, and I probably deserved it. Although I'd known Rafa was coming to my debut race, with the court case and the testing—and let's be honest, the brain-melting sex—it had kind of slipped my mind.

I definitely hadn't mentioned that I was sharing my wife with two other guys to Rafa. That wasn't something my extremely traditional family would approve of.

We sat around in the hotel restaurant awkwardly—except Hayes, who'd feigned being tired and volunteered to take Bobbi-June upstairs and put her down to sleep. While I wanted to curse him for his cowardice, if I'd had the option, I also would have run for the hills.

Luckily, Jesse was super relaxed about the whole thing. Actually, Jesse was pretty relaxed about most things.

Rafa dropped his voice low. "You didn't think you

should tell me that your wife has her own… is it mistresses? Masters? Side pieces? Whatever. And they all live under your roof?"

Tally frowned. "The more important question is 'shouldn't you have told your wife that your brother was coming to the race, so his first impression of her wasn't that she was some kind of cheating whore, and she'd have a chance to make a good impression before you *dropped the whole polyamorous thing on him?*'" She hissed out the last words.

Jesse just laughed. "Man, you're in so much trouble right now."

I glared at him; he didn't need to seem *quite* so entertained right now. "I apologize, but I just… forgot."

Rafa looked at Tally. "He forgot."

Tally slowly blinked in my direction. "You just forgot. Of course. Understandable."

I was never getting laid again. "The important thing is now you both know, and you've met. Maybe we can just move on?" It sounded so hopeful, and just made Jesse laugh more.

"Can we just move on?" Rafa imitated me in a high voice. It always used to piss me off when we were kids, and it didn't piss me off any less now. "No, we *can't* move on. I'm going to need you to explain it to me. How does this polyamory thing work? Is it popular over here in this godless country?"

Jesse indicated to the waitress that we all needed another round of drinks, and I'd never been more thankful for a person, even if I did want to punch his smug face every time he laughed.

Tally flushed and stared pointedly at me. I just shrugged. This four-way relationship thing was her forte. After one final glare at me, she schooled her face into something a little more socially nice. "It wasn't something I was searching out, and I wouldn't say it is even something popular in this country, though it's becoming less taboo." She swallowed hard. "Jesse and Hayes were there for me when no one was. They're best friends, who went out of their way to help me when everyone else had ostracized me. I didn't want to repay their kindness by coming between them. Not when we could *all* be happy, you know?" Her eyes slipped to me. "Your brother was meant to be a business decision," she said softly. "But he's too fucking lovable."

"*Ti amo, Stellina,*" I murmured, picking up her hand and kissing her knuckles.

Rafa made a gagging noise. "Okay, okay, enough with the mushy crap." He looked at me like I was a stranger. "Who the fuck *are* you? It's like you've been body snatched."

I didn't bother telling him he'd been exactly the same when he met Theresa. I'd made fun of him for weeks for following her around with calf eyes, but clearly, revenge was a dish best served with a side of humiliation.

"I don't expect you to understand, Rafa. I just need you to accept that this is how it is." I implored him not to make this a big deal, and his face softened. Rafa had been many things growing up. A typical brother who would thump me if I stole his console controllers. An asshole who definitely gave me one or two of my neuroses. But more than all that, he was the man who would do absolutely anything for me, if it made me happy.

He sighed, downing the glass of red wine the waitress had just delivered to the table. "I think we can all agree on one thing. Thank god I didn't bring Theresa or Mamma like you suggested."

I saluted the sky. "*Grazie a Dio*."

We flew with Rafa from Tampa down to Miami, though we stayed at a resort on the beach and not at the hotel that was housing all the Formula One teams and drivers. If I could avoid them for a little longer, I would.

Instead, we took the week off to spend it as a family. I did a lot of video calls with the team about tweaks to the car I'd like, though. But I also spent hours by the pool with my beautiful wife in a bikini, and found out Bobbi-June was, in fact, part-mermaid. My little *Bambolina* loved the water and spent a long time splashing around, as did her mamma.

I was holding the sleepy baby now, my brother beside me under the shaded cabana lounge on our suite's balcony, and I didn't have to see him to know he was giving me an incredulous expression. "Would you like to take a photograph for prosperity, brother?"

Rafa laughed. "I never would have believed it if I

hadn't seen it with my own eyes. You've changed, Rocco. You've grown up."

I couldn't pin all that on Tally and our marriage; it had started long before that, when I'd been helpless to help Lucia, because she wouldn't help herself. When I'd been booted from the team as a bad teammate with a terrible reputation, yet it was an open secret that Mattias beat his wife. The world wasn't a dichotomy of black and white, right and wrong, winning and losing. It was complex, and kind of a shitshow. The rose-colored glasses had been torn off and crushed beneath the heel of reality, and that had made me grow up more than anything.

"Love, right?" was all I said, though, and he made a noise of agreement in the back of his throat.

There was movement in the suite, which was probably Tally getting dressed and ready to walk the paddock. I'd avoided quali days; I was only obligated to show my face on race day, according to my manager, but I still wasn't looking forward to it.

Rafa would be there, and I was hard launching Tally as my wife to the media that followed the elite championship around. It was a media far more interested in my relationships than the American tabloids had been.

Most of the trackside pundits traveled the world in the Press Pack. They were people who'd insinuated that I was having an affair with Lucia. They'd followed me to clubs, photographing me with random models, or falling down drunk. They'd formed an opinion of me over the previous decade, and I couldn't even say they were wrong. I'd been a manwhore who partied far too hard, who let the fame and success go to my head. Who lost sight of what was important, just like they said.

I just hoped they didn't bring that shit up in front of Tally. I wasn't stupid enough to think she'd never heard of that reputation before; it wasn't exactly hush-hush. But that wasn't the man I was anymore.

The door slid open, and Jesse was there. "She's nearly ready. Here, let me take Junie." I sat up slowly, and we did a gentle handover, like she was a suitcase of uranium and not a small, sleeping baby. Giving him a mental high-five when we did it without her opening her eyes, I stood.

Rafa was still shaking his head. "I can't wait to tell the family about this." He frowned. "When are you coming home to introduce your wife to your family?"

I shrugged. "The next off-season, I think. They'll love Italy. Jesse will love the food, Hayes will love the cars. Tally will love the family, if they let her." Because there was just as good a chance that they'd reject us completely. I'd hate that, but I wasn't going to make Tally choose between us to keep my family happy.

Rafa narrowed his eyes. "I thought you were just trying to keep Tally happy by letting the guys live with you, but you really do like them. You're a real little family unit."

I slapped his shoulder. "I really do. I'm as surprised as you, but they're like living with your best friends and not having to worry they'll ghost you when they get a girlfriend," I said with a laugh. I needed to finish getting ready, so did Rafa. "We'll meet you in the lobby?" Nodding, he walked back along the balcony to his room, while I stepped through the sliding doors. "Are you almost done?" I shouted into the suite, and Tally's voice called back from the bedroom.

"Just putting on my shoes!"

I slipped on a white linen shirt that was hanging in the coat closet, and tucked it into my black jeans messily. Or artfully, depending who you asked. It was the first time I'd walk the paddock as a guest and not as a driver, so it was kind of weird. I slipped on a pair of sneakers and ran a hand through my hair. Done.

Tally bounced out of the bedroom, and my breath caught in my throat. She looked effortlessly beautiful, like a golden goddess made of cream and sunshine. "Is this outfit okay? I didn't want to pretend I was high fashion, but also didn't want to embarrass you," she joked, but I could see the nerves in her eyes.

She was wearing wide-leg pants in olive satin that were high-waisted, a thick band with small pearl buttons down the front the only ornamentation. She'd coupled it with a little beige knit top that showed off her milky skin, and a tiny sliver of her upper stomach. She looked classy and effortless.

I stepped toward her, pulling her into my arms. "You look perfect in anything you wear. You couldn't embarrass me if you went out in a sack." I kissed her softly, and she pulled back after barely more than a brush of our lips. She was a few inches taller than normal, which probably meant she was wearing heels under those pants. I ran my hands over the silky curve of her ass. Man, I really liked these pants.

She shoved gently at my chest. "If you kiss off my lipstick after I just put it on, we'll be late." She ran to get her purse, and Hayes and Jesse appeared in the living room. They were staying home to look after the baby and to give us this moment.

Tally danced over to kiss each of them in turn. "Gorgeous," Hayes breathed, and did the same thing I did, ran his hand over her ass in those satin pants. "We need to get more of these, I think."

Laughing, Jesse kissed her too. "Have fun, sweetheart. Remember, you're a badass, and he loves you, even though he tried not to."

I chuckled softly, because he was right. I might have been attracted to her, but that was a base urge, a bodily response to an attractive woman. However, falling in love with her was completely involuntary and probably quite inconvenient, given that I'd have to share her forever.

I had zero regrets. Holding out a hand, I tilted my head toward the door. "Let's go."

FORTY-THREE

TALLY

WE'D HIRED a car when we arrived in Miami, so we joined the traffic heading toward the race track. In the front, Rocco and his brother talked Formula One, and it was passionate enough for me to know that while Rocco had come to IndyCar, his one true love remained Formula racing. I guess he'd lived and breathed it for so long—probably since he was born—it was insane to think half a year of IndyCar could shift his allegiance.

It was gridlock as we approached the autodrome, but luckily, there was valet parking. Rafa gave us guest passes that got us through the gates and into the paddock, and I tried not to look nervous. It was insane, with people and cameras everywhere. It was like Daytona met Milan Fashion Week or something, with beautiful people walking along toward the garages, and cameramen and press just standing there in the middle of the walkway, doing interviews as people hustled around.

Rocco reached down and gripped my hand. "Are you ready?"

Fuck no. Was it too late to go home and splash around in the pool with Bobbi-June, or maybe snuggle with the guys on the bed?

I didn't say any of that, though. "Yep, I'm ready!"

He raised an eyebrow as if to call bullshit, but squeezed my hand. Rafa took up my other side, and as soon as one of the cameras spotted us, a buzz rippled through the crowd.

Someone with a long camera stopped in front of us. "Rocco! It's good to see you. Can I just grab a quick photo?" Rocco merely lifted his chin, wrapping an arm around my waist, his fingers curling possessively on my hip. "Is this the new wife?"

He was talking about me like I wasn't there. Or like I was a blow-up doll that Rocco was merely preventing from blowing away in the sea breeze.

"This is Tally Palmer-Passero, yes."

The photographer snapped a few more pictures, but Rocco was already leading me away. We must have stopped and posed at least six more times before we came across a driver giving an interview.

"...the conditions are perfect and we'll try to—holy shit, it's Rocco Passero." The driver grinned, and I realized it was Harry Weiss, one of the British drivers. "How are you doing, man?"

Rocco gave him a genuine smile and a bro-hug. "Good, good."

Harry turned back to the guy giving the interview.

"Only reason I podiumed last race is because this guy defected to the US. We'll catch up later, yeah?" Harry asked, and Rocco nodded.

We continued down the track, getting closer to the garages. More people came out to talk to Rocco, as well as Rafa, who I'd found out worked for the Teams Association. I was relegated to the background, but Rocco kept me close. If he wasn't wrapped around me, he was holding my hand tightly. I didn't know if I was offering him support or if he was offering it to me, but either way, we remained connected, no matter who we spoke to.

It was going fine, until we got to the area around Rocco's old team. That part was nearly painful, as the mechanics gave sad little waves like children in a messy divorce. These people would've been with Rocco through most of their careers, and I could only imagine how awkward it was to have to turn your back on someone you considered a friend. Not everyone was as loyal as Hayes, who'd quit over my former team's treatment of me.

But on the flipside, Hayes hadn't been getting paid the insane amount of money these mechanics were raking in every year. I didn't blame them for their choices really, though I did think it made them chickenshits.

Rocco's jaw was tense, and I just wanted to hug him. So I did, wrapping my arm around his waist and dragging him close. "I'm sorry."

He kissed the top of my head. "I'm not. It was meant

to be." Rafa suddenly reappeared beside us, his posture stiff as he stared down the paddock. I searched the crowd, and tensed too.

Mattias and Lucia Christian were swanning up the paddock, Mattias signing autographs and smiling like a politician. Lucia posed for photos, but was firmly relegated to the background, a pretty ornament for Mattias.

Rafa said something stern to Rocco in Italian, and it didn't take a cunning linguist to know that he was telling him to be cool and not to throw any punches. We continued walking; I was kind of hoping that we'd pass like ships in the night, but I should have known better.

The journalists in the area saw their opportunity and began to shout both their names. Mattias's eyes whipped up and found Rocco, his gaze then traveling down to our clasped hands, and his lip curling before he straightened it back into its generic smile. He grabbed Lucia by the waist and paraded her over to us.

"You've got this," I murmured to Rocco, squeezing his hand in support. "You're the better man." He looked down at me, and there was no faking the look of love on his face.

"Passero. It's good to see you." Mattias Christian spoke with about as much enthusiasm as I did at the doctor's office before a pap smear.

"Christian." It was short and laced with so much venom, it was a wonder the other man didn't drop dead. Rocco turned toward Lucia, his face softening slightly. "Lucia. You look lovely."

He wasn't wrong; Lucia Christian was gorgeous.

Tall and lithe, she looked like a Mediterranean beauty queen. Her hair fell down her back like warm, liquid chocolate. Her eyes were like sparkling gold gems. Her teeth were perfect. I was inconsequential in the face of her beauty.

But behind that perfection, you'd have to be blind to miss the dead look in her eyes. I'd thought Rocco had been exaggerating, but there was no way people looked at Lucia Christian and thought she was happy. She was a doll. A beautiful trophy, but probably not as well cared-for by her husband.

"Thank you, Rocco." She turned to me, her eyes flicking over me quickly, envy crossing her features. "This is your wife? I saw all over social media that you were married, but I'm not sure I believed it until now."

Mattias looked at me appraisingly, giving me a smarmy smile as he put out his hand for me to shake. Or maybe to kiss his rings—he had the same level of imperiousness about it. "Lovely to meet you. You are beautiful. Passero, you're a lucky man."

Incredibly aware of the cameras, I shook his hand quickly and resisted the urge to wipe my palm on my satin pants.

"Tally's beauty is the least of her defining qualities. She's strong and a talented racer in her own right." Rocco looked at me lovingly, and I felt myself flush. "We best get to the hospitality tents. Have a great race today," he said lightly, though you'd have to be an idiot to miss the dark undertones of the statement.

Mattias nodded. "Thanks. The team is good this year—very competitive with the new cars and fresh blood." He threw the barbs like they were poisoned darts.

Oh no, he didn't.

I smiled kindly at him. "I love your optimism. We're only a race or two into the season, and I'm sure that the whole team is aiming for some better results than, ah… what were you in the last race?" I looked up at Rafa, who had a brow raised in my direction as I defended his brother. "P9?" Rafa nodded at me, but didn't say anything. "I'm sure you'll find your feet. We all know it's hard when there's a shift in driver talent within the team. Klaus's P5 was quite good, though; you're right about that. I don't see him being in the second seat for much longer."

Yeah, I'd been paying attention, even if Rocco wanted to pretend this part of his life didn't exist anymore. A petty part of me wanted to see his team suffer for what they did to him, and apparently, if there was a Petty Fairy Godmother, she was making all my wishes come true.

Rocco worked very hard to keep the smirk off his face, but couldn't keep it from his eyes. "We best go. Christian. Lucia." He stepped around them, and as we continued to move down the track toward the Paddock Club, he lifted our clasped hands to his lips. "Fuck, you're so beautiful when you verbally take down grown men." He kissed me deeply. "When we get home, I'm going to show you just how much I enjoy it. I want you screaming my name so loud, everyone will know you belong to me."

I smirked up at him. I'd have his back, for now and for always.

FORTY-FOUR

JESSE

THE GRIP TALLY had on my cock was going to drive me crazy. I clutched her hips, staring at the place where our bodies met, watching my cock slide in and out of her like the most filthy ASMR. Except the only thing tingling was my balls as they pulled up tight. I was going to blow, but I wasn't ready for this to end.

Her fingernails pierced my skin, scraping raw lines that I knew I'd feel all day, which would send me back to this very moment when she was bouncing on top of me, her breathy little moans driving me to the brink and back again. I had to hold her still, deep breathing through the pleasure, so I didn't embarrass myself by unloading deep inside her before she'd even gotten off.

I ran my thumb around her hips and over her clit, using our combined rhythm to maintain the pace as I fucked up inside her.

"Fuck, Jesse. More. I need just a little more. I'm so

close," she panted, and I gripped her hips and thrust wildly, aiming for so deep that she'd taste me on the back of her tongue. I mean, I knew that's not how biology worked, but we all needed goals in life.

Her tits bounced, sweat making her skin glow, and I had to close my eyes before the visuals had me toppling over the edge. I recounted all the different parts of a bike, holding off my release for just a second or two longer, and then another second more, until she was fluttering around me, my name somewhere between a moan and a yell as she climaxed like some kind of beautiful goddess.

Finally able to let go, I gave some rough, deep thrusts as if I could bury myself in her soul through my dick, groaning my release as I shot my load deep inside her. I fucking loved the primal feeling of unloading in my girlfriend, inside the love of my life. My hindbrain that controlled my cock didn't understand that we couldn't really get her pregnant, and luckily, there wasn't a whole lot of higher reasoning going on when Tally was riding me.

She flopped down on my chest, her body heaving as she sucked in lungfuls of air. I stroked my hand up and down her back. "Uh-oh."

She lifted her head. "Uh-oh what?"

"Look at the time."

As if on cue, Hayes hollered at her from downstairs. He was a hollerer. It was from living with a bunch of sisters—I'd met them, and I could promise you, if you weren't shouting in their household growing up, you weren't going to be heard.

"Tally, let's go! We're going to be late!"

I sighed and kissed both her cheeks. "Come on, before Hayes gets his panties in a twist." Shooing her into the bathroom to wash up quickly, I picked out her favorite work uniform: a VANT Racing polo and a pair of well-worn dark jeans that cupped her ass like my hands loved to do.

When she emerged from the bathroom a couple of minutes later, you'd never guess that I'd just fucked her within an inch of my life a moment ago. She looked so put-together that I wanted to drag her back to bed and ruin it all over again.

"Stop looking at me like that," she groaned, coming over to kiss me as she threw on her clothes. "Hayes will have a coronary if we're late again."

I pouted, but didn't protest. I just watched her get dressed, like this was a reverse strip show. She stopped and eyed me suspiciously. "What?"

Shrugging, I picked at my nails, like I wasn't thinking completely debaucherous thoughts. "Oh, I was just realizing that my cum will be dripping from you all day."

She came to lean across my lap, straddling my thighs. "You like that idea, don't you? Marking me so everyone knows I'm yours?"

Fuck. If she didn't stop right now, I was going to have an uncomfortable boner that I'd need my own cold shower to hide.

Grinning because she knew she had the upper hand, she slid from my lap and held out a hand. "Come on, handsome. Let's go find the others."

Bobbi-June wasn't in her room, so I assumed she was already downstairs with the guys. This was confirmed when I saw Hayes feeding her a bottle on the couch.

"We have that nine a.m. meeting, so we'll have to hustle." He stood, still feeding the baby as he handed her over to me. Rocco kissed Bobbi-June's head, then handed Tally a coffee in a travel mug, as well as a muffin.

"I thought you may be hungry after your morning workout," he said with a wink, and I grinned smugly.

Popping Bobbi-June over my shoulder, I burped her as I followed everyone to the door. "Have a good day," I called as they walked down into the garage, climbing into the monstrous Lincoln SUV that Rocco had bought Tally so she could return her loan car back to VANT Racing. It could fit us all very comfortably if we needed to go somewhere together.

Rocco had also gotten me a Volvo so I could drive around with Bobbi-June, because it was safer for the baby than my truck. I hadn't even protested, because there was very little I wouldn't do to keep Bobbi-June safe, and on that, both Rocco and I could agree.

Did it make me feel like a kept woman? Maybe a little. But honestly, who the fuck cared?

"Okay, kiddo, what's on the agenda today? I think we

should watch that show with the dogs first, then breakfast, and then we might head out to look at a place I want to flip out near Palo Alto. And then, we might go to the grocery store and buy some stuff for Dada Hay-Hay's homemade chili for dinner and see how tough Papa Rocco is, hey? That stuff will put hairs on your chest." Junie gurgled happily, and I laughed. "You little troublemaker. I love it."

After I made myself a coffee in my travel mug, we sat down to watch a colorful show about Australian dogs, then another one with a woman in a bright pink shirt and some dungarees. At nearly four months, I felt like Bobbi-June paid better attention to things around her now, and I wasn't sure if that was advanced or not, but it *felt* advanced. A few short weeks ago, she'd basically been a fragile little potato that cried and pooped and slept. Now she smiled at me, and it was the greatest feeling in the world.

"You're the cutest baby in the world, do you know that? I bet you do." Sliding her up and into my arms, I grabbed the morning dishes and stacked them in the dishwasher. The housekeeper didn't come until tomorrow, and we'd quadrupled her cleaning quota so I tried to help out at least a little. "Okay, let's go get dressed and get on with the day, Junie."

I'd just put her in a tiny little yellow dress, with a pair of striped pink tights and a sweater when my phone rang. I wiggled it out of my pocket to see an unknown number lighting up the screen.

"Hello?"

"Hello, is this Jesse Banks?" an official-sounding voice asked from the other end of the line.

I juggled Bobbi-June into one arm so I could clutch the phone tighter to my ear. "Yeah, speaking?"

"This is Officer Chrissimos of the Redwood City Police Department. There's been an accident."

FORTY-FIVE

TALLY

"DO you think we should look into getting daycare or something for Bobbi-June? Just, like, a day or so a week, so Jesse can have some time off? He can go out and do stuff he likes to do, maybe ride his bike or something? I feel like I've trapped him at home. Maybe I should talk to Antony about working from home one day a week."

I was sitting in the back of the giant Lincoln, glad that Rocco was driving it. The thing was like a tank and almost impossible to park, not that I'd ever admit that out loud.

Rocco shrugged. "He seems to enjoy it. I caught him watching that kids' program with the dogs the other day while Bobbi-June was asleep."

Hayes snorted in the passenger seat. "It is pretty funny. But you can always ask him. Besides, we both know if you stay home and look after Bobbi-June one day a week, Jesse isn't going on rides anywhere. If anyone will be riding, it'll be you."

I laughed, but Hayes was probably right.

"I could always look after *Bambolina* a few days a week. It will give me a good reason to tell my agent no. I do enjoy that," Rocco said wistfully. I didn't envy his PR firm. Some days, I wondered if we should send them chocolates and a condolence card.

We'd started a little late today, and the traffic was insane. There was a pileup on the freeway, so we were going the back way to East Palo Alto.

Nodding, I slumped back in the seat. "We'll talk to him tonight. Man, we are going to be late. My bad." I didn't actually regret it, though, because that thing Jesse did with his tongue was totally worth it.

Rocco cursed as the railway crossing boom gate came down and we didn't make it across. I texted Antony that we'd be a couple of minutes late for the meeting, due to the traffic. I mean, traffic *was* a contributing factor. The other factor was Jesse's dick, but that was a far less socially acceptable excuse.

Traffic built up behind us, and I sighed. I missed Miami and the sun.

Rocco looked in the mirror with a frown. "This guy behind me is right up my ass." He hit the brakes a couple of times in warning, muttering swear words in Italian. For a professional driver, Rocco had a fair amount of road rage. He always protested that it was the Italian passion, but I just thought perhaps he'd spent too long being chauffeured around places.

"Yeah, the only person allowed to ride that ass is—"

The truck behind us suddenly rammed forward,

rear-ending us with so much force that my head snapped forward before my seatbelt locked and flung me back. It also pushed us through the boom gate onto the tracks, the airbags deploying with violent speed.

The next ten seconds happened so slowly, it was like a horror movie. Deployed airbags pushed Hayes and Rocco back in their seats, and the car turned off. The train horn blared through my brain like an echo of death, the sound so loud I couldn't think. Hayes was shouting at me to get out, even though we all knew there was no time. I couldn't even find my belt buckle before the rattling noise of a hurtling train was piercing my eardrums.

I screamed, but you couldn't hear it. There was just the crunch of metal and glass, and my head slamming into the window, sending everything black.

I opened my eyes again to yelling and screaming. Sirens in the distance made me squint as a hand reached through the glass. "She's alive. Help me get her out!" someone yelled, and I distantly thought they were talking about someone else.

Was someone else in the accident? Rocco. Hayes.

"Help," I moaned, the world dimming at the edges.

A woman's face came into my view. "Hey, it's okay. Stay with me." She had a nice face. Maybe she was a guardian angel. I needed one of those. But at least Bobbi-June wasn't in the car.

"My name is Malia. What's your name?" the angel asked.

"Tally," I groaned out. Fuck, it felt like my whole body was bruised. I could hear other people talking, but I didn't recognize any voices. "Hayes. Rocco. Are they okay? My husband?"

"Everyone is gonna be fine, Sugar. Just you wait there and be still. Does anything hurt?"

I did the assessment I'd done every time I crashed in NASCAR. Could I wiggle my toes? Yes. That was good. I could take a deep breath, but while my body felt sore to move, nothing felt broken. "I think I'm okay. Sore."

"I bet you're sore. It'll be all right. Help is coming right now."

Finally, someone appeared, gently moving Malia out of the way. "Miss, my name is Chadwick and I'm from the fire department. I'm just going to put this collar on you as a precaution."

"Okay. Can you see my partners? Hayes? Rocco?" I yelled for them, but there was no response. Dread made my gut sour. "*ROCCO! HAYES!*" I yelled louder, but Chadwick the paramedic hushed me.

"It's okay. My colleagues are taking care of them, I promise. What's your name?"

"Tally. Tally Palmer-Passero."

"All right, Tally. You know what year it is?"

"2024."

"How about the day?"

"Monday."

Chadwick listened to my chest. "That's great. Good

work, Tally. Any pain?" I answered his questions, but I kept trying to look into the front seats. All I could see was crumpled metal. "We're going to send you to hospital for scans, but you're extremely lucky."

Someone got out a machine that popped the doors off the car, and they pulled Hayes out the passenger side. "Hayes!"

His face was coated in blood, and he had a collar on his neck too. "Tally," he breathed, before his eyes closed again. I tried to stand, to go to him, but Chadwick pushed me back down.

"He's okay. He's going to the same place as you, and they'll let you know when they know more. Now, let's get you on the board and into the bus."

They were still working on the driver's door, and I wanted to vomit when I saw it. It was completely caved in, like a monster had put his foot through it. "Rocco," I breathed. But then Chadwick was shutting the doors and driving away.

"You have to tell me about my husband, Rocco Passero," I asked the nurse for the hundredth time.

She patted my hand. "He's in surgery, but it's going well. I promise you, Mrs. Passero, as soon as I know more, I'll let you know."

Hayes was in the room next door to me, with three broken ribs, a fractured tibia and a concussion. But he was alive. He would heal. They wouldn't let me see him, but I knew he was okay.

I heard shouting from the halls, and then Jesse was in my room. "Sir, you can't—Sir, that's the wrong room!"

Jesse burst toward me with a wild and frantic look in his eyes, and Bobbi-June in her carseat, frowning, her lip jutting out like she was about to cry. "Tally," he breathed, coming over to the bed and kissing me firmly.

"Mr. Banks, the person we contacted you about is one room over." A pissy nurse, not mine, appeared in the doorway. She blurred in and out of focus, and I realized I was crying.

"This is my partner. That's my baby."

My nurse looked so confused. "Your husband is in surgery." She was definitely going to give me another cognitive test, like I'd lost my mind.

I nodded, pointing to the next room. "That's right. And the guy in there is my partner too. Jesse, please, go check Hayes is okay. I need to know."

He nodded, not asking any more questions as he disappeared into the room next door, taking Bobbi-June with him. The ER administrator who'd chased him down followed along with a sigh.

My nurse came in and took my blood pressure once more. "I think, perhaps, you're going to have to explain it to me slowly. So the guy who just left is…"

"My boyfriend. Well, more than that. My partner. It's not a throwaway thing."

"And the guy next door?"

"Same thing. Also Jesse's best friend, which is why he was his emergency contact and not me yet. We didn't expect…" I choked back the sob that wanted to bubble out. "We didn't expect something like this to happen."

The nurse patted my hand. "Of course not. Now, the guy in surgery, Rocco Passero, he's your…"

"Legally wedded husband. I can only marry one of them, but if I could, I would marry all of them."

The nurse nodded, adjusting everything. "I don't blame you," she said conspiratorially. "We're just waiting for your scans to come back, but everything looks good."

I still didn't know what had happened. One second, we'd been waiting for a train to pass, and the next, we were on the tracks and in its path.

My brain was given the all-clear, and my nurse walked me next door into Hayes's room, giving me another chair even though it was against policy. He looked way worse than me, his face all swollen and a cast on his leg. I burst into tears.

"Fuck, Tally. Fuck. I'm so thankful you're okay," he breathed, though it was slurred because his face was swollen. "Come here." I gently laid my head on his, trying not to touch him too much and hurt him more than he'd already been hurt. "I heard you yelling about Rocco. Any word?"

I shook my head, the hollow pain in my chest making me fear the worst. I looked over at Jesse, who was holding Bobbi-June, though the baby was still frowning. I kissed her face over and over and over as I cried. It had been so fucking close. So close.

"I love you, baby. So, so, so much. Both of you." I

shifted to kissing Jesse, and he returned it with the taste of fear and pain on his lips. He looked like he'd aged a hundred years.

"I'll take her outside and feed her, and call Rafa. Rocco's family will want to know what happened and that he's in surgery."

I nodded, kissing him hard on the lips once more. "Call Will and Colin too." He stood, and even just the idea that they'd be out of my sight made anxiety climb up my throat. "I love you so fucking much, Jesse," I told him. I would tell him every two minutes, because for a split second, there'd been a chance I could never tell him again.

Just as he stood, two uniformed cops knocked at the door. "Tally Palmer-Passero? Hayes Davis?" I nodded. "We'd just like to ask you a couple of questions."

FORTY-SIX
ROCCO

I FOUGHT my way out of the darkness slowly. Someone was praying over me, and I followed along in my mind, more out of habit than anything. When I blinked my eyes open, Mamma was standing over me, rosary beads in hand.

"Mamma?" Fuck, my body hurt. Maybe I was dead.

She crossed herself. "*Grazie a Dio.* Rocco!" She kissed all over my face, like I was a tiny boy again. "I've been so worried. They said you would wake, but then nothing. You just sleep on and on and on. Let me get the nurse." She pressed the button on the wall, still thanking God.

A nurse appeared with a smile. "Good to see you awake, Mr. Passero."

I was in a hospital room—that was obvious—and it was filled with flowers. But no Tally. "Mamma, where's Tally?"

Mamma frowned. "Who?"

I tried to sit up, and pain raced up and down my body like a whip. "Tally, Mamma. My wife. Where's my wife?"

It was coming back to me now, like a horror sequence in an action film.

The train.

Her screams.

The roof of the car crumpling in on me.

The nurse pursed her lips in my mother's direction. "Easy, Mr. Passero. Your wife has just gone home to shower and sleep. She'll be back soon. She hasn't left your bedside."

"She's okay?"

The nurse smiled. "She's okay. Banged up, but miraculously uninjured. The other gentleman, Hayes…" She flushed pink. Clearly, Hayes was pretty handsome in that All-American kind of way. "He has a fractured leg and more than a few busted ribs, but he's also okay. Your wife tells me he's at home recuperating."

"Yes, your wife's other boyfriends are all fine, *Tesoro Mio*."

Is it too late to pretend to be in a coma again?

I sighed. "Not now, Mamma."

Rafa came into the room, pulling up in surprise when he saw me with my eyes open. "About time you woke up from your nap, brother." He strode over and kissed both of my cheeks. "You scared the shit out of all of us there."

Sucking in a shaky breath, I just wanted to hold

Tally, but it was probably best to get this all out of the way before she came back. "What happened?" I looked down at my body, at my broken hands and my leg in a cast.

It was Rafa who answered. "You got the brunt of the train. You'd taken your seatbelt off, which was probably what saved you, but your big head was what broke Hayes's ribs. It was also lucky that the airbags had already deployed, because it cushioned you all a little. You broke your left hand and wrist, and your right leg. They said it was lucky that you have such great neck muscles, or you would have snapped your neck. You did have some swelling on the brain, and they put you under to allow it time to heal." He shook his head. "How you all got out of there alive is nothing short of a miracle."

Mamma sent up a prayer of thanks again.

"We were waiting. We got rear-ended onto the tracks." It was hazy. So fucking hazy.

Rafa nodded. "The cops have come by a couple of times, and now that you're awake, they're going to want to talk to you. Tally was awake for nearly all of it, so she filled them in on most of the accident. You'll just have to corroborate."

"It was an accident?"

His jaw tightened. "They aren't treating it as such."

I blinked at him. Maybe my brain was still sluggish. "Are you saying someone tried to kill us?"

He shrugged. "The police are treating it as a malicious event. From what Tally says, the eye witnesses

said there was a truck that rear-ended a car three vehicles behind you. They said it didn't even try to slow or
stop. If anything, it sped up. It injured the people in the
two cars behind you too, but not quite as badly as you
guys."

I was being dragged back down into the darkness
again, and the more I struggled, the harder it was to
stay awake.

"Sleep, Rocco. Heal," Mamma murmured, and just
like when I was a baby, her voice sent me off to sleep
again.

The next time I woke, it was to raised voices.

"No offense, Mrs. Passero, but I'm sitting beside my
husband. Why don't you go back to the hotel and rest?"

Mamma made a rude noise. "What, so you can
finish the job? Kill him for his money? American
women…. I've seen the late-night shows."

A sigh reverberated around the room. "Mamma,
please. There's a difference between murder documen-
taries and real life. Come back to the hotel with me so
we can rest." Rafa sounded exhausted.

I blinked my eyes open to see Tally, her face battered
and bruised, standing toe-to-toe with my mother. Actually, Mamma was a full four inches shorter than Tally,
but she made up for it in… personality.

"Tally," I mumbled, and every face in the room
snapped toward me.

Tally dodged my mother and was at my bedside in

an instant. "Rocco." She leaned forward and kissed me softly. "I was so fucking worried," she swore softly, probably so my mother couldn't hear. "Your mom scares the shit out of me."

I chuckled, because if I was honest, Mamma scared the shit out of me too. "You're really okay? Hayes?"

She nodded, her eyes wet with tears. "We're all fine."

I tried to lift my hand to cup her cheek, but winced. That's when I remembered how fucked I was. "But not perfect?"

This time, she did cry. She laid her head on my chest and just wept.

"*Stellina*, my love, don't cry. It'll be okay. I'll heal."

Rafa, who was a sucker for women's tears too— maybe it was hereditary—rubbed her back while Mamma huffed. "He'll be fine. We got the best surgeon in to repair his hands and wrist. His leg is pinned, and with a little rehab, it'll be fine too."

Well, that's good to know. I breathed a sigh of relief that my career wasn't over, though when I'd woken up and Tally hadn't been in the room, my career had been the last thing on my mind.

She shook her head, not lifting her face from my chest. "You don't understand. It's my fault."

I looked up at Rafa, who shrugged. "What do you mean, Tally?"

She met my gaze, guilt sitting in heavy, dark circles under her eyes. "The cops, they said that the truck had been stolen earlier in the day from around our area.

That the truck followed down the motorway behind us. That it had rammed us onto the train tracks, in front of a train, on purpose."

My mind whirled about what she was saying. Was it a deranged stalker? An angry fan? A jilted ex? Who would do such a thing?

And even as I thought it, as I took in Tally's devastated face, I knew. "No. He *wouldn't.*"

I didn't know the man, not like Tally and Hayes did, but I knew his reputation. He was a shark, and he liked to color a little outside of the lines, but to resort to murder? Unlikely.

She was nodding, as she pulled back to stand up. "The detectives are fairly certain he did. The detective told me he believed Brick Willtot hired some kid, promised him a seat in NASCAR and more money than this kid had ever seen, and told him all he'd have to do was ram us into a wall, or off a bridge, or into traffic or something. An accident—that's what he wanted. The kid ad-libbed a little when he saw the train, and panicked, rear-ending a car at the back, causing a chain reaction that led to us on the tracks."

She swallowed hard. "That's what the kid told the police after they picked him up. Brick is categorically denying ever meeting the guy, or knowing him at all."

I shook my head, feeling like I'd woken up in the twilight zone. My brain was sluggish, and my heart was thundering so fast, it felt like it would fly right out of my chest. She was backing away now, back toward the door.

"*Stellina*, come back here," I ordered, as my chest got tight. But she continued backwards.

She shook her head. "No. Until Brick is behind bars, I'm going to tell the world that we're getting a divorce. He won't have a reason to come after you then." She licked her lips. "I'm going to take Bobbi-June away for a little while, until the cops figure everything out."

"Tally, *no.*"

"Not forever, I promise. We aren't really breaking up. I love you." She choked out the words on a sob. "But you almost *died*, Rocco. You almost died because of me, Hayes almost died because of me, and this time, Brick would be right—it would be all my fault." She let out a pained gasp. "As soon as the detectives tell me they have enough to arrest him, I'll come back, I promise."

She ducked out of the room, and I threw a helpless look at Rafa. "Go after her. Talk some sense into her or something!"

My brother gave me a curt nod and disappeared into the hallway behind my wife. She wouldn't be my ex-wife *ever*.

"Maybe this is for the best, *Tesoro Mio.*"

I growled in my mother's direction. "She's the love of my life, Mamma. Learn to live with it or go home." I closed my eyes, like I could block out the pain that had nothing to do with my damaged body. "I'm tired. I'm going to sleep."

I closed my eyes, but Tally leaving just played over and over in my mind.

FORTY-SEVEN

TALLY

WITH THE BABY hooked over one arm and the phone pressed to my ear, I just felt tired. So fucking tired. "Thank you again for this," I said to the person on the other end. "I know this probably seems insane, but I just needed somewhere no one would find me, you know?"

Charlotte chuckled darkly. "Don't even stress it, girl. If anyone knows anything about having psycho exes, it's me." There was history there, and normally, I'd want to know. But right now, I was at capacity for drama with my own bullshit. "Besides, that apartment is just sitting there empty, so you're doing us a favor really."

I'd sent a message to Charlotte in the hopes she could help me out, which, now that I thought about it, was stupid. But it had paid off.

Shaking my head, I tuned back into her words down the phone. "Now, Pieter is the doorman, and he'll help you take your stuff upstairs. I'm going to tell you the code to get in the door, and you can't forget it, all right? But you also can't write it down; that's not very secure. If you forget, call me and I'll remind you, or talk to Pieter and he'll walk you through resetting it."

I would not cry. I would not cry.

Finnegan, the absolutely giant bodyguard Rocco had insisted I have, hulked behind me. The guy was easily forty, but he had muscles on his muscles. He did nothing for me, though I appreciated his presence when I jumped at shadows in the parking garage.

"Thanks, Charlotte. And thank the guys too."

I hung up and typed the code into the door. It popped open like magic, and I breathed a sigh of relief. I wasn't leaving this apartment until Brick Willtot was no longer a threat. The detective had assured me that it would be over soon, that they were compiling irrefutable evidence, but I couldn't help looking over my shoulder.

Finnegan checked out the apartment, before he put my suitcase in the bedroom. "I'll go and get the rest of the stuff from the car. Don't open the door for anyone, okay?" Something about Finnegan gave me safe vibes. Maybe it was the completely impartial way he looked at me. I'd seen that look before, as a teenager, with my best friend.

Nodding, I waited until he'd left to flop down onto the couch and unbuckle Bobbi-June from her carrier. Propping her against the cushions, I kissed her tiny feet.

"It's just for a little while, baby. And then we'll go back and see your daddies."

Her sparkling blue eyes gave me a concerned look, as she looked around the room. Obviously, she wasn't really concerned, because she had no idea that her biological grandfather was trying to kill me.

This apartment was furnished with high-end stuff, and I was already worried about ruining it with assorted baby vomit. Or one of those poo explosions, like last month, which had traumatized us all, including Norton the dog.

"We're just going to hang out, have a girls-only holiday and hope for the best. First, I have to call my boss and tell him I'm on the run. Should be fine, right? I'm definitely not getting fired."

Bobbi-June looked skeptical and sucked on her fist.

Antony answered on the second ring. "Tally, are you okay?"

I let out a choked, bitter laugh. "I'm fine. I'm sorry to run out on you like this, especially when you're already down a driver, but I'm going to need a little bit of time off."

There was silence at the end of the line, and I could hear Antony standing and shutting his office door. "Are you safe?"

I didn't deserve this man's kindness. "I'm safe. I, uh, I don't know what Hayes or Rocco told you—"

"They told me that Brick Willtot has lost his godforsaken mind and that you've... left to keep them safe.

That's very noble, Tally. A little silly, but noble all the same."

I made a rude noise, my emotional turmoil apparently making me stupid. "Like you wouldn't do the same if someone was threatening Vanessa, or any of the guys."

"Touché, kid. Your job is here, once that whackjob is behind bars." He paused. "You should have come to me, come to us. We would have kept you safe." His voice was soft and kind, but the idea of putting them in danger too made me want to vomit.

I sucked in a shuddering breath. "Rocco made me get a big, hulking bodyguard, so I'm fine."

"Hopefully, you're back before next weekend, because we're going to need our reserve driver," he said pensively. "Don't worry about anything, Tally. You're part of the family here, and we've always got our family's back."

After we hung up, Finnegan and Pieter the doorman appeared with the rest of the baby stuff. Bobbi-June was too big for the bassinet now, but it would have to do for a couple of more weeks as we figured everything out.

Once I'd set everything up, I put her down for a nap and climbed into the bed beside her. I was exhausted, and I couldn't see it getting better anytime soon.

Three days later, I was going out of my brain for a whole different reason. I was still keeping in touch with the guys, sending little updates, but refusing to enter into any conversations about me coming home. I just promised I would, once this was all over.

I was also in contact with Willy, who was losing his absolute shit and not half as worried about chasing me off. He'd told me I was being damn stupid, that I could either tell him where I was or he'd hunt me down personally. Eventually, I'd had to cave and tell him where I was before he tore apart the whole town, looking for me.

Willy had no concept of boundaries when it came to the people he loved, and if I was being honest, I really needed someone. Finnegan was great, but in the same way that the fridge was great. Or the occasional lamp was great. He was there, doing his job, but his job wasn't to keep me entertained. It wasn't to hold the baby so I could take a pee. It wasn't any of that.

If I let one of the guys come over, not only was I painting a target on his back, but they'd all want to come over. And if that happened, I may as well have just gone home to Rocco's mansion.

Some days, I needed Willy. Willy had known me when I was a scared little kid, whose dad had just been stabbed in a carjacking and died. Willy had held me together when I realized I was an orphan with no friends. I loved my guys, with all my heart and soul, but sometimes, I just needed my best friend to hold me together and tell me everything was going to be okay.

Finnegan had not been impressed. But eventually, after I'd pulled an extremely diva-ish "I'm your boss and you do what I say" move, he relented. I felt like an asshole. I was not that person. But I needed my best friend right about now.

The knock on the door had Finnegan pulling his gun and directing me toward the master bedroom. I hoped it was Willy, but just in case it wasn't, I picked up Bobbi-June and hid in the bedroom.

"Who the fuck are *you?*"

The very clear baritone of Willy had me sighing with relief. Stepping out of the bedroom, I ran across the living room straight toward him, the baby clutched in my arms. He turned from trying to stare down Finnegan just in time to catch me.

"Aw, Tally." He didn't tell me it would be okay. He didn't tell me that he could make it all better. He just walked me backwards into the living room and hugged me and Bobbi-June tightly. "Who's the big, gay Goliath?" he murmured in my ear, probably to distract me from my crying, and I gotta admit, it worked. My eyes snapped toward Finnegan. I mean, I'd suspected, but it was interesting to hear it confirmed by Willy.

I pulled back, sniffling a little. "I'm sorry. Willy, this is my temporary bodyguard, Finnegan. Finnegan, this is Will, my best friend."

They continued to eye each other in some kind of macho standoff. I wasn't exactly sure who won, because Willy tore his focus back to me. "Rocco made you get security?" I nodded. "Good. I might forgive him one day for driving you in front of a train and halving my life expectancy. God, the idea of losing you, Tally. You're my best friend—you know that, right?"

I nodded again, snuggling into his chest and letting his comfort soothe me. He let me relax there for a little while, until finally, he let out a large sigh.

"Babe, I mean this in the nicest possible way, but you need to give me the baby while you go and have a long, hot shower. And I mean *long*. I'll make you dinner and feed this little cherub. You smell like an old bag of Doritos. Go take a minute to collect yourself."

I laughed, because that was such a bitch thing to say. Willy would always tell it to me straight.

"It's going to be okay, isn't it?" I asked him softly, my voice small and pathetic.

He wrapped an arm around my shoulders. "It's going to be okay. I promise."

FORTY-EIGHT

HAYES

THE DOWNFALL of Brick Willtot was almost anticlimactic.

After chasing off my girlfriend and nearly ending my life, Brick was picked up for conspiracy to commit murder on a Sunday morning, while he was asleep in his pajamas. His house was raided, and all sorts of shit was seized.

Nothing was a smoking gun, per se. There was no shrine to the baby, or photographs of Tally with her eyes scratched out, or anything like that. What they did find was a burner phone, the only number in the phone book being that of the kid who'd been charged with attempted murder.

According to the detectives, the only communication on it was a message from the kid, saying he wasn't sure he could do it. Brick had messaged back that the best NASCAR drivers were decisive. If he couldn't commit to his word, how could he commit to a team?

None of it said *Murder Tally Palmer to get a job,* but it was enough to charge him.

The final nail in Brick's coffin, however, was that the private investigator had come forward to say that Brick had offered him two million dollars to kill Tally and Rocco. With both witnesses corroborating, it didn't look good for Brick.

I hoped he rotted in the pits of Hell, personally.

The press had picked it up quickly, and there were news vans parked outside the gates of the community, which meant we were trapped here for a little while longer. I missed Tally with a physical ache that was far worse than the one in my ribs. We all did, and it was making us mean and testy. How Jesse hadn't smothered us both in our sleep was actually a miracle.

I rolled out of bed with a wince. I'd be glad when the ribs healed completely. Norton sat at the nursery door, whining softly. If I could have reached down and scratched his head, I would have. As it was, with the boot and the ribs, I couldn't do any more than rub my toes along his rump.

"Don't worry, boy. I'm going to get our girls today."

Some of my pining for her was negated by the fact that I knew wherever she was, she was safe. Rocco had hired some ex-mercenary to make sure no one got within ten feet of her or Bobbi-June.

Jesse was sitting on the couch when I walked into the living room, the television blaring. *"The charges laid against NASCAR giant Brick Willtot have shocked the motor racing world, with some coming out in support of the man, but many more condemning his actions."*

Ryker, my old boss, had been stopped outside his house, apparently. *"It's terrible, the whole situation. Brick has been suffering since the death of his son, and I hope that he gets the help he needs."*

Well, it wasn't an out-and-out condemnation, but I'd take it.

Jesse huffed, muting the TV. "I've been trying to call Tally all morning, but she hasn't answered." Fear and doubt crossed his face. "What if she doesn't come back?"

I shook my head. I refused to believe that. She would return now that it was safe. She loved us.

I patted his shoulder. This whole thing had been as hard on him as it had been on Rocco and I, even though he hadn't been injured. It was in the way he hovered around, and how he looked longingly in Tally's room or the nursery.

"We won't give her a choice. We'll show her how much we love her, and she'll come back to us. I better go check on Rocco."

Rocco's mom was in the kitchen, and honestly, I wasn't sure how I felt about her. It was obvious she loved her son, but she gave us suspicious looks all the time, like we were somehow waiting for him to die of surgical complications so we could steal his money.

I also didn't like the way she'd treated Tally. I knew it would take some adjustment—she was old, so the idea of one woman with several men would be as foreign as not asking to see the manager. But she'd have to get used to the idea, and damn quickly, because Tally loved Rocco, and I loved Tally. Her happiness was paramount to me.

"Good morning, Mrs. Passero."

She narrowed her eyes. "You need to explain."

Okay, so I talked a big talk, but as soon as she used that tone of voice, I wanted to say, "Yes, ma'am," and run in the opposite direction. "Explain what?"

"This *relationship* you have with my son and his wife."

Eesh. Was it too late to pretend my ribs were so sore I couldn't get out of bed? "Maybe that's a discussion you should be having with Rocco?"

She shook her head, waving a spatula at me. Whatever she was cooking smelled freaking amazing. She grabbed a plate and loaded it with biscotti, then shoved a coffee in front of me. "Eat." She turned back to the stovetop. "When I ask my son, he says, 'It's none of your business, Mamma. I don't want to talk about it, Mamma.'" She huffed. "Like it's bad that I want to know about how my baby lives his life! So you'll have to explain it to me."

It didn't sound like I had much of an option, and did I mention she was terrifying? "Uh, what exactly do you want to know?"

"It is best to start at the beginning, no?"

This is so fucking weird. "I met Tally back when she was a NASCAR driver. She was in love with another racer…"

I was on my second cappuccino and stuffed full of pastries by the time I got to the part where we'd all come to an agreement that we loved and respected each other enough to make sure that Tally was always loved and cared-for, as well as Bobbi-June.

The older woman looked pensive as she sipped her own coffee. "Marriage can be lonely. No one tells you that when it's you and him against the world, it is wonderful. But sometimes it's also you *against* him, and then who has your back? You're alone, and once upon a time, you were stuck."

I nodded like I could understand, but honestly, I couldn't. I was from the wrong generation, the wrong gender. I was well aware that I had life easier than so many people, just by some weird twist of fate.

"It still takes a lot of work, even more so because there's a lot of people with a lot of feelings that can get hurt. You have to put your pride aside a lot."

She nodded. "And the baby?"

I met her eyes, because I wanted her to know how serious my next statement was. "Bobbi-June is ours. She's Tally's biologically, but she's also mine, and Rocco's, and Jesse's. Each one of us wants to be a father to that baby."

"And future children?"

"They'll be ours too. Doesn't matter to me who they belong to genetically. I will raise them. Be their dad, regardless."

She straightened, running the cloth from over her shoulder across the counter to clean up the crumbs.

"Okay. Yes. What are you still doing here? Go and get my daughter-in-law and my grandbaby, so I can show them some love before I'm forced to go home. My husband does not do well on his own." That was a loaded statement I didn't really want to unpack. "He will probably starve to death if I don't return soon, and I'd like to get to know them first."

Nodding, I was already backing out of the room. "Yes, ma'am." I hobbled out of there as fast as my busted-up leg could carry me.

Jesse found me in the hallway, his eyes wide as he saw me traveling like the hounds of Hell were on my heels. "Everything okay?"

I shook my head. "Sorry. I got caught in the kitchen explaining polyamory to Mamma Passero."

He cursed beneath his breath. "Are you emotionally okay?"

I laughed, but it was a nearly hysterical sound. "I think I am. Call Will. I want my family back now."

I paced around the front foyer as I waited for Tally to arrive, and it was making my ribs ache. Jesse kept opening and closing his mouth as if he wanted to tell me to go back to bed, but then changed his mind.

I'd go back to bed when Tally could come with me.

Finally, an SUV pulled up in front of the house, and it was too much. I burst through the door and hobbled down the front steps, Jesse right beside me in case I pitched forward and ate gravel. I knew it was killing

Rocco to still be up in bed and not down here too, but he'd get his turn soon enough.

She burst out of the car and ran toward us, wrapping an arm around each of our necks, and I kissed every inch of her face I could reach. I had days worth of kisses that needed to grace her skin.

"God, I hated being away from you," she grumbled, holding us tightly. "It's finally all over."

Well, mostly. Brick had been remanded without bail, considered a flight risk, and was being extradited to California. There'd be a long-ass trial eventually, where he'd probably plead insanity and not get nearly long enough behind bars.

That was a future problem, and I didn't want to borrow tomorrow's trouble when we finally had the opportunity to be happy. She was back in my arms, and I wanted to drag in lungfuls of her scent. "I missed you *so fucking much.*"

A huge dude appeared—who must have been her security—as well as Will, who was carrying a sleepy baby. I held out my hands, and he handed her over. "Short Stack, I missed you!" I kissed Bobbi-June's chubby little cheeks, the ache in my side pushed to the background as I healed the ache in my heart.

Jesse and I swapped, and I went back to kissing my wife. Because legally, she mightn't be able to be mine but in my heart, she was it for me, forevermore. "I love you, Tally Palmer. I never want to be apart again."

She shook her head, her eyes shining with unshed tears. "Never again."

Jesse walked back up the steps, Bobbi-June clutched against his chest. "Welcome home." Stepping aside, he lifted his chin toward the stairs. Tally raced up to the second floor so fast, I was a little worried she'd miss a step and fall down. We followed along behind at a much more reasonable pace, mostly because getting up the stairs was slow as hell for me.

Jesse walked with me, making me feel all soft. "I don't tell you this enough, man, but I love you too. You're the best guy I know."

Giving me a crooked grin, he rolled his eyes. "One near-death experience, and he's finally in touch with his feelings." He slapped my back gently with his free hand. "I love you too, man. When I thought I'd lose you all…" He shuddered.

I couldn't imagine. That split second of panic when I woke up in the ambulance had been the worst. At least until they told me that Tally was okay. I couldn't even imagine what it would've been like getting a call like the one he'd gotten. It would have messed me up for good.

We finally made it to Rocco's room, and Tally was in bed beside him, clutched to his chest as he kissed her over and over again. I was kind of glad that Mamma Passero had gone back to her hotel.

"*Non posso vivere senza di te,*" he crooned at her between kisses. "I can't live without you, Tally Palmer-Passero."

She was crying softly now, but her smile was wide. "You'll never have to."

EPILOGUE

TALLY

"WELL, Frank, it's a beautiful day here in Long Beach, and the crowds are looking excited for a great day of IndyCar racing ahead."

"That's right, Steve. And some of that buzz is due to the brand new VANT Racing team. After all that nastiness that's been happening around their drivers, it's good to see them out here, getting on with business, even if their star driver is out for at least twelve weeks. But Tally Palmer-Passero has a good racing pedigree, and you can't argue with her qualifying times."

The interviewer nodded sagely. "They might not be Rocco Passero times, but they are pretty darn good for a driver on her IndyCar debut."

I tried not to eavesdrop, but they were literally standing right outside the garage.

"With Mickey Macguire finding his feet, I think the team might have a chance of getting some points, even without Passero there. How long until they become a three-car team, do you think, Frank?"

"They'd be crazy not to foster that talent. VANT is known for its fostering of women in sports, so I think we'll see a double Passero race team before long."

Pride flooded through my veins. Qualifying had been insane, and I'd been so nervous that I'd almost thrown up a kidney, but it was all fine in the end.

I tuned out the pundits and their kind words as I prepared for the race. I pulled my suit up, my last-minute sponsors on badges across my chest. Vanessa had gone to bat for me, approaching people to sponsor me, and I'd managed to secure three, one of whom was VANT Enterprises.

Surprisingly, there was also a bull's head logo, with the team at Dark Storm Rodeo Academy sponsoring me. Well, T.M. Moore was sponsoring me. An investment company in New York was another one, though I'd only met with a lawyer named Tobias Lecter to sign the contracts.

"Are you going to puke again?" a voice asked next to me, and I turned to smile at Hayes. He wasn't allowed to be in my pit crew today, but you couldn't have kept him from the garages if you tried.

I leaned into him. "Not yet, but it's still early days. Who knew I'd be back here?" I said lightly, like my stomach didn't feel fizzy and my heart wasn't about to beat out of my chest.

Hayes kissed me. "I knew, baby. I never had any doubt in my mind you'd be back here, better than ever." He kissed me softly. "I'm so fucking proud of you."

I shook my head, emotion choking me. "I wouldn't be here without you, Hayes." He opened his mouth to protest, but I put a finger over his lips. "No, it's true. I would have crawled into a hole and just existed, but my dream would be dead if it weren't for you. You believed in me when I didn't believe in myself. The best thing fate ever did for me was put you in my path." I kissed him hard. "I love you."

"I love you too, baby." He slapped me on the ass. "Now go out there and show them what they've been missing this last year. You've got this."

Sucking in a deep breath, I walked into the garage as they were wheeling the car out to its place for the anthem and the pre-race ceremonies. Ari Rome appeared in front of me, a frown on his face, but with a calm demeanor. I was pretty sure Ari had been frowning one day when the wind changed, and his face stayed like that, just like Mom always said it would.

"You good, Palmer?"

Nodding, I grabbed my helmet. "Yes, sir."

"Feeling confident?"

"Yes, sir."

"Good. Go out there and show them that you aren't just Rocco Passero's wife. Or Buck Willtot's girlfriend. You're a fucking competent driver with good instincts. You've got this."

I let out a shaky breath. Maybe I *did* need to puke. Honestly, if I didn't think I'd lose the tiny bit of respect

I'd just garnered, I might burst into tears. "Thank you, sir."

He gave a sharp nod. "Go smile for the cameras and then eat these fuckers for dinner."

I moved out of the garage, toward the straight. I signed hats thrust my way and took selfies with fans, and it was a heady experience.

"Excuse me, Miss, can you sign my baby?" I looked over and saw Jesse close to the wall, with Bobbi-June strapped to his chest. Beside him was Rocco in dark sunglasses and a cap, totally in incognito mode. Useless really, if you judged the side-eyes everyone in the crowd was giving him.

I shook my head. "I can't sign your baby, but I can give her a kiss." Kissing both of Bobbi-June's chubby cheeks, I soaked in their loving looks. I kissed Jesse too, then leaned over further and kissed Rocco.

The man in question frowned. "Don't forget to watch them coming into that first corner. They like to go wide and push you out."

"I know, Rocco."

"The brakes might lock up early too, because they'll be cold. Just keep it off the wall and it'll get easier."

I cupped his cheek. "I've got this."

He turned his face and kissed my palm. "This is far less stressful when I'm on the track."

Jesse laughed and patted his back. "Come on, man. We'll go get our seats. See you at the finish line, sweetheart."

I went and stood by my car after they rolled it into

the starting position in the pitlane, and a girl down the front sang the national anthem. I mouthed the words, but my brain was already running the track, thinking about the drivers in front of me and behind me.

Finally, it was done. Time to get my head in the game. Someone appeared with my earbuds, and I slipped them in. I did the tests and climbed in the car, letting them strap me in.

Antony appeared beside me, squatting down so he was eye height. "You got this?"

I gave him a crooked smile. "I was born for this."

He pulled my head sock down and laughed. "I know you were. Go out there and make us proud, kid."

Then I was one hundred percent a driver. The nerves disappeared as I ran through my lists. The car was started, and the pit crews moved back to safety. As we pulled out behind the pace car, I let myself feel the thrill of the adrenaline coursing through my veins.

This was for Bobbi-June.

For my dad.

For Hayes, who believed in me.

For Jesse, who supported me.

For Rocco, who challenged me.

But most of all, this was for *me*.

"Green! Green! Green!" The voice came through my earbuds.

It was time to race.

ABOUT THE AUTHOR

Grace McGinty is eclectic. She has worked as a chocolatier, a librarian, a forensic accountant, and finally, a writer. Like her professional career, the genres she writes are chaotic and out of control. From contemporary new adult to smutty reverse harem novels of every sub-genre, if you like it, she's probably written it.

Except dark romance. She's a marshmallow, and somehow the mean guys always end up cinnamon rolls.

Grace lives in rural Australia with her crazy family, an entire menagerie of pets, and will one day be crushed by the giant piles of books that litter every room.

Head over to www.gracemcginty.com and join the mailing list for sneak previews into what she is working on and to stay up-to-date with new releases and giveaways!

Want more badass women chasing their dreams? Turn over for a sneak peek of 8 SECONDS TO FLY: A Bull riding Romance

8 SECONDS TO FLY

CHAPTER ONE

"You're not supposed to be here, Nugget."

My bright pink Chucks were covered in dust, but I had my boots in my backpack. I wondered if I had time to put them on so when I kicked Branch Watson in the nuts, it'd hurt more.

"My name isn't Nugget, asshole," I replied through gritted teeth. Branch grinned, flashing perfectly straight white teeth that looked like they'd been selected from a catalogue. I hoped a horse kicked him in his perfect face so he wouldn't be so distractingly pretty anymore.

Me and Branch's teeth had a long history. In the third grade, he'd lost his two top front teeth because CJ Dempsey had called me a bitch. Branch hadn't liked that, because apparently he was the only one who was allowed to be an asshole to me. So they'd gotten in a fight and CJ had landed a good hit. A year later, I'd knocked his bottom two out with a rock.

Much like his teeth, me and Branch had a long and

complicated history that was basically intertwined since birth.

"I know your name, Tessa, but it doesn't change the fact that your daddy will kick your ass all the way to the border if he catches you back here. This is no place for girls and 'specially not you."

I shifted my duffle bag and glared. "Fuck you, Branch. I deserve to be here just as much as you. Maybe more. This," I waved a hand at the area behind the chutes. "This shit is in my blood."

"You shouldn't swear."

I flipped him the bird. "Eat a dick."

Finally the stupidly handsome boy in front of me lost his cocky grin, the frown on his brow chasing away his disarming dimples. "It's dangerous, Nugget."

I sighed at his use of my nickname again. I was never going to escape it. My dad had called me Nugget ever since I was a kid, because my hair was the distinct color of gold, and back then it had sat on top of my head in a riot of barely tamed curls. In the sun, it had looked like a, yep you guessed it, gold nugget. So Nugget had stuck.

It didn't help that Branch's dad and mine were best friends and business partners, so he'd always called me Nugget. I hadn't even minded until middle school, when I started to grow boobs and Branch and his friends had started calling them chicken nuggets. I hated him and his gorgeous damn face.

"You need to leave," he repeated like I hadn't heard him the first three times.

I clenched my jaw. "And you need to get the hell outta my way."

The atmosphere around us started to penetrate the red haze of my anger. The distinct scent of dust, sweat, and cow shit, so thick you could taste it on the air. The booming roar of the crowd and the slow drawl of the announcers were all drowned out by the snorts and grunts of the thousand pound beasts in the pens beside me. It was a symphony that I loved.

The rodeo. There was no other place like it.

I was born and raised at these events; took my first steps on this muck colored dirt. My first pet had been an eighty pound bull calf. It wasn't such a weird pet to have when your daddy bred bulls for the rodeo. Once he even had a bull that ranked in the WBRP, that was the World Bull Riding Professionals circuit. That bull's name had been *Dark Storm*, and he had been a beast in the ring. Outside the ring? Total softie. It happened like that sometimes though. Some of the animals just knew that they were there to perform and they stepped into the ring to play their parts like Oscar winning actors.

I'd been a kid when *Dark Storm* had made it big in the WBRP. I'd watched guys try to ride him, not even conquer him, but be one with him for all of eight seconds. That was when I knew that I wanted to be a bull rider. In the middle of the ring, just me and a beast made of nothing but pure muscle.

I'd been nine at the time.

Now, eight years later, stupid Branch Watson stood between me and my dream. I stepped around him, but he caught me by my waist. "The ring is no place for a woman. Turn that cute ass around and head back to the stands. You don't belong here." If he'd sounded smug or condescending, I'd have elbowed him in the balls and then stomped his pretty face. But his voice was full of concern, and that stilled my temper, just a little.

I gritted my teeth and jerked away hard, but Branch was strong. You had to be, to be a bull rider. He wrenched me back and not-so-gently slammed me into the wall of the pit beside me, pressing his whole body right along mine to keep me still. He may only have been 18 to my 17, but he had raw strength that I lacked, and I'd be damned if that didn't make me mad as hell.

It was better to be mad than the other emotion that was flowing through my veins right now. Fire burned in my belly that had nothing to do with my rage and everything to do with the fact that Branch Watson had his delicious body pressed against mine.

I didn't even have the good sense that God gave me to be fearful of the fact that a much larger, much stronger man had me trapped. Because I knew him as well as I knew myself. Branch was many things; arrogant, cocksure and sometimes a bit of a bully, but he would never raise a hand in violence to a woman, and especially not to me. His mother would castrate him publicly, his own father would kick his ass and mine would finish the job.

"If Daddy catches you pressed against me like this, me wanting to ride will be the last thing on his mind." My voice was unintentionally husky, and I watched

Branch's eyes hood. This was no longer Branch, the gapped toothed kid who'd chase me around with sticks when we were kids. No, this was Branch the man, and I wanted to simultaneously climb him like the tree he was named after, and run away screaming.

"Branch! Leeroy is callin' for you. You're almost up," someone yelled, and I subtly hid myself behind Branch's shoulders. If anyone else knew I was down here to ride, they'd share Branch's opinion on the matter. His eyes didn't leave mine, their normal sparkling blue now as dark and ominous as the sea. The look didn't scare me. I quirked an eyebrow at him and he made a frustrated sound deep in his throat.

Then he kissed me. A hard, punishing kind of kiss. No tenderness, just a shit load of frustration. He whirled away on his boots and left, striding down the path between the pens. I stood there gaping after him like a catfish out of water.

I don't know how long I stood there, staring in the direction I'd last seen him before Mickey stood beside me, clearing his throat. "Nugget," he hissed. "I did what you asked. You drew *Black Hurricane*. I mean, I drew *Black Hurricane*."

Fuck.

I shook my head, shaking away the fog of that damn kiss and looked over at Mickey. He was the same height as me, and he was weedy. I knew he was about due for his growth spurt, otherwise he might look like a bean pole forever.

I reached into my back pocket and pulled out a

hundred bucks. I'd paid Mickey to sign up for me because he had two advantages I didn't. One, he was eighteen and you had to be eighteen to ride at this event. Two, and the one that peeved me off the most, was that he was a boy. The misogynistic old bastards who ran this league didn't care that he was so weedy that he'd basically be a toothpick for a bull like *Black Hurricane*. As long he had a dingleberry that could flap in the breeze and the brass ones to sign up, he was good.

"Branch is right though, Tessa May. It is dangerous."

I rolled my eyes at him as I headed towards the livestock trailer that Daddy had brought the bulls in. In my duffle I had everything I needed to ride. It was time to prepare.

"I know how dangerous it is, Mickey. I've been sitting on top of bulls since before I could walk." Mickey followed along behind me, stuttering out protest after protest.

"I'll give you your money back, ya know. You don't have to do this."

I whirled around, smiling at Mickey because no matter how annoying his protests were, they were kind of sweet too.

"Thanks, but we had a deal, and an Everett never backs out of a deal. Just go home or hide or something Mickey, so you don't get spotted and all this is for nothin'.'"

Mickey looked like he wanted to protest more, so I do the only thing I can think of that would guarantee him leaving. I started undressing. By the time I pulled my shirt over my head, Mickey was gone.

I slipped on the clothes Mickey had loaned me. Ariat jeans that didn't cling to my ass too much and a loose chambray shirt that hid my boobs which I'd strapped down tight. Not that you'd be able to see them under my protective vest, but better safe than sorry. Between the vest and the helmet, I hoped no one would know I was not Mickey.

I attempted to strap on my chaps, wishing I hadn't sent Mickey away so fast when I had to basically twist like a pretzel to get the buckles at the base of my asscheeks done up. I put my plainest boots on, then slipped on the spurs I stole from Daddy. My vest and helmet went on last.

I looped my rope over the rail in the trailer and pull it tight so I can rosin it up. I'd practiced this a thousand times, hidden away in the barn. I knew every step back to front. I'd been goofing around with Branch and the other ranch kids for as long as I could remember, wrestling and riding young steers. I had this.

I huffed out a breath. I pinned my number, well Mickey's number, to my chest, and stepped out of the trailer. I stuck to the shadowy areas of the arena, and headed to the back of the chutes. I kept my head down, not even acknowledging the other riders as they paced and talked shit about drinking beer and getting laid at the bar later on. Because everyone wanted to ride a bull rider, right?

My height wasn't so out of place, because riders in

general weren't too tall. They were usually 6'1, like Branch, or under, and I was tall for a girl.

"Next up we have a local boy. Branch Watson. We gotta watch this kid, Earl, because if I've ever seen a contender for goin' pro, it's Branch," the announcer said over the PA.

"I agree, Tom. This boy has been riding bulls since he was in diapers. What he doesn't know about riding bulls probably ain't worth knowin'," Earl fired back.

They'd say that shit about me too, if I had a dick.

People bustled around the chute, there were at least four at all times, as Branch settled in. I had to watch, stepping out of my darkened corner for a second, seeing Branch sitting atop that ball of muscle and meanness.

He slammed his hat down on his head a bit better, and nodded to the latch guy. The bull bursts out of the gate in a twirling, twister of fury.

"Vickery," someone yells, but I don't take my eyes off Branch as he rides the bull like he's on the coin slot pony in front of the grocery store. So much damn natural talent. Fuck, I hated him.

"Vickery," someone yells again, and my eyes snap back to the Chute Boss when I realize he's calling for me. I'm Mickey Vickery, for today at least.

I raise my hand and the overweight and obviously stressed man waves me over.

"Your bull has been stalled. Get your rope on him."

I'd fixed my rope already. The joy of being the daughter

of a stock contractor was that I knew these bulls, these athletes on four legs, just as good, if not better than anyone. When girls were going crazy over the cowboys, I was always judging and appreciating the performance of the bull. *Black Hurricane* was one of ours, sired by *Dark Storm*. I'd watched him be trained, knew his moves, knew how he liked to spin, and what direction he liked to do it in.

I had this.

I tilted my hat lower as I stepped up to the chutes and a grizzled old cowboy helped me secure my rope over *Black Hurricane's* shoulders, pulling it tight. Hurricane didn't mind. He knew it wasn't time yet. He'd been around long enough to know he had to save it for the arena.

The crowd was going wild and I thanked the cowboy for his help. I saw Branch walking back, a grin on his too pretty face that gave him dimples as deep as wells.

I hid behind the chutes unashamedly. The bulls got corralled through into their chutes and my heart started to thud hard against my ribs.

This was it. A small, sane part of my subconscious told me that it wasn't too late to back out now. No one knew it was me. I wouldn't lose face.

Instead of running away, I squared my shoulders and slammed my helmet down on my head, obscuring my face. I tugged my vest, checking that it was strapped on tight.

I headed to chute one, my turn was coming up. My

destiny fucking awaited, and I was going to take it with both hands and my head held high.

I climbed up on the chute, running my foot over Hurricane's back to let him know I was coming. I settled in, and a hand behind me grabbed my vest.

I didn't look over my shoulder at them. I knew they were there to grab me up in case the bull did something crazy. They'd yank me out of there before I got crushed, if they needed to. As if he knew the direction of my thoughts, Hurricane kicked around in the chute, testing the metal. Hands dragged me up until I could get my feet back on the rails. Hurricane settled back down and I slid back on, running my hand over the rope to warm the rosin. I did the loop and nodded to the rope guy to pull tight.

He did, and I made the mistake of looking up to thank him. I met a pair of familiar warm whiskey eyes. Beau, Branch's long time best friend. My friend. Fuck.

He reared back in shock as recognition rocked through him, and I knew if he opened his mouth, I was fucked.

"Go!" I yelled at the gate man, and then it was eight seconds to fly or fall.

Hurricane burst out of the chutes, twisting to the left. I leaned into the movement, trying not to get sucked into the well. But Daddy bred his bulls well, and the strain on my arm was insane as I struggled to get my seat. I knew in another two rotations, *Hurricane* would stop and try and throw me forward. But *Hurricane* decided to fucking adlib today, rapidly changing direction and throwing me off the side.

I hit the ground with a thud, the wind getting knocked out of me even as hooves flew around my head. I scrambled to my feet, but *Hurricane* decided he was being ornery and had me in his sights. He ran after me, ignoring the bullfighters and charging after me. His giant head caught me in the ass and he flipped me like a rag doll. I knew how to fall, but I would never forget the faces of the crowd as I shot six feet in the air over the back of an enraged bull. I even saw Beau and Branch's faces on the way down, the horrified expressions would have been comical if I wasn't about to be severely injured.

Leaving my body loose, I still felt a pain in my shoulder as I landed hard on it in the sand. The clowns corralled *Hurricane* back through the gate, and then Branch and Beau were over the fence, running toward me.

I just laid there, staring at the sky. I'd done it. I'd fucking done it.

When the faces of Beau and Branch crowded out the sky, I tuned back into the roar of the crowd and their voices.

"Fucking hell, Nugget. Are you okay?" Beau yelled over the sound. Branch grabbed my helmet and pulled it off.

When he saw my huge shit eating grin, his face morphed from concern to anger. "Are you fucking insane, Tessa May? You could have died," he roared, and I had no problem hearing him over the crowd.

I sat up, still grinning. "Yep, so could you. How long did I stick it for?"

Beau's lips twitched. He wasn't as big of an asshole as Branch. "Five-three. It was a good ride."

Branch slapped him on the back of the head then stood, reaching down to haul me to my feet. He frog-marched me out of the ring and I hoped none of the crowd could see I was a girl. I didn't want it to detract from my ride. I'd stuck it for five seconds.

The rodeo medic was there when I walked out of the arena, and his face as he recognized me was hilarious. I'd known the doc since I was an infant. "Tessa May, what are you doing?" he gasped, and I knew that in exactly two minutes, word would get back to Daddy.

"I was flyin', Doc," I grinned.

He shook his head in bemused worry. "Let's see if that fall knocked any sense into that head of yours, shall we?"

Branch stormed off, but Beau stood beside me as the Doc checked me over. When the door opened and closed, Beau's face went pale and I knew who stood there. Uh oh.

"Tessa May!" The roar rattled the windows, and I looked over my shoulder at my father, and I smiled softly.

"Did you see me ride? Did you see?" I whispered, and his face melted. He loved me. He loved me more than anything in the world. He wouldn't stay mad at me, but he would ground me for life for this.

He shook his head. "I saw. Get in the damn car. We are going home."

Thirty minutes later, I was sitting in the front seat of my Daddy's truck with an icepack pressed to my shoulder. I couldn't wipe the smile off my face, despite the absolutely thunderous expression on my father's face.

"Why Nugget? Why the hell do you test me like this? Have I not been a good father?"

I rolled my eyes at his theatrics. "You're the best, and you know it. I want to ride. I don't think it's fair that I can't because I'm a girl."

Daddy shook his head. This was an argument we'd had a million times. "That's not the only reason Nugget, and you know it."

I made a rude noise. "If I was your son and not your daughter, you'd be proud as hell of me right now."

Daddy grunted. "It'd make no difference. I am proud of you, Nugget. So damn proud. But it scares the shit out of me that one wrong kick and you'd be taken from me too." His voice cracked, and I knew he was thinking of Mama. She died when I was a baby. Brain aneurysm. Daddy had come home from work one day, found me sound asleep in my bassinet and Mama dead on the couch, a smile on her face.

But it had devastated him, and a little guilt ate away at my happiness. "I'm sorry. But it's what I want to do. I'll wear all the protective gear. I'll bail early. But Daddy, on the back of that bull? I felt more alive than I've ever felt in my life."

Daddy shook his head, but a small smile tilted his lips. "So damn headstrong. Alright, Nugge-"

Whatever he was going to say died in his throat. A car crossed into our lane, and Daddy yanked the car to the right. I screamed as the car plowed into our truck. As it flipped end over end, I thought how much this looked like coming off that bull only an hour earlier.

Eight seconds to fly or die.